Praise for Ted Dekker's Novels

"*Saint* reads like *The Borne Identity* (Robert Ludlum) meets *The Matrix* meets *Mr. Murder* (Dean Koontz)."

—5 OUT OF 5 STARS FROM THE BOOKSHELF REVIEW

"Fans of Dekker and supernatural suspense will relish this creative thriller."

—LIBRARY JOURNAL

"Dekker's in fine form here, delivering another blockbuster of action, mystery, and suspense, while serving up some of his most heart-rending scenes ever. This latest plot is a breathless, winding maze of intrigue, and his tightest non-stop thrill ride since *Thr3e*."

—INFUZEMAG.COM

"Dekker only continues to improve on his prodigious storytelling skills. Highly recommended."

—CHRISTIANFICTION.COM

"A master of suspense reminiscent of Dean Koontz and John Grisham, Ted Dekker keeps readers on their toes trying to solve the mystery of Saint's identity."

—ROMANCE JUNKIES

"Their [Dekker and Peretti's] collaboration [in *House*] is as big of a deal as Tom Clancy and Clive Cussler getting together to co-author a spy novel."

—PAT CURRY, *PAGES*

"Toss away all your expectations, because *Showdown* is one of the most original, most thoughtful, and most gripping reads I've been through in ages . . . Breaking all established story patterns or plot formulas, you'll find yourself repeatedly feeling that there's no way of predicting what will happen next . . . The pacing is dead-on, the flow is tight, and the epic story is downright sneaky in how it unfolds. Dekker excels at crafting stories that are hard to put down, and *Showdown* is the hardest yet."

—INFUZEMAG.COM

"[In *Showdown*] Dekker delivers his signature exploration of good and evil in the context of a genuine thriller that could further enlarge his already sizable audience."

—PUBLISHERS WEEKLY

"[*Showdown*] strips the veneer of civilization to the darkness of the soul, revealing the motivations and intents of the heart. This is a difficult book to read and definitely not for the squeamish. It brings home the horror of sin and the depth of sacrifice in a way another book would not—could not."

—AUTHOR'S CHOICE REVIEWS

"Calling [*Showdown*] unique is an understatement. Ted Dekker has successfully laced a contemporary thriller with searing spiritual principles."

—IN THE LIBRARY REVIEWS

"Only Peretti and Dekker [in *House*] could have delivered this full-tilt supernatural thriller. They had me ripping through the pages . . . then blew me away with a final twist, I never saw coming. Can't wait to see the movie!"

—RALPH WINTER, PRODUCER: *X-MEN 3* AND *FANTASTIC FOUR*

"[In *Obsessed*] an inventive plot and fast-paced action put Dekker at the top of his game."

—LIBRARY JOURNAL

"One of the highlights of the year in religious fiction has been Ted Dekker's striking color-coded spiritual trilogy. Exciting, well written, and resonant with meaning, *Black*, *Red*, and now *White* have won over both critics and genre readers . . . An epic journey completed with grace."

—EDITORS, BARNES & NOBLE

"Dekker is a master of suspense and even makes room for romance."

—LIBRARY JOURNAL

"[With *THR3E*] Dekker delivers another page-turner . . . masterfully takes readers on a ride full of plot twists and turns . . . a compelling tale of cat and mouse . . . an almost perfect blend of suspense, mystery, and horror."

—PUBLISHERS WEEKLY

SAINT

www.teddekker.com

OTHER BOOKS BY TED DEKKER

Skin
House (coauthored with Frank Peretti)
Showdown
The Martyr's Song
Obsessed
Black
Red
White
Three
Blink
When Heaven Weeps
Thunder of Heaven
Heaven's Wager

COAUTHORED WITH BILL BRIGHT
Blessed Child
A Man Called Blessed

SAINT

TED DEKKER

THOMAS NELSON
Since 1798

NASHVILLE   DALLAS   MEXICO CITY   RIO DE JANEIRO   BEIJING

Published in Nashville, TN, by Thomas Nelson. Thomas Nelson is a trademark of Thomas Nelson, Inc.

Thomas Nelson, Inc. titles may be purchased in bulk for educational, business, fund-raising, or sales promotional use. For information, please e-mail SpecialMarkets@ThomasNelson.com.

Publisher's Note: This novel is a work of fiction. Names, characters, places, and incidents are either products of the author's imagination or used fictitiously. All characters are fictional, and any similarity to people living or dead is purely coincidental.

Library of Congress Cataloging-in-Publication Data

Dekker, Ted, 1962–
    Saint / Ted Dekker.
      p. cm.
    ISBN 10: 1-59554-006-7 (hardcover)
    ISBN 13: 978-1-59554-006-5 (hardcover)
    ISBN 10: 1-59554-228-0 (ie)
    ISBN 13: 978-1-59554-228-1 (ie)
    ISBN 10: 1-59554-297-3 (trade paper)
    ISBN 13: 978-1-59554-297-7 (trade paper)
    1. Kidnapping—Fiction. 2. Christian fiction. I. Title.
    PS3554.E43S25 2006
    813'.6—dc22

                                              2006010191

Printed in the United States of America

07 08 09 10 11 RRD 7 6 5 4 3 2 1

1

I see darkness. I'm lying spread-eagle on my back, ankles and wrists tied tightly to the bedposts so that I can't pull them free.

A woman is crying beside me. I've been kidnapped.

My name is Carl.

But there's more that I know about myself, fragments that don't quite make sense. Pieces of a puzzle forced into place. I know that I'm a quarter inch shy of six feet tall and that my physical conditioning has been stretched to its limits. I have a son whom I love more than my own life and a wife named . . . named Kelly, of course, Kelly. How could I hesitate on that one? I'm unconscious or asleep, yes, but how could I ever misplace my wife's name?

I was born in New York and joined the army when I was eighteen. Special Forces at age twenty, now twenty-five. My father left home when I was eight, and I took care of three younger sisters—Eve, Ashley, Pearl—and my mother, Betty Strople, who was always proud of me for being such a strong boy. When I was fourteen, Brad Stenko slapped my mother. I hit him over the head with a two-by-four and called the police. I remember his name because his intent to marry my mother terrified me. I remember things like that. Events and facts cemented into place by pain.

My wife's name is Kelly. See, I know that, I really do. And my son's name is Matthew. Matt. Matt and Kelly, right?

I'm a prisoner. A woman is crying beside me.

CARL SNAPPED his eyes wide open, stared into the white light above him, and closed his eyes again.

Opening his eyes had been a mistake that could have alerted anyone watching to his awakening. He scrambled for orientation. In that brief moment, eyes opened wide to the ceiling, his peripheral vision had seen the plain room. Smudged white walls. Natural light from a small window. A single fluorescent fixture above, a dirty mattress under him.

And the crying woman, strapped down beside him.

Otherwise the room appeared empty. If there was any immediate danger, he hadn't seen it. So it was safe to open his eyes.

Carl did, quickly confirmed his estimation of the room, then glanced down at a thick red nylon cord bound around each ankle and tied to two metal bedposts. Beside him, the woman was strapped down in similar manner.

His black dungarees had been shoved up to his knees. No shoes. The woman's left leg lay over his right and was strapped to the same post. Her legs had been cut and bruised, and the cord was tied tightly enough around her ankles to leave marks. She wore a pleated navy-blue skirt, torn at the hem, and a white blouse that looked as if it had been dragged through a field with her.

This was Kelly. He knew that, and he knew that he cared for Kelly deeply, but he was suddenly unsure why. He blinked, searching his memory for details, but his memory remained fractured. Perhaps his captors had used drugs.

The woman whose name was Kelly faced the ceiling, eyes closed.

Her tears left streaks down dirty cheeks and into short blond hair. Small nose, high cheekbones, a bloody nose. Several scratches on her forehead.

I'm strapped to a bed next to a woman named Kelly who's been brutalized. My name is Carl and I should feel panic, but I feel nothing.

The woman suddenly caught her breath, jerked her head to face him, and stared into his soul with wide blue eyes.

In the space of one breath, Carl's world changed. Like a heat wave vented from a sauna, emotion swept over him. A terrible wave of empathy laced with a bitterness he couldn't understand. But he understood that he cared for the woman behind these blue eyes very much.

And then, as quickly as the feeling had come, it fell away.

"Carl . . ." Her face twisted with anguish. Fresh tears flooded her eyes and ran down her left cheek.

"Kelly?"

She began to speak in a frantic whisper. "We have to get out of here! They're going to kill us." Her eyes darted toward the door. "We have to do something before he comes back. He's going to kill . . ." Her voice choked on tears.

Carl's mind refused to clear. He knew who she was, who he was, why he cared for her, but he couldn't readily access that knowledge. Worse, he didn't seem capable of emotion, not for more than a few seconds.

"Who . . . who are you?"

She blinked, as if she wasn't sure she'd heard him right. "What did they do to you?"

He didn't know. They'd hurt him, he knew that. Who were they? Who was she?

She spoke urgently through her tears. "I'm your wife! We were on vacation, at port in Istanbul when they took us. Three days ago. They . . . I think they took Matthew. Don't tell me you can't remember!"

Details that he'd rehearsed in his mind before waking flooded him.

He was with the army, Special Forces. His family had been taken by force from a market in Istanbul. Matthew was their son. Kelly was his wife.

Panicked, Carl jerked hard against the restraints. He was rewarded with a squealing metal bed frame, no more.

Another mistake. Whoever had the resources to kidnap them undoubtedly had the foresight to use the right restraints. He was reacting impulsively rather than with calculation. Carl closed his eyes and calmed himself. *Focus, you have to focus.*

"They brought you in here unconscious half an hour ago and gave you a shot." Her words came out in a rush. "I think . . . I'm pretty sure they want you to kill someone." Her fingers touched the palm of his hand above their heads. Clasped his wrist. "I'm afraid, Carl. I'm so afraid." Crying again.

"Please, Kelly. Slow down."

"Slow down? I've been tied to this bed for three days! I thought you were dead! They took our son!"

The room faded and then came back into focus. They stared at each other for a few silent seconds. There was something strange about her eyes. He was remembering scant details of their kidnapping, even fewer details of their life together, but her eyes were a window into a world that felt familiar and right.

They had Matthew. Rage began to swell, but he cut it off and was surprised to feel it wane. His training was kicking in. He'd been trained not to let feelings cloud his judgment. So then his not feeling was a good thing.

"I need you to tell me what you know."

"I've told you. We were on a cruise—"

"No, everything. Who we are, how we were taken. What's happened since we arrived. Everything."

"What did they do to you?"

"I'm okay. I just can't remember—"

4

"You're bleeding." She stared at the base of his head. "Your hair . . ."

He felt no pain, no wetness from blood. He lifted his head and twisted it for a look at the mattress under his hair. A fist-sized red blotch stained the cover.

The pain came then, a deep, throbbing ache at the base of his skull. He laid his head back down and stared at the ceiling. With only a little effort he disconnected himself from the pain.

"Tell me what you remember."

She blinked, breathed deliberately, as if she might forget to if she didn't concentrate. "You had a month off from your post in Kuwait and we decided to take a cruise to celebrate our seventh anniversary. Matthew was buying some crystallized ginger when a man grabbed him and went into an alley between the tents. You went after him. I saw someone hit you from behind with a metal pipe. Then a rag with some kind of chemical was clamped over my face and I passed out. Today's the first time I've seen you." She closed her eyes. "They tortured me, Carl."

Anger rose, but again he suppressed it. Not now. There would be time for anger later, if they survived.

His head seemed to be clearing. More than likely they'd kept him drugged for days, and whatever they'd put into his system half an hour ago was waking him up. That would explain his temporary memory loss.

"What nationality are they?"

"Hungarian, I think. The one named Dale is a sickening . . ." She stopped, but the look of hatred in her eyes spoke plenty.

Carl blocked scattered images of all the possible things Dale might have done to her. Again, that he was able to do this so easily surprised him. Was he so insensitive to his own wife?

No, he was brutally efficient. For her sake he had to be.

Their captors had left their mouths free—if he could find a way to reach their restraints . . .

The door swung open. A man with short-cropped blond hair stepped into the room. Medium height. Knifelike nose and chin. Fiercely eager blue eyes. Khaki cotton pants, black shirt, hairy arms. Dale.

Carl knew this man.

This was Dale Crompton. This was a man who'd spent some time in the dark spaces of Carl's mind, securing Carl's hatred. Kelly had said Hungarian, but she must have meant someone else, because Dale was an Englishman.

The man's right arm hung by his side, hand snugged around an Eastern Bloc Makarov 9mm pistol. The detail was brightly lit in Carl's mind while other details remained stubbornly shrouded by darkness. He knew his weapons.

Without any warning or fanfare, Dale rounded the foot of the bed, pressed the barrel of the Makarov against Kelly's right thigh, and pulled the trigger.

The gun bucked with a thunderclap. Kelly arched her back, screamed, and thrashed against her restraints, then dropped to the mattress in a faint.

Carl's mind passed the threshold of whatever training he'd received. His mind demanded he feel nothing, lie uncaring in the face of brutal manipulation, but his body had already begun its defense of his wife. He snarled and bolted up, oblivious to the pain in his wrists and ankles.

The movement proved useless. He might as well be a dog on a thick chain, jerked violently back at the end of a sprint for freedom.

He collapsed back onto the bed and gathered himself. Kelly lay still. A single glance told him that the bullet had expended its energy without passing through her leg, which meant it had struck the femur, probably shattering it.

"I hope I have your attention," Dale said. "Her leg will heal. A similar bullet to her head, on the other hand, will produce far more satisfying results. I'd love to kill her. And your son. What is his name? Matthew?"

Carl just stared at him. *Focus. Believe. You must believe in your ability to save them.*

"Pity to destroy such a beautiful woman," Dale said, walking to the window. "Just so you know, I argued to tie your son next to you and keep Kelly for other uses, but Kalman overruled me. He says the boy will be useful if you fail us the first time."

Englishman put the gun on the sill, unlatched the window, and pulled it up. Fresh breezes carried a lone bird's chirping into the room. *It's spring. I can smell fresh grass and spring flowers. I can smell fresh blood.*

Englishman faced him. "A simple and quite lethal device has been surgically implanted at the base of your hypothalamus gland. This explains the bleeding at the back of your head. Any attempt to remove this device will result in the release of chemicals that will destroy your brain within ten seconds. Your life is in our hands. Is this clear?"

The revelation struck Carl as perfectly natural. Exactly what he would have expected, knowing what he did, whatever that was.

"Yes."

"Good. Your mission is to kill a man and his wife currently housed in a heavily guarded hotel at the edge of the town directly to our south, three miles away. Joseph and Mary Fabin will be in their room on the third floor. Number 312. No one else is to be killed. Only the targets. You have two cartridges in the gun, only two. No head shots. We need their faces for television. Do you understand?"

A wave of dizziness swept through Carl. Aside from a slight tic in his right eye, he showed none of it. Beside him, Kelly moaned. How could he ignore his wife's suffering so easily?

Carl eyed the pistol on the sill. "I understand."

"We will watch you closely. If you make any contact with the authorities, your wife will die. If you step outside the mission parameters, she dies. If you haven't returned within sixty minutes, both she and your son will die. Do you understand?"

Carl spoke quickly to cover any fear in his eyes. "The name of the hotel?"

"The Andrassy," Dale said. He withdrew a knife from his waistband, walked over to Carl, and laid the sharp edge against the red nylon rope that tied Carl's right leg to the bed frame.

"I'm sure you would like to kill me," Dale said. "This is impossible, of course. But if you try, you, your wife, and your son will be dead within the minute."

"Who are the targets?"

"They are the two people who can save your wife and son by dying within the hour." The man cut through the bonds around Carl's ankles, then casually went to work on the rope at his wrists. "You'll find some shoes and clean clothes outside the window." With a faint *pop,* the last tie yielded to Englishman's blade.

Kelly whimpered, and Carl looked over to see that her eyes were open again. Face white, muted by horror and pain.

For a long moment, lying there freed beside the woman he loved, Carl allowed a terrible fury to roll through his mind. Despite Dale's claim, Carl knew that he stood at least an even chance of killing their captor.

He wanted to touch Kelly and to tell her that she would be okay. That he would save her and their son. He wanted to tear the heart out of the man who was now watching them with a dispassionate stare, like a robot assigned to a simple task.

He wanted to scream. He wanted to cry. He wanted to kill himself. Instead, he lay still.

Kelly closed her eyes and started to sob again. He wished she would stop. He wanted to shout at her and demand that she stop this awful display of fear. Didn't she know that fear was now their greatest enemy?

"Fifty-eight minutes," Dale said. "It's quite a long run."

Carl slid his legs off the bed, stood, and walked to the window, thinking that he was a monster for being so callous, never mind that it was for her sake that he steeled himself.

I'm in a nightmare. He reached for the gun. But the Makarov's cold steel handle felt nothing like a dream. It felt like salvation.

"Carl?"

Kelly's voice shattered his reprieve. Carl was sure that he would spin where he stood, shoot Dale through the forehead, and take his chances with the implant or whatever other means they had of killing him and his family. The only way he knew to deal with such a compelling urge was to shut down his emotions entirely. He clenched his jaw and shoved the gun into his waistband.

"I love you, Carl."

He looked at her without seeing her, swallowed his terror. "It'll be okay," he said. "I'll be back."

He grabbed both sides of the window, thrust his head out to scan the grounds, withdrew, shoved his right leg through the opening, and rolled onto the grass outside. When he came to his feet, he was facing south. How did he know it was south? He just did.

He would go south and he would kill.

2

Carl found the clothes in a small duffel bag behind a bush along the outside wall. He dressed quickly, pulled on a pair of cargo pants and black running shoes, and tied a red bandanna around his neck to hide the blood that had oozed from a cut at the base of his skull, roughly two inches behind his right ear. Odd to think that a single remote signal could take his life.

Odd, not terrifying. Not even odd, actually. Interesting. Familiar.

He snatched up the Makarov, shoved it behind his back, and set out at a fast jog. South.

He was in a small compound, ten buildings in a small valley surrounded by a deciduous forest. Three of the buildings were concrete; the rest appeared to be made of wood. Most had small windows, perhaps eighteen inches square. Tin roofs. No landscaping, just bare dirt and grass. To the west, a shooting range stretched into the trees farther than he could see, well over three thousand yards.

The day was hot, midafternoon. Quiet except for the chirping of a few birds and the rustle of a light breeze through the trees.

On stilts, a single observation post with narrow, rectangular windows towered over the trees. There were eyes behind those windows, watching him.

All of this he assimilated before realizing that he was taking in his surroundings in such a calculating, clinical manner. His wife lay on a bed with a shattered femur, his son was in some dark hole in one of these buildings, and Carl was running south, away from them in order to save them.

Three miles would take fifteen minutes at a healthy jog for the fittest man. Was he fit? He'd run a hundred yards and felt only slightly winded. He was fit. As part of Special Forces, he would be.

But why was he forced to rely on instinct and calculation instead of clear memory to determine even these simple facts?

He brought his mind back to the task at hand. What were the consequences of entering a hotel and murdering a man and his wife? Death for the man and his wife. Orphaned children. A prison sentence for the killer.

What were the consequences of allowing this man and his wife to live? Death for Kelly and Matthew.

He was in a black hole from which there was no escape. But blackness was familiar territory to him, wasn't it? A pang of sorrow stabbed him. There was something about blackness that made him want to cry.

Carl ran faster now, weaving through the trees, pushing back the emotions that flogged him, and doing so quite easily. When the blackness encroached, he focused on a single pinprick of light at the end of the tunnel, because only there, in the light, could he find the strength to hold the darkness at bay.

He had no way to know with any certainty when the hour he'd been given would expire, but time was now irrelevant. He possessed limits and he would push himself to those limits. Any distraction caused by worry or fear would only interfere with his success.

He crested a gentle hill outside the forest roughly fifteen minutes into the run. He pulled up behind a tree, panting. There was the town. Only one neighborhood in his line of sight contained multistory buildings—the Andrassy would be there. After a quick scan of the country leading to the town, he angled for the buildings at a jog, slower now, senses keen.

His shirttail hid the gun at his waist, but nothing else about him would be so easily hidden once he encountered people. Was Kelly right? Were they really in Hungary? He didn't speak Hungarian but doubted he looked much different from any ordinary Hungarian. On the other hand, he was sweating from a hard run and his neck was wrapped in a bright bandanna—these facts wouldn't go unnoticed.

The hotel was heavily guarded, Englishman had said. How could Carl possibly race into a completely foreign town, barge into a well-guarded hotel, shoot two possible innocents, and expect any good to come of it?

Images of Kelly flooded his mind. She was strapped to the bed, right femur shattered, face stained with tears, praying desperately for him to save her. And Matthew . . .

He ran past farming lots that bordered the blacktop entering the town from his angle of approach; past people milking a cow, raking straw, riding a bicycle, kicking a soccer ball. He ignored them all and jogged.

How empty his mind was. How vacant. How hopeless. How disconnected from the details swimming around him, though he noticed everything.

He slowed to a fast walk when he reached the edge of town and searched for a hotel matching Englishman's description.

None. No hotel at all. And time was running low.

Carl flagged the rider of an old black Schwinn bicycle and spoke quickly when the older man's blue eyes fixed on him. "Andrassy Hotel?"

The man put his feet down to balance himself, looked Carl over once, and then pointed toward the west, spouting something in Hungarian.

Carl nodded and ran west. On each side of the asphalt ribbon, people stopped to watch him. Clearly, he looked like more than a commoner out for an afternoon jog. But unless they represented an immediate threat, he would ignore them. For the moment they were only curious.

Assault has three allies: speed, surprise, and power. Carl didn't have the power to overwhelm more than a few guards. Speed and surprise, on the other hand, could work for him, assuming he was unexpected.

The Andrassy was a square four-story building constructed out of red brick. A Hungarian flag flapped lazily on a pole jutting out from the wall above large revolving doors. Two long black Mercedes waited in the circular drive—possibly part of the guard.

Carl veered toward the back of the hotel. A large garbage bin smelled of rotting vegetables. The kitchen was nearby.

He bounded over three metal steps and tried a gray metal door. Unlocked. He pushed it open, stepped into a dim hallway, and pulled the door shut behind him.

He followed the sound of clattering dishes down the cluttered hall and through a doorway ten paces ahead on his right. He grabbed an apron from a laundry bin against the wall and wiped the sweat from his face. He slipped into the apron. Barely there long enough to answer a casual glance from a passing employee.

It was all about speed now.

If he was right, there would be a service elevator nearby. If he was right, there would be guards posted outside the third-floor room that held the targets. If he was right, he had roughly ten minutes to kill and run.

Carl took deep breaths, calming his heart and lungs. The soft *ding* of an elevator bell confirmed his first guess.

Kill and run. Somewhere deep in the black places of his mind, a voice objected, echoing faintly, but his mind refused to focus on that voice. His mind was on the killings because the killings would save his wife and son.

There were two ways to the third floor. The first required stealth—assuming a server's identity on a mission to deliver room service, perhaps. He dismissed this idea because it was predictable, thus undermining his greatest allies, speed and surprise.

The second approach was far bolder and therefore less predictable.

Carl breathed deeply through his nostrils and closed his eyes. He'd been here before, hadn't he? He couldn't remember where or why, but he was in familiar territory.

Unless the guards were exceptional, they would hesitate before shooting an unarmed man who approached them.

There were towels in the laundry basket. Carl quickly pulled off his shoes, socks, apron, bandanna, and shirt, pushing them behind the laundry bin. With a flip of his fingers, he unsnapped his cargo pants, let them fall around his ankles, and tied the pistol to his thigh using the bandanna. He pulled his pants back up and rolled up the legs to just below his knees.

Bare feet, bare legs, bare chest, bare back—no sign of a weapon, even to a trained eye.

Satisfied, he draped a large white towel over his head and around his neck so that it covered the blood at the back of his neck and fell over his chest on either side. A man who'd just come from a swim or a shower. Unusual to be found walking through a hotel, particularly one that didn't have a pool, which he suspected to be the case here, but not so unusual as to cause alarm. He had taken a shower upstairs, come down on a quick errand, and was headed back to his room.

Carl grabbed the towel on each side, strolled down the hall, and walked into the open, whistling a nondescript tune.

LASZLO KALMAN drummed his thin fingers on the table, a habit that annoyed Agotha more than she cared to admit. His uncut nails made a clicking sound like a rat running across a wooden floor. They were all firmly in this man's grasp: she as much as his killers.

Agotha loved and hated him. Kalman could not be defined easily, only because he refused to explain himself. But then, evil rarely did explain itself.

Still, she could not ignore her attraction to the raw power that accompanied Kalman's exceptional lust for death. He feared nothing except his own creations, killers who could slay a man with as little feeling as he himself possessed.

Of all his understudies, Englishman was the one he feared most, although soon enough Carl might surpass even Englishman, a fact that wasn't lost on anyone. It was this tenuous nature of the game that brought Kalman satisfaction, not the millions of Euros this X Group of his was paid for its assassins' skills.

"How much time?" Kalman asked.

Agotha glanced at the wall clock behind them. "Thirty-five minutes. Perhaps I should call Englishman."

"He knows the price of failure."

"And if he does fail? We've come so far."

Agotha rarely got involved in any of the operations directly. Her place was here, in the compound's hospital. But now they were on the verge of something that even she struggled to understand.

"Englishman won't fail," Laszlo said.

"I was speaking of Carl."

Laszlo hesitated. "That's your department. I don't care either way."

Agotha bit her lower lip. To fail now would be a terrible setback. The shooting of two people was all that stood in the way. Correction: the shooting of two people by this one man who had been meticulously selected and trained was all that stood in the way.

"There's something different about Carl," she said.

Kalman looked at her without emotion. Without comment.

He returned his gaze to the monitor and resumed clicking his fingernails on the wood.

3

Carl strolled toward the service elevator in bare feet, hoping that his wet bangs looked like the work of a shower rather than a hard run. In the event he raised an alarm prematurely, he would resort to force.

He'd timed his approach by the elevator's bell, but by the time he caught sight of it, the door was already closing. Empty or not, he didn't know.

At least a dozen people were staring his way from the main lobby on the right. Casual stares, curious stares. For the moment.

Carl stopped his whistling and ran for the door—a man hurrying to catch an elevator. The towel slipped off his neck and fell to the ground. He reached the elevator call button, gave it a quick hit with his palm, and reached back for the towel as the door slid open.

The car was empty. Good.

He stepped in, pushed the button for the fourth floor, and resumed his whistling. The door slid closed, and he shut his eyes to calm his nerves.

Who are you, Carl?

He didn't know precisely who he was, did he? He knew his name. Scattered details of a dark past. He knew that Kelly was his wife and that Matthew was his son, and he knew that he would give his life for them if he needed to.

But why was his past so foggy? Who were his captors? Why had they chosen him to do their killing? Whatever they'd done to his head was more profound than a mere drug-induced effect.

He grunted and shoved the questions aside.

Do you believe?

"I believe," he said softly.

What do you believe?

"I believe that I will kill these two to save my wife and son."

Belief. Something about belief mattered greatly.

The elevator bell clanged.

He stepped onto the fourth floor, reached back into the elevator, pushed the button for the third floor, and was running toward the stairwell at the end of the hall before the elevator doors closed.

Despite the absence of specific memories, he seemed to be able to access whatever information he needed for this killing business from a vast pool of knowledge without a second thought. For example, the basic fact that going to a target's floor by elevator was unwise on two counts: First, because all eyes watching the elevator call numbers above the doors on any floor would know where it stopped. Second, because the elevator's arrival was almost always preceded by a bell, which would naturally warn any posted guard.

Better to take the stairs or the elevator to a different floor. Carl had chosen the elevator because that's what would be expected of a nutty tourist who'd gone down to the lobby for a candy bar or something after a shower.

These kinds of techniques didn't require any thought on his part. His training in the Special Forces had clearly become instinctive.

Carl ran down the stairs, pulled up by the third-floor access door, and waited for the sound of the elevator bell, heart pounding. This was it.

Kill and run. *What am I doing?*

The bell sounded. He pushed the door open and stepped into the third-floor hall.

Two guards dressed in dark suits stood across the hall, twenty yards down. Neither sported a weapon. Their heads were turned away from him, toward the elevator.

He hurried toward them, covered half the distance before the closest guard turned his way.

Carl cried out in pain, doubled over, and grabbed his right foot. Without hesitation, he inserted his thumb between his second and third toes and dug his nail into the skin with enough force to draw blood.

He pulled his hand away, red with a streak of blood.

The guard demanded something of him in Hungarian.

Carl ignored him. Examined his foot, feigning shock. Muttered loudly.

Another question, this one from the second guard.

He gave them a quizzical look. Both had their eyes on his foot. He hobbled toward them. "Sorry. Sorry, I just . . ."

Carl was three paces from them when one of the guards reached under his jacket. Carl took two fast strides, smashed his left palm under the closest guard's chin while stepping past him. The second guard had pulled a pistol clear of his coat when Carl's right fist slammed into the man's gun hand. Using his momentum, Carl propelled his head into the guard's chin.

No one else dies, Englishman had said.

The first guard slumped, unconscious, hopefully not dead. The second stood dazed. Carl grabbed a fistful of hair and jerked the man's head into his rising knee.

The man grunted and dropped like a sack of coal. Carl broke his fall with his right leg. The tussle may have been heard inside, but he couldn't change that now.

One of the two should have a key card to gain access to the room if needed. He quickly searched both men, found the card in the second guard's jacket.

Hall still clear.

No need for the Makarov tied to his leg. Carl retrieved both of the guards' guns, shoved one behind his back and checked the other for a chambered cartridge, slipped the key card into its slot, and twisted the knob when a green light indicated he'd successfully unlocked the door.

He stepped into the room, gun extended.

THE ABSENCE of a bed indicated that the room Joseph and Mary Fabin had rented was a suite. He'd been prepared to shoot from the threshold if necessary—time was running short and there was a chance the guards would regain consciousness soon.

He stepped into the room, gun still leading.

That distant voice in his head was asking him questions—such as whether he should reconsider shooting two people in cold blood, challenging how he could do this without considerable turmoil. He shut the voice down.

Two doors led out of the room, one on each side. Voices from the one on the left. He broke toward the left, turned the door handle slowly, and then crashed through with enough force to bury the doorknob in the wall plaster.

A black-haired Caucasian with gray bangs and sideburns sat across a table from a lanky woman with straight blond hair rolled into a bun. They looked at him, not surprised. He hesitated, thrown off by their calm demeanor. Carl knew the look of a man about to die. This wasn't it.

"Hello, Peter," the man said.

No *head shots*. Carl leveled the gun at the man who'd spoken. "Joseph and Mary Fabin?"

"Yes," the woman said. "Please lower the weapon, Peter."

American accent. No fear, only calm resolve. The man and woman had been expecting him. And they both called him Peter, not Carl. On their own, neither of these facts would have kept Carl from squeezing the trigger. Together, they presented an obstacle that distracted him from the light at the end of his tunnel, from killing and running and saving his wife and his son.

Joseph Fabin stood. "They told you your name was Carl Strople, am I correct?"

One hour. Kelly's and Matthew's lives hung in the balance, and he was standing here contemplating nonsense from an American who should be dead by now.

Carl didn't answer.

"But your name isn't Carl. It's Peter Marker. You were an independent contractor for the CIA before you went missing two years ago. It seems that you have more stored up in that mind of yours than the agency is willing to surrender."

Carl doubted he had more than twenty minutes left.

"Remove your jacket," he said to Joseph.

Fabin's eyes narrowed barely, but after thinking his situation through, he peeled off his jacket.

"I have something I think you should hear," Joseph said. He reached into his jacket, which now lay over his right arm. "May I?"

Carl hesitated.

Joseph pulled out a small black tape recorder, tossed the jacket on the couch to his right, and pressed the Play button. A woman's voice spoke through a light static.

"Peter, it's Kelly. I'm begging you, please come home to us. Matthew cries at night . . ." Her voice trailed off, then came back stronger. "I don't care what they've done to you, you hear? I need you, Matthew needs you. Please, I'm begging you. I'm making this recording for a Mr. Joseph Fabin with the CIA. Please come home with him, Peter. If you can hear me, please."

Fabin turned the tape off. "Do you recognize her voice?"

The room faded for a brief moment, then sprang back into focus. Was it Kelly? He couldn't tell. Impossible! Kelly had been bound by his side today! He'd seen her eyes and known the truth.

"It's your wife," Mary said. "I talked to her this morning by phone in Brussels, where you were stationed. Two years is a long time. Longer than I would wait for a missing husband. She obviously loves you. Our orders are to take you home."

"I saw my wife less than an hour ago," Carl said.

"Whoever you saw an hour ago wasn't Kelly. Impossible, my friend. Kelly is in Brussels."

"How did you know I would be coming here? If you're with the CIA, why the guard outside?"

Joseph studied him for several seconds, then sighed and sat back down. "Have a seat, Peter." He indicated a third chair.

Confusion swarmed Carl, but he refused to let the light at the end of the tunnel wink out. His palms had gone sweaty and his tongue was dry and his heart was pounding, but he forced his mind to the point.

The hour was expiring. Even if he left now, he would have trouble returning to the compound in time.

"Fine, stand. But lower the weapon. Really, Peter."

Send the bullet. Send it now.

"We've been closing in on a highly specialized underground operation known only as the X Group, which was founded by a man named Laszlo Kalman," the man said. "They have been known to kidnap government operatives, agents, even military regulars who fit a certain profile, strip their minds of memories and identities, and then retrain them as assassins. You were sighted six days ago after a two-year absence, which explains the tape recording."

Carl hit a wall. He knew he was faced with a decision that couldn't wait more than a few seconds. Either the woman who'd been strapped down beside him had been lying and wasn't his wife, or the man before him was lying.

"We know everything, Peter. We know you were sent to kill us, and we let you come because we know something that neither you nor Kalman could possibly—"

Carl shot the man in the chest.

Joseph Fabin grunted and grabbed at a red hole in his shirt. Carl swiveled the gun to the woman. His slug knocked her clean off her chair, like a mule kick to the gut. They both hit the ground at the same time, only because the man's fall had been stalled by his chair.

The sound of his gunshots lingered, chased by a high-pitched whine in his ears.

He didn't know who Joseph and Mary Fabin were, but he knew they were lying. Not because they'd slipped up, but because he knew that the woman who'd looked into his soul while they were strapped to a bed back at the compound was the woman he loved.

He'd come to save Kelly and Matthew, and their lives depended on his ability to kill these two and return within the hour. Carl hurried to the couch, slipped into Joseph Fabin's jacket, and headed out.

The killing had been a strangely emotionless affair. That was the last analytical thought that Carl allowed himself before running from the room. He stopped long enough outside the door to return the guards' guns and pull the Makarov from his thigh.

No sign that anyone had heard the shots. He sprinted to the stairs and descended quickly, shoving the Makarov into the waistband at his back.

Carl exited the stairwell and walked directly toward the kitchen, nodding once to a maid who watched him casually. Still no pursuit.

Shoes. He needed his shoes for the run. He snatched them from behind the laundry bin and stepped out into the sunshine.

A thin layer of sweat coated his body, and the base of his skull throbbed with pain. These he could deal with easily enough. But he required more than mental strength to reach the compound in time to save Kelly.

He shrugged out of the jacket and donned his shoes. For a moment he felt panic edge into his nerves. He wasn't going to make it, was he? *And what if the man I just killed was speaking the truth?* The thought fueled his panic, but just as he had done a dozen times in the last hour, he shut the emotion out.

When Carl stood from tying his shoes, his hands were shaking. He could actually see them quivering in the afternoon light, as if connected to a circuit that had been thrown. The sight didn't correlate with his thin reality. There was more, so much more to what was happening to him than this mission revealed. Somewhere deep below his consciousness, the voice protested.

Carl clenched his hands to still the tremor, turned north, and ran toward the light at the end of the tunnel.

HE DIDN'T know how long he'd been running. Every nerve, every muscle, every brain wave was focused on reaching that light as fast as humanly possible.

He tapped reservoirs of strength that exceeded reasonable ability. Deep in the blackness of his own mind, he found a place of power. He knew because he'd been there before.

The realization gave him some warmth. Hope. Whoever he was, Kelly would help him understand. He'd looked into her eyes and seen love. And Matthew . . .

The thought of his son filled him with an unexpected burst of love and energy. He whispered Matthew's name as he ran.

To his surprise, the emotion grew until he thought he might cry. He was still running, but his focus had been shattered and his vision blurred. Allowing himself to feel this kind of love for his son was intoxicating—like a drug equally pleasing and destructive.

He caught himself, steeled his mind against the destructive power of the emotion, and refocused on the tunnel.

The compound looked vacated when Carl crested the hill that hid it. But it wasn't. The buildings were all there, hiding their secrets, like Jonestown in the jungles of Guyana.

He sprinted toward the building that had held Kelly. The window he'd climbed from an hour ago was still open, as if it, too, had been abandoned. He reached it and pulled up, panting hard.

The bed was there, red nylon cords cut and dangling from the metal frame. Kelly was not.

Carl dove through the window, smashing his knee in the process. He landed on the floor.

"Kelly?"

Only his hard breathing answered him. He was too late!

The tremble returned to his hands and spread to his whole body. For the briefest of moments, he felt shame, not for failing Kelly, but for being overcome. He staggered to his feet and let a new emotion crowd his mind. Anger. Rage.

"Kelly! Where is my wife?"

He was wheezing. Standing with fists tight, wheezing like a . . .

Ssssss . . .

Carl spun to his right. A translucent vapor hissed from a small hole in the wall. They were gassing him. He knew this because he'd been gassed before. And he also knew that it was too late to run from it. He would pass out in less than five seconds, no matter what he did, or where he went.

Kelly is alive.

It was his last thought before he fell.

4

"Carl?"

The sound of her distant voice came to him like an angel.

"Carl."

His mind began to clear. How many times had he awakened with the sound of an angel in his ear? This time Kelly was here, which meant that . . .

Kelly?

Carl opened his eyes. He was on a hospital bed with the bright round lamps above him and the large humming machines on each side. But he wasn't restrained.

He sat up.

"Hello, Carl."

He turned to the voice and saw a familiar man. Tall, thin, dark hair that was graying on the sides. Bushy eyebrows. Did he know this man? Yes. This was Kalman. Laszlo Kalman.

Beside him stood the doctor. Agotha Balogh. She wore a white smock over a blue dress and held a cup of tea, which she now set down on the counter.

"Hello, Carl."

Carl looked to his right. Kelly leaned against the counter, arms crossed, smiling. There was no sign of any injury on her leg where he'd seen Englishman shoot her. She wore black dungarees, much like his own. A brown cotton turtleneck.

"Welcome home," she said.

His first impulse was relief. Sweet, sweet relief. Enough to make him feel weak. His wife was safe.

But why no wound?

"Kelly?"

"Yes. Kelly." Her eyes flashed blue like the sea. She stepped away from the counter. "You did well. I'm very proud of you."

Carl stared at her leg. It supported her without any sign of weakness. *How . . . ?*

He looked into her eyes, suddenly terrified by confusion. "Is Matthew—"

"You have no son," Kalman said. "Kelly is not your wife."

Familiar voices screamed through his mind, but he couldn't make out what they were saying. He'd been here before, but he didn't know where *here* was.

Had he killed two people in the Andrassy Hotel, or was that all part of an elaborate dream? He lifted his hand to the back of his head and felt the small cut at the base of his skull. Real. He wiggled his toes and felt the small pain of the wound between them. Real.

Kelly stepped closer and stopped five feet from him, still looking into his eyes with pride. Still smiling.

"The drugs are still in your system, but they'll wear off. You did very well this time, Carl. I knew you could do it."

Did he love this woman? Or was that a deception?

Agotha spoke with a distinct Hungarian accent. "Your name is Carl Strople. Do you remember?"

He hesitated. "Yes."

"You've been in training here for nearly a year. The mission you just completed was your tenth of twelve before we put you into the field. Do you remember?"

Now that she'd said it, he did. Not the missions specifically, but the fact that he had been here a long time. Training. His mind was still on Kelly. What did she mean to him? What had he done for her?

He couldn't think clearly enough to ask, much less answer, the questions.

"We call you Saint," Agotha said.

The name ignited a light in Carl's mind. He blinked. Saint. He'd been covertly recruited for Black Ops and given his life to the most brutal kind of training any man or woman could endure. He was here because he belonged here. To the X Group.

"You remember?"

"I remember."

"Good," Agotha said. "The mission you just executed was an important test of your skills. You must forgive us for deceiving you, but it was necessary to test your progress. Naturally, Englishman didn't actually shoot Kelly in her leg. It was only made to look like he did. The two people you shot at the Andrassy wore vests with pockets of red dye. The woman suffered a broken rib, but otherwise they are quite alive."

Carl stared at her, stupefied. *No head shots. No one else may be killed.* The whole mission was a setup.

"You performed exceptionally well," Agotha said. "We are proud of you."

"Thank you." He lowered his eyes and rubbed his fingers, trying to fill in a thousand blanks. But he couldn't. "Why can't I remember?"

Agotha nodded once, slowly, as if she had expected this question. "Our training is invasive. We train the mind as much as we train the body. You knew this when you agreed to the Group's terms. It was what you wanted. And you have proven that our techniques produce results. And rewards. You are important to your country, Carl."

"Which country?"

"The United States."

Kalman seemed satisfied to study Carl with a dark stare. There was something about him that struck Carl as obscene. But in a good way, perhaps.

Carl held Kalman's gaze for a long time, trying to understand his confusion. But he was trained not to trust his feelings, wasn't he? He was, in fact, trained to *control* his feelings by shutting them down entirely.

He didn't know how he felt about Laszlo Kalman.

Or Kelly, for that matter.

"The implant is real?" he asked Agotha.

"Yes. You've had it for many months. It is our way of tracking you."

"Or terminating you," Kalman said.

So Englishman had spoken the truth on that count. Carl avoided Kelly's eyes. For some reason she alone was able to penetrate his emotional guard.

Agotha frowned at Kalman. "We made a small incision this morning to create the impression that it was recently inserted."

"I'm being trained as an assassin," he said.

"You already are one. But you're much more than just an assassin. Only seven of more than a hundred recruits have ever finished all twelve training missions and entered the field."

"The rest?"

"Are dead," Kalman said.

Carl remembered that now. He was quite sure he'd asked these same questions dozens of times.

"As you will be if you fail."

"You kill your own recruits?"

"Only when they fail. We all die."

Maybe this was why he found Kalman obscene. But he didn't think so—deep down he understood what the dark man said.

"You'll spend two days in regression before your next training exercise," Kalman said. He walked toward the door. "Take him to his quarters." The director of the X Group left him with Agotha and Kelly, whose eyes he still avoided.

Agotha put her hand on his shoulder. She seemed enthralled by him, a scientist examining her prize specimen.

"I knew you could do it," she said. "One day you may be stronger than Englishman."

Agotha glanced at Kelly, then walked out of the room.

"You're upset with me," Kelly said.

"Am I?"

"Yes, you are."

Carl looked at her. "I'm confused. I'm not quite sure who I am. Or, for that matter, who you are."

"Then I'll tell you who we are."

She stepped up to him and reached out her hand. He took it only because she offered it in such a way that suggested she'd done so many times before.

Kelly led him from the room into a long, familiar concrete hall, offering no explanation of who either of them was.

His thoughts returned to the outburst of love he'd felt when he heard his son's name. Matthew. Even now the name pulled at his heart. How could that be, if it was only a name?

"I don't have a son named Matthew."

"No. But we helped you believe that you did for the sake of this test. You acted under that pretense and you did precisely as you should have done. I'm very pleased."

They walked through a door at the hall's end, onto a cement landing, then down five concrete steps that led to browned grass. She waited until they were twenty yards away from the building before speaking again.

"We have recording devices in all the buildings. I wanted to speak to you without being heard. I'm sorry for the confusion, Carl. I really am. Every time they do this to you, you forget that you can trust me."

How could he answer that? She'd lied to him; he could never trust her. And yet he knew already that he not only wanted to trust her but would.

"What I did was horrible," she continued. "I laid next to you and convinced you that I was your wife. That we had a child. Terrible, yes, but I did it for you." Her grip on his hand momentarily tightened. "You have to succeed, Carl. My greatest gift to you today was convincing you beyond any shadow of a doubt that you loved me and would do anything for me, including shooting two people who offered you a plausible alternate truth. If you failed to show complete loyalty to the set of facts you were fed, you would be dead now, and I couldn't live with that."

She looked at the forest, jaw clenched.

Carl's confusion lifted like a fog before the sun. He'd been here before, too, which only made sense. He was undoubtedly practiced at stepping out of the fog when presented with the right information.

In that moment, Carl heard the sincerity in her voice and knew that Kelly had done precisely what she said she'd done. She'd saved his life. There was a bond between them, which explained the emotions he'd allowed himself when he looked into her eyes as they laid tied to the bed.

"I'm sorry," he said. "It's just . . ." He didn't know what to say.

"Confusing," Kelly said for him. "Their invasive techniques are designed to strip you of your identity and reshape you. They spent three days force-feeding you the fabricated memories prior to this last test. Now they've taken those memories from you with a simple injection. They've trained your mind to respond to their manipulation. But there are some things they can't take from you. Trusting me is one of them. Remember that, Carl. Please remember that."

"I will." He swallowed, unsure how he felt about anything, including the woman who led him across the browned field toward the bunkhouse.

Familiar. The bunkhouse made his stomach turn, but such an emotional reaction was unreliable. "Tell me who I am."

"You're Carl Strople. Also known as Saint. Your memory has been stripped and reconstructed many times, and each time it becomes more difficult for you to remember who you really are. I won't bore you with the science behind it, but it's based on the relationship between memory and emotion that every human experiences. Here, a normal lifelong process is compacted into days, weeks, and months."

"But *who* am I?"

"You were in the United States Army, Special Forces, when you were recruited for this assignment. You've never been married and have no children. When you first came to the X Group, a man named Charles was your handler. He was terminated and they gave you to me."

"Why are you here?" he asked.

Kelly hesitated, then answered in a distant voice. "Because I survived the training just like you."

"Then you're what they made you?"

Another break. "I suppose. I won't be deployed in the field. I'm here to help you make it in the field."

"This is all an elaborate extension of the Special Forces? Why in Hungary?"

As soon as he'd asked the question, the answer came to him from his own memory. He answered himself.

"Black Ops. No one in the United States government has officially approved of these operations."

"You're remembering. Good. And you'll quickly remember that Englishman is the most dangerous person in this compound, perhaps more than Kalman. You won't see much of him, but he's stronger than you. Be careful around him. Play by the rules and I'll make sure you survive."

"I can't remember who my father is," he said.

She didn't answer.

"Or my mother."

Still no answer.

They walked up to the bunkhouse. It was made of concrete blocks with a single door. This was his home. The darkness inside, under the first floor, was bittersweet to him. He remembered. Once bitter, now sweet.

Kelly walked up to the door and pulled it open. "Do you remember your specialties?"

Carl followed her into an empty building with a concrete floor. A stairwell descended to their right. Kelly walked toward it.

He stopped and stared at the concrete steps. "I can walk into a dark tunnel," he said. "Nothing will hurt me."

She reached the rail and turned back. Their eyes met. "Yes, you have a strong mind. Stronger than you think. Are you coming?"

He stepped after her, focusing anew. Shutting down his uncertainties. Once bitter, now sweet. He had to remember that it was now sweet, or he might be tempted to think it was still bitter.

"What else?" she asked, walking down the steps.

Carl followed. "I can kill with almost anything. But I am first a sniper."

"Not just a sniper. You can handle a rifle like no one in recorded history. Do you remember?"

Her voice echoed in the narrow cement stairwell. She unlocked a metal door at the base and pushed it open. It was cool down here. Damp but not wet. The musty smell of undisturbed earth filled his nostrils. He walked through the door into a long tunnel lit by a single caged incandescent bulb.

"It's okay," she said, reaching back for him. "I've been here too." He took her hand and walked beside her, deeper into the tunnel.

His fingers began to tremble, so he squeezed her hand tighter. She let him walk without speaking now. This journey to the pit was always a quiet one. Bittersweet, but sweet now. Lingering ghosts that had once been memories tried to haunt him, but he refused to succumb to their power.

They walked past two gray metal doors, one on the left and one on the right. The door on their right led to the training room, which featured a large sensory-deprivation tank that they'd used many times in his early training. When they lowered him into the warm salted water with headgear that masked his sight and hearing, he floated weightless without sensory perception, left only to the dark spaces of his mind. Terrible, beautiful, comforting, lost. But in the end he always found himself.

The other room had a small kitchen, a refrigerator, a shower, and a hard bunk without a mattress. When he wasn't in the pit, he slept and ate here.

The hall took a sharp right turn, then descended one more flight of stairs into the pit. They called it the pit, but it was really just a small, square concrete room with black walls. A single metal chair was bolted to the floor in the center of the room. There was a small metal door to an access tunnel at the back of the cell, but it was always locked. No other features.

No lights.

He paused at the open door, then stepped in, walked to the chair, and turned around.

Kelly stood by the door, staring at him. If he wasn't mistaken, she looked sad. She didn't like his being here. Why not? It was what he needed to succeed. And it wasn't nearly as bad as the hospital bed or the electricity.

They controlled the temperature of the room by heating or cooling the floor. He was forced to spend most of his time in the chair with his feet off the floor. The only way to survive the extended periods of time was to sleep sitting in extreme temperatures, something he could do only with considerable focus.

They monitored his vital signs with remote sensors.

"How long will I be here?"

"Two days."

He slipped off his shoes. Tossed them to the floor by her feet. She picked them up by the laces and tossed them onto the steps behind her.

"And then more training?" he asked.

"Yes. I want you to forget everything that happened at the Andrassy."

He nodded. They stared at each other for a few seconds.

"Be strong, Carl. You have to make it. We're almost done. I'm so proud of you. You know that, don't you?"

"Yes."

"They'll try to break you this last month. Promise me you won't break."

"I won't break."

"I think that you'll change the world. They have something very special in mind for you. All of this will soon make sense."

"It already does," he said. "Why are you helping me?"

Kelly walked into the room, put her right hand on his chest, and kissed him gently on the lips. "Maybe this will help you remember," she said.

Then she walked out and shut the door behind her. An electronically triggered bolt slammed into place. Familiar silence settled. He couldn't hear her ascending the stairs.

Carl stood with one hand on the chair, staring at the blackness. It made no difference in here whether he had his eyes open or closed. The darkness was like a pool of black ink.

He stood without moving for a long time, at least an hour. The questions that had plagued him up in the light no longer mattered. He'd spent countless hours asking those questions and never received answers, only frayed emotions, which he could not afford.

The only way to survive for Kelly was to shut down.

The floor began to cool, and he knew it would soon be covered in ice. He climbed onto the chair and sat cross-legged.

It was time to enter the safe tunnel in his mind.

5

The president of the United States walked along the long bookcase in his office at Camp David and ran a finger along the leather-bound titles. How many presidents before him had added volumes to this collection? It contained the expected law books, history books, countless classics. But it was the eclectic mix of fiction that intrigued him most.

Stephen King. Which president had taken the time to read Stephen King? Or had *The Stand* simply been placed on the bookshelf unread? Dean Koontz, John Grisham, James Patterson. A book called *This Present Darkness* by Frank Peretti. He had heard the name.

Behind him, Secretary of State Calvin Bromley cleared his throat. "I think it's a mistake to underestimate the polls, Mr. President. The country isn't where it was ten years ago."

"Robert, Calvin. My name is Robert Stenton. If I've learned anything from my son, it's that even presidents have to be real." He faced the two men seated in the overstuffed leather chairs flanking the coffee table. "I feel more like a real person when my friends use my given name in private."

"And when will you feel the realness of being the leader of the free world?" David Abraham asked, stroking his white beard.

The president frowned, then cracked a grin. "Give me time. I've only been at this for a year." He walked to the couch and sighed. "I know the polls are leaning toward the Iranian defense minister's proposal to disarm Israel, but I can't ignore the fact that it goes against every bit of good sense I've ever had."

"Mr. Feroz's proposal makes some strategic sense," Bromley said. "I'm not counseling you to throw in the towel, but more than a few nations are backing this initiative. I think the American people see what the rest of the world is seeing—a plausible scenario for real peace in the region. And you are the people's president."

Robert looked at the secretary of state. Calvin Bromley, graduate of Harvard, two years his elder, but they'd known each other through the track-and-field program. The large Scandinavian man's blond hair was now graying, and he'd put on a good fifty pounds in the last thirty years, but his clear blue eyes glinted with the same determination that had served him so well throughout his career.

All three were Harvard men. David Abraham, retired professor of history and psychology who'd taught three of Stenton's undergraduate classes, now served as a confidant, a kind of spiritual adviser. The professor had experienced a spiritual renaissance later in life and had reconnected with Robert when Robert was the governor of Arizona.

The seventy-year-old mentor sat stoically, one leg crossed over the other. David had called this meeting. The weekend had originally been scheduled as a time to unwind, but when David suggested that the secretary of state come as well, Robert dismissed the hope of rest altogether.

"You're right, Calvin, I am the people's president. The minute I put my leg over the Harley and thundered down the highway to that infamous rally in Ohio, I became the people's candidate. I don't intend to ignore them. But that doesn't mean I'm always going to agree."

"I'm only suggesting you reconsider your judgment."

"I reconsider my judgment every day of the week," the president said. "I spend half my nights wondering if I'm making the right decisions."

"Forcing Israel to disarm in exchange for the mutual disarmament of all her neighbors, assuming it all could be reasonably executed and verified, would go a long way in reducing the risk of a major conflict in the region."

"Assuming it could be executed and verified," Robert said. "And enforced. That's a significant assumption, isn't it?"

"Both the French and the Germans will aid us in enforcing the Iranian initiative, should it be approved."

"The initiative isn't officially Iranian."

"No, but it's been proposed by their minister of defense, and they are backing him. The United States is now the *only* Western nation openly opposing the plan."

"And how many Middle Eastern countries are paying lip service with no intention to disarm?"

"If they don't disarm, Israel doesn't disarm." Bromley shrugged. "The execution could stall and fade into oblivion like every other treaty signed in the Middle East. But by backing the plan, we gain considerable political capital."

The president closed his eyes and rubbed the back of his neck. There was some good logic behind the plan. Each Middle Eastern country would be allowed an army large enough to carry out regional defensive operations only. No air forces, no nuclear programs, no mechanized armies.

The United Nations would establish a full-scale nuclear defense in the region under the strict obligation to deal immediately and force-fully with any threats.

It was a bold, audacious, improbable plan that made sense only on paper. But his staff had analyzed it for nine months now, and the fact remained, it did indeed make sense on paper. The Iranian minister of defense, Assim Feroz, might be a crook to the bone, but he certainly wasn't short on intelligence.

All of Europe and Asia had provisionally endorsed the plan.

Israel had rejected the plan outright, but that only played into the hands of her enemies.

"Our alternative is to dissent along with Israel, further degrading our good standing with Europe and Asia," Bromley said.

"The Israelis will never agree."

"If we back the UN force, they may have to."

Still no comment from David Abraham. The man was biding his time. He sat in his black tweed suit, legs still crossed, one hand still rubbing his beard.

"The initiative will come to a head at the United Nations Middle Eastern summit next month," Bromley said.

David Abraham spoke quietly, but his voice was thick. "This is unacceptable. If you agree to the terms of this initiative, pain and suffering will haunt the world forever."

They stared at him in silence. David had never really concerned himself with policy—why the strong reaction now? What had prompted him to suggest the meeting in the first place? Robert gave him space.

"I'm not sure I understand," Bromley said.

"Without an army, Israel is powerless against an enemy sworn to her destruction. I don't profess to be an adviser of world politics, but I am a historian. A simple glance down the corridors of time will reveal the foolishness of any disarmament on this scale. You can forcibly disarm a country, but you can't disarm the heart. The hatred of Israel's enemies will find its own way."

"Which is why the United Nations—"

"You assume the United Nations will always have Israel's interests in mind." David lowered his hand from his beard and drilled Bromley with a stare. "Don't forget that the United Nations is made up of Israel's enemies as well as friends."

"I think the secretary's suggesting that we play ball without intending to follow through," the president said.

"Assuming that's possible. You agree one day, and the next day you are bound by your word. You must not do this, Robert. As your adviser on spiritual matters, I cannot overemphasize my strenuous objection to agreeing to this initiative."

David was now out of character. He was known to give strong opinions at times, but always with a smile and a nod. Robert couldn't recall ever seeing the man so agitated.

"You see this as a spiritual matter?" the secretary asked.

David settled back in his chair. "Isn't everything? At the risk of sounding arrogant, let me suggest that I know of things in this matter that would make no sense to either of you." He shifted his gaze to Robert. "Words can become reality, Robert. And when those words are evil, someone had better be fighting the good fight, or the world could very well be swallowed up by evil."

The president felt his heart pause. *Project Showdown.*

There was far more here than David was saying openly. The secretary's presence was now a liability.

"Could you give us a minute, Calvin?"

Bromley glanced at David, then stood. "No problem."

"Dinner's in an hour. Join us?"

"Of course, Mr. President."

"Robert."

"Right." He left without another word.

Robert and David sat in silence for a few seconds. Robert wasn't sure how to draw out his mentor. When he'd invited David to serve as his spiritual adviser, the professor's first response had been that he couldn't, not until he told the president everything.

It was then, nearly a year ago now, that David had sat down with Robert in the Oval Office and told him about Project Showdown. The story spun by this man on that day had sounded like something out of the Old Testament, a series of fantastic events of mythical proportion. Such an account made it seem as if Joshua were a real man who really had knocked over the walls of Jericho with a blast of horns. As if John's Revelation were a real possibility, in literal terms.

David had insisted that Robert know the full extent of Project Showdown, because he wasn't sure that the president of the United States would want someone with such a résumé to serve as his spiritual adviser.

At first, Robert wasn't sure either. He commissioned a private study to determine if the events described by David Abraham could possibly have happened as the man claimed. The man he'd put in charge was a proud agnostic with the FBI named Christian Larkin.

One month after receiving the assignment, Larkin had walked into Robert's office a changed man. The only copy of his report, simply titled *Showdown*, was now in Robert's closet at the White House residence.

Larkin had analyzed satellite images of Colorado, which showed some spectacular anomalies if you knew what to look for. He had conducted hundreds of interviews, analyzed the material from many of the buildings, and explored the canyon in question with ultrasonic equipment.

In the end, there was no room for doubt. Evil had indeed visited the small town of Paradise, Colorado, in a most stunning fashion twelve years earlier. What started out as a covert experiment to study the noble savage in a controlled environment had spun horribly out of control. The shocking events of Project Showdown required three hundred pages.

Robert had called David Abraham within an hour of reading Christian Larkin's full report and insisted that he fill the role of his personal spiritual adviser.

He looked at David, who was watching him, calm now.

"Okay. Tell me what's on your mind."

"I have," David said.

"You know what I mean, Father. I'm not making the connection here."

"I'm not a priest," David said. "But I appreciate your confidence in me. Can you look past the simple ways of man?"

Meaning what? Robert wasn't a man of subtleties—he never liked it when David employed them to make his points. "Don't tell me this decision I'm about to make has anything to do with what happened twelve years ago."

"Maybe yes, maybe no. But I have a feeling. I haven't had a feeling like this for twelve years. I can tell you that this Iranian defense minister, this Assim Feroz, is not where he is by accident. He will be the destruction of Israel if you allow him."

David stood and walked across the room, staring at the books. He'd always been a great lover of books. He collected them, tens of thousands of them. Some said that his was the most valuable private collection of books in the world.

"There is an evil stirring, Robert," David said behind him. "I realize you would prefer some evidence, but nothing I can tell you would satisfy your demand for plain facts. I came here to tell you and the secretary that you must not, under any circumstances, yield to Feroz."

"What do you suggest I do?"

"I suggest you pray, Robert. You do still pray, don't you? For your son?"

"More than you know."

"Then pray more. And know that Assim Feroz is your enemy." He turned and faced the president. "Have you ever heard of a man named Laszlo Kalman?"

"Doesn't ring a bell, no."

"The X Group, then?"

Robert frowned and shook his head. "No. Should I?"

"Yes, I think you should. But not from me. You should talk to the CIA."

"What does this have to do with the initiative?"

David hesitated. "I believe they're connected. I can't prove it any more than I can prove any of this has anything to do with Project Showdown, but I have a very strong feeling, Robert. A feeling I haven't had in twelve years."

"So you said."

A soft knock interrupted them. He knew that knock—two raps. It was his son, Jamie, who had carte blanche permission to join him in any unclassified meeting he wished during these last few months of his life. The doctors had given him two, but they all knew he would outlast any doctor's prognosis. He had lived eighteen years with a very mild case of Down's syndrome complicated by a congenital thyroid dysfunction that was supposed to have killed him before he turned four. Other than being short for his age, he showed no physical clue of his illness, unusual for those with Down's.

His mind was a different matter. Although Jamie was eighteen, he had the mind of a twelve-year-old.

There was nothing that Robert and Wendy, his wife, loved more about their son.

"It's Jamie," he said.

David nodded once. Smiled. He had his own affection for children, didn't he? *It's why he and Jamie have struck up such a friendship,* Robert thought.

"Come in."

The door swung open. A short boy, blond and sweet, stared at them with wide brown eyes. "Can I come in?"

"Of course. I've been expecting you."

Jamie walked in and shut the door. His one love in life was politics. He lived and breathed the business of government, which in his simple world primarily meant scanning the news channels, listening to a good three hours of talk radio each day, and sitting in on whatever meeting his father would allow him to. It didn't matter that half of it flew over his head; Jamie had a way with politics. His outlook on life gave him a unique insight into the public psyche. If Robert wanted to know how the American public felt about a certain initiative, nine times out of ten Jamie's perspective would tell him.

In ways his staff would never truly appreciate, Robert credited Jamie for his ascent from Arizona governor to president. At his son's suggestion, he'd revamped his entire campaign during the primaries, bought himself a Harley, and become the people's man from Arizona. And that was only the beginning. His wife, Wendy, had once teased him that he'd won the presidency by thinking like a twelve-year-old.

The very least he could do for his son was to allow him unfettered access to a political life that most could only dream about. He took Jamie anywhere and everywhere that he could.

Jamie looked sheepishly from his father back to David. "Heavy discussion?"

"David thinks that Assim Feroz isn't who he says he is," Robert said. "What do you think?"

"I think Feroz is a bad goat," the boy said. "I think he's lying and won't disarm anyone but Israel."

"Really?" Robert lifted a brow and smiled. "What brings you to this conclusion?"

Jamie shrugged. "I don't believe him."

David put his arm around Jamie and faced the president. "Listen to your son, Robert. For the sake of his generation, listen to Jamie."

6

Deep in the darkness beyond the black tunnel, a terrible enemy had gathered and was waging war against the light.

The light was a tiny pinprick at the end of the tunnel, and Carl's mind and soul were fixated on that light. Two days or maybe ten days ago—he'd lost his sense of time completely—that light had been the murder of two people in the Andrassy Hotel. But he'd extinguished that light, as Kelly had asked him to. He'd learned long ago that if he didn't obliterate certain memories, Agotha would, and he didn't favor her methods.

Now the light at the end of his tunnel was survival.

He'd learned how to ignore the darkness and focus on the light by disciplined repetition. His ability to control his mind and by extension his body was his greatest strength.

In fact, his mind, not a gun or a knife, was his greatest weapon, and his handlers had helped him learn how to wield his mind in a way that few could.

The enemy changed shape regularly. Right now it was an intense heat that threatened to suck the moisture out of his body and leave him so dehydrated that his organs might stop functioning. But if he forced his mind to accept the impression that it was cool in the room rather than hot, he could maintain his energy for an extended period of time.

He sat cross-legged on the metal chair, willing his flesh in contact with the chair to stay cool, sitting perfectly still so the rest of his skin would not be unexpectedly scalded.

He'd slowed his heart rate to fifty beats per minute to compensate for the heat in the same way that he increased his heart rate to compensate for extreme cold. He did not eat or drink or pass any waste. These were the easiest functions to control. More difficult were his emotions, which seemed predisposed to rise up in offense at such treatment. In the worst conditions, he resorted to turning his emotions to Kelly. To her blue eyes, which were pools of kindness and love. The only such pools he knew.

All of this information registered as part of his subconscious, like a program that ran in the background. The light at the end of his tunnel remained at the center of his attention. Carl was so used to the torturous conditions of his pit that he no longer thought of them as torment. They were simply the path to the light.

Agotha had asked him recently whether he thought he could ever step outside the mental tunnel. "If your tunnel protects you from threats, could you not deal with those threats offensively rather than merely defensively?" she'd asked.

"I *am* offensive," Carl replied. "My aim is to survive."

"Yes, and you achieve that aim very well. But have you ever tried to deal with the threats more directly?"

"I'm not sure what you mean."

"You ward off the heat by controlling your mind and changing the way your body reacts to it. Have you ever tried to change the heat itself?"

Was she suggesting he try to lower the room's temperature? It was absurd, and he politely told her as much.

"Is it? What if I were to tell you that it's been done?"

"How? When?"

"In many documented cases studied by science. The pH balance of water, for example, can be significantly raised or lowered strictly through focused thought. This was first published by William Tiller, PhD, in a book titled *Conscious Acts of Creation*. There have been dozens of studies by quantum physicists since. None of this fits well with the older understanding of Newtonian physics based on sub-atomic particles, but it makes sense in accepted quantum theory, in which waves of energy, not particles, form the foundation of the world we know. It is possible, Carl, to affect these waves. They are connected to your mind."

"I can push an object with my hand and make it move," he said. "I can't do that with a wave from my mind."

"Because you don't think of the wave as an object." She walked to the chalkboard and drew a dime-sized circle. "Imagine that this is an atom, one of the smallest particles we know, yes?"

He could remember this now that she said it. "Yes."

She drew an arrow to the end of the board. "If an atom were enlarged to the size of a dime, the space between it and the next closest atom would be ten miles in every direction. There are a countless number of atoms that make up your hand, correct?"

"Yes."

"But in reality, most of your hand is this empty space *between* the atoms." She tossed the chalk into its tray. "This space, which was once thought of as a true vacuum, is actually a sea of energy. This is the zero-point field, most evident at a temperature of absolute zero. But it rages with energy at all times. Does this make sense?"

"This is all proven?"

"Yes. Finding ways to predictably influence this field is where theory takes over."

The light in Agotha's eyes was infectious. She smiled. "Do you know how much energy the empty space between atoms holds?"

"No."

"A single cubic yard of this so-called empty space, this sea of raw energy known as the zero-point field, holds enough energy to boil away all of the earth's oceans."

Hard to comprehend, much less believe.

"I want you to begin thinking of ways to step past your safe walls into this sea of energy. Imagine that your mind is connected to other objects through the zero-point field, just like islands are connected to each other by the sea. Can you do that?"

The thought of going beyond the black tunnel of safety unnerved him.

"If you were to stand on your island—your mind—and send out a large wave toward another distant mountain in the sea, could you destroy that mountain? Or at least move it?"

"I suppose you could."

"With an idea the size of a mustard seed, you could move a mountain," she said. "It's all a matter of perspective. When you first tried to see the light at the end of your tunnel, what did you see?"

"I closed my eyes and saw nothing but blackness."

"And what did you feel?"

He hesitated. For some reason the memory of failure had never been stripped away. The first time they'd inserted a needle through his shoulder, he screamed until he passed out.

"Pain," he said.

"But you found a way to construct the tunnel by pushing through the blackness to the light."

"Yes."

"Maybe you should try to punch a hole in the side of the tunnel and push back the sea of heat. Change the heat, rather than just protect yourself from it. It's theoretically possible."

The discussion with Agotha had been a few days ago, perhaps a week, perhaps a year. No, it was recent, very recent. Now in the safety of his tunnel, seated on the metal chair in the very hot/cold place, Carl decided that he would try again. He'd managed to take part of his mind off the light without the tunnel collapsing around him only three or four times, but each time, finding a way beyond the black tunnel's walls had proven too difficult.

It wasn't easy to take even a fraction of his focus off the light. The light was his survival, his comfort, his life. He'd become very good at giving it his complete attention.

Splitting the mind's eye was not unlike moving his physical eyes independent of each other, something he'd learned with great difficulty as a sniper. He moved now with caution, first allowing the tunnel wall on his right to come into his field of vision while never breaking contact with the light far ahead. He gradually began to isolate features on the tunnel wall.

The process was slow but fascinating. The tunnel protected him from the heat beyond. So far so good. He lingered there for an hour or ten, growing comfortable with his divided focus.

What if he could form a second tunnel to punch through the first tunnel?

The thought took him by surprise. The light faded, and for a moment he thought the tunnel had collapsed. But it remained straight and true, and the distant pinpoint of light came back into sharp focus.

He considered this new thought. Maybe a *second* tunnel of focus could break through the walls he'd constructed.

KELLY LARINE sat at a round metal table in the main laboratory, watching the monitor as the lines of numbers ran by. Carl's vitals had held rock steady since he'd gone deep, nearly three days ago now. In terms of controlling his emotions, he was better than Englishman, who, although the more accomplished killer, seemed to have less control over his mind, which could in time make him the lesser of the two.

Then again, Englishman had appeared on the scene a full month after Carl and was already well ahead of him. He had come to them practically ready-made, which only eroded her own trust of the man. On occasion she couldn't escape the vague notion that he was far more than who he said he was. More than even Kalman or Agotha knew. A puppet master who was simply playing games here while he waited for his true purpose to reveal itself.

Laszlo Kalman fears the man, she thought.

There were never more than three assassins in the X Group at any one time. Sometimes up to a dozen were in training, but in operation, only three. At the moment only two: Dale Crompton, known as Englishman; and Jenine, the dark-skinned, soft-spoken feline from the Ukraine. Neither of them had the same control over their emotions as Carl, but both more than compensated with skill and determination.

All three had full control of their vitals and had developed nearly inhuman thresholds for pain, although how Englishman and the Ukrainian managed so well without mastery over emotion was still a bit of a mystery to Kelly.

On the other hand, maybe their achievements weren't really that much of a mystery. The training methods perfected by Agotha were all founded on a guiding principle that had yet to fail: the appropriation of identity. The assassins thought they were surrendering their memories, but Agotha wasn't concerned with erasing memory as much as erasing identity.

Identity was the linchpin.

Commandeering a person's identity allowed Agotha to manipulate the memories associated with who a person was and what he had done without compromising his knowledge of how things worked. How to operate a car, for example, or brush teeth, or kill a man in the most effective way depending on the circumstance.

Agotha Balogh wore the same yellow dress she so often wore, always half-covered by a white lab apron. At the moment she was calibrating the powerful spinning magnets that she used in conjunction with powerful drugs to rewrite the identities. The machine was a common MRI machine, the kind found at any decent hospital, but its magnets had been adjusted to Agotha's specifications. The drugs she'd been testing for the last decade, however, were evidently nothing so common.

Everything about the X Group was extraordinary, from the operatives they'd managed to sequester away in the hills of Hungary, to their incredible success rate, to the highly controversial techniques they used to train, to the personalities at the helm. Kalman. Agotha. And now she could add her name to that list. Kelly.

"No change?" Agotha asked.

It was a rhetorical question, to add some noise to the room. "None," Kelly said. They returned to silence.

Kalman. Kelly knew little more than what Agotha had told her about his background. He'd killed his first man when he was eight. The dead bodies in his wake could not be counted, Agotha had said. Somewhere along the line he'd become convinced that the mind was man's most powerful weapon, not a gun. His interest in manipulating the mind had started when he met Agotha at the University of Newcastle in the UK.

"What is this?"

Kelly looked at Agotha, who was staring at the monitor. She glanced back at Carl's vitals.

"What's what?"

"His heart rate," Agotha said.

Kelly saw the numbers blinking on the screen. Saint's heart rate had risen from roughly fifty beats per minute to ninety. They stared, caught off guard by the sudden change.

"How long?" Agotha asked. "Were you watching?"

"It was fifty less than five minutes ago. It's been fifty since I came in half an hour ago. Did you check the logs from the last twenty-four hours?"

"Yes. He's been static for more than forty-eight hours. Something's happened." Agotha hurried over to the computer and punched up his record. "Less than a minute ago. The rest of the indicators are steady."

Carl's pulse steadied at ninety-one beats per minute. Kelly watched for thirty seconds. The rate changed again.

"It's dropping."

"So it is."

"What do you think caused that?" Kelly asked.

Agotha watched as Carl's heart rate fell to sixty, then held steady.

"We're not dealing with the known here," Agotha said. "It's amazing enough that Carl can alter his vitals as easily as he does."

"A simple break in concentration could be enough to cause this."

"True, but he's not given to simple breaks. I would guess that it was emotionally induced. Controlling the receptor cells' ability to receive peptides in response to various stimuli is practically unheard of. Carl is the first candidate we've had who's demonstrated a capability to do this."

The chemical reactions of emotions were one of Agotha's primary areas of research. Because emotions were in essence chemical reactions in the brain, science had long accepted the fact that it was possible to manipulate the chemicals and therefore the emotions. A number of drugs on the market did this. But for a person to exercise control over his brain's chemicals was a different matter.

"You know that he's progressed in other areas," Agotha said.

"Such as?"

"His marksmanship. You know that he's matched the limits of ballistics accuracy out to two thousand yards. He placed ten consecutive rounds within a twelve-inch grouping at one and a half miles. According to all conventional knowledge, Saint can't possibly improve. The bullet would require its own guidance system to do any better."

Kelly knew of his latest scores—she'd overseen the testing herself. Her involvement with him was primarily to manipulate, and she was playing her role well, building his trust, earning his love so that her power over him would be unchallenged. His only weakness was her, and it was a weakness by design.

But lying awake late at night, she wasn't sure that all of her emotions were as calculated as they had once been. She couldn't tell Agotha, of course, but what if Carl was now becoming her greatest weakness?

Impossible. But if it became true, Kalman would eliminate her.

"Why doesn't Kalman trust Saint?" Kelly asked.

"Who said any such thing?"

"No one. I see it in his eyes. And he's called up another ten recruits."

At present, Carl was the only recruit. They had been confident enough in him to stall the solicitation of more, but Kalman had put out an order for ten new candidates to be filled within sixty days. Only one in ten would survive the first three months of training. The rest were killed and their bodies incinerated. Clearly, Kalman was thinking that either Carl, Dale, or Jenine would need replacing soon.

Agotha nodded absently. "A man like Carl presents certain risks. Frankly, his relationship with you could become a concern. Has he asked about his father since the last treatment?"

Kelly blinked. "It was your plan that we bond. And yes, he said he couldn't remember who his father was."

"Yes, my plan, but I'm not sure the bond is strong enough. If his bond with you is ever compromised, he may become obsessive about knowing his origin, this father figure of his."

"You want me to strengthen his bond with me?"

"I didn't say that. If the bond is too strong and something happens to you, we may lose him. It's a tenuous balance."

"With Carl as my guardian, it's unlikely anything will happen to me. Right?"

"Regardless. With Saint going on his first mission in two weeks, we need a new recruit."

"Two weeks? So soon? You have the mission?"

Agotha turned back to the monitor. "We've had it for a long—"

She froze, eyes on the monitor.

Kelly scanned the stats. "What?" For the second time in ten minutes, something about Carl's situation had changed. This time it had nothing to do with his vitals.

"Did you change the room temperature?" Kelly asked.

"No. It should read 150. You did nothing?"

"Nothing."

The temperature was now 140.

"It must be a malfunction," Kelly said. "It's happened—"

"The control hasn't moved. How could it be a malfunction?"

The same system that regulated the temperature in Carl's pit fed a small closet that was measured by separate sensors. In this control, the temperature was still 150 degrees.

"Then the thermometer has malfunctioned?" But she knew three separate meters measured temperature, and a quick glance at the computer told her that all three were down to 138.

Agotha grabbed the phone, called Kalman, and then promptly hung up.

"It's going back up," Kelly said.

They watched as the temperature rose and finally settled at 150.

"How's that possible?"

"By the same physics that allow a monk to change the pH balance in water through meditation," Agotha said excitedly. "By affecting the zero-point field. Let me know if it changes again." Agotha changed screens, ran a quick diagnostic test for any system anomalies, then walked to the printer and watched her report print on continuous-feed paper. The printer stopped and she ripped the paper off the spool.

"Changes?" she demanded.

"Still 150."

The door behind them opened, and Kalman stepped in. He approached them, expressionless.

Agotha handed him the report. He glanced up and down, then eyed her. "What is it?"

"The graph showing room temperature."

"So you changed the temperature."

"We didn't change it." The fire in Agotha's eyes betrayed her passion. She was a scientist, not easily excitable, but at the moment, no matter how she tried to hide her feelings, she looked as if she might explode.

He glanced at the chart again. Studied it in silence. His eyes lifted, but he did not lower the paper. "You're suggesting that he did this?"

"Do you have another idea?"

He obviously didn't.

"When is he scheduled to come out?" Kalman asked.

"He has an afternoon drill with the others," Kelly said.

Kalman set the report on the table. "Bring him out now."

Agotha had talked often about the quantum physics behind the brain's ability to affect its surroundings, but Kelly had never seen evidence of it. Focusing the mind, stripping memory, shutting out pain, seizing control of typically involuntary bodily functions, controlling emotions—mastery over these was unusual but had been demonstrated for years among the greatest warriors and spiritual masters.

The notion that Carl had actually managed to control the temperature in his pit by affecting the zero-point field was altogether earth-shattering. It may have been proven that the empty space between atoms was filled with large amounts of energy, but she wasn't sure she was ready to believe that Carl could affect this field.

"Put him on the range," Kalman said. "Let's see what he can do."

"He'll need a few hours to normalize and eat."

"He shoots before he normalizes."

"Every man has his limits."

"We've broken his limits many times."

"The drill he faces this afternoon will test his shooting in an optimum setting before stretching him to his limits," Kelly said. "I suggest we wait as planned."

Kalman looked at her, and the darkness in his eyes made Kelly regret her suggestion. But he didn't object.

He simply turned and left the room.

7

The Englishman watched the man cross the compound with his typical nonchalant amble. Tall and well toned, with shortcropped hair and a small nose that made him look boyish. He had become ruthless as required, but his soft eyes contradicted his stature.

I am lost, I am found—Carl was trapped between the two without the slightest clue as to how lost and found he would truly be before it was all over. Lost to himself, found to the darkness that waited below hell.

Englishman wanted to grin and spit at the same time. It was all growing a bit tedious, but he'd known from the moment he walked into this terrible camp that he would grow bored before the fun began.

Soon. Maybe he could change his name from Englishman to Soon. *Soon* rhymed with *noon*, as in Daniel Boone.

There was no way he could adequately describe the depths of his hatred for the man who was stealing the show with all of his move-this-move-that emotional control nonsense. Englishman could and would drop Daniel Boone the moment he felt good and ready.

Which would be soon.

He took a deep breath and shifted his eyes toward the pretty girl. Kelly. She was playing her part well enough, but he wasn't sure she could toe the line. Her emotions could get in the way, despite all her training. Did she know the true stakes? He wasn't sure. Either way, he wouldn't trust her. He'd come here to make sure Carl did what was expected of him, or kill him if he didn't, and Englishman was hoping it would be the latter, because he hated Carl more than he thought humanly possible.

If they only knew why he was here, what lay in store for them, how he would do it all . . . My, my.

Hallelujah, amen, you are dismissed.

NEARLY FIVE hours had passed since Kelly liberated Carl from his pit. She'd hooked him up to an IV and pumped enough glucose and electrolytes into his system to wake the dead. He'd been in his pit for two days, she told him. A meaningless bit of trivia.

He ate a light, balanced meal, then showered, shaved, and dressed in his usual training clothes per her instructions. A short run brought him fully back to the present, the physical world outside the tunnel.

Kelly had asked him to meet her and the others at the southern shooting range precisely at three for a drill. He wandered the compound for half an hour, then made his way south, past the hospital, which doubled as the administration building; past the barracks; past a small mess hall that they rarely used and a weight room that they frequently used.

He supposed that he spent an average of three days every week in the pit, but he rarely recalled anything about them. In the beginning his training was filled with the pain required to break him. Needles and electricity and drugs. They still used electricity, but once he'd learned to control his body, his training had turned more to his mind.

The mental training sessions, like the kind he endured in the pit, were now hardly more than a good, hard run. So long as he success-fully blocked the pain. But today was different. At some point, he'd tried to split his focus and succeeded. Then he tried to break through the wall in his tunnel and, to his surprise, again succeeded. In fact, if he wasn't mistaken, he had pushed back the heat crowding his safe place.

He wondered if Agotha had noticed anything in her detailed charts. Kelly hadn't said a word of it, but if he wasn't mistaken, the light in her eyes was brighter. Regardless of what caused this, he was glad for her. She was pleased with him, which made him happy.

Where do I come from?

The stray thought surprised him. He briefly wondered who his father was, then put the question away. There was no answer to it, he remembered.

They were waiting by the sandbags when Carl made his way down the slope to the shooting range. The vegetation had been cleared four thousand yards to the south—he could see the trees bordering the encroaching forest but no detail from this distance.

There was something ominous about those trees, he remembered now. Oh yes. The compound didn't need a fence to keep them in, because if any of them stepped beyond the trees, their implants would send a debilitating electrical charge into their brains. He'd tried it on two occasions with disastrous effects, but he couldn't remember any-thing beyond that.

At least a dozen assorted personnel drifted in and out of contact with him in any given week, guards and scientists and the like. He knew a few by name, but most existed like ghosts in his mind, beyond the scope of his immediate concern, which was survival and success.

Two of these personnel stood fifty yards to each side of the sand-bags now. Carl focused on the three people who were in the scope of his immediate concern. Kelly, Englishman, and Jenine.

The recruits were not allowed to talk to one another except as required by their training. As far as he remembered, he'd never spoken to either Englishman or Jenine without Kelly present.

Jenine. The sight of her standing in black slacks and brown pullover, facing the south with her arms crossed, evoked nothing but curiosity in him. Did she have a pit? Jenine looked at him without expression. Her hair was black, shoulder-length, framing a face with fine features browned by the sun. The Ukrainian, as they called her, was always quiet and hard to read. She could smile softly and slit your throat before you realized that her smile had left her face.

Carl wasn't sure if he liked her or not.

Englishman. From twenty yards he looked angry, but this was nothing new. The man often looked angry, as if he resented being in Carl's company. This wasn't a weakness necessarily. He compensated for his lack of emotional control in other ways. There was something profoundly unusual about the sandy-haired man who stared at him over crossed arms, wasn't there? Whereas Carl could shut out distractions and focus on his intentions, Englishman seemed to join the distraction and use it to his advantage. He didn't strike Carl as a man who needed to be taught anything by either Kalman or Agotha. Kelly said that the exercises kept Englishman's skills sharp. One day, when Carl was truly skilled, maybe he would learn to do what Englishman did.

"Hello, Carl." Kelly smiled. "You look refreshed."

"Thank you. I feel good."

Not a word from the other two. Though often pitted against one another, they rarely trained together with a common objective. By the looks of the three sandbags set thirty yards apart, the X Group was going to be shooting downrange. *That will change before the end of the training exercise,* Carl thought. Beside each shooting post lay a crate. He had no idea what these were for.

Kelly faced all three of them. "The reactive targets are set at twelve hundred yards. You will each use the M40A3 with a 150-grain boat tail bullet today. All three rifles have been sighted in at four hundred yards."

She walked to the left, eyeing Jenine. "You will expend ten rounds on the reactive targets. Consider it a warm-up. Beyond the yellow reactive targets are the static targets. Do not shoot these targets. Dale, take the far left; Jenine, center; Carl, on the right. Take your places, find the targets, and fire at will."

Carl turned to his right and walked to his sandbag. He'd shot more rounds on this field than he could count, much less remember. What he could remember with surprising detail were the technical specifications of the rifles, handguns, and cartridges that he'd spent so many hours with.

The rifle leaned against a small fiberglass rack by the sandbags. It wasn't just any M40A3, he saw. It was his. He'd sighted it in at four hundred yards himself; he could remember that clearly now.

Warmth spread through his chest. He wanted to run for the weapon, to pick it up gingerly and examine it to be sure they hadn't scratched it or hurt it in any way. His heart began to pound, and he stopped, surprised by his strong emotional reaction to the weapon.

A hand touched his elbow. "It's okay," Kelly said softly. "Pick it up." She looked at him sheepishly, as if she'd given him the very gift he'd been waiting for so long. And she had, he realized.

Kelly winked. "Go on, it's yours."

Carl walked to the rifle, hesitated only a moment, then picked it up and turned it in his hands. So familiar. Yet so new. The sniper rifle fired a .308 round through its free-floating twenty-four-inch barrel. Internal five-round magazine, six including the one chambered.

He ran his hand over the well-worn fiberglass stock and noticed that his fingers were trembling. He had to seize control, but these feelings were so comforting that he allowed them to linger.

Did he always feel this way when he picked up his rifle? Did the others feel this way?

He lifted his eyes and saw that Kelly was watching him with interest. Maybe some understanding.

SAINT

He knew that the rifle he held was nothing more than a tool formed with precision, but then, so was a woman's hand. Or an eye. It was what he could do with this rifle that fascinated him.

"Thank you," he said.

"You're welcome. Shoot well today."

"I will."

She walked back toward the others.

Carl picked up a box of .308 rounds and set his emotions aside. Shooting well, as she put it, was like the beating of his own heart. Both could be controlled, both gave him life, both could be performed without much conscious thought.

He dropped to one knee and set the box of cartridges on top of the sandbag. A quick examination satisfied him that the mechanisms of the rifle were in perfect working order. He pressed five rounds into the magazine, disengaged the bolt, slid a cartridge into the barrel, seated the bolt, and took a deep breath.

He was eager—too eager. After the jumble/void of the last day/week, he felt fully alive, kneeling here, staring downrange. A slight, steady breeze, five miles per hour, he estimated, from the east. Temperature, seventy Fahrenheit. Low humidity.

It was a perfect day for killing.

Carl unfolded the bipod and lay down behind the rifle. Scope cover off. The thin thread that hung from the barrel to indicate wind barely moved. He drew the weapon back into his shoulder and glassed the field.

Three rubber cubes—yellow, blue, and red, each five inches square—sat on the ground. The yellow was his. When hit, the cube would bounce, thus its identification as a reactive target.

Carl snugged the weapon and swung the Leopold's familiar crosshairs over the target. He knew the charts for dozens of rounds intimately. The 150-grain boat tail bullet had a muzzle velocity of twenty-nine hundred feet per second. It would take the projectile just under half a second to reach twelve hundred feet. In that time the bullet would fall 22.7 inches and slow to nineteen hundred feet per second.

But his target was thirty-six hundred feet away. Twelve football fields. In that time the bullet would slow below one thousand feet per second and fall more than five feet.

If he placed the crosshairs directly on a target that was four hundred yards out, he would hit it precisely as aimed. But at this distance, he had to place the crosshairs more than five feet above the target.

He steadied his aim, lowered his heart rate, released the air in his lungs, and focused on a spot roughly five feet above and slightly to the left of the yellow cube.

A round went off to his left. Englishman. The red target leaped. All of this was peripheral to Carl. He slowly increased the tension in his trigger finger.

His rifle jerked in his arms. It took the bullet almost two seconds to reach the yellow cube. When it did, the cube bounced high, rolled to the left, and came to a rest.

Carl ejected the spent shell and chambered a second cartridge.

A breeze cooled his neck. A musty odor from the dust under his chin and the gun oil mixed with the sharp smells of burned gunpowder. His body hugged the earth. He was a killer. His preferred instrument was the rifle, and his weapon was his mind.

Carl shot the second round, waited for the target to bounce, reloaded quickly, and reacquired the yellow cube.

He was a man who loved and hated only if and when it facilitated his objective to kill. To kill he had to survive. Survive and kill, this was his purpose.

He sent a third round speeding down the range.

"Do you know what happened today?" Kelly asked behind him and to his right.

He held the scope over the target until it settled for a fourth shot. "No," he said.

"In the pit, do you know what you did?"

Carl considered the question, trusting his instincts on the fourth shot. She was talking about the heat. Rifle cracks filled the air in rapid succession. Three cubes bounced downrange, like three puppets on strings.

"No."

"Did you try to lower the temperature in your pit?"

"Yes."

She lay down beside him, glassing the field with binoculars. "You succeeded, Carl."

So. His mind was connected to his immediate environment through this quantum field that Agotha had told him about.

He shot the target for the fifth time. Successfully. Chambered his last round.

"Do you see the white target on the right farther down range?"

He moved his scope. "Yes."

"It's over three thousand feet. Can you hit this target for me?"

She knew he could—he'd done so many times in a row. Carl answered anyway. "Yes."

"But by the time the bullet reaches that distance, its parabolic rotation will be nearly ten inches in diameter. You can't control the bullet's wobbling to place it where you want in that ten-inch circle."

"Correct."

"But if you can lower the heat in your pit, can you affect the flight path of a bullet?"

Carl eased off the scope and looked at her. Was she serious?

"I want you to shoot your next five shots at the static target. Shoot for the center."

"I was in a different place when I lowered the heat."

"Go there now."

"I was in the pit for three days. My mind was focused. And I don't know what I did. I created a second tunnel, but beyond that I don't really know what happened."

"You can't create a second tunnel now?"

He didn't know. Even if he could, he had no idea how to affect the flight path of a bullet leaving the end of his barrel at twenty-nine hundred feet per second.

"Please, they insist."

He would try, of course. He would do whatever they wanted. He would do it for Kelly, but he was quite sure he would fail.

And what were the consequences of failing this time?

"They don't care if you succeed or fail; they only want you to try."

Carl nodded.

The 150-grain bullet would fall much farther over two thousand feet. And the target looked much smaller, barely more than a white speck in the distance.

He spent a full minute bringing his focus into alignment and entering his tunnel. The light at the end was the target. It was here, on the range, that he'd first thought of consciousness as a tunnel.

The air had become still; there were no shots from the others. There was a path between where he lay and the white target. He walked that path, feeling the wind, the humidity, and the trajectory that the bullet would take, arching over the field to fall precisely into the porous white electronic board.

He lowered his heart rate so that he would have enough time to shoot between beats. Made his muscles like rubber so there would be no movement conducted through his bones into his shoulder, or forearms, or trigger finger.

It was time to send the bullet. He knew that he would hit the target if he shot now.

But they wanted more.

Carl tried to form a second tunnel as he had in the pit. But no matter how he focused his mind, it refused to form. *Why?*

Maybe he didn't need a second tunnel. Maybe he could just focus on the bullet and force it to fly straight.

He brought all of his mind to the bullet. For a moment everything around him simply stopped. His breathing, his heart, the air itself seemed to pause.

Carl sent the bullet.

He couldn't see the impact on a static target at this distance, but through her scope, Kelly could.

"Again," she said.

"Did I hit it?"

"Again," she repeated.

Carl reloaded and repeated the same shot five times to her urging.

"Did I hit it?"

She lowered her binoculars. "You did fine, Carl. I'm very proud of you."

Kelly handed him the binoculars and walked toward the others, who were watching patiently.

"We're going to play a game," she said loudly enough for all of them to hear. Carl lifted the binoculars and quickly studied the target.

He'd hit it, he saw, but in a scattered pattern, with no more accuracy than any other time. The marks winked out as the target electronically cleared itself. He lowered the binoculars. Kelly had reset the target with the remote in her hand. She offered him a small smile and continued.

"Each of you will lie down in a crate with your weapon. The crates have been treated with a chemical that agitates hornets. You have a six-inch opening in the front panel through which to shoot at the reactive twelve-hundred-yard targets. Once you are ready, three dozen black hornets will be funneled into each of your crates. Their stings will adversely affect your muscles. The first to place five rounds into the target will win this contest. Do you understand?"

None of them responded.

"Good. The winner will be freed and given a knife. The next one to succeed will be armed with a handgun and will hunt the winner until one of you is either killed or incapacitated. The third will be left in the crate for an additional five minutes and then taken to the infirmary."

Carl dropped the binoculars on a sandbag and picked up his rifle.

8

Robert Stenton ruffled Jamie's short blond hair and hugged him tight with one arm. "You're smarter than most of the senators in Washington, buddy. That's why I insist you hang around."

Jamie smiled sheepishly, then pulled away.

They were in the Oval Office, where the secretary of commerce had just briefed the president on the progress of a White House initiative to increase import tariffs. Jamie had sat on the couch and fidgeted through most of the meeting. He'd had a bad night, the first in a week. The pain in his stomach hadn't settled until he finally vomited at three in the morning.

"Can I go?" he asked.

"Sure." *He's not himself,* Robert thought. "You sure you're okay?"

His son shrugged. "I'm tired is all."

"Okay, go get some rest. Mom will get you something to eat."

"'Kay."

Candace poked her head in the door. "Your next appointment is here, Mr. President."

"Send him in."

Jamie turned back. "Who's that?"

"Classified, buddy."

"'Kay."

Jamie passed a thick, short, dark-haired man at the door and was gone.

"Sir?"

"Come in, Frank. Have a seat."

"Yes, sir."

It was clear that Frank Meyers wasn't accustomed to visits to the White House, particularly not the Oval Office. The few times Robert had met with the CIA had always been with the director, Ed Carter. This time Carter wasn't even aware of a meeting.

"Drink?"

"No, sir."

Robert seated himself on the sofa facing the director of special operations. "What do you know about the X Group?"

Frank Meyers blinked. Clearly he hadn't expected the question.

Robert grinned. "No sense beating around the bush. I realize that most of what you do is classified and rarely discussed with us political types, but it's a direct question and I want a direct answer."

Meyers cleared his throat and clasped his hands together. "The X Group. I'm not sure I know precisely what they are. Or precisely—"

"I don't need you to be precise. Just tell me what you know. If you don't know, then give me the word on the street."

"Well, I'm not sure there is a word on the street. Very few are even aware of their existence."

"But you are."

"Don't misunderstand me; I'll tell you everything I know. It's just that this group is an unusual animal. We aren't sure where they're located or which hits they carry out, but—"

"So they are assassins."

"Yes, sir."

"Ordered by?"

"They have no apparent political or ideological interests. Strictly guns for hire. Mercenaries. They're run by a man named Laszlo Kalman. Hungarian descent. From what we know, they use cutting-edge psychiatric science to train their people. Phase-three memory wipes, torture, extreme forms of psychological manipulation. But they get results."

"Phase-three memory wipes?"

"There are three levels of memory manipulation. The first pertains to specific memories, dates, occurrences—the kind that comes with age. The subject forgets what has happened. The second involves time-space disorientation. Not knowing who you are or where you are. The third and most invasive is forgetting that you *should* know who you are or where you are. The Chinese proved fifty years ago that even otherwise healthy men can be effectively reduced to a phase-three memory wipe in less than forty days. The assassins employed by the X Group are first reduced to shells of their former identities and then trained as extremely loyal and lethal killers."

"So this group has been used?"

"By us?"

Robert lifted an eyebrow. "That would be illegal, right?"

"Under most circumstances, yes."

"Most?"

"I have to say, sir, I'm not sure—"

"I know that both the military and the CIA have been known to take out a bad guy now and then."

"The rules change under declared war."

"So we declare war on drug lords and take out a cartel in Colombia. Just give it to me straight. To your knowledge, has the CIA ever employed the X Group to carry out an assassination?"

"That's not the way it works. We hire people who hire lawyers who have clients protected by their attorney-client privilege who have other clients who hire assassins. Follow?"

Robert grinned. "I'll take that as a yes."

"Some of our offshore interests have contracted the X Group. The fact of the matter is there's no organization as isolated and as sure to give us the desired results. Some people say they've never failed in the ten years they've been on the market."

"I wasn't aware the market was so well organized."

"On the contrary, the black market requires more organization than the open market to avoid authorities."

So the X Group peddled assassinations on the black market. David Abraham not only knew about them but thought they were somehow linked to Assim Feroz.

Robert stood and walked behind the couch. "Who do they typically target?"

"At five million dollars a hit, the targets are pretty far up the food chain. High-level executives. You heard about the death of Sung Yishita, president of the Bank of Japan? It was reported as an accident, but it wasn't. His throat was cut two minutes after a high-level speech in Tokyo."

"Government officials would make natural targets," Robert said. "Heads of state."

"Yes. Which is why we have established an agreement with them to reject any contract on a United States federal government official."

The revelation surprised him. It was tantamount to paying off terrorists. At the same time, it gave him some comfort. He hated to ask how much they paid.

"Sounds like the agency's in pretty deep with them," Robert said.

"In this regard it's unavoidable."

Robert walked to his desk, wondering how far he really wanted to go with this.

"You have any reason to believe there might be any connection between Assim Feroz and the X Group?" he asked, facing the man.

Like most politicians, he'd learned to judge people by how they reacted to questions. Being asked this run of questions by the president of the United States was usually disarming even for someone as practiced as the director of special operations. Meyers showed no visible sign of surprise, but his answer was too long in coming. He stared at the president, mute.

Robert pushed. "I have reason to believe that there is a connection. I want to know whether there's any plan on or off the books to deal with Feroz using the X Group."

A pause. "There's been some discussion. Only that. I'm afraid I simply can't say more."

"You can't possibly think that killing Feroz would resolve the dilemma we're facing with the Iranian initiative."

"No."

"It would only fuel their fires."

"I agree. But killing a man isn't the only way to remove him from the scene."

"What, you wound him? Give him a disease that turns him into a vegetable? Poison him?"

"They've all been done, but no." Frank Meyers averted his eyes. "With all due respect, I really don't know of any operational plan involving the X Group. I've already said way more—"

"Remember which office you're in, Mr. Meyers."

A direct stare. "That's my point."

Robert knew he'd pushed the topic to its limits. He already knew more than he wanted to know.

"You're right. I'm sorry, I don't mean to compromise your position. But I assure you that the last thing we need is to make the Iranian defense minister a martyr."

"Absolutely, I agree."

But there was still a plan. What then? It would make no sense for anyone to attempt to kill Feroz or him. Or, for that matter, the Israeli prime minister.

"Does Director Carter know about this 'discussion' with the Group?"

Another slight pause. "I believe he's aware of some things."

Then a formal plan existed. A plan that was being considered at the highest level. And his spiritual adviser seemed terrified by this business. Which part of it, David himself probably couldn't explain. The man operated on spiritual discernment as much as on facts. Evil was lurking.

Then again, David Abraham had come face-to-face with evil and lived to tell of it. The president of the United States had Gandalf the White as a spiritual adviser.

Robert regarded the director of special operations steadily. "You know that I've decided to oppose the Iranian initiative at the UN summit in two weeks?"

"Yes, sir."

"Please tell whoever you need to that I want no agency involvement in this. Are we clear? If I have to, I'll talk to the director, but the last thing we need is some kind of cover-up in a matter as critical as this."

"Understood, sir."

"Thank you, Frank."

9

Carl lay on his belly in the narrow crate, rifle extended, ready, with the barrel an inch from a small wooden door he assumed would be opened when it was time to shoot. A strong medicinal scent made it hard to breathe.

The implications of his predicament were clear. He was expected to win. Neither Jenine nor Englishman could place five rounds in a target at two thousand yards as quickly as he could.

And if he won, one of the others would hunt him. He would have less hornet venom in his system, but the hunter would have a gun. He wasn't sure which he preferred, to be the hunter filled with poison, or the hunted with far less poison. They both sounded like a kind of death. The thoughts crashed through his mind as he tried to focus.

A gate opened behind him, and a faint, then loud, buzzing swarmed in his ears. Closing his eyes would compromise his accuracy now and his sight later. He wondered briefly if a hornet could sting someone in the eyeballs.

He searched for his tunnel, ignoring the soft bump of frantic hornets along his legs, then up his back. He shut down methodically, easing into the safe place of darkness.

A hornet buzzed past his right ear and slammed into the crate in front of him. For a moment it came into focus. A large black insect with gangly legs and appendages sticking out in every direction. It ricocheted off the wood and struck his right cheek.

The gate slid open in front of him. He peered through his scope at the tiny white target. The hornets were slamming into his shoulder blades now, buzzing loudly around his head.

A sharp pain cut into his neck, and he gasped. This pain had sliced past the wall of protection he'd erected. How?

Panic crowded his mind. He'd felt fear before, and he knew how to shut it down. It had to go first, before he could shut down his nerves. He couldn't hope to hit the target until he'd rid himself of pain.

The buzzing became a roar. Carl reluctantly took his eyes off the target and closed his eyes. He felt another bite, this one on the small of his back.

He disassociated his mind from the pain and let himself fall into a soft black pillow. There he formed his tunnel from the blackness.

Another sting on his shoulder, but this one hurt less. The poison would affect him more than the pain now.

Slowly the sound faded.

Slowly the pain eased.

Then he was in.

He snapped his eyes open and peered through the scope, no longer noticing the blur of insects streaking by. He didn't even know where they were biting him now, only that they were.

Carl found the target as he would on any other day, adjusted for the same range and wind factors he had earlier, and walked the trajectory the bullet would take. Then he squeezed his trigger finger and sent the bullet away.

The report crashed against his ears in the enclosed space, but he took strength from it. His rifle was his savior, speaking to him with undeniable power.

He chambered another round and sent it down the same path. Kissing cousins.

Bullets were his dear friends, following his every instruction until they had wasted all of their energy in his service. There was no loyalty greater than a bullet's, speeding to a certain and willing death.

The sensation of hornets stinging him felt like popcorn popping on his skin. A dull ache spread beyond the tunnel.

Carl didn't know how long it took him to fire the five rounds; he only knew that he was finished. And that the crate's lid had been pulled off.

He clambered to his feet and handed Kelly his rifle. Pain flared through his body. Kelly was yelling something at the guards. "Two pills only. Handgun, remember."

She placed a knife in Carl's right hand, two pills in his left. "These won't help the pain, but they'll minimize the swelling and keep you alive. I will go with you."

He shoved the pills into his mouth and stumbled forward, glancing back at the other two crates. The buzzing inside would cover any sound he made now, but it wouldn't take either assassin long to find his tracks.

He cleared his head, turned to the north, and ran into the compound with Kelly close behind.

THE SUN would be down in three or four hours. *Nothing matters more than survival.* This one thought hung before Carl, calling him forward. A buzz lingered in his mind, not from the hornets, but from their venom.

He understood less of the world than he once had, but some things he understood better, and one of them was survival.

The other was killing.

Kelly ran lightly on her feet beside him, trusting him completely. At one time she would have offered him advice, but those days were behind them. He could now survive by instinct.

"Do you have the key to my pit?" Carl asked.

"Yes. Do you think—"

"To the door in the wall behind my chair?"

Hesitation. "Yes."

The guns were still booming behind them. Carl veered west and ran for his bunkhouse.

"Carl, are you sure—"

"We have to get in before they're out. Faster."

They sprinted the last hundred yards, then flew up the steps and into the concrete barracks. The air was suddenly quiet. One of them, likely Englishman, had completed the task.

Carl spun back to be sure they'd left no marks on the cement steps. None. He closed the door.

"Into the pit," he whispered. They descended the stairs on the fly.

Kelly didn't need her key for the pit; it was open. But the small door at the back was secured tightly with a dead bolt, which he assumed could be operated from either side of the door.

"Where's the key?"

She pulled out a small ring of keys from her pocket. "I hope you know what you're doing."

"I do."

He pulled the door open, revealing a dark earthen tunnel reinforced with wooden beams. He stepped in and pulled her in behind him.

"Do you know where this leads?" she asked.

"No. Lock the door."

"There's no light. The door on the other end is locked."

"Hurry, please. Lock it."

Kelly pushed the door shut, fumbled for the lock, and engaged the dead bolt.

"Is there anything in this tunnel?" he asked.

"No. It's for emergency evacuation. Leads to the hospital."

"It's a direct path? Straight?"

"Yes."

Carl turned and walked into the darkness.

"I can't see a thing. Where are you going? There's nowhere to go."

He reached back for her, felt her stomach, then her hand. Together they walked into the inky blackness. "Tell me when you think we've reached the halfway point."

She stopped him in twenty seconds. "Here." He knew that they were nowhere close to halfway, but he decided it was far enough, so he stopped. Released her hand.

Silence engulfed them. He listened for any sound of pursuit but expected none. Even if Englishman or Jenine stumbled into his pit, neither had a key to the tunnel. There was no way they could verify his presence here.

"Now what?" Kelly whispered after a minute.

A tension in her voice betrayed her insecurity. She'd been through training similar to his own, but he didn't know how far they'd pushed her. And she hadn't been in a pit since his coming. Perhaps that explained her fear of it.

"Now we wait," he said. "Please don't talk."

Carl squatted. And waited. Home.

"HOW LONG are we going to stay in here?" Kelly whispered.

They'd only been in the tunnel for an hour.

"Until I've rested and have the advantage," he said aloud, thankful for the dirt walls that absorbed the sound of their voices.

He could hear Kelly moving toward him. Only now had she realized that he'd moved away from her during the last hour so that he could hear above her breathing. It occurred to him that he was her protector here. In the tunnel, he was the master and she was the student. It made him proud.

Do you believe?

The soft voice echoed through his mind. Believe in what? In the Group, of course. His belief in everything he'd learned here was the fabric of his survival. He'd actually lowered the temperature in his cell! Imagine that.

"Why did you move away from me?" Kelly asked, closer now.

"I wanted to be able to hear," he said, standing.

"And?"

"They entered my pit, walked around, and then left."

"This is like your mental tunnel," she said.

"Yes."

Her hand felt for him, touched his chest, his neck, and then drew back.

"How are the bites?"

He hadn't given them much thought, but he felt his neck now. "Gone mostly."

For a long while they stood in silence.

"When do you think you will have the advantage?" she asked.

He shrugged in the darkness. "A day."

"A day? That long?"

"Patience is always—"

"I know about patience. I taught you that, remember? But how will a day help you?"

"Do you want to leave now?"

"I'm only the observer. I stay with you."

"Maybe it'll be less than a day," he said.

He really was in complete control, not only of her safety, but in some ways of how she felt. Kelly settled to the ground, and he joined her.

For several hours neither of them spoke. Carl was doing what he did best. He didn't know what Kelly was doing.

"Do you mind if I touch you?" she finally asked. "As much as I hate to admit it, the darkness is a bit disorienting."

"Okay," he said.

She felt for his knee, then found his hand. "Okay?"

"Okay."

They held hands in the dark for a while.

"Do you know what's so special about you?"

He didn't answer.

"Your innocence. You're like a child in some ways."

A child? He wasn't sure what to think about that.

"But there's a man inside, waiting to be set free," she said. "I'm very proud of you."

Her statement confused him, so he still said nothing.

"Do you remember Nevada?" she asked.

"Yes."

"I've always wanted to go to the desert. It's so vast. Uncaring of the rest of the world. It's just there, no matter what else happens. Golden sands and towering rocks. Coyotes that roam the land, free. When this is all over, I think I'd like to go to the desert in Nevada."

"When what is over?" he asked.

She didn't answer for a while. "It's just a fantasy," she said. "Something stuck in my head. I can imagine you and I walking into the desert like this, hand in hand, away from all of this. Do you ever think about leaving?"

"To the desert?"

"Not necessarily. Just leaving this place."

"I can't leave."

"I know, but if you could. If you didn't have the implant, would you go?"

"I don't know. It's not so bad here."

"I once lived in the desert," Kelly said. "In Ethiopia when I was ten. I was born in Israel and sold on the black market. To an Afghan warlord who loved me for my fair skin and hated me because I wouldn't do what he wanted. I escaped into the desert when I was fifteen and ended up in Hungary, where I met Agotha. I studied under her, you know."

Another long stretch of comfortable silence filled the tunnel.

"You're scheduled to go on your first mission in two weeks if you succeed in your training," Kelly said.

"I will succeed."

She didn't immediately agree, and he wondered why.

"I've always succeeded."

"The final test will be very difficult. If you fail, Kalman will kill you, assuming the challenge hasn't killed you already. Kalman doesn't want anyone to succeed—it's his way of making sure only the best enter the field."

She tightened her grip on his hand. "But I want you to succeed."

"I always succeed," he said again.

"If you do, you'll be leaving this place."

"But with you. And then we'll return."

"Yes, with me. Always with me."

"Will I always be in training?"

"Is there any other way to stay sharp?"

"Do you enjoy hurting me?" he asked.

Carl had no clue where the question had come from. He was talking without really thinking. Half of his mind was still in the darkness, focused on the current objective, listening for any sound of approach. The other half was asking this odd question.

She wasn't answering him.

"I know that your hurting me leads to strength," he said, ashamed that he'd asked. "You're helping me be strong. I'm thankful for that."

Kelly removed her hand from his. He'd hurt her feelings! She was upset with him. He wanted to shut his emotions down now, but he wondered if he really should. There was a strange life in this terrible empathy that had suddenly overtaken him. He wanted to comfort her heart. He was her protector, every part of her, which meant he could only protect her emotions with his own.

It was the first time he'd thought of his role this way. But he felt powerless to do anything, so he just sat in the darkness and let himself feel uncomfortable.

Kelly started to cry. The sound was very soft, a sniffing followed by a nearly silent sob.

Carl reached his hand into the darkness. When he found her, he realized that she'd rolled over to her side and had curled up in a ball. She lay on the tunnel's dirt floor, sobbing softly.

But why? Didn't she know that he loved her? Maybe she didn't.

Carl rested his hand on her hip, frozen by awkwardness. He couldn't remember her ever being so hurt. It reminded him of a time, long ago, when he lay sobbing on his cell floor, overcome by his training. They'd cut him and inserted needles into him and placed electrodes on different parts of his body and forced him to look into light for long hours and then left him alone in his pit for two days. These things had made him want to die, and he cried like Kelly was crying now.

It made him want to cry again.

Carl laid his head on her hip. Before he could stop himself, he was crying with her. He didn't know why.

She cried harder then, which made him feel an even deeper sorrow. A flood of anguish gushed from the darkest place of his soul, and he couldn't stop himself. He began to shake with sobs.

It must have lasted for a full five minutes. Strange and terrifying minutes.

Kelly sat up and wrapped her arms around him. She cried into his neck. "I'm sorry, Carl. I don't want to hurt you. I hate myself for hurting you. I just . . ." Her voice was choked off by sobs.

Carl sat back against the tunnel wall like an emptying sandbag, still unable to stop the flow of unidentified grief. He loved Kelly. He loved her so very much. The pain she was feeling was his fault. How could he have done this to the only person who cared about him?

They held each other for a very long time until their crying finally subsided. Then stopped. Then they sat in silence.

And Carl began to forget the way he'd felt. Englishman was out there somewhere, waiting.

"IT'S TIME," Carl said.

They'd been in the black tunnel for almost a day, he guessed. Exhausted by his time in the pit leading up to this day, he'd fallen asleep and rested for ten hours. Kelly had slept through the night as well, although they couldn't tell day or night down here.

They didn't speak of their emotional outburst, but Kelly kissed him on the lips and assured him that it wasn't his fault. She loved him very much. They'd left it at that, much to his relief.

"Can you open the door that leads to the hospital?"

"You don't want to exit through the hospital."

"My opponent, likely Englishman, is either there or waiting upstairs in my barracks."

"How do you know?"

"He'll know by now that we hid close, beyond the reach of the GPS monitors, which he's likely examined. The monitors are in the hospital. My guess is that he's there, waiting for me to show my signature, or above, waiting for me to show my body. I'll show myself in the barracks, and if he's not there, I'll backtrack through here and come around behind him."

"If Englishman isn't in the hospital?"

"Then I'll hunt him. Either way I have to go on the offensive."

She considered this for a moment, then agreed. "I'll exit through the hospital and leave the door unlocked."

Carl started to leave, but she held his arm. "No matter what happens here, Carl, remember that I love you."

"I will."

She reached up in the dark and kissed him on the cheek. "Remember."

Carl waited until she opened the door at the far end before walking toward his pit. He hurried up the stairs, found the barracks empty, and waited by the window, eyes on the hospital a hundred yards away. From his vantage he would see anyone who attempted to leave the building.

Five minutes passed. Then ten. Still no sign. If he was right, there should have been a sign by now. He had to change his course of action now, before—

The door to the hospital flew open. Kelly ran out. Still no sign of Englishman. Was there a problem? Maybe something had happened after they'd gone into hiding. Why was she sprinting toward his bunker?

He retreated to the stairwell so that his field of vision covered both the hall below and the door. If Dale came either way, he could make an escape under cover.

Kelly pulled up to the door and threw it open. "He's not there!"

She was telling him this? Ordinarily she would only observe, never report. She'd unlocked the door for him only at his suggestion, not hers. The games were always between the recruits, never the handlers.

Yet she was telling him that Dale wasn't at the hospital.

And then he knew for himself that Englishman wasn't at the hospital, because he stepped up behind Kelly.

Carl dropped into the stairwell. He landed on the fifth step and saw then that Englishman didn't have the gun trained on him.

He'd shoved it into Kelly's temple and was pushing her into the bunkhouse.

"You go, she dies," Englishman said.

Carl's first thought was that this maneuver had been planned by both of them. Why else would Englishman have waited for Kelly to arrive before stepping out? The coordination was too tight.

Englishman smiled and jerked Kelly's head back by her hair. "She's right. I'm not in the hospital because I'm here, and I'm here because I knew within the hour yesterday that *you* were here, in your pathetic little pit. I've been waiting too. I didn't expect such eager assistance from your lover. In the middle of the room, or she gets a bullet."

"He's lying!" Kelly cried. "What do you think you're going to do, shoot me? Agotha will kill you with the flip of a switch in a matter of seconds."

"I didn't hear anyone say that I couldn't use you to get to him. I have more than forty bites on my body, and they all tell me I should kill Saint. Why not the woman who loves Saint as well? We all know she's nothing more than a mouthpiece for Kalman. I doubt he'd miss her that much."

To Carl he said, "Get up here, wonder boy."

Something was wrong, drastically wrong, but Carl couldn't identify it. Surely Kelly had no role in Englishman's appearance. She seemed genuinely frantic. Never mind that; she would never betray him!

He came out of the stairwell in two long steps.

"Knife on the floor," Englishman said, pressing the gun into Kelly's cheek.

Carl backed toward the middle of the room.

"Knife on the floor!"

He raced through alternatives. In the moment Englishman removed his gun from Kelly's head to adjust his aim, Carl could and would throw the knife. Englishman knew this. A quick flip of Carl's wrist, and Englishman would have a knife buried in his eye.

Carl could throw the knife now, while the gun was pointed at Kelly's temple, but a simple spasm from Englishman and she would die.

There were several other alternatives, but the only ones in which both he and Kelly lived depended on Englishman. Would he really hurt Kelly? The man would kill him, Carl was sure of that, but killing a handler was another matter.

Unless there was more to it.

There was a way for Kelly, Carl saw. She might be able to get them out of this situation. But would she? If he dropped his knife now, he would be completely dependent on her to move at the right time, or Englishman would likely kill him.

Their eyes met, but he saw no encouragement in Kelly, only fear.

"Now I count, and her shoulder goes first," Englishman said. "Please don't make this difficult on yourself. Just drop the knife."

Carl opened his fingers and let the knife clatter to the floor.

Englishman smiled. He licked Kelly's ear. "Had to throw in some cliché, you know."

Cliché? Something to be expected.

"Now it's time for me to shove her to the side. That's the way it always goes. The villain shoves the princess to one side, thus making a convenient opening for the prince to kill the villain without hurting the princess."

His words seemed out of place. But that was exactly what Englishman wanted. Carl had been here before.

Englishman shoved Kelly to his left. "No interference, princess. I haven't hurt you, remember that. I simply used you the way Carl used you to escape. No penalties."

He was right. She wouldn't interfere. She couldn't, not without facing consequences from Kalman. The training protocols were inflexible.

Kelly glared at Englishman but stayed where she was.

The man leveled his gun at Carl. "You do know that I've been given permission to kill you. *Incapacitate* or *kill* were the words used, I believe."

Carl said nothing.

"The fact that you stand there like a piece of wood makes me think

I should just get it over with. On the other hand, a bullet through the leg would be a little more interesting, wouldn't it?"

For a long moment he stared at Carl. Then he tilted the gun down and aimed at Carl's thigh.

The room rocked with a thunderclap.

But it wasn't Dale's gun. It was Kelly's. She had a gun in her right fist, pointed at Englishman, who was looking at a bloodied hand. His gun had flown across the room.

"No," Kelly said. "It doesn't end like this. Carl had you beat."

The man lowered his hand and let it bleed on the floor. His face was white, but he showed no other outward sign of pain.

Kelly walked over to Englishman and slammed her gun into his temple. He dropped, unconscious.

She's broken the rules. She's saved me but only by breaking the rules at terrible risk to herself.

"No one hears about this," Kelly said in a low voice. She stared at him with shining eyes. "Not a word, you hear, Carl? Remove this from your memory. Remember only if you ever doubt my loyalty to you."

"Why did you do this?"

"He was going to shoot you through the leg. I love you."

"My leg would have healed."

"Not in time for your mission. As far as Kalman's concerned, you shot Dale."

"What will Englishman say?"

"What I tell him to. Agotha's waiting for you."

Carl stepped past them, but he paused at the door and turned back. Kelly's blue eyes searched his soul.

He would die for her.

10

David Abraham paced Air Force One's conference room, stroking his beard. Robert had never seen the man so bothered. Gone was that stoic confidence that came with his seasoned spiritual father persona. Gone was the calm and collected demeanor of wisdom. The man before Robert and CIA Director Ed Carter looked downright tormented.

"Please, David, sit. You're making me nervous."

"And you should be nervous. *I'm* nervous."

"I can see that. But I don't think I understand why. Nothing you've said sounds as ominous as you're suggesting."

Robert had invited David to ride along for the sake of this conversation with the director, but he was beginning to think that it was a mistake.

Carter clearly wasn't comfortable speaking frankly with David in the room, and David hadn't clarified his concern regarding Assim Feroz in any way that made sense, perhaps because Carter was still present.

"Sit, David, I insist."

David pulled out a chair and sat. "Forgive me, Robert. I simply don't have the kind of details that would justify my concern to any-one other than myself. I can only say what my son saw."

"In this"—the president waved his right hand through the air—"this foggy vision Samuel had nearly a year ago."

"Yes, it was quite some time ago, and yes, what he saw was admit-tedly rather general. But he's not given to visions. It's the first one he's ever had, I think. But what he saw is now knocking on our door."

"None of this strikes you as a bit . . . absurd? It was just a vision—"

"Not *just*. No more than you're *just* the president."

"I wasn't in this vision of his, right? I don't understand the con-cern." It couldn't possibly be a sound idea to base a policy or deci-sion on a vision, even if it came from a source like David, even if it contained alarming details about the X Group that no ordinary per-son could have possibly stumbled upon.

"Assim Feroz will destroy whoever crosses his path," David said. "You're now in his path, so yes, you were in the vision, if only by association."

"Either way, the summit is sponsored by the United Nations. There'll be no lack of security."

David Abraham took a deep breath and nodded, but his eyes were heavy with concern. *He isn't telling us everything,* Robert thought.

He faced Carter. "Well, Ed, now you know how the president of the United States makes decisions that change history." He winked at David. "Sorry about that. I couldn't resist."

David was too involved to find humor in his comment.

Robert leaned back, sighed, and regarded the director. Ed Carter was well over two hundred pounds and had a double chin that looked exaggerated below his small round spectacles.

"So would you mind telling us this plan involving the X Group, Ed?" Robert asked. He'd already told Ed Carter about his earlier conversation with the head of special operations, but this would be the first confirmation David would hear that any such plan was afoot.

David gave them both an alarmed look.

"Don't worry, I think we're past secrets here," Robert said. "We all know about this little assassination club. According to Samuel's vision, the X Group is connected to one of my greatest enemies. I think that qualifies me to hear everything and anything, don't you?"

Carter looked as if he was still trying to figure out whether to take the whole business of this vision seriously. But then, so was Robert.

Carter cleared his throat. "Well, some ideas have been thrown around. I'm not sure you'd approve—"

"Just give it to me straight. We'll go from there."

"Okay." Carter spread both hands. "No plans at this point, actually. I think you'll see why."

"Please. Just tell me."

Carter frowned. "What if, and I really do mean *what if*, Assim Feroz were eliminated? His death could fatally undermine his initiative."

"First of all, any such plan would be highly illegal and morally reprehensible. Second, he'd become a martyr. His death would probably energize support for his plan."

"Unless Feroz was eliminated because he was attacking innocents. As a terrorist."

"Terrorist? I don't follow."

"What if Feroz was killed while attempting to assassinate one of his enemies?"

"Such as?"

"Such as you, sir."

Robert wasn't sure he'd heard correctly. He coughed once. "You can't just tell the world that such and such a leader was planning on killing me and so we took him out. We're not at war."

"Assassinations are provoked by policy rather than war. In this case, we're talking about a policy that would threaten the national security of our ally Israel. I'm not suggesting or defending this course of action; I'm merely explaining the rationale." He put his palms on the table. "As for the world believing, you're right. The assassination attempt would have to be real. If it was, and we could produce definitive evidence linking Mr. Feroz to the attack, we would win world sympathy by taking him down."

"You're actually suggesting that we stage an assassination attempt on me and blame it on Feroz? And then kill him?"

"That was the idea, sir. Not the plan, mind you. There are some problems, of course, but it does have some merit if you consider—"

"No. It would never work. And even if it did, it breaks more international laws than . . . Forget the laws—it's murder."

"As are all assassinations. Maybe you could declare war on Iran to cover our moral quandaries and send a hundred thousand men and women to their graves instead. Forgive the sarcasm. My point is, assassinations save lives. Kill one drug lord, save the hundred men he will kill. Kill one tyrant, save a hundred thousand of his subjects. In the case of Feroz, I'm not sure I follow Dr. Abraham's reasoning, but I think we all agree that this man's life will cost the world dearly."

"Tell me straight, Carter. You've been with the agency for what, fifteen years? Does every president hear this assassination speech?"

"Yes. And are made aware of its merits. What was the human cost of removing Hitler or Saddam Hussein by war rather—"

"Point made," Robert said. "But Feroz isn't Saddam or Hitler."

"Not today, no. Maybe David has some thoughts on this."

They both looked at David Abraham, who regarded them with an ashen face. He pushed his chair back. "Forgive me, gentlemen. I'm afraid I must excuse myself from this discussion. I would say you're both right, but I'm not in a position to inform your final decision. Do you mind, Robert?"

He'd never known David to refuse a good philosophical debate. Clearly the man was plagued by more than he'd revealed. And just as clearly he wasn't going to divulge any more.

"Feel free to use my quarters to get some rest if you need it."

"Thank you, but I think I'll be fine. Please, continue." David left the room and closed the door behind him.

Robert turned to Carter. "What happens to the people involved in the assassinations, or fake assassinations as the case may be?"

"They would probably need to be eliminated."

"So more innocents die."

"Soldiers, guns for hire, not innocents."

"And this is where the X Group comes in," Robert said. "You're planning on hiring the X Group to take out Feroz as a matter of foiling his nonexistent assassination attempt on me."

"It's a thought. You would need to agree, of course."

"Exactly when were you planning on discussing this with me?"

"I believe I have a meeting scheduled with you this Friday."

Robert pushed back his chair. "Cancel it. The answer is no. I don't care what rationale you throw my way, I won't be involved in this. If you can find a way to turn Feroz into a bumbling idiot who makes a fool of himself at the summit, I'm all ears. But I don't play politics with bullets."

"Of course, sir. It was just an option."

"An option you were ready to recommend."

"Not without your endorsement. Consider it a nonstarter."

11

Because Kelly had told him that he was going to be tested and then, if he succeeded, go into the field in two weeks, Carl kept track of the days for the first time in months.

After speaking with Agotha for a long time, he went into the pit again, to fight the cold this time. And he was able to nudge the cold back each time, but not much. He could add a few degrees to the room's temperature. Maybe five, once ten, she told him. This was like someone changing the pH balance of water through meditation, she insisted, something that had been proven possible.

She was trying to help him believe, but he already did believe, so he mostly just listened. Agotha was sure that he could do more, but he couldn't.

On three different occasions, they brought him to the hospital for additional training, as they had for many months. They asked him to lie on a metal bed with his head inside the large white magnetic resonance imaging machine, put drugs into his veins, clipped electrodes to his toes and fingers, and then asked him to repeat what he knew for long periods of time. If he got the answers wrong, they turned dials and sent sharp shafts of electricity through his body.

He couldn't turn off the pain easily when they did this, because he had to focus on the right answers. In the early days, he'd passed out nearly every time. Now he rarely gave them a wrong answer. His memory was very good.

When he wasn't in the hospital or in the pit, he was with Kelly, practicing. He would often be put into a room with several objects and a fixed amount of time to create a weapon. Next to focus, improvisation was the assassin's greatest asset. He'd learned to make weapons out of almost anything that was small enough to wield:

A sharp knife that could be held and used like any blade made from an aluminum soda can in under ten seconds.

A stiletto made from a coat hanger in even less time.

A bomb with enough power to gut a man at three paces made out of chemicals available in most bathrooms.

These tasks came easily. Kelly told him that both Jenine and Dale could do the tasks as easily. In fact, they were better than he in many disciplines, particularly Englishman, who had more natural strength and speed. But Carl had the better mind, she told him. And the mind is an assassin's greatest weapon.

Whenever they were pitted against each other, Englishman always held the edge. In hand-to-hand, in knife wielding, in strategic field exercises that challenged both reaction time and decision making, Englishman was better. The only clear edge that Carl had was his ability to control his emotions and his bodily functions, which in turn made him the better sniper.

If all three were compared head-to-head in all disciplines, their rank would fall thus: Englishman, Saint, and then the Ukrainian, but not by much.

Agotha was eager for him to shoot straighter at a long range. Each day that he wasn't in the pit, he sent hundreds of bullets toward the static target at two thousand yards.

Each day he landed more than three hundred of them in the twelve-inch circle. There was always the bad bullet that strayed because of poor construction. Carl didn't let the few wayward bother him. The rest were reliable. In the field, he would inspect each round before using it to be sure it met his standards, but on the range he didn't bother.

For some reason Kelly didn't tell him whether he was actually able to make the bullet defy its physical ballistic limits and fly straighter. There was no way for him to know, even by looking at the target. Just because a bullet landed in the bull's-eye didn't mean he'd made it go there. At two thousand yards, the bullet was wobbling in a ten-inch circle and could land anywhere in the target.

But a computer was tracking his every shot to see if he was beating the odds. He didn't think he was. They would be shouting about it if he was.

In all of Carl's training, a single word called to him, like a father urging him forward. Through his tunnel.

Believe. Just believe, Carl, and you will find the light at the end of the tunnel.

When Kelly came for him in his pit on the tenth day, he knew by the fear in her eyes that the day for his final test had arrived. He'd survived the last two—the hornets, and before that the Andrassy Hotel. Today he would face the ultimate measure of his skill.

"Shower, eat, and report to the hospital," she said.

They stood on the floor of his pit, looking at each other. Carl had always thought he'd be proud on this day, but the darkness in her eyes ruined his confidence.

"You're coming with me?" he asked.

"No, not this time, Carl."

"Do you know what they'll ask me to do?"

"They wouldn't tell me. They insist that I remain here."

"In my pit? Why?"

"Not down here, necessarily. Just in your bunker. They said it wouldn't be long."

Carl put his hand on the metal chair, unsure he wanted to leave her here and cross the field to the hospital alone.

Kelly moved closer to him, eyes fixed on his. "You can do this, Carl. I know you can. You will succeed. You always have."

She took his hand and kissed him on the cheek. "You'll succeed for me. There's nothing you can't do for me. Promise me."

"I promise."

"Kiss me, Carl."

He leaned forward and kissed her lips. The warmth of her mouth seemed to swallow him. They lingered, hot, wet, sharing the same space deep in his mind where everything was safe.

"Go to them," she finally said, smiling softly. "Keep my face and my smile with you."

"I love you," he said.

"I love you too."

THE HOSPITAL had three floors including the basement. Carl had never been to the basement or the third floor, both of which were off-limits. The main floor had four smaller examination rooms and the main laboratory, where Agotha administered her drugs and electric shock treatments that helped her subjects forget and remember.

Carl felt well rested and full of energy. He'd eaten twenty carrots, half a bag of jerky, and a chocolate bar to give him the energy he might need for the test. Then he'd showered and dressed in black fatigues and a brown nylon pullover. The shoes he wore were also black, made of canvas with rubber soles. Agotha was in the laboratory when he entered it.

"Hello, Carl."

"Hello."

"Thank you for coming."

"Kelly told me to come."

She studied him with eyes that seemed to move too quickly. Concern. "Kalman is waiting downstairs. Please follow me."

They walked down the hall to a staircase that descended into the basement. Agotha opened the metal door that led into the lower floor, and a strong medicinal odor stung his nose. Three large picture windows lined a long white cinderblock hall. Each looked into a room.

Agotha opened the door into the first room and waited for him to enter. Carl walked past her and studied the room.

Kalman sat in a brown leather chair with wooden arms, smoking a cigar, watching him. Next to him was a large metal chair with buckled straps on the arm and leg rests. A round leather bowl was suspended above the chair, and from this headpiece extended several large electrical cords.

It was an electric chair.

Three guards stood to the left of the electric chair.

"Hello, Carl."

Carl stared at the chair, at a loss. He'd been told that to fail meant execution, but he'd always imagined a bullet to the brain. The chair didn't make him afraid—he had no intention of failing.

"Today you will either become the third assassin, or you will die," Kalman said. "I've decided that I will electrocute you when you fail. I think you have some considerable strength and should put on a good show, but not even a bull could withstand the electricity that will boil your blood when you fail us today. Do you understand this?"

"Yes."

Kalman shifted the cigar from one side of his mouth to the other, then stood. He ran a finger over the leather headpiece, removing dust, which he smelled and then wiped on his pants.

"If you execute your mission successfully, you won't have to face the chair, but I don't expect it. Tell me, what is your primary objective?"

"To survive."

"To survive why?"

"So that I can execute my mission."

"Good. Your first assassination was to be in five days, but I've decided to make it today. Today you will find and kill your handler. If you fail, I will kill you."

"My handler . . ." Carl wasn't sure he'd heard correctly. He had to be sure that he had the right target.

"Kelly Larine," Kalman said. "The one who has ordered you around for ten months. She knows too much and is too valuable to you. It's good to cleanse the system now and then. You know where she is?"

"Yes."

"You have one hour to kill her and bring her body to the hospital." Kalman pulled out a stopwatch and thumbed the knob on top.

Carl could not focus. He knew his mission, but he wasn't sure how to execute it.

"You may kill her however you wish," Agotha said.

"You may go," Kalman said.

"Thank you, sir." Carl dipped his head and ran down the hall. Up the stairs, out into the sunshine.

"LEAVE US," Agotha ordered.

The three guards left the room. The only thing more reliable than the assassins they sent into the field was one of their personnel. They were paid significant sums of money for their cooperation and threatened with significant consequence for any failure. Mostly thugs, but not stupid ones.

The door swung shut. "I want to voice my final objection to this," Agotha said. "Both are too valuable."

"She cares for him too much."

"Which only ensures that she will keep him safe. She knows that if he ever betrays us, we'll kill him with the implant. You're stripping away everything I've worked for!"

Kalman did not reply. He knew what he was taking from her and took pleasure from it. This was his twisted way.

"You think she's weak?" she demanded. "What would you know about a woman's weakness for a man? And this is no ordinary man whose life you're toying with. His shooting scores have improved all week. He's manipulating the field, for heaven's sake! You would kill a man like that?"

"Then perhaps he's too dangerous."

"Not if you leave his loyalty to me. We've led him to believe that she's his savior. Our manipulation has been extensive and effective. Last week he gave up a knife to save her in a test I designed for Kelly. He's dangerous, but not to us, not as long as we have his loyalty. But today you may compromise that."

"One of them has to go. I don't care which."

"Are you listening to me? Their emotional bond is a good thing. I'll leave the killing to you, but you will leave the manipulation to me."

Kalman drilled her with a dark stare.

"He's been carefully programmed both to survive and to love Kelly," she said. "This scenario presents no solutions for him. We are fighting ourselves with this mad game of yours."

"Then we will kill both of them."

"And accomplish what?"

Kalman rose, impatient. "If he is what you say he is, then let him prove it, and he will live according to the terms."

"He's a gold mine."

"You favor this one too much. We both know that Englishman is the better man. It takes more than good marksmanship to make a good assassin."

Agotha walked to the door and pulled it open. "Englishman could kill Saint easily enough now, but in a year or two?"

"If he survives today, we'll give him his year or two. If he dies, he wasn't meant to live."

12

Carl walked toward the bunker on legs filled with lead. His head swam in dizzy circles. He couldn't seem to make sense of the mission that lay ahead of him, much less form a tunnel of security from which to execute it.

So he just walked. He didn't feel the urgency to run. He didn't feel the need to use stealth. He just walked.

Birds chirped from the nearby forest. He wondered if Englishman had been faced with a challenge similar to this one. Or Jenine. They had both passed their final tests and been deployed. Soon he would join them.

But without Kelly?

Kelly was his life as much as the blood that coursed through his veins. Killing her was the same as killing himself. He couldn't kill himself. So he just walked.

But he had to kill her. If draining his blood was the only way to complete his mission, he would drain his blood.

Why would he agree to kill Kelly? Why did he long for an assassin's life? The answers, clear on some days, eluded him now. But he knew with more certainty than he knew anything else that his role in this operation was far more important than the dilemma immediately before him. His failure to execute the task would end badly for everyone, including Kelly.

If killing Kelly was the only way to become the assassin he was meant to be, he simply had to kill her, no matter how much he cared for her. She herself would insist.

The truth of the notion suddenly struck him as insane.

She was standing in the corner when he entered the bunkhouse. "You're finished?" She hurried over to him. "What's going on?"

Carl closed the door, heard it clank shut, surprised by how loud it sounded. He looked into her wide blue eyes and knew then that he couldn't kill her—not here in the light where he could see her eyes.

When he spoke he could barely hear his own voice. "Can we go to my pit?"

"Sure. What is it? Are you finished?"

"Maybe we should go to my pit," he said.

Her eyes searched his, concerned. "Sure, Carl."

He let her lead. They descended the stairs, walked down the long hall with its single caged incandescent light, down the concrete steps that led to his pit.

Kelly paused at the entrance, then entered the dark room lit only by the open doorway. She turned around by his chair and waited for him to follow her in.

But even here, in the safest place he knew, Carl felt powerless to kill her. He needed to go deeper.

"Do you have the key to the tunnel?"

She glanced at the locked door behind her. "Yes."

"Could we go inside?"

"Tell me what's happening, Carl. You're scaring me."

"I will tell you. But we have to go inside the tunnel where it's dark."

She found the key on a ring that she withdrew from her pocket, opened the door, and stepped aside to let him pass first.

He walked into the inky blackness a full fifty yards before stopping and turning back. She'd left the door open, but only a pale beam of gray followed them in. She reached for his arm and stared into his face. He couldn't see her eyes.

"I've never seen you like this. Whatever it is, you can do it, Carl. I believe in you. You have to believe in yourself."

"My final test is to kill you."

They were surrounded by silence and darkness, and ordinarily Carl would have found comfort in both. But he could feel the heat drain from her fingers around his arm, and the sensation terrified him.

"They want you to kill me?" she asked.

"If I don't kill you, they will kill me," he said.

They stood still for a full minute. *When she has the solution, she will give it to me,* he thought. But he knew that there was no solution. He would have to choose between killing her or being killed. If it was Agotha or Kalman or anyone else, the choice would be simple.

But his need for Kelly was as great as his need for his own life.

She placed her free hand on his chest. "How long did they give you?"

"One hour."

Kelly lowered both hands and swore in a whisper. "You can't let them kill you!"

She might as well have screamed the words, because in his mind they were deafening.

Her voice trembled. "You know very well that I'm expendable. What am I, just a slave girl that came to Agotha off the streets of Budapest—"

"Did you really shoot Englishman?"

He still couldn't see her eyes. "No. We used special effects to make it look like I shot him. The test was ordered by Agotha to test your loyalty to me."

"And is this a test too?"

"No! Kalman will kill you with pleasure. No doubt, we've destroyed your mind, I'm so sorry, but you have to listen to me. This is it—you have no choice. You have to kill me. It will be my penance."

"But you said yourself, you only deceived me to save me. It's why you hurt me. And when you did hurt me, you hurt yourself, not just me. We're linked, see? If I kill you, I'll be killing myself. I can't do that."

She looked at him without speaking. Then she lowered her head so that her forehead rested against his shoulder. "Dear Lord, what have I done?"

"I'll go to the hospital and see what they do."

"No."

"I've survived electrical currents running through—"

"No!" She slammed her fist against his chest. "No, no, no! You will not let them kill you!"

Then what? What could he do? She loved him; he believed it now. Whatever lingering doubts he'd had were denied. He could not kill her. He would not.

Either way, he would die. But there was a way for her to live.

Carl broke away from her and began to pace. "Time is running out." He still had forty-five minutes, but it seemed like only a second. "I have to do something. I can't . . ."

Desperation was an enemy he'd beat long ago. But this time there was no light at the end of this tunnel. It was black to the bottom, no solution, no objective that could be achieved in this place where he no longer knew who he was.

"It's the end this time, Carl," Kelly said softly. "There's no way out. No tunnel that will lead both of us to safety. I won't let you go to your death. Use the drugs on me. They're the kindest."

Something moved in Carl's mind. Something Kelly had said. He stopped pacing and peered into the darkness. "What did you say?"

"Drugs. They're—"

"No! You said there's no tunnel."

"Is there?"

He began to pace again as the idea blossomed.

Carl grabbed her arm and ran past her, jerking her after him. "Is the tank full?"

"The isolation tank? Yes, why?"

"I have to go in. We have to hurry!"

She ran behind to stay up with him. "What about the mission?"

"I can't kill you."

13

His plan was simple, but it made no sense, and Kelly told him that a dozen times before he lowered himself into the huge cast-iron ball they called the isolation tank.

It contained warm, salted water, heated to 98.6 degrees. In this water the body felt nothing. Carl would wear a modified deep-sea diving mask that effectively cut off all sensory input to the ears, the eyes, the mouth, and the nose, leaving him completely sense-free.

The isolation tank provided the simplest, easiest, and quickest way for most subjects to enter stasis. They rarely used it anymore because Carl had advanced beyond the need for such an unwieldy tool, but with it he could move most quickly, and time was now an issue.

He was going deep, he said. Very deep. Deep enough so that he would remain in partial stasis for some time after he came out.

As agreed, Kelly left him in the tank for thirty minutes before pulling him out, dripping wet. Despite an almost uncontrollable urge to ask him how successful his trip had been, she worked quietly. She dried his body and dressed him in a dry pair of pants. She did all with the ring of insanity in her ears. In many ways she felt as if she were performing last rites on an animal to be sacrificed in a sick ritual.

He had no more than ten minutes to complete his mission when he followed her back into the tunnel, shirtless and shoeless.

Kelly led him toward the hospital, groping through the darkness with her free hand. She could hear his breathing, a full fifteen seconds between each breath, and she knew that he was still deep in the safety of his world.

She, on the other hand, was in a world of more peril than she could remember ever experiencing. She could no longer deny the fact that she felt deeply for him. She was meant to earn his love, and she had, but in the process, he had found a way to earn something from her. It made everything she was doing feel like a betrayal.

Leading him in silence now, she couldn't hold back quiet tears.

He was going to die. She had tried to tell him as much, but he was adamant. Even angry. Now any attempt on her part to change his mind would only compromise his concentration.

She unlocked the door at the end of the tunnel and led him up the stairs into the hospital basement, still vacated of personnel. The door to the execution chamber was open. His breathing now came once every twelve seconds. He was normalizing!

Moving as fast as she could, Kelly strapped him in as Kalman had shown her several months earlier when he was in an especially cheerful mood. Each contact had to be coated with gel to ensure conductivity. Normally they would shave the head, but there was no time. She attached the electrodes to his forehead and to the back of his neck.

THE PLACE was as black as any Carl could remember.

He had formed his tunnel within seconds of entering the tank. He knew that he had a limited amount of time, but time ceased in here, so he didn't think of himself as in a race against the clock.

He was here to protect the tunnel. A terrible force would come to destroy it, he knew. An enemy far greater than any he'd ever faced.

He would have to do something new. He couldn't rely on the wall to protect him.

This time he would have to go outside the wall in a new tunnel, as he had recently, but with far more focus. His one advantage was that he knew how the attack would come. The force would come through his hands and skull.

If he could lower the heat in a room; if the pH balance of water could be altered so easily; if the faithful could walk into the fiery furnace and not be burned by flames or walk on water without drowning, then his mission wasn't impossible.

It had been done before.

Carl swam outside the tunnel, sending wave after wave of the sea to his extremities, to the place where the enemy would attack. It was all in his mind, of course, but the mind was his greatest weapon.

He remembered being led down the underground tunnel and being strapped into the chair, but these were noises and sensations of another world.

Then voices. Urgent. Arguing, perhaps. Excited, perhaps.

He smiled. Did they know that he was outside the tunnel? Agotha would be proud!

The voices ceased, and he knew that the attack was going to come.

And then it did, in a red-hot wave that took his breath away and flooded his eyes with blinding light.

"TEN, ELEVEN . . ." Agotha stared at the jerking body through the picture window. There was no way he could possibly survive!

Inside Kalman continued his count. "Thirteen, fourteen, fifteen." He nodded at the operator inside. "As agreed."

A loud clank signaled the break. The hall lights brightened, then one sputtered and winked out. Kalman stood beside the chair, wearing a look of fascination. At times like these Agotha hated him.

She pulled the door open and stopped short. The smell of burned hair was strong. He was surely dead. If not physically, then mentally. A vegetable. They'd found no record of a man surviving fifteen seconds at this voltage, the only reason Kalman had agreed to the terms.

"Carl?"

He was slumped against his straps, headpiece firmly in place.

"He's dead," Kalman said on her left.

The hall door crashed open, and Kelly pulled up by the large window. She rushed into the room and brushed past Agotha, not caring that her face was still wet with tears.

"Carl? Carl, please tell me you can hear me." She frantically unbuckled the leather mask and flung it from his head. She ripped the blindfold off his face. Then she went to work on the attachments on his arms and legs, practically tearing them free.

Agotha blinked. Carl's cheeks and lips were dry, not wet from tears or saliva. *Surely his eyes would be gone,* she thought. *Surely his—*

His left hand twitched. Residual current.

"Carl?" Kelly's voice was filled with desperation. She had deeper feelings for the man than even Agotha had guessed.

"He's not breathing!" Kelly cried. She dropped her head against his chest and listened for a heartbeat. But if he wasn't breathing now, a full minute since they'd turned off the electricity, he was dead.

As if in response to her thought, Carl's left hand lifted an inch from the armrest. Stopped. Then it twisted, and his forearm slowly rose.

Agotha was no longer breathing. Carl, on the other hand, had to be! Kelly had seen none of it, not yet.

Carl's hand rose slowly and touched the back of Kelly's head. Her whole body froze.

Carl smiled. "Hello, Kelly."

His eyes snapped open.

Kelly began to cry.

Behind Agotha, Kalman grunted.

"I OWE you my life," Kelly said.

"And I owe you mine." It was true. Without his love for her, Carl didn't think he'd have survived the last ten months, assuming that was truly how long he'd been in training.

They sat at a round table for four in his bunker kitchen, eating nuts and jerky.

"You know what this means, don't you?" she asked.

Carl put a peanut in his mouth and bit into it around a big grin. Honestly, he couldn't remember feeling this happy, so he let the feeling ride. "That I'll go into the field."

"Yes. Agotha is thrilled. If you were her pet project before, you're her golden calf now."

"And Kalman?"

She shrugged. "Kalman is Kalman. He lives for killing."

"Like a good father," Carl said. "Sets the rules and makes sure they're kept."

She gave him a strange look. Picked up a piece of jerky and tore off a strip. "You're not angry at him?"

"That would be impractical. He's only doing what he thinks is best. Can any of us argue with the results?"

She nodded. "What else can you do?"

"What do you mean?"

"If you can protect your body against the currents of an electric chair, shouldn't you be able to do more?"

"Anyone can ignore heat. I just do it better than most. That doesn't mean I can fly."

She laughed at that, and he joined her. The pleasure in her blue eyes, the soft curve of her neck, the shine in her wavy hair—he found her stunning. And he'd saved her, hadn't he? He had saved the one he loved.

"I have your mission, Carl," she said, flashing a mischievous grin.

"You do?"

"I do." But she didn't offer it.

"When?"

"In five days."

"Where?"

"New York City. They say it's a wonderful place. I can hardly wait."

"Who is it?"

"An Iranian leader named Assim Feroz."

Carl slapped the table with his palm. "Finally," he said and snatched up his glass for a toast. "To Assim Feroz. May he accept the bullet I send him with grace." Even as he said it, he wondered if such eagerness was appropriate. Was he really so excited to kill?

Kelly lifted her glass and clinked it against his. "To Assim Feroz."

14

The United Nations Middle Eastern summit attracted a large number of protesters, as expected, but the media kept most of their coverage focused on the conflict brewing inside the UN rather than on the street. *Viewers can look only so long on a nineteen-year-old woman with stringy hair waving a banner that reads "Stenton Kills Babies,"* David Abraham thought, flipping through channels.

In his way of thinking, such slander should have to defend itself with logic. Even minimal logic. No panel of jurors in the country would convict Robert Stenton of killing fleas, much less babies. And yet too frequently, highly educated journalists reported such accusations as serious charges worthy of attention.

He should have gone to New York, even though he could not stop whatever might happen. Now all he could do was pray that God would save those who needed saving and let the rest find their own way.

He sat on the couch in his Connecticut home and switched to FOX News. The president was holding a press conference. David turned the volume up.

President Stenton was saying, ". . . that I strongly objected to forcing Israel into a corner where her national defense rests in the hands of a foreign government, which is what the United Nations would be doing in this situation. As I see it, the Feroz initiative threatens Israel's sovereignty."

Steven Ace of NBC asked, "Sir, the United States is now the only country that opposes the plan. Does that fact pose any problem for you?"

Stenton replied, "Uniting world opinion always poses problems. Clearly we have a ways to go. But when it comes to standing up for an ally that's facing potential extermination, I think those problems are worth grappling with, don't you?"

"I have a follow-up, if that's okay," Ace said.

"Go ahead, Steve," Stenton replied.

"I understand that there's growing support in Congress for the initiative. Are there any plans for a congressional vote on the matter?"

"No," Stenton said, excusing himself with a nod. "Thank you, that will be all." With that, the most powerful man in the world stepped away from the flashing lights and walked through a blue curtain behind the podium.

David grinned. *That's it, Robert. No mincing words.*

Then again, they both knew that the president was indeed being strong-armed to reconsider by members from both sides of the aisle. Robert had told David two days earlier that the price he was paying for his immovability was turning out to be much higher than he'd expected. There was talk on Capitol Hill of shelving his domestic agenda altogether.

World opinion boiled down to what each government thought of the United Nation's charter. In this new role suggested by Feroz, the United Nations would become the strongest government in the Middle East. Why the leaders of Europe and Asia didn't feel threatened by this was beyond David.

Unless, of course, they saw Israel as their enemy as well.

David sighed and switched to another news channel. Protester coverage.

Another channel. Commentary on the president's brief conference.

Another channel. ABC was interviewing none other than Assim Feroz outside the Waldorf-Astoria, where the UN was hosting several major social events for the dignitaries.

David sat back, crossed his legs, and pressed the DVR record button. The Iranian was tall and gaunt with eyelids that hung lower than most. Fair skin and dark hair, clearly of Persian descent. That the Iranian minister of defense had worked his way into the spotlight with this transparent initiative disgusted David.

Feroz was answering the questions with a polite smile.

"Naturally, it's unacceptable. But we believe that the United States will soon see the wisdom of stopping the ongoing bloodshed in the Middle East through this peace initiative. You cannot turn your back on suffering for too long."

"What will you do if the United States vetoes the initiative at the summit?" the ABC anchor asked.

A crowd of security personnel and reporters was gathered around the defense minister. A limousine door gaped open behind him, apparently waiting on him.

"We will not rest until we have peace. How can one man stand against so many?" Feroz answered. "Now the whole world will unite and bring peace where there has been no peace for centuries."

"Thank you, Mr. Feroz."

"Thank you," he replied.

David saw the reporter, Mary Sanders, for the first time as the camera faced her. "There you have it . . ."

David muted the television. Another journalist in a black sports coat faced the camera, then abruptly turned his back and walked away. The man was familiar to David, but then, so were the faces of a hundred reporters.

Stenton had a fight on his hands. The summit was clearly doing him no favors. David had expected nothing else.

But there was something out of place about that reporter in the sports coat. Strange how the memory worked. Déjà vu?

David started to change the channel. Instead, he pressed the rewind button on the DVR. The reporter's face came and went.

Forward, slow motion this time. David paused the picture as the man turned. He stared for five full seconds before recognition struck.

"No . . ."

It was him!

David stood, studied the profile on the screen. Could he be mistaken? His heart was pounding at twice its normal pace.

He was at the interview with Assim Feroz. There, in New York!

Still gripping the remote control in his left hand, David ran around the couch and snatched up the phone. He dropped the remote on the desk. Dialed the president's number with a shaky finger.

"Dear Lord, help us . . ."

"Brian Macteary."

"Brian—Brian, it's David. I must speak to the president."

"David? David Abraham?"

"Yes. Please tell him it's important."

"I'm sorry, he's unavailable. Is there something I can help you with?"

"No, I have to speak with him. It's very important."

"I'm under strict orders not to interrupt them. He's just gone into a short meeting with the British prime minister. I can pass him a message when he comes out. Shouldn't be more than fifteen minutes."

David quickly considered his options and settled on the only course that presented itself with any clarity.

"It's very important that you tell him something in the strictest of confidence. Tell him that I have reason to believe that there will be an attempt made on the life of Assim Feroz. The security is tight, I'm sure."

"I've never seen more security." Brian paused. "You're saying that someone may be trying to kill the Iranian defense minister?"

"Yes."

"Nothing more? How—"

"Never mind how I know—tell him! I'm taking the first flight I can into New York. Tell him that."

"I should pass this through the Secret Service."

"No! Please, just tell the president and let him decide how to proceed."

"I'm obligated—"

"No, Brian. This isn't a formal threat. Just the president. Promise me!"

The president's press secretary was hesitant. "I'll tell him," he finally said.

15

Carl had never been as happy as he was now, walking the streets of New York with Kelly.

He'd been in many exercises that felt like true assignments at the time, but walking down Park Avenue toward the Waldorf-Astoria with such a show of security as far as the eye could see swept away any lingering suspicions, however small, that this, too, was simply an exercise.

He really was here to kill Assim Feroz. And that was good. Better than he'd dreamed. He told himself so on many occasions.

Kelly had taken care of a number of details that facilitated his mission, but in the end, it would be his finger on the trigger, sending the bullet on a trajectory determined solely by him. It would make them both proud. And he wanted to be proud, he'd decided. This was now an emotion that he embraced whenever it presented itself.

As with any assassination, it wasn't only the opportunity to kill but the opportunity to kill and then escape to one day kill again that drove the preparations leading up to this day. Prior to leaving Hungary, Carl had spent dozens of hours with Kelly, viewing video footage provided by the X Group and planning the hit. They had a good plan.

He made his way toward a security line at Park Avenue and Fifty-second Street, two full city blocks from the Waldorf. He wore a foreign press badge that identified him as Armin Tesler, Ukraine, KYYTP Television. Beside him, Kelly was identified by a similar badge as Ionna Petriv. *We play our roles flawlessly,* he thought.

But not as flawlessly as all the others who had delivered them to Park Avenue as two Ukrainian reporters. This feat had required substantial support from Kalman and his host of contacts, none of whom Carl knew or cared to know.

They'd left Hungary by train three days ago, bound for the Ukraine, where their current covers—complete with passports, history, and press identification papers—had been previously arranged. Their fingerprints had even been registered with the CIA and Secret Service. Kelly told him that these kinds of details had been handled long in advance through an extensive identity-requisition program that Kalman had fine-tuned over the years.

From Kiev, they'd flown through London into New York, arriving two days earlier.

First order of business: establishment of an operations center out of a hotel in Manhattan. This task required renting three separate rooms in their assumed names. Two were dummy rooms, in which they'd hidden miniature video cameras that sent signals to the third room, in which they would actually sleep and operate. In one of these dummy rooms, #202 in the Peking Grand Hotel, they'd left several spent rifle cartridges and a red message painted on the wall: "Death to America, Praise Be to Allah." They'd made the room appear lived in and demanded that housekeeping not disturb them. Strategically planted clues would lead investigators to this room and slow down the post-assassination investigation. The delay would buy them time to chart an alternate escape if their planned route was cut off.

Another dummy room, #301 in the Chinatown Best Western, was reserved in the event that they needed to switch operational centers.

They'd bagged several weapons and hidden them in the toilet tank. Otherwise the room was left undisturbed.

The hotel they selected as their actual operations center was a seedy place in Chinatown called the New York Dragon.

Second order of business: weapons. There was only one weapon Carl needed for the actual operation: a rifle. Anything else he might need, he could fabricate out of materials at hand.

Kelly had obtained the rifle he would use from a contact in New Jersey. An M40A3, nearly identical to the one Carl preferred in Hungary, sighted in at four hundred yards, with a Leopold Vari-X 4x12 scope, three-inch eye relief, and nonglare lens. The rifle had been modified for quick disassembly. It fit neatly into a soft-sided tripod bag normally used for a camera.

The host of assassin's tools common to the trade was useless in this setting. No vest, no night-vision equipment, no knives, nothing that smelled or looked anything remotely like something an assassin would wear. In this kill, Carl would simply be a shooter who pulled off a shot that only a couple of living souls could pull off.

Third order of business: reconnaissance of both the kill zones and the general area of operations. They'd spent the better part of the previous day walking the streets of midtown Manhattan, riding the subway from Central Park to Chinatown and taking taxis to a dozen destinations both in Manhattan and the two kill zones.

Fourth order of business: rehearsal of execution. Essentially a walk-through of the actual assassination. Carl had developed two alternate plans: one for a dinner of dignitaries at the Waldorf, which Assim Feroz was expected to attend; and one for a press conference scheduled at Central Park the following day, which Feroz would also participate in.

Each zone had been identified by Kalman—how, Carl didn't care. His task had been to find a place from which to shoot and escape during a narrow window of opportunity. He'd scouted both zones on foot in the dead of night, and then again the following day while the streets were crowded with cars and pedestrians. One shot would be made from a hotel room. The second, if required, would be made from a garbage bin.

Fifth order of business: performance of their roles, which they were doing now. Part of the X Group's training had involved role-playing, not simply on a conscious level, but deep down where belief was formed. Because he'd frequently been manipulated into assuming a particular identity, Carl now found that willfully playing a Ukrainian correspondent came easily.

He took a deep breath and regarded the bustle of the crowd around him. He judged each face that passed into his field of vision to determine if any threat might hide behind the eyes.

"We should go into the hotel," he said softly.

Kelly cast him a natural glance. "It wasn't planned."

"Then we should change the plan. We have time."

She didn't respond. Any changes were his prerogative—she trusted him. Her trust made him proud.

A line of police cars and construction barriers cut off the street ahead. Carl walked toward the security check.

The guard eyed him with a steely stare, and Carl smiled gently. "Busy day," he said, shifting to a nondescript European accent. With the blending of cultures in Europe, nearly any would do.

"Yes, it is. Can I see your identification?"

Carl unclipped his badge and handed it to the man. They were using a scanner that matched the thumbprint on the card to the thumbprint of the person carrying it. The information was relayed to a central processing station, where the authorities monitored the comings and goings of authorized cardholders.

The guard held out a small scanner, and Carl pressed his thumb on the glass surface. A soft *blip* sounded. After a few moments, the man nodded.

"Thank you, Mr. Tesler."

It took only a minute for Kelly to pass in the same manner. Then they were in the outer security barrier. They would have to watch what they said here. Randomly placed recording devices monitored conversation. According to CNN, not all in the press were thrilled with the new security measure. Evidently they wanted to keep their comments private.

They'd passed through the second security checkpoint and were approaching the entrance to the Astoria when Assim Feroz stepped out with a small entourage and was swarmed by journalists.

Carl felt his pulse spike. Beside him, Kelly stiffened slightly—he felt it more than saw it.

It was the first time they'd seen the target in the flesh. Tall, gaunt, dark-haired, Iranian. This was the life that Carl would end, because that's what he did.

For a brief moment Carl wondered why they wanted him dead. *Who* wanted him dead? *What* had this man done to invite the bullet? And *why* was he agreeing to kill this man?

The last question came out of the blue, uninvited and unwelcome. The answer was obvious, of course—he wasn't so much agreeing to kill this man as he was agreeing to be himself. He was a killer. He was a man who knew nothing except killing. He could no more not kill than a heart could arbitrarily not beat. If he hadn't always been a killer, he was one now. And he'd been one for as long as he could properly remember.

His exposure to this noisy, confusing city was interfering with his focus. He blinked and shut out the thought.

"Closer," he said, angling for the man who was now taking questions from an ABC correspondent. Kelly followed, pulling out a notebook.

Carl slipped between a heavyset reporter and a woman in a purple blouse, eyes fixed on the man. They were behind and to the right of the Iranian defense minister and the camera that captured the interview.

It took little effort to work his way to the front of the other journalists who were yielding space to ABC for the moment. Carl stopped ten feet from Feroz.

This was his prey. From his right, the scent of a flowery perfume. From his left, the smell of the asphalt and pollution and cooking meat. Feroz himself had practically doused himself in a spicy cologne laced with nutmeg.

Carl stepped from the circle, eyes fixed on the man's dark hair and gently working jaw. Assim's jaw was sharp and pitted, from acne, perhaps. His voice was low and gravelly. His dark, purposeful eyes cut through the crowd.

". . . not rest until we have peace. How can one man stand against so many? Now the whole world will unite and bring peace where there has been no peace for centuries."

An interesting voice. Carl wouldn't risk detection, despite the strong urge to pass closer to this man in his perfectly tailored suit.

Carl turned back and eyed Kelly. She stared at him, emotionless. He started to face Feroz again, saw that the camera was panning, and thought better of being caught in a full shot in the proximity of the target. Their appearances and identities would be changed immediately after the assassination, but his instinct warned him off.

A thin sheen of sweat covered Kelly's face. She wasn't comfortable with his admittedly unorthodox approach in this surveillance mission. They'd come to walk the perimeter, not enter the hotel. They hadn't expected to see the target, let alone make such a bold approach in the event that they did.

Carl guided her toward the Waldorf's revolving entry doors.

"I hope you know what you're doing," she said.

"I wanted to know who he is."

She didn't respond.

I want to know him so that I can know myself. I am a killer. Who and how I kill define me.

They waited in line fifteen minutes before security would allow them to enter the hotel. It seemed that only a limited number of people were allowed inside at any given time. They walked up marble steps and entered a large atrium with towering pillars. Exotic floral arrangements that stood twice the height of a man blossomed in huge urns every seven paces.

Carl stopped below the arches that opened to the lobby and allowed the room to soak in. Magnificent. The old walls and ceiling were inspiring.

He scanned the room, detected no threat, and walked out to the center. Being taped by the hotel security cameras was actually to his benefit. The typical assassin would never be so bold. He faced the ceiling, where he knew the cameras hid, and examined the intricate designs etched into the wood.

Here was a building with a history. Unlike him.

Carl turned, refreshed by a sense of destiny. He was going to find himself here, in New York. The ceiling seemed to be staring down at him like a proud father. Rotating to his right like a camera on a wire. And in the center, him, staring up, lost to the world.

Are you my mother?

A hand touched his elbow. "We should go."

Carl lowered his head. She was right. They'd come inside to see the reception hall on the tenth floor, where Assim Feroz would die this very night.

But a single sign made that impossible. A white placard etched in black calligraphy that read "No Press Above Lobby Floor." Two guards stood at each elevator and beside the stairwell to enforce the restriction.

Carl walked toward an archway that led to specialty shops, the first of which he could see at the hall's end. "Should we go shopping?"

Kelly walked abreast and talked quietly. "Are you feeling all right?"

"What do you mean?" he asked. There were fewer people back here. "I'm feeling what I choose to feel."

"You seem a bit erratic."

"Because I'm making erratic choices. If it's any comfort, I can assure you that every one of these guards has been trained to pick out the calm, cool behavior of a potential assassin. It's better to play the part of an awed foreign correspondent, don't you think?"

"It just feels . . . odd. The way you're acting."

"I don't feel odd. This building fascinates me."

"And that's not odd? When was the last time you were fascinated by anything?"

Carl gave her a shallow grin. "I'm fascinated by you."

Her face went red, and try as she might, she couldn't hide a grin. It was the first time he'd ever seen her so embarrassed, and strangely enough it thrilled him.

They walked by a shop window displaying gold and silver jewelry, something that held no fascination for him at the moment. The next store looked as if it sold dolls and stuffed animals. Toys. More fascinating.

"We should get back to the hotel," Kelly said.

"I agree."

A tall, dark-skinned man in a black suit stepped from the toy shop and faced them, eyes skittering along the hall. Secret Service.

A boy half Carl's height walked out after him, holding his purchase: a pair of compact binoculars. Polaroid XLVs—Carl knew of them. From where he couldn't remember, but he knew the binoculars. Perhaps he'd owned a pair himself when he was younger.

The boy turned blue eyes toward Carl and stopped. For a moment they exchanged stares.

"You're from the Ukraine?" he asked in a small but confident voice.

Carl wasn't sure how to respond. He should acknowledge the guess, but something about this boy struck a reverberating chord deep inside him.

"Yes," Kelly said.

"That's good. I hope you support our president's position on Israel."

Had he seen this boy before? No, he didn't think so. As far as he knew, he hadn't really known any boys before. At least none he could remember.

The sound of feet clacking down the hall reached him. *Seven, maybe eight pair,* he thought absently.

The Secret Service agent stepped around the boy, shielding him from Carl and Kelly. "Your father's coming, Jamie."

Jamie.

They came around the corner, five agents and a lean, blond-headed man whom Carl immediately recognized as the president of the United States, Robert Stenton.

The boy was his son. Jamie.

The boy's guard put a hand on his shoulder and eased him forward, toward his father, who beamed at the sight of his son.

"What did you get?" the president asked, stopping twenty yards away.

Jamie hurried to his father and held up the binoculars.

Secret Service agents circled father and son like hens gathering chicks. Carl and Kelly had been scanned by every one of them, including the two responsible for the president's back.

Robert Stenton took the binoculars and held them up. "Fantastic!" He peered through them, past Carl, down the hall. "Perfect choice," the president said.

Then he put his arm around his son's shoulders and walked back the way he'd come. The entourage disappeared around the corner, trailed by Jamie's dark-skinned agent, who turned and cast one last look at them before following.

Carl stared after them, mesmerized by the interaction between father and son. What was it about them that confused him?

He smiled at the guard, dipped his head, and turned around. "We should go," he said.

"Yes. We should."

16

Robert Stenton glanced at David Abraham, who was watching him like a hawk. For the first time the president was beginning to understand his mentor's distress. Accepting Samuel's vision might require any ordinary person to jump through mind-blowing mental hoops, but there was a resounding ring of authenticity to everything David had just said.

One of his aides handed him a phone. "Ed Carter is on the line for you, Mr. President."

Robert took the cell phone. "Thank you." He walked to the window overlooking Manhattan and spoke softly to the director of the Central Intelligence Agency.

"Thank you for stepping out of your meeting, Ed."

"Of course, sir."

"I have a very simple question, Ed, and I want a simple answer. Is there an agency plan to deal with Assim Feroz? And when I say plan, I mean of any sort, technically sanctioned or not."

That question caught him off guard, Robert thought. Carter hesitated, then spoke plainly. "Not to my knowledge, no. We discussed this—"

"I know what we discussed. Now I'm being sure. I assume the bulletin that went out an hour ago was brought to your attention?"

"Yes."

"Does the subject match anything you have?"

"We're still running the comparison against our database, but nothing on the list of priors matches. If this guy's an assassin, he's never been spotted."

"Regardless, we have reason to believe there may be a threat to the Iranian defense minister's life. Do you know how badly this could go if he were killed on American soil during this summit?"

"I couldn't agree more. Wrong place, wrong time."

"There is no right place or right time. I thought I made that clear."

"A figure of speech. The security surrounding the minister's schedule would be difficult to penetrate."

"Unless there was an inside operation," Robert said. "But you're telling me that there isn't."

"That's correct. None whatsoever."

"If anything happens to Assim Feroz while he's in our country, you'll answer, Ed. I assume you understand that."

"I don't think we have a problem, sir."

"Please make sure of it."

He hung up and faced David. "I don't know what else we can do at this point."

"Nothing. You have to prevent him from killing Feroz, but you can't pick him up. Not yet."

"So you've said." David's explanation had taken a full fifteen minutes, laying out details that explained far more than Samuel's vision. What David revealed was tantamount to conspiracy. Their discussion still made his head hurt.

It was no wonder David Abraham had been wringing his hands for the last month.

"Are you absolutely sure the person you saw was him?"

"Yes," David said. "I could never mistake that face, trust me."

The president took a deep breath and set the cell phone on the lamp stand. "I have to be honest, David. I'm having a hard time buying into all of this. It's a stretch."

"It's only a stretch for a mind that hasn't been where mine's been."

"Well, if you're right about all of this, you've taken immeasurable risks and overstepped your place. I'm not sure how I feel about that."

"Let's pray I made the right decision, then," David said. "I'm sure you understand why I've said nothing about this before now."

"That doesn't make it right."

"Only time will tell. You can decide then whether to burn me at the stake or build a statue of me."

17

Manhattan offered a dozen possible sites from which Carl could kill Assim Feroz while he dined on the Waldorf-Astoria's tenth floor, but after only short consideration, he'd agreed that shooting from a hotel room would best facilitate the objective. There were numerous advantages to the protection offered by a room, chief among them silence and isolation. The room would absorb much of the sound, critical because a sound suppressor would affect the bullet's path and therefore would not be used.

There were as many disadvantages, perhaps the greatest being that most hotel rooms weren't conveniently positioned to offer a shot into the Waldorf. As far as Carl could see, there were only seven possible rooms, four of which were aligned vertically in the hotel in which he now prepared himself.

Seven hotel rooms, seven different shots, seven escape routes. But of these seven, only one was available—the one he now occupied. Regardless, it was an excellent choice. An obvious choice. Obvious because it was far *too* obvious to be taken seriously by even well-trained security personnel.

Carl sat cross-legged on the bed, staring at the round oak table next to the window. His rifle rested on its bipod, pointed at the pulled curtain less than a foot beyond the muzzle. He would wait until the three-minute mark to pull the curtain and prepare the window for the shot.

He kept his eyes on the rifle and his mind in his tunnel.

Strange and wonderful and frightening emotions swam in the blackness beyond the pinprick of light that was his mission, but he held them all at bay easily enough. He didn't have to control fear, because there was none. He hadn't expected any. Instead, there was excitement, an emotion that could easily affect his pulse and by extension his accuracy.

And there was some empathy, an emotion he'd expected even less than fear. He was about to send a bullet toward a man who had done nothing to harm him. Kelly had told him what a danger this man was to the world, but none of her words mattered. Carl was simply a killer who would kill whomever she told him to kill. He needed no other motivation to please her.

Yet now, just a few minutes from doing precisely that, he was aware of this strange empathy lingering beyond his tunnel. He dismissed it and kept his mind on the light ahead.

Carl stared at the barrel of his rifle, allowing peripheral elements to stream into his vision without distraction. A four-inch LED monitor on the table captured the high-bandwidth video images transmitted from a small camera he'd positioned under the room's front door, peering into the hall. In the event his location was compromised, he would see any approach in enough time to make a quick exit into the adjoining room.

The room was warm. He'd turned off the air conditioner when he first entered in order to equalize the pressure between this room and the air outside. A part of him wished he could turn the heat up to better simulate his pit when it was hot.

He missed his pit.

But he'd left the safe world of that pit to fulfill his purpose. As soon as he'd reached the light at the end of this tunnel, he would be allowed to return to Hungary.

The light. That circle of white now beckoned him. Excitement tried to enter his tunnel again, but he deflected it without conscious thought and stared at the light.

He would kill the Iranian defense minister while the man ate his dinner on the tenth floor of the Waldorf, and he would do it with a bullet that came from the tenth floor of the Crowne Plaza on Broadway, roughly twelve hundred yards away. It would be a two-shot kill.

His first bullet would leave the hotel room Kelly had reserved for him, cross over one of the busiest streets in Manhattan, and travel down Forty-ninth Street for five blocks before crashing into a thick window. The bullet's soft, hollow point would allow the projectile to spread at first impact and blow the window inward.

His second bullet would follow on the heels of the first, free to fly unobstructed through the broken window, through an open doorway, and into a second room, where Assim Feroz would be seated.

The second shot had to be fired within two seconds of the first so that it would reach the target before the sound created by the exploding window elicited any reaction.

The strings that Kalman had pulled to give Carl a line of sight into the kill zone could have been pulled only by very influential people. Being sure that Feroz was seated at one of three tables facing the doors, for example. Making sure the doors were open. The drapes pulled. But none of that concerned Carl.

His task was to place the bullet in the target's chest at 9:45 p.m.

Kelly's soft voice spoke through his radio headset. "Four minutes." The frequency was scrambled on both ends, allowing them untraceable communication.

"Four minutes," he repeated.

He didn't need a spotter at this range, so Kelly coordinated the mission from the Dragon in Chinatown. Her contact inside the Waldorf had two tasks. The first was to raise the blinds on the window. The second was to make sure the double doors that led into the dining room were opened at 9:45 p.m., a far more difficult task in this security-rich environment than in any other. The server was being paid $100,000 in U.S. currency, a good payday, Kelly said.

A thousand men could hit a target at twelve hundred yards. But very few could shoot a bullet into a window, chamber a second cartridge even as the glass fell, acquire a target seated next to twenty other dignitaries through a narrow doorway, and place a bullet in the target's chest in the space of two seconds.

This was the light at the end of Carl's tunnel.

"Three minutes."

Two minutes and fifty-nine seconds by the clock on the table.

"Three minutes," he repeated.

Carl waited a beat. He unfolded his legs and stood. The only emotion that now threatened him was excitement, and he blocked it out forcefully.

He stepped up to the window, pulled the heavy curtains a foot to each side. A sea of lights filled his view. Times Square was two blocks south, Central Park a half mile north. A hundred feet below him, heavy traffic ran along Broadway, refusing to sleep just as the brochure Carl had studied claimed.

Two minutes and thirty-five seconds.

He lifted a black cutting tool from the table, pressed five suction cups against the glass, and ran the glass cutter's diamond bit in a two-inch circle. Three full turns and a gentle tug. The glass popped softly.

He set the glass cutout on the table and lowered the bit so that it rested on the window's outer pane.

A soft gust of air blew through the two-inch opening as he pulled the second circle of glass free. No wind in Manhattan, as forecasted. Wind had been Carl's greatest concern during the planning, but no more.

One minute and thirty-two seconds.

He eased into the chair, took the rifle gently in his hands, leaned over the table, and aligned the barrel with the hole. The weapon's smooth, cool barrel and familiar trigger brought him comfort, and he accepted it.

He peered through the light-gathering scope, quickly found the corner window that he would punch through in just over one minute, and let the air seep from his lungs.

The hot gases blown forward by the .308 cartridge would create both sound and light. The first would be absorbed in part by the room, baffled by the glass, and then muffled by the heavy traffic below. The fire would be dimmed by the flash suppressor affixed to the end of his barrel. Unless someone was peering directly at this window, the shots would likely go unnoticed.

He would escape easily enough either way.

"One minute."

"One minute," he repeated.

A stray thought penetrated his consciousness. *Is this just another test?* And then another thought. *It doesn't matter.*

Carl let his mind go where it now begged to go, into the scope. Into the tunnel. Through the dark passage toward that light. He walked his bullet's trajectory as he had a thousand times before.

"Thirty seconds." Kelly's voice sounded distant.

As agreed, he did not reply now, but he wanted to. He wanted to say, "I'm in, Kelly. I'm going to kill Assim Feroz for you."

Carl went deeper. His breathing slowed. His heart slogged through a gentle beat. Absolute peace. If called upon to do so, he thought he might be able to walk the bullet into a quarter at two thousand yards.

Yes, he could do that, couldn't he?

"Abort."

The shade was up, but the window was still dark. At any moment the doors would swing open and reveal the dining . . .

"Carl, do you hear me? Abort the current shot. There's been a change. There's a new target."

Only now did her first word penetrate his dark place. *Abort.*

No. No, he couldn't have heard it correctly.

I'm inside, Kelly. I will kill Assim Feroz for you. Please let me do this one thing for you. For us.

"Carl, acknowledge! You can't kill Assim Feroz. Do you hear me?"

The urgency in her voice made his vision swim for a brief moment.

"Acknowledged," he said.

"There is a new target. Acknowledge."

He could hear his breathing now, not a good thing. "Acknowledged."

"Your new target is the president of the United States, Robert Stenton. Acknowledge."

Light suddenly filled the open window five blocks away. He could see through the window, through the open doorway into the dining room now. Several dozen men and women, most in dark suits, seated at round tables.

Assim Feroz sat on the right, precisely where he'd been told to sit. But this wasn't the man Carl would kill. There was another. He hadn't known the president would be in the room. Where was this new target of his?

"Acknowledge, Carl."

"Where is he?" Carl asked.

"Third from the right at the long head table."

Carl eased his aim up and over. Third from the right. The president's torso filled the scope. Dark suit—too far for any other details. This is where he would send his bullet.

"Do you have him?"

"Yes."

He raised the crosshairs above the man's head, allowing for the drop of the bullet.

"Take the shot," Kelly said.

The president leaned to Carl's right. He was listening to the boy who sat on his left. This was his son, the one who'd purchased binoculars from the toy shop on the main floor.

Do I know this boy?

Jamie. *Do I know Jamie?*

Jamie looked as if he was laughing with his father.

The image froze in Carl's mind. He stared at father and son, mesmerized by the strange and wonderful display of affection.

"Take the shot, Carl."

His tunnel wavered, and he knew he couldn't take the shot without reacquiring perfect peace. The first shot would be easy; it was the second that concerned him. Under no circumstances could he jeopardize the mission by compromising the second shot. Any failed attempt would result in the target's immediate evacuation.

Carl dismissed the unique tension that had come from seeing father and son together. His body obeyed him.

He would take the shot now.

Why had they changed targets? Had they changed their minds? No. They'd known all along that the president was the target.

Then why hadn't they told him earlier?

Because they are afraid I won't kill the president of the United States. It was the only answer that made any sense.

"What's going on, Carl? Do you have a shot?"

Fear spread through Carl's body. Something about the father and son shut his muscles down. An instinctive impulse that screamed out of his dark past.

He would take the shot now. He had a clear shot. Less than an ounce of pressure and the president would be dead.

But this wasn't just the president of the United States. This was the boy's father. How could he possibly kill Jamie's father?

"Listen to me, Carl." Kelly's voice came gently, calming his confusion. "Whatever's going through your mind right now, let it go and send your bullets. For me. For us. They won't allow us to live if you fail."

She was right. He had to shoot.

"My heart is pounding, Kelly," he said. The realization that his tunnel was breaking down only made the matter worse. "I don't know if I have the shot."

She didn't respond.

"Kelly?"

Silence in his headset.

Now the fear that he'd hurt Kelly joined his confusion and sent a visible tremble through his fingers.

I'm breaking down!

For the first time in many months, Carl began to panic.

"Kelly!"

"Shh. Shh . . ." Her voice fell over him, milky soft.

"What's happening to me, Kelly?"

"It's okay, Carl."

But it wasn't okay, he knew that. The doors had been open for more than a minute already—at any moment the lapse in security would be identified and the opportunity for his shot would be closed.

Who is your father, Carl? You can't shoot this father.

A figure stepped into the doorway, peered out, then crossed to the window and pulled the shade closed.

Carl closed his eyes.

"They've pulled the shade," he said.

There was no response.

A terrible remorse swallowed him. He held his rifle tightly, feeling the familiar surfaces on his cheek and shoulder and in his hands. This gave him some comfort. He could have taken the shot. He could have killed the president for Kelly.

You can't shoot this father.

"Come home, Carl."

Her voice was like an angel's to him, calling him from the valley of death.

"Repair the glass, scrub the room, and come home. I'm here for you."

18

The New York Dragon was located a block west of the East River, where the small boat that would depart Manhattan Island waited in hiding. The authorities would undoubtedly shut down both bridges and tunnels as soon as they learned of any assassination attempt, thereby trapping all suspects on the island.

A withdrawal under cover of darkness was preferable, but the point was now moot. There was no need for a withdrawal.

Kelly watched Carl pace over the worn brown carpet. He'd returned at eleven, one hour earlier, after gluing the circles of glass back into the window, wiping down all surfaces, and packing his tools into the golf bag.

She felt ambivalent about his failure. A part of her ached with him. He was struggling to control his emotions, which threw him into a terrible funk. Confusion raced through his eyes. Her own feelings for him had grown far deeper than she had expected over the last month. Not only could she feel his pain; she found herself wanting to lighten it.

But she now suspected that she was *supposed* to feel this way. Her own feelings were part of the design. Surely they knew she would come to respect, perhaps even love Carl.

"Do you mind if I tell you what I think happened?" she asked.

Carl slid into the metal chair at the table and formed a teepee over the bridge of his nose, eyes lost on the wall.

"I think you've progressed exactly how Agotha expected you would. She told me that you'd fail the first attempt. She told me that you were meant to."

His eyes darted toward her. "That makes no sense."

"Neither did any of your training at first. But look at you now."

"Why was the target switched? They want me to kill the president—"

"Does that matter to you? Or does it matter more that you trust me? You've always believed in me, and nothing's changed now."

"I failed now."

She took a deep breath and told him what she'd been waiting to say. "You failed by design, to strengthen your resolve."

He didn't look her way.

Kelly walked over to the table and sat down across from him. "Listen to me, Carl. Look into my eyes."

His round brown eyes turned to her.

"I'm about to tell you something that might confuse you, but I want you to resist that confusion. For my sake. It's very important that you trust me now, like you've never trusted me before."

"I've always trusted you."

"I know you have. But you have to dig even deeper. Can you do that?"

"I love you," he said.

"I know you do. And I love you. We trust each other, even when the worst happens."

Kelly reached across the table's Formica top and offered him her hand. He took it.

"Do you remember your last treatment in the hospital?"

He thought for a moment. "No."

"No. You always put them behind you, don't you? But you were treated with drugs and shock therapy on the hospital bed the day before we left Hungary. During that treatment, you were led to believe that you could never take the life of Robert Stenton because he's the father of Jamie, a son. You, too, want—need—to be a son. That's why you hesitated. Only because Agotha wanted you to hesitate."

"Why?"

"Because this is your first real mission for the X Group. You may not think you can differentiate between real missions and the training, but your subconscious mind can. It's important that you understand that even in the field, you will feel only what Agotha wants you to feel."

"She wanted me to feel confusion."

"Yes."

"But I still failed."

"Yes, you did. But the next time you feel any hesitation or confusion, you'll remember that those feelings can't be trusted. You didn't really have any feelings for the son or the father, did you? The feelings were planted by Agotha."

A light grew in his eyes.

"The next time you feel anything in the field, you'll know. Even the feelings that break through aren't to be trusted. You'll know that they are simply tests from Agotha and you'll have the strength to set them aside."

"I'm not sure I understand. I don't want or need a father?"

"No. Why would you? You're twenty-five years old."

He grunted, then frowned at his own failure to recognize this.

"Agotha's methods are strange, but only because they are so advanced. I think you hold a special place in her heart. For all practical purposes, *she's* your mother. You can trust her with your life."

He grunted again. Shook his head and grinned sheepishly. "So it was all planned. I haven't failed, then."

Kelly stood and walked behind him. She placed her hands on his neck and messaged lightly. "Not really, no. You're as strong as ever. Even stronger."

She bent over and spoke gently behind his right ear. "How do you feel?"

"Foolish."

"Can you set this feeling aside?"

"Yes."

"Then please do it. How can the man I love feel foolish if he knows that I love him?"

Carl turned his head and looked into her eyes.

"If you're foolish, is your love for me also foolish?" she asked.

"No."

"Then you're not a fool."

"No."

She leaned around him and kissed him on the lips. "I didn't think so," she breathed. Carl's breathing thickened.

The idea that I can generate this response from him is without question the most satisfying part of loving him, she thought. And she did love him.

She was meant to.

Kelly straightened, unable to hide the coy smile on her face. She returned to her chair and sat slowly. "The president is scheduled to speak from the same stage that Assim Feroz will use tomorrow. One hour earlier."

"Then I should get into position," Carl said, standing. He walked to the window, pulled back the curtain, evidently saw nothing of interest, and turned to face her.

"If you fail tomorrow, they will kill us both," Kelly said. "You know that, right?"

"Why would I fail?"

"You won't. The only reason they haven't triggered the implant yet is because they expected you to fail. If you want proof that all of this is by design, there's your proof. You're still alive."

He nodded. "Then I'll kill the president of the United States tomorrow as planned."

"And then we can go home."

Carl pulled back the curtain again. "I like it here," he said. "The city is a good place to hide."

"So is the desert," Kelly said. "Nevada isn't so far from here. When all this is over, maybe we can go to the desert where no one will bother us."

"When what is over?"

"A figure of speech. We both know this will end only if we fail."

"I won't let that happen," Carl said. "I will never let them hurt you."

19

The garbage trucks picked up trash along Avenue of the Americas every two days. Today was not one of those days.

Night still darkened Manhattan when Carl pushed the steel manhole cover off its seating. Unlike the first hit from the hotel, this one required far more direct coordination between Kelly and him.

Carl slid the heavy steel lid aside. He lit the portable acetylene torch, adjusted the flame until it was a bright blue, and began his cut into the bottom of the large garbage bin that Kelly had rolled over the hole.

The sound of wheels peeling along the street on his left muted the soft crackle of cutting steel. Kelly had pulled the bin into the alley and taped a rubber skirt around the bottom before pushing it into place. She was now playing the role of a janitor from the adjacent towers on Thirty-eighth Street, loading the bin with spent rags and rearranging the garbage already inside to make his entry possible.

It took Carl less than a minute to cut the two-foot hole and remove the hot steel plate from the bottom of the bin.

It took him a full three minutes to push his equipment through the hole and climb in after it, only because even with Kelly's efforts, he was forced to make room by shoving the bags around.

Once in the bin, he reached down to the sidewalk, slid the cover back into place, and rapped on the side of the bin.

Within seconds, the metal box was rolling. Twenty feet before it came to rest at the corner of the alley as planned, he heard the rubber skirt pull free. For several minutes Carl waited in the darkness.

The half-filled container smelled like spoiled milk, but he'd expected worse. He placed his feet against the wall he expected to work through and crammed the garbage to his rear.

Kelly's voice spoke quietly into his headset. "You copy?"

"Copy."

"You're clear."

Carl lit the torch and cut a seven-inch hole from the sidewall, leaving a half-inch section connected at the top. Using a screwdriver, he pried the lid that he'd cut in and up. The alley gaped in darkness, empty.

Satisfied, he pushed the metal plate back down into place.

"Ready," he said.

"Copy."

Thirty seconds later he heard a scraping sound around the hole he'd cut. She was filling the crack with putty and spraying it green.

"All clear," she finally said. "You're good?"

"Good."

"Still clear."

Kelly would watch the box from a dozen surveillance vantages, some of which they'd already selected, others she would find as the day passed.

Carl pushed the torch under the garbage behind him and extracted his rifle from the golf bag. He rested the gun on the metal floor, careful not to jar the scope. There was only one way to position himself for the shot—on his belly with his legs bent up and his rifle inside his elbow, resting on its bipod. He maneuvered slowly, shoving and rearranging bags as he moved. The hole he'd cut in the floor of the bin clipped his left forearm—unavoidable. He would have to reposition himself just before shooting. Once in place, he pulled the bags of rags over his head, shaping a clearing around the scope as he did so.

He snugged the weapon to his shoulder and peered into blackness. Kelly would move the bin into position and open the hole he'd cut for his shot thirty seconds before the kill.

Once again, the level of information that the X Group had secured to facilitate this opportunity was beyond his ability to comprehend. Feroz would be standing on the stage they'd erected just inside Central Park South, on Avenue of the Americas. He knew now that it would be the president of the United States, not Assim Feroz, but nothing else about the kill had changed.

The street would be closed to both pedestrian through-traffic and cars at Thirty-eighth Street three hours prior to the press conference. The unprecedented security measures would require an enormous effort on the part of the NYPD. But any security envelope could be penetrated by the right person.

In this case, Carl was that person.

Their effort might remove most conceivable threats to those who took the stage, but it would also clear a corridor down Avenue of the Americas for an improbable shot. Perhaps impossible.

To all but him.

"I'm in position," he said.

"It's 4:36 a.m.," Kelly said. "You have just over ten hours before the press conference. I'll check in every hour unless we have a problem."

He would have preferred to set up closer to the target, but there were no garbage bins suitably located for both the shot and the escape. His shot would be just under two thousand yards. As long as the weather cooperated and he was able to acquire the target, he would have a good shot.

"You're okay?"

"I'm fine."

It was now time to wait.

OUTSIDE, CARS roared by and pedestrians rode a wave of indistinct voices, but in the pitch-black container, Carl lay facedown on a cushion of darkness, shut off from everything except the hourly sound of Kelly's gentle voice.

They didn't talk. She called him on the hour and asked for acknowledgment, which he offered and then retreated into his darkness. He was in his pit, right here on Avenue of the Americas. Truth be told, he was more comfortable in this place than he'd been anywhere since leaving the compound. *In the future, I'll shoot from the darkness whenever I have the opportunity,* he thought. Maybe always.

The pressure on his elbows and hip bones, the cramping of his muscles, and the stuffy heat reassured him that very few could withstand such discomfort. He alone could satisfy Kelly with success, because to him the pain wasn't pain at all—he'd shut it down. How many men could do that?

Even though he couldn't yet see the target, he walked an imaginary path from the garbage bin to Robert Stenton. He'd selected a 150-gram full-metal jacket for the task, preferring the increased accuracy it offered over a bullet that would flatten upon impact, even though the latter would increase the likelihood of a kill should the bullet miss the chest.

He had no intention of missing the target's chest.

The father was about to die.

Could he kill Jamie's father? Of course he could.

The sound of traffic ceased at noon, when they closed the street fifty yards behind him.

"One o'clock," Kelly said. "We're on schedule."

"One o'clock."

Time drifted by. Twice someone opened the bin, threw some garbage in, then let the lid clang noisily back in place, oblivious to his body hiding below the bags.

At times like this, deep in stasis, he felt as though he might actually be hallucinating. The darkness seemed to touch him as if it were matter.

Agotha had once told him that he drew all of his power from his own mind, that a person who finds silence and solitude boring is a person who is himself boring, empty of anything worth consideration. "These empty shells require outside stimulation to keep them from blowing away in a gentle breeze," she'd said.

"Two," Kelly said.

Carl grunted.

In one hour he would send the bullet into the father's chest.

Less than a week ago he'd been strapped into an electric chair and survived an onslaught of electricity. How? By going very deep and affecting the zero-point field that connected him to the objects around him. It was nothing more than mind over matter. Not so different from embracing the dark or slowing his heart rate.

With belief as small as a mustard seed, you can move mountains—a famous teacher had said that. But what if Agotha was wrong about the source of his power? What if he'd tapped into something far greater than the dark musings of quantum theory?

Whatever it was, it had worked. Could work. Would work. More important, his success pleased both Agotha and Kalman. And even more than either of these, it pleased Kelly.

Carl wasn't even aware of the last hour. It was simply there one minute and gone the next.

"Five minutes."

He methodically reached up and flipped a small switch on the side of his scope. Battery-powered light filled the glass. Without it, his vision would be distorted by the flood of light when Kelly opened the metal flap. He let his pupils adjust.

"We have a go. The target has just taken the stage. I'm coming in."
No need to answer.

The bin swayed once and then began to clatter along the rough concrete. He was like a battleship being maneuvered to bring its guns to bear.

Kelly's boot kicked the metal circle, forcing it inward a few inches. He reached forward and bent it all the way up. Now Carl had a clear view of the street and, thanks to the blockade behind him, the distant park.

"Clear?"

"Clear," he said.

Avenue of the Americas fell and rose between this point and the park, but on balance it dropped about ten feet on its way to the stage. He would have to compensate accordingly.

Carl peered through the scope, down the street, all the way to the park, a mile and a half away. The bullet would fly a second and a half and drop nearly eight feet before striking the target.

And now Carl could see that target.

The last time he'd seen this view was two days earlier, when he dropped to one knee while picking up a dropped pen to study this line. Then, he'd had to visualize the street vacant of cars and pedestrians. Now a dozen obstacles rose between him and the president—street lamps, light posts, a few tree branches at the end—but the target's torso was in plain view. His bullet would pass under a branch that cut the target off at the neck and enter his chest for a kill. There were no obstacles between his barrel and the father. He studied the man's chest.

"It's your call, Carl. Take your shot."

Again, he felt no need to respond.

His pulse slowed. His breathing stalled. He was home.

A man in a blue suit stood to the target's left. Secret Service. An older man in a tweed blazer sat behind the president.

I know this man.

He stared, transfixed by the older man. Aside from the man's beard and general features, he couldn't make out fine details, but he was suddenly and forcefully certain that he knew this man. It was the way he sat with arms folded. The way his head sat on his shoulders. The way he crossed his legs.

Carl blinked, stunned. His heart thumped, ruining his aim, forcing him to reacquire the stillness the bullet would need as it sped down the barrel.

But he knew this man! As a father. The man was his father?

You can't kill the father.

Carl stilled his body. Raised the barrel ever so slightly. Found the light.

But there was more than light in his mind. There was a voice, and it was screaming bloody murder, raging through his concentration.

You cannot kill the father!

Carl began to panic.

KELLY WATCHED the president through powerful binoculars from her perch half a block behind the garbage bin in which Carl lay, wondering why he hadn't taken the shot.

She'd wheeled the green steel box onto the sidewalk and left it directly above the manhole as planned. Carl would make the shot, drop into the service tunnel, discard the weapon, and run one block south, where he would exit through a manhole in an alley and then meet her at the Dragon.

As they'd suspected, the NYPD was too busy rerouting traffic and dealing with mobs of pedestrians behind the barricades to care about a single garbage bin half a block up the street. A handful of workers from nearby office buildings still loitered on Avenue of the Americas, occasionally passing near the bin. Although through-traffic had been cut off, these people were allowed. The streets of New York were accustomed to change. The presence of a garbage bin ten feet from its normal resting place attracted no attention.

So far, so good.

According to the media, the summit had accomplished little or nothing—neither side budged. The president was already into his speech, presumably pitching his final position to the media.

Take the shot, Carl. Now, take the shot!

Most of the expanding gases responsible for the noise of Carl's shot would be baffled by the bin's metal wall, but the few dozen pedestrians within a hundred yards would hear the sound clearly enough. Still, it would take them many seconds to isolate the sound's source and react. By then, Carl would be gone.

This was the plan.

But she wasn't sure that Carl was following the plan.

The president had been talking for several minutes now, and still no shot. She knew he had a clear line for the simple reason that he hadn't said otherwise.

"We are clear." She spoke deliberately but very softly. "It's time, my dear."

No shot.

It was this business about his father. She cursed under her breath. *Please, Carl, please shoot.*

What if this was a profound weakness in Agotha's training? *What if Carl simply cannot bring himself to fire upon a father figure because he, like me, really does need—*

A muffled explosion stopped her thought short—the sound of a car backfiring. But today it wasn't a car.

Carl had fired!

Her hands trembled, momentarily distorting the image on the platform a mile and a half away. The bullet would travel for two seconds before—

Robert Stenton grabbed his chest. He sat hard, then dropped back.

For a brief second there was no movement. Then the stage blurred into a picture of confusion as Secret Service swarmed the prone body.

Kelly jerked the binoculars from her eyes. Two dozen people were scattered down the street. Some had stopped what they were doing and were looking around for the source of the sound. Others had probably concluded that a taxi had backfired. None were paying any special attention to the green garbage bin. By now Carl would have already shoved the green metal flap back into place.

She lowered her eyes to the gap between the bin and the sidewalk just in time to see Carl drop through. Then he was gone.

Saint had just killed the president of the United States.

20

Carl pushed his rifle through the manhole, heard it splash below. To abuse a weapon so intentionally struck him as profane, but this was the plan. His plan.

He swung his feet into the hole, dropped down to the fifth rung, and pulled the manhole cover back into place. Dim light filtered through a thin gap around the heavy metal plate. He descended the ladder quickly.

Who had he shot? What had he done? *Father*—the word refused to stop pounding through his skull.

Father, father, father. Father!

A foot of dirty water ran down the passage, soaking his canvas boots. He felt for the rifle, found it, and ran south along the walkway on the east side of the tunnel.

The bullet had followed a perfect trajectory, he knew that. What he didn't know was whether he'd succeeded. Or who the old man was. His need to know smothered his judgment.

He had to escape, and he would. But he also had to know what had happened. Why he'd believed with such certainty that he was peering through the scope at his father!

He threw the rifle into a deep alcove two hundred yards south as planned and ran on. They would find the rifle without a serial number and without prints.

Heart pounding like a sledge, Carl reached his exit ladder and climbed from a manhole in the alley two blocks south of the barricades. His radio should work now.

"Are you there?"

Kelly was breathing hard when she responded. "I'm here. You did well, Carl."

He turned up the alley and ran eastward.

"I'll meet you as planned," he said.

"Hurry."

Carl ripped the headset from his ears and threw the device into a garbage can at Thirty-seventh Street and Fifth Avenue. They'd blockaded Fifth as well, but the traffic would be flowing freely on Third.

Bellevue Hospital was located on First. Although South New York Hospital was technically closer to Central Park, they would take the president down Avenue of the Americas to Bellevue, he'd been told.

He wasn't sure why he hadn't told Kelly of his impulsive change in plan, but the five-block side trip would hold him up for only ten minutes and wouldn't compromise their exit, which wasn't planned until nightfall anyway.

He had to go to Bellevue Hospital because he had to know.

A host of sirens wailed through the streets. If the bullet hadn't killed the president outright, toxic shock soon would. They would waste no time speeding to the trauma unit.

But Carl was much closer to Bellevue than they were.

He sprinted down Thirty-seventh, ignoring the casual gazes of pedestrians, clearly clueless about the events behind him. The city exploded back to life at Third Avenue, but no one in this part of town had heard the news that the president had just been shot twenty-two blocks north. They still sold their magazines and walked briskly to their meetings and hailed their cabs.

Carl ignored the red lights and tore across the street, ignoring a long horn blast from a motorist. The chorus of sirens reached him above the street noise. The ambulance and its police escort were behind him on Avenue of the Americas, screaming toward him.

What are you doing, Carl? You think you're going to find your father? Every step is a step closer to death.

Left on First Avenue. He could see that they'd already closed the Midtown Tunnel in an attempt to cut off escape routes. Confusion was backing up. News was spreading.

Carl reached Bellevue Hospital on First and Thirty-fourth ahead of the piercing sirens. He stepped into an alley opposite the emergency ramp as the first police swept around the corner, sped past the alley, and squealed to a stop one block north. Another car joined the first. Two others peeled south to cut off any approach from Twenty-third Street.

The ambulance slowed to take the corner, then accelerated toward the emergency ramp, directly across from Carl.

He eased back into the shadows, panting from his run. But he couldn't stay here; there was no direct view of the ramp.

He glanced behind, saw that the alley was clear all the way to Second Avenue, shoved his hands into his pockets, and headed directly for the ramp, head down.

Why are you risking exposure, Carl?

I'm not. I'm simply a curious bystander, oblivious to the contents of that ambulance.

You'll be seen.

I've already been seen at a dozen events. My face is undoubtedly on film. Faces can be changed.

You haven't mapped this escape route. If they grow suspicious, you'll be running blind.

I do well running blind.

Do you think the old man is your father?

He couldn't answer the question.

Then Carl was behind a waist-high retaining wall, staring down a slight incline at the red ambulance. The doors flew open. A paramedic spilled out and was quickly joined by six medical staff who'd been waiting.

The gurney slid out. The man he'd come face-to-face with yesterday in the Waldorf lay on his back with a green oxygen mask over his face. A silver pole with a bag of fluid was affixed to the gurney.

But it was the blood that held Carl's attention. The sheets draped over his chest were red with blood. This had been his bullet's doing.

The old man in tweed stepped from the back of the ambulance, and Carl's heart skipped a beat. *Father.* Surely this couldn't be his father!

The man hurried beside the gurney as they wheeled it to the open doors. He seemed to be praying.

The distant features that had transfixed his mind as he settled for the shot now confronted him in full color at less than fifty paces.

He did know this man!

He didn't know who he was, or how he knew him, or even how well he knew him, but he did know him.

As a father.

Carl stared, wide-eyed. His father? Or his spiritual father?

They call me Saint.

A STRANGE calm had stilled David Abraham's heart the moment Robert dropped to the stage floor. He knew then that one of two things had happened.

Which meant that he'd been right all along.

Or dreadfully wrong.

He was second to reach the president, just behind an agent who ran between Robert and the audience to intercept a second shot.

But one look at the president, and there was no doubt that a second shot would not be needed. Robert Stenton lay on his back, eyes closed, red blood spreading from a small tear in his white shirt.

David's inexplicable peace quickly changed to an urgency. Perhaps some panic. The president of the United States had been assassinated, right here in front of a hundred cameras. And he had played a role!

He began to pray, loudly and fervently, pausing every few seconds to demand they work on him faster, load him faster, get to the hospital faster.

Now they had arrived at the hospital, and the singular calm returned to him. He prayed as he hurried to stay by Robert's side. Disbelief gripped the staff as they rushed him in. A doctor spoke urgently, issuing orders, but David wasn't listening. His own prayers crowded his mind.

Not until he'd crossed the threshold did he notice a lone figure in his peripheral vision, watching them from behind. He turned his head.

David froze. Dear Lord, it was *him*!

They exchanged a long stare.

Someone touched his elbow. "Sir—"

"I'll be right in."

David turned and walked toward the man, who still stood with his hands in his pockets, mesmerized by the scene. He stopped less than ten feet from the man, separated from him by a waist-high barrier.

David found his voice. "Do you know who I am?"

The man searched his face, eyes blank.

"Do you know what's happening?"

"Are you my father?"

The sound of his voice—he would never mistake that voice!

"No. My name is David Abraham. Do you know who I am?"

No response.

"I know who you are," David said.

The air was thick between them.

"Who am I?" the man asked.

David glanced back and satisfied himself that they could not be overheard. A part of him demanded that he call security. Unless he was wrong about everything up to this point, he was facing the man who'd assassinated the president of the United States.

But if he wasn't wrong, calling out for help would be the worst thing he could do.

He jerked his head back to the man. "You're more than I can tell you here. Did you kill the president?"

"Was that the president?"

"Yes. He was shot. Did you do the shooting?"

"No."

As far as David could see, the denial wasn't a lie. But that meant nothing; he couldn't see into the mind.

"Do you know my father?" the man asked.

"No, I don't."

The man hesitated a moment, then turned to his right and began to walk away.

"They've lied to you," David said. "It's all a lie."

The man stopped and turned back.

He knew it! David pushed forward while he had the advantage. "Tell me where I can find you. I'll send a boy to talk to you. He's my son. No one else, you have my word."

The man stood still, considering. Then he pulled his hand out of his pocket and dropped something on the ground. Without a word or a glance, he jogged across the street and into the alley.

David hoisted his leg over the short wall and struggled over. It was a matchbook, he could see that now. He ran to the matches and picked them up.

Peking Grand Hotel. Chinatown.

Hands trembling, lips mumbling in prayer, David pulled out his cell phone and made the call.

21

Carl unlocked the hotel room door, stepped in, and eased the door closed.

"Thank goodness you made it! Is everything okay? You're late."

He felt lost but refused to show it. "I'm here, aren't I?"

A wide smile split Kelly's face. She hurried over to him, threw her arms around his neck, and kissed him on the lips.

Her enthusiasm washed over him, and the desperation that had plagued him for the last hour faded.

"We did it, Carl." She kissed him again, and this time he kissed her back. It was a great moment, wasn't it? They'd completed their first mission together. Kelly had never been so happy when he'd successfully executed an exercise, but now, in the field, her joy was practically spilling over.

It was a very good day to be alive.

Carl suddenly wanted to see their work. "Is it on the news?"

"Are you kidding? They've been playing it nonstop. A perfect hit, Carl. Agotha will be so proud."

"I don't care about Agotha," he said. He clarified his statement when she raised her brow. "Not like I care for you."

"She's your mother," Kelly said. "I'm your lover."

He winked at her. Imagine that, he actually winked at her. He wasn't used to being so forward with her, preferring instead to let her take the lead. She was, after all, his handler as well.

But he was emboldened by his tremendous success. "One day we should get married," he said.

Her eyes lit up. "And run off to Nevada?"

"Why not? We're lovers. Isn't that what lovers do? Run off?"

They stared at each other.

"You want to see it?" Kelly plopped down on the bed and faced the television.

Carl sat next to her and watched the muted images. A reporter was speaking below a large graphic that read "President Stenton Shot." At the bottom was a disclaimer that the images were graphic.

He stared as the footage of his kill played in slow motion. It looked surreal. The president talking, pointing to someone in the crowd. A sudden tug at his shirt, his mouth caught open in a gasp, clutching a growing red spot on his chest. He dropped to his seat hard, then toppled back and lay still.

Kelly was biting her fingernail when Carl looked at her for approval. "Amazing," she said.

He shrugged. "Just a day on the range."

But there was more to it, wasn't there? Far more. He was playing her game now, as he always had, but if she knew he'd spoken to someone at the hospital, she wouldn't be so happy.

Carl knew he faced a predicament that could end his life. He had to tell her. She would help him figure it out—she always had. But he couldn't bring himself to ruin her happiness.

"What's wrong?" Kelly asked.

He looked at her. "Hmm? Nothing."

"You're sweating."

"Am I?" He drew his fingers across a moist forehead.

"What's wrong?"

Here it was, then. He couldn't lie to her. Never. Yet he'd just lied, hadn't he? He felt nauseated. He'd felt this way before, many times. When he lied to Agotha while on the hospital bed. When he'd mistaken the truth about who he was and answered incorrectly. In that moment before they turned up the electrical current to help him understand the truth, he'd often felt nauseated.

"What is it?" Worry laced Kelly's voice.

"Our lives might be in danger," he said.

Kelly stood up. "They know?"

"No, not from them. From Kalman."

She looked at the television. "But you've executed the hit perfectly."

Carl blurted the truth as he knew he must. "I talked to him, Kelly! I went to the hospital and talked to the old man. He said his name was David Abraham."

"What old man? What on earth are you talking about?"

Carl pointed at the television, which was replaying the scene.

"Him. The old man behind the target. I recognized him. I felt as though I had to be sure . . ."

"Sure about what? The hit? We can verify through the media! You . . . You're saying you went to the hospital?"

"They took him into the emergency room. The man was there. He said he knew who I—"

"You *talked* to him?"

"I told him I didn't shoot the president."

"He actually asked you that?" Kelly stared at him, face white, eyes round. She was angry. Or shocked. Both. At moments like this Carl felt nothing like the hero who could kill any man he wished. He felt more like a child.

Kelly walked to the laptops that showed the views of the dummy rooms, slammed them closed.

"What are you doing?"

"We're getting out of here! You've been identified. It's only a matter of time before the old man matches you to file footage taken over the last few days. They'll have your face on every television in the world by tonight."

"He gave me his word that he wouldn't do that. He's sending his son."

Kelly faced him, aghast. "Here?"

"No. To the Peking."

"How could you do this? You've just killed the president of the United States! Do you think some old man loyal to the president will let you walk away because you told him you didn't kill the leader of the free world?"

Carl fought the nausea sweeping through his stomach. He'd never seen her so distraught. He'd made a terrible mistake, he knew that now. They would terminate him as soon as they discovered it.

And Kelly with him.

He stood and paced in front of the television. "I'm sorry, Kelly. I don't know why I did it. He *knew* me!"

"And I know you," she said quietly.

"Then tell me what to do."

She studied him. She loved him—he could see it in her eyes. Even when he made such a terrible mistake as this, she loved him.

Kelly closed her eyes, trying to think. "Okay. Forget what happened. Right now we have to survive." Her eyes drilled his. "You tell me, what will increase our likelihood of survival now?"

He'd already thought this through. Perhaps, if the cards fell in his favor, he could undo the damage before Kalman discovered the truth. "Even if the man sends his son to the Peking, they have no idea where we are. Our exit window is still four hours away. We should watch the room. If the boy arrives, we may be able to use him. We may also choose to ignore him."

"How will we know if the boy arrives?"

"Before coming here I went by the Peking and opened the door for him." Carl pointed at the computers she'd closed. "We'll see him enter the room."

"We could never trust him. It's likely a trap."

"He could have alerted the police at the hospital, but he didn't. If the son comes, it won't be a trap."

She considered his logic. "We have no way of knowing he's really the man's son. I don't understand why we would need the boy in any case."

"We may need him to kill the president."

"The president's dead!"

"No, I don't think he is."

DAVID ABRAHAM walked briskly down the corridor, following the signs to radiology. Dr. Tom Davis was the chief radiologist. He would be the first to know what the X-rays showed.

They were working on Robert Stenton with an urgency that called for the immediate dismissal of all well-wishers, regardless of their political clout. Two Secret Service staff were posted outside the private room, and the hall was lined with staff, but not even his closest advisers knew the president's condition. All they knew was that he'd arrived at the hospital with a very weak pulse.

It wasn't great news. Many victims of gunshot wounds managed to hang on to life for an hour, even two, before expiring. In the case of such a prominent figure, no word on his condition would be given until it was certain.

The only thing the world knew at this point was that the president of the United States had been shot in the chest.

But David had to know more. He pushed open the door to the main radiology reception room. A dozen patients waited their turn.

The door twenty yards down the hall marked Authorized Personnel

Only would lead into the same department. David hurried to the door and walked through.

"May I help you?"

He faced a nurse who'd stopped in the hall on his right. "Yes, I must see Dr. Tom Davis immediately. Can you tell me where—"

"Dr. Davis is tied up. Have you checked in at reception?"

"I don't think you understand. I'm with the president. It's a matter of life and death."

She wasn't impressed. "You'll have to—"

"Now!" He started to walk. "Another minute and he could be dead. Now!"

She hurried after him. "Sir, they specifically—"

"I'm President Stenton's spiritual adviser, for heaven's sake. I don't have time for this!"

She hesitated only a beat. "Third office on the left. He's in his reading room."

David reached the door and put his hand on the knob. "This room?"

"Yes."

"Thank you."

He stepped into a dimly lit room with four large monitors on one wall and a large vertical light surface on the opposite wall. The man he presumed to be Dr. Tom Davis stood in front of a row of large flat-screen monitors, reading a dozen X-rays. He didn't seem to notice David's entry.

"You're Dr. Davis?"

No response. The man was clearly focused.

David approached, scanning the backlit negatives. "My name is David Abraham. I'm the president's spiritual adviser. Are these his X-rays?"

"CAT scans. I've already sent the digital images down to surgery," the radiologist said without looking over. "Interesting."

"What do you see?" David asked.

Now the radiologist looked at him. "Spiritual adviser, huh?"

"That's correct. I must know if you've found any anomalies."

"Not that I can see."

"Nothing?"

"Nothing."

"Show me nothing."

The radiologist picked up a telescoping pointer, stretched it out, and tapped the image in front of him. "The bullet entered here, between the seventh and eighth lateral ribs. No break. If you want to consider that an anomaly, be my guest."

"That's unusual?"

"It happens sometimes. Depends on the entry angle."

He rested the point on a dark spot just below what looked to David like the president's heart. "Missed the heart and the lungs by a hair. We have some minor bleeding here, but I would guess it's from the surface wound. You could also call that an anomaly, I suppose."

"That's not unusual?"

"It happens. But yes, it's unusual."

He tapped a third image. "The bullet exited here, between the fifth and sixth vertebrae."

"No breaks in the spinal column?"

"No."

"So that, too, is unusual?"

Dr. Tom Davis put his hands on his hips and stared at the three images he'd just pointed out. "None of these is particularly unusual. Put them all together, and I would say you have an impossibility."

David's pulse strengthened. "Meaning what?"

"Meaning that I've never seen anything like it. The bullet entered his torso in one of the only places it could have to miss all the internal organs and exit without so much as breaking a bone. Normally I'd expect to see the bullet break up and tear things to shreds. Most exit wounds leave holes large enough to put your fist through."

The radiologist faced him with a grin. "This is no anomaly, my friend. If I were a man of faith, I'd call this a miracle."

He knew it! David could hardly contain himself. Waves of relief washed over his body.

"And what injuries did he sustain?"

"You'll have to take that up with the surgeon. By what I can see, I'd say he sustained two flesh wounds. No internal bleeding. Nothing but a couple of minor cuts to his chest and back."

"Then why surgery?"

"For starters, they just got these pictures. They'll sew him up. His greatest danger was from toxic shock, but they got to him pretty quickly. If I were a betting man, I'd say the president will be up and out of bed in two or three days."

"And this isn't an anomaly?" David cried.

"I once read the X-rays of a skydiver whose chute failed to open. He sustained one broken finger and bruises. Unusual, yes; anomaly, no."

David hardly heard him. He whirled toward the door. "I have to talk to him."

"He's in surgery."

David exited the reading room and suppressed a temptation to run. He hadn't felt so full of life in twelve years. There was no telling how Robert would react to this turn of events, but David would tell him everything. Today. As soon as he woke up.

Project Showdown was breathing still.

22

He wasn't sure, he said. His mind had entered a strange place, and he didn't know what had happened, because he really, really didn't want his bullet to kill the president. But he would now make it right. He would; he swore he would.

Kelly's worst fears were realized half an hour later when an NBC reporter giving a live report on location at Central Park was cut off by the anchor.

". . . was here on this platform, where a forensic team is still looking for the bullet that—"

"I'm sorry to interrupt, Susan, but we have a live update on the president's condition. Reuters is reporting that the president of the United States has survived the assassination attempt that took place an hour and a half ago. I repeat, it appears that the president has survived the attempt on his life. The report goes on to say that the bullet resulted in flesh wounds only."

Kelly stared at the screen, disbelieving. "How's that possible?"

Kelly muted the television and sat on the bed, stunned. Kalman would receive the news soon enough, if he hadn't already. It would be the end.

Behind her, Carl remained silent.

"Do you know what this means?" she asked.

"That I've failed," he said. "But I can fix it."

She stood with her back to him. "Agotha will know."

"She'll know what?"

"That your failure was intentional."

"*I* don't even know that!"

Kelly could feel her world collapsing around her. So much training, so many hard nights—in one moment, gone. Both she and Carl were now expendable.

Was this also part of the plan? She sometimes found it difficult to determine what was real and what was part of the game.

She looked at Carl, who was still staring at the silent news broadcast. "You affected the bullet's trajectory the same way you have been for the last two weeks."

He refused to look at her.

"Today you placed the bullet precisely where it had to travel to knock him down without killing him. We taught you more about the anatomy of the kill zones in the human body than most medical students ever learn. Now you've used that information to save your target. And by doing so, you've signed our death warrants."

"We don't know that," he said. "If it was intentional, I would remember."

"Then what do you remember?"

"That I didn't want the president to die. I thought that the old man behind him might be my father. Or that the president himself might be. I was confused and knew that Agotha had probably put these ideas in my head to test me. As you said."

"But you couldn't overcome the confusion?"

"I thought I had."

She sighed and closed her eyes. "It doesn't matter. Kalman will assume that you've countermanded his order to kill. He will never accept such a failure."

Her cell phone chirped.

"That will be him." Kelly picked up the phone. "Yes."

Kalman's distant, gravelly voice spoke into her ear. "I see he missed."

"Yes. We're working on a third attempt."

The phone hissed.

"Carl's leading the son of the president's adviser—"

"I don't want the details," Kalman said. "Englishman is standing by. You have until midnight. If I haven't received confirmation by then, your man must be eliminated." He paused. "I want you to do it personally. I'll give you two hours following any such failure on his part. If you don't follow through, I'll trigger the implant and hold you responsible. Are we clear?"

She hesitated. "Of course."

The line clicked off.

Kelly kept her back to Carl and gathered her wits. He couldn't see her face flushed.

"If the boy shows, can you do what you've suggested?" she asked, setting the phone down slowly.

He'd formulated a simple plan for a third attempt, but she had her doubts about his willingness to finish the job. If he didn't, she would.

"Why wouldn't I?"

Carl's mind is so fried that he can hardly hold a conviction for an hour, she thought.

"You've failed to finish the job twice now, both times because you associated the target with a father figure. None of this will change."

"But I know why now," Carl said. "Agotha put the desire in me."

"That knowledge didn't help you execute the hit today."

He didn't respond to her obvious point. It didn't matter. Her psychological manipulation had failed to affect him as she'd hoped. Perhaps the truth would work better.

"I have a confession to make," she said. "I lied to you yesterday. Agotha didn't plant the thoughts of your father. I needed you to feel strong about today's attempt, so I gave you a plausible reason for your failure. It seems that this father business is coming from your own mind on its own terms."

Carl looked lost. Stunned.

"Maybe it's my fault you feel so conflicted. I was trying to help you."

"And I would have done the same for you," he said. "It must have been horrible to have to lie. Yet you did it to protect me. Thank you."

She couldn't bear this manipulation. What had they done to him? The mental stripping was one thing in the compound, but here in the middle of New York, it seemed inhumane.

"Can you do it?"

"Send the boy back with a message for the president?"

"Unwittingly armed with a toxic canister," she finished. "It would kill everyone in the room."

"Of course I can do it. It's what I've been trained to do."

"You were also trained to put a bullet in a target's heart, yet you willfully missed."

"I don't remember willfully—"

"There he is!"

The laptop showed a short boy standing inside their room at the Peking, looking around.

Carl walked up to the desk, studied the image for a few moments, then slammed the laptop closed.

"Let's go," he said and strode toward the door.

THE PEKING Grand Hotel was a five-minute walk. With any luck the boy would find Carl's note instructing him to wait ten minutes.

They walked quickly, silently.

He was less sure of what he was doing now than at any time in his memory. His response to the confusion was to retreat. There were many times when survival depended on retreat. It was how he defeated the heat in his pit. The hornets on the shooting range. The hospital bed under Agotha's care. There was always a safe place in his mind somewhere. He just had to find it.

At this moment, that safe place was probably execution without thought. They had until midnight to undo the mess he'd made. Poison was the preferred weapon of many assassins, and tonight Carl would remember why.

If his plan failed, he would be left with only one alternative. He would find a few more-familiar weapons and go after the president in the hospital. His chances of survival were minimal, but he would be dead at midnight anyway. If he was going to die, he would die fighting for Kelly's survival. He owed her his life.

They entered the Peking through a rear door that required a plastic key card to open. Second floor. First door on the right, room 202.

The small device that Kelly carried in her purse consisted of a remote triggering device and a small canister of colorless, odorless hydrogen cyanide gas, potent enough to kill any living creature in a ten-by-ten room within five minutes. The boy's mission would be a simple one: in the president's hospital room, he would call a given telephone number and then verbally relay a message intended only for the president. In this way, they could reasonably believe that the boy was talking to the president, not a third party.

There would be no message, of course. As soon as the boy confirmed the president's presence, they would trigger the canister hidden on the boy's person with a certain degree of confidence that both were in the same room. A similar method using explosives rather than gas had been used successfully among drug cartels in South America. Certainly not infallible, but with nothing to lose, Carl was willing to assume the odds before he attempted anything more direct.

The door was still cracked open. He entered the room, followed by Kelly.

It was empty. David Abraham's son had left?

"Hello, Johnny."

Carl turned to face a blond-headed boy standing in the bathroom doorway. He looked to be thirteen or fourteen. A sheepish smile curved below bright blue eyes.

"My name is Samuel," the boy said. "You don't remember me, do you?"

"Should I?"

Carl had no intention of remembering anything. Memory only brought confusion and contributed to his failure.

"They've stripped you of your identity," Samuel said. "You really don't know who you are anymore. Amazing. We knew . . ." His eyes shifted to Kelly, then returned to Carl. He carried himself with surprising confidence for such a small boy.

"We knew you couldn't do it. The truth runs too deep in you, Johnny. We always knew that you could only go so far."

A ringing bothered Carl's ears. "Why do you keep calling me Johnny?"

"Johnny Drake. That's your real name. You were a chaplain in the army when the X Group took you. You were on leave in Egypt."

"A chaplain?"

"You're mistaken," Kelly said. "You're confusing him with someone else."

"Don't let my appearance deceive you," Samuel said. "I'm much older than I look. And I can prove all of this if you give me the chance."

The ringing in Carl's ears had become a soft roar. He'd been a chaplain who was now called Saint? How would the boy know? Why would the boy lie?

He tried to think of himself as Johnny. The name sounded odd.

"Do you mind excusing us for a moment?" Kelly asked Samuel.

"Now?"

"Yes. Could you step outside? Just for a moment."

"Okay."

The boy stepped out into the hall, and Kelly closed the door behind him. She returned, motioning silence.

"Do you know this boy?" she whispered.

"I don't remember."

"It's Kalman. I can smell it on him."

"I don't understand. How could Kalman know—"

"The old man knew you. Who's to say that he's not with Kalman?"

Carl's mind spun. He'd faced and accepted more confusion in the last twenty-four hours than he'd allowed himself in many months. The nausea he'd felt earlier made a comeback.

"It's like Kalman to put redundancies in place to deal with the possibility that you will fail to assassinate the president. Why not the old man and the boy?"

"Why two people instead of just one? And why would he use a boy?"

"What better way to gain your trust and lead us to a place where Englishman can kill us both? The one thing that Kalman fears more than anything else is his own assassins." She took a deep breath. "I've seen this before, in Indonesia once. If I'm right, the boy will suggest you go somewhere."

"I don't understand why—"

"Then trust me! I lied to you once, but I won't lie to you again. Kalman knows your weakness for a father figure and he's exploiting it."

"Kalman doesn't need the boy. He could kill me with the implant."

She nodded and paced. "True. But I don't like it. Kalman is a suspicious snake. This would be like him. I think the boy is lying!"

"What are you suggesting?" he asked.

"That we walk away from this boy. We can't believe his lies, and we can't use him the way we planned. If he's connected to Kalman, there'll be a trap waiting for us."

Carl nodded. It made sense in a twisted way. He'd never considered betraying Kalman, but at the moment he was desperate for any sense at all. He accepted her truth and felt his nausea ease.

"Then we'll dismiss him and I'll go after the president on my own."

"It's the only way we can prove ourselves to Kalman without risking being caught in a trap," she said.

Kelly let the boy back into the room.

"You don't trust me, do you?" the boy said. "I came because my father and I know what you did, Johnny. You shot a bullet through the president's chest in a way that wouldn't kill him. They found the garbage bin that you shot from. Hitting a man at two thousand yards is very difficult. Sending a bullet through a precise point at that distance is impossible. Yet you did it."

The boy knew all of this? Carl glanced at Kelly. She was as confused as he.

Samuel continued. "You may think there's some kind of scientific explanation for your abilities, but the truth is not so simple. Your real power is much greater than anything you've seen. In fact, you were more powerful before they took you. By messing with your mind, they messed with your power."

"How do you know this?" Kelly demanded.

"Because I've been watching Johnny ever since he left Paradise."

A strobe ignited in the back of Carl's mind. Paradise. It was familiar. Terribly familiar. But he couldn't place it.

"Do you remember?" Samuel asked. "I'm here because I want you to go to Paradise, Johnny. Your mother still lives there. Her name is Sally, and she's been sick about your disappearance."

Samuel's words fell into his mind like bright flashes along a line of lost history. *Sally. Paradise. Colorado. Chaplain.*

Johnny.

Johnny.

My name is Johnny.

But he couldn't remember any of it!

"If I were Kalman, I would tell you to say all these things," Kelly said. "Be careful, Carl."

"His name is Johnny," the boy said. "Not Carl."

"And why are you speaking as if you know more than any boy should?" Kelly demanded.

"Because I am no ordinary boy," Samuel said. "And now I have to go."

He turned and walked to the door. "Remember, Johnny," he said, turning back. "Go to Paradise. It'll all become clear in Paradise. Project Showdown still lives."

And then the boy was gone.

23

The president wants to see you."

"Thank you."

David Abraham brushed past the nurse and hurried toward the guards posted outside Robert's room. The president had been out of surgery for forty-five minutes, and David knew that the local anesthetics hadn't dimmed his mind in the least. If he knew what David had for him, he'd have told the nurse to let him through sooner.

He dipped his head at the guards, one of whom opened the door for him. "Thank you."

"David!" The president grinned from his hospital bed as David crossed the room.

"Miracles never cease," Robert said.

"Clearly. How are you feeling?"

"Sore but otherwise surprisingly well. They're using local anesthetic at my request, but I'm not sure how well it's working."

"Your mind's clear, then. That's good. Your prognosis?"

"I'll be up in two days, they say."

David glanced at two aides who sat by the window. "I need to speak to you privately."

"Give us a moment."

David waited for the aides to leave before he spoke again.

"Do they have any leads?"

"You're asking if I told anyone about this man you recognized?"

"Yes."

"I've only been conscious for an hour, half of that time on a table with bright lights overhead. The game's changed, I'm sure you understand that. Someone just put a bullet through me. An attempt was made on the life of the president of the United States—this is far bigger than either of us."

David knew that what he had to say wouldn't be easy. Knew that Robert might very well reject it. Most sane men would.

"Robert, please. What I am about to tell you may offend you at the deepest level. God knows that I am culpable in matters you know nothing about, and I'm willing to suffer any fitting consequences when this is all over. But I'm begging you to open your mind."

The president studied him for a moment, then looked at the ceiling. "God willing, this *is* over. Whoever's behind this will be dealt with in a manner expected by both the office and the nation."

"Of course. But you're wrong—it's not over. In some ways it's just beginning."

"I'm a reasonable man, David. But you've caught me in a down moment. Please don't patronize me."

"Down but not dead. That's the point, isn't it? Why are you down but not dead? You know the details of the shooting?"

"I was shot. The bullet missed my internal organs. Evidently somebody up there still wants me around."

"You were shot from a garbage bin at over two thousand yards. There are only a handful of shooters in the world who could accomplish such a feat. Do you know what a bullet's trajectory looks like after it's traveled a mile and a half?"

"I didn't realize you were so interested in shooting."

"I've become interested as of late. I'm sure that the FBI will get around to filling you in on this, but let me put it in layman's terms. When a bullet leaves a barrel, it's spinning. That spinning motion eventually forces the bullet to move off its axis and rotate in circles. They call it parabolic rotation."

David moved his finger through the air like a corkscrew.

"At two thousand yards, the diameter of the bullet's parabolic rotation is about a foot. There's no way the shooter can know which part of the rotation the bullet will be in when it strikes a body, only that if it's perfectly aimed, it will strike somewhere in a twelve-inch circle. Did you know this?"

"No. Go on."

"Since the bullet is moving in a circular pattern, it will enter the body at a slight angle and tear the flesh in that direction. Like a corkscrew. Lateral tear."

"Okay, so what's the point?"

"The point is that I've seen the images of your wound. The path of the bullet was perfectly straight. It entered and exited your body in a perfectly straight line. And that straight line happened to be through one of the only paths a bullet could travel without causing significant injury."

"Like I said, a miracle."

"The lack of damage was intentional, Robert!"

"That's impossible."

"Of course it is. Which is why you have to listen to me."

David had pushed Robert to the edges of his reasoning many times, and he knew the look of a man being stretched. Robert was being stretched.

The president sighed. "I'm listening."

David stood and walked to the end of the bed, dragging his hand on the bed rail. "You're alive because the shooter is a man named Johnny Drake. Do you recognize the name?"

"That's the name of the man you recognized in the footage of Assim Feroz?"

"Yes."

"Then he's in custody? You thought he was after Feroz!"

"No, he's not in custody. And I was wrong about Feroz being the target. In hindsight, I realize I should have known. Samuel didn't know *who* would be killed, only that a very powerful man would be assassinated, resulting in Israel's disarmament and downfall. Either way, this doesn't change the fact that the killer made an impossible shot. I believe that the only man alive who could do this is named Johnny Drake."

"This has to do with Project Showdown."

"Johnny was one of the children in Paradise, yes."

Robert closed his eyes, brought both hands to his forehead, and swept his hair back, sighing. "David . . ."

"I'm not finished. Please, you know about Project Showdown. You of all people should consider what I'm telling you. Without reservation!"

"I thought the children were all placed in homes with strict confidence so that they couldn't be tracked."

"They were, all but a few who were special cases."

"It's one thing to believe that dragons once existed. It's another to actually go hunting for one because someone believes they still exist!"

"You won't have that problem long, my friend. You'll believe soon enough. I have a feeling that you're going to meet more than a dragon before this is over."

"It *is* over!"

"Not until you die, if you go after the only man who can save you. Johnny Drake *must* be allowed to follow the path he is on. No charges, no media leaks, not a word."

He'd said it. Prematurely, perhaps. Not as part of a carefully constructed argument that had the president eating out of his hand, but there it was.

"I should let the man who tried to kill me walk? Please, David, you're—"

"You're alive because Johnny Drake wants you alive. If he wanted you dead, believe me, you would be dead. He's capable of far more than even he knows. Take him out of the equation, and another man will shoot you. That man will shoot to kill. You will die."

"This . . ." Robert stalled. "You're making an assassin out to be some kind of hero."

"Call him what you like. He's the only thing standing between you and death."

"Based on a vision—"

"Based on what I know!"

A knock sounded. One of the guards opened the door. "Is everything okay?"

"Unless you hear a scream, assume I'm fine," the president said.

The man bowed out.

"Forgive me for raising my voice, but I can't overemphasize my conviction on this matter. I'll explain everything when we have more time, but for your sake I'm begging you to do everything in your power to thwart any investigation that leads to Johnny as the shooter."

Robert closed his eyes again. He wondered if David knew what kind of stress he had just put Robert under.

"What else are you not telling me, David?"

"Only what makes no difference to you."

"You're right, you are culpable. What makes you think Johnny has this supposed power?"

"Besides what he just pulled off? Read the report again. We didn't pick up on it until three years ago, but it makes sense. He has . . . a gift."

He couldn't read the president's reaction to this.

"And what made you so sure he wouldn't kill me?"

"I thought he was after Feroz, and I *wasn't* sure Johnny wouldn't kill him. As for killing you, it's not in his nature. Again, read the report and you'll understand far more than I can convince you of. We are dealing with matters that reside between the head and the heart, Robert. I had faith in Johnny. Enough to put the world on his shoulders."

"Including my life?"

"Samuel's vision saved your life. If we hadn't intervened, you would be dead right now. I would expect some gratitude when this finally sinks in."

"Intervened? How did you know Johnny was with the X Group?"

David took a deep breath. He bit his lip and answered slowly, with a tremble in his voice.

"Because we put him there."

The president kept his eyes locked on David for a long moment. "My, my, you have been busy."

"For your sake. For the sake of Israel."

"Based on a *vision*."

"Based on Project Showdown, which gave me the faith to believe in this vision."

"And would you happen to know who ordered my assassination?"

"No. The X Group has no political agenda."

"If you had to guess?"

David hesitated. "Assim Feroz. Impossible to prove. It's not over, Robert. The X Group will not accept failure."

"And neither will I."

"I don't think you can neutralize them. Certainly not in the time we have. How long did it take to deal with Al Qaeda? From what I understand, the X Group is far more organized."

"Then what?"

"Keep a heavy guard. Make sure everyone around you is armed to the teeth. And pray that I'm still right about Johnny."

24

JOHNNY.

The more Carl allowed the name to reside in his mind, the more disoriented he felt.

He and Kelly had walked back to their hotel room in a dizzy silence. She'd fashioned her own theory as to how and why the old man David and his son, Samuel, would make such outrageous claims, and she convinced him to follow a logical course based on that theory. But he knew her own confidence was shaken.

He also knew that he would follow whatever direction she gave him, but he couldn't dislodge a terrible suspicion that something was wrong.

Kelly left him sitting at the table and went for a list of weapons that he needed for his final mission against the president. Using Samuel was no longer an option. He would have to do this himself. She did her best to assure him that everything would be okay. That they were only doing what they were both destined to do. That the only truth was the truth he knew when he looked into her eyes.

Carl believed her. She was Kelly. She was the only person who truly loved him. He would die for Kelly.

But would *Johnny* die for her?

Would Johnny believe her?

Would Johnny kill the president of the United States?

Then there was Samuel, a boy of maybe thirteen who talked and acted like someone twice that age. An apparition from Johnny's past, or another lie sent from Agotha to challenge Carl. Or an associate of Kelly's like Englishman, playing some deep psychological game that would ultimately manipulate him into a position of yet deeper loyalty.

His body began to sweat thirty minutes after Kelly left. He tried to stop it by retreating into the safe blackness of his mind, but his face continued to flush with heat.

Frightened by his inability to control the emotions or his response, he hurried into the bathroom, stripped off his clothing, and took a cold shower. The water felt like heaven on his body, and for a few minutes he successfully put Samuel out of his mind.

Satisfied, he dried and donned the black pants and shirt he would wear tonight. He didn't have to form a plan as much as select one from several dozen already waiting on the edge of his consciousness, then modify it to meet the current situation. The fact that he didn't know the hospital's layout limited him. He would have to make adjustments during the operation.

Johnny. Your mother's name is Sally. She is waiting for you in a town called Paradise. My name is Samuel. I'm not an ordinary boy.

The sweat returned five minutes after he'd dressed. Buckets of it, soaking his shirt in less than a minute.

He quickly stripped and jumped back in the shower. This time the cold made him shiver. First sweat, now shivers—he was losing his self-control!

Carl stepped from the shower and attempted to forcefully towel away the gooseflesh. But he wasn't successful. He stared at his reflection in a full-length mirror affixed to the inside of the bathroom door. Pale from the months in darkness. Lean, ribbed with muscle, marked by dozens of scars on his shoulders, hips, and feet—Agotha's little gifts to him. But it was the way his skin prickled with a thousand goose bumps that fascinated him now. More accurately, the fact that he wasn't able to make them go away.

He should ask Kelly to give him a treatment! Maybe she carried some of the drugs with her. She could strap him to the bed and use the electricity from the wall outlet to encourage his mind to react as it was trained.

No, no, what was he thinking? He had to complete the mission tonight, before midnight! And it was always Agotha, not Kelly, who administered his lessons—he doubted Kelly would want to shock him.

"Who are you?" he asked the shaking image in the mirror.

He answered himself. "My name is Carl."

"And who is Carl?"

"Carl is Johnny."

The thin sheen of sweat glistened on his skin. Somewhere deep in his mind, where he erected walls of blackness and formed friendly tunnels that led him to the light, his understanding of truth seemed to have shut down.

Carl who was Johnny began to panic, and this time he couldn't stop himself. He stood before the long mirror, shaking and sweating and panicking.

He had to get to the bed! Lying down would allow him to relax and focus. He stumbled to the bed, still shaking, and lay down on his back. The white ceiling dissolved into a sea of lights that made him dizzy.

Why was his body doing this? Why was he afraid? He was afraid because he was shaking, and he was shaking because he was afraid, because he couldn't stop sweating.

He heard the door open and close, but he couldn't seem to do anything about it. He couldn't stop shaking.

"Carl?"

"Kelly . . ."

"Carl!" She dropped her bag and rushed over to him. "Carl, it's okay. Shh, shh, shh. You're shaking!"

She placed her hands on his chest and face. "You're burning up! What's happening? Please, you're scaring me."

"Kelly . . ." He couldn't seem to say any more past his violent shakes.

"Shh, shh, shh . . . I'm here now. I'm home. It's okay. I'm so sorry."

"I'm afraid," he managed.

Kelly lowered her head to his chest and began to cry. "Johnny," she whispered.

Johnny?

"Please, Johnny. I'm so sorry, I'm so sorry. Please stop."

He closed his eyes and let his mind fall back into blackness. He suddenly didn't feel anything. No hot, no cold, not even Kelly on his chest.

She was calling him by his name. His real name. In a moment of stunning clarity, he knew what was happening. Kelly was loving him as she'd never loved him before. She was speaking a deep and personal truth. Something he himself didn't even know.

Her soft whisper, calling him Johnny, cut to his soul in a way that no kiss ever had. He was swallowed by a profound sense of intimacy that he'd never imagined could exist between two people.

Carl stopped shaking. He opened his eyes. Kelly was weeping. In that moment he knew that she'd wept with him in the tunnel because she was torn by this terrible secret.

The secret that he was Johnny.

She carried the burden for him because she loved him. He put his hand on her head and stared at the white ceiling, moved by her great love. And by this revelation that he really was Johnny Drake, not Carl Strople. They stayed that way for a long time.

It was Kelly who broke the spell, long after she'd stopped sniffing, long after her breathing settled. She lifted her head from his chest, searched his eyes, then retrieved his clothes from the bathroom and set them on the end of the bed. Carl sat up slowly.

"Dress," she said, walking to the window. She pulled back the drapes and stared out at the darkness.

He dressed, numb and directionless.

"Your name is Johnny Drake," she said, crossing her arms. "You were a chaplain with the United States Army. They took you by force when you were on leave in Cairo. That's the way the X Group works."

"Then . . . Then the boy was right?"

"Yes. I'm sorry, I panicked. I didn't know what to do. I'm so sorry. I lied to you."

"My name is Johnny," he said.

"Yes."

"Johnny Drake."

"Yes, yes. I'm so sorry. I—"

"I'm from Colorado?"

"I don't know." She turned around and looked at him with cried-out eyes. "I don't know about the rest. Please, please, I beg you to forgive me."

Carl felt as if he was going to burst into tears. But he wasn't Carl, was he? He was Johnny.

"You have to leave me, Carl. I don't care what they do to me, you have to run."

"I could never leave you. I have to finish this or they'll kill you!"

"No, listen to me. It's not too late for you to reclaim your life. We can never be together again, not after what I've done. You have to—"

"No!" Rage welled up in his chest. This is why she'd been so quiet while she lay on his chest. She'd been convincing herself that she had to leave him, although she loved him desperately. "You can never leave me! I need you."

"You think you do, but you don't." She walked to him, keeping her eyes locked onto his. "Please, Carl, you're an innocent child, don't you see? Agotha's turned you into an innocent child and then abused you. And I've been her accomplice. You even talk like a child!"

"Tell me one thing. Do you love me?"

Her eyes pooled with tears. "Yes."

"You're sure?"

"Yes. At first it was one of Agotha's games. But it's become much more. I love you very much."

"Then don't hurt me more by leaving me. I don't know who I am. If I'm a child, you can't leave me alone!"

His words rang in the small room, silencing with their truth. There were only two things that Carl knew about himself. The first was that his name was Johnny. The second was that apart from names and places, he was totally and terribly lost.

His identity had been stripped.

"I'm lost," he said. "And without you, I'm hopelessly lost."

"I've *tortured* you!"

"And now you will help me heal. I'll do what they've asked me to do. With your help, we can play their game and find a way to beat them."

Kelly paced between Carl and the bathroom door, staring intently at the floor. Then at him.

"You can't finish this mission. You may not understand why now, because your moral compass has been dashed, but you can't."

"They'll kill me with the implant."

"Unless . . ."

"Unless what?"

She was anxious now. "Unless you can block the implant. Long enough for it to be removed."

"I couldn't even stop myself from shaking. How can I block—"

"That's why Kalman is so nervous about you! You survived the electric chair, why not the implant? It's designed to detonate if tampered with in any way, but what if you could shut it off just long enough for a surgeon to remove it?"

"Because the tunnel is gone!"

"Then I'll help you find it again."

"Electric shock?"

"No, not that way!" She grabbed his hand and kissed it, then held it against her cheek. "Never that way again, I promise."

Carl considered her words. What choice did he have? He could either kill the president or take his chances with the implant. She was right, there was no real choice. He would have to set his mind on shutting out the implant long enough for a surgeon, assuming there was one, to take the implant out, assuming such an operation could be done without damaging his brain.

"They'll still come after us," Kelly said.

"And without me, you don't have a chance."

Her eyes searched his, side to side. He felt a moment of deep empathy with her. She would pay such a price to love him.

What if all of this is just part of the game?

Carl dismissed the absurd thought. See, he could still control his mind. He'd just done it.

He leaned forward and kissed her. "I will die for you, my love."

"No, you won't. If you die, then I die. They'll never quit. It's forever, Carl. Do you understand that? If we do this, we'll be on the run together for the rest of our lives."

"Maybe we can find some life before we die."

"Maybe."

"Then we should go to Paradise."

Kelly grabbed the bag of weapons off her bed. "Not until we take care of the implant. We have six hours. There's a doctor outside the city that we've used before. The implant sits behind the brain, set to trigger if exposed." She glanced at him. "You'll have to remain conscious so you can block—"

"Kalman will trigger the device before then."

"Not if we leave now. We still have some time."

"Does this doctor have a pit?"

She looked surprised that he'd asked the question. It was a ridiculous question, of course. He didn't know why it came out.

"This is New York. There will be no pits in New York. Ever."

"Okay. I'll find another way to block the pain. And the implant."

"You'll have to find a way to block the tracking device for a few hours, or he'll know we've left the city. Can you do that?"

"I can try. Do we have a choice?"

Kelly shook her head and closed her eyes. "I can't believe we're doing this. Even if we get rid of the implant, Kalman will send Englishman after us."

"I've beat him before."

Her eyes opened. "Not in real life, you haven't." There was a strange darkness in her eyes that bothered him. "Not when he pulls out the stops. We'll have to find a hole to live in."

"I love the dark," he said.

"And I hate it."

They quickly packed two duffel bags, one for weapons and one for the rest. This was their collective material wealth, this and $87,000 in U.S. currency remaining from the $250,000 Kelly had brought with her.

Kelly scanned the room after they'd wiped it down. "One last question before we leave. Should I call you Carl or Johnny?"

He thought for a moment.

"Carl," he said. "I don't know who Johnny is."

25

He is called Englishman. He's not *the* Englishman, of course. Neither is he Dale Crompton. He doesn't really know who he is anymore, so he is who he wants to be, which is far more and far less than any Englishman.

The man taps his thumb on the leather steering wheel in the Buick he took from a nameless parking lot this morning. The radio is on. He dislikes the song's lyrics, but the beat fills him with energy.

Pain is in the game,
And the game is in the name

The singer has no idea what pain is. If Englishman had enough time, he might find the singer's home and rearrange his view of pain.

The name is Slayer
If you really want to know
He hunts in the dark and kills in the light

Any man who can sing such words without knowing their meaning deserves to be hunted down. Still, the beat is good and Englishman hums with the guitars, unbothered by his butchering of the tune.

He's not Englishman. He's Jude Law. He's Robert De Niro. He's Hannibal Lecter. He's whoever he wants to be . . .

The one called Englishman cracked his neck and cleared his mind. His drive to tell the story perfectly dogged him like those irritating hornets. And by *perfectly* he meant in a way that kept them forever in the dark where they belonged.

The story had to be more personal. First person. He started again.

I am called Englishman. I'm not the Englishman, of course. Neither am I Dale Crompton. I don't know who I am, so I am who I want to be, which is far more and far less than any Englishman. An Englishman has a history; I do not. An Englishman is weak; I am not.

I look like Jude Law. I smile like Robert De Niro. I laugh like Hannibal Lecter. Dust to dust, ashes to ashes. Hallelujah, amen, you are dismissed.

Englishman nodded and repeated the words that had become a kind of mantra to him. He'd touched the hand of the gas station attendant fifteen minutes earlier when he'd stopped to fill his tank. Did the girl have any idea whose hand she was touching? No.

Did she know how many throats he'd cut? No.

Did she even suspect that he hated women? No.

Did she want to kiss him? Yes.

Did she love him more than she loved Jude Law? Yes.

Did she realize how much he liked corn nuts? No.

Would he return and kill her for wanting to kiss him? He didn't know. Probably not—he wouldn't have much idle time in the next few days.

Englishman paused. He understood the plan, but he'd never liked it much. Yes, he embraced the idea in the very beginning, but that was before he understood that he had the power to find a better plan. Like telling a better story.

Playing the part of Englishman had grown stale and tired. The killings had become boring. How many ways could you kill a person anyway?

There would come a time when he would walk into Kalman's hospital and take off his head with a machete. Better yet, shave him bald and fry him in that electric chair of his.

Johnny had picked up some skills, but he was still weak. The showdown ahead made Englishman's skin crawl with anticipation.

I look like Jude Law and I'm . . . He didn't bother finishing the thought because he drew a blank.

It didn't matter; he was close to the target now. He would kill the doctor as Kalman had ordered, and then, with any luck at all, the true game—the one he'd waited so patiently for—would begin.

He'd been watching Johnny's progress since he and the woman, whom he hated only slightly less than Johnny, set foot in New York. They'd gone off the reservation last night, leaving the hotel room spotless. Even so, Englishman knew their ultimate destination and in fact had anticipated that Johnny would do what he was now doing.

Englishman knew not only where they were heading but *how* they would get there, based on the last few tracking signals emitted by the implant before it had stopped transmitting.

He exited the freeway, backtracked a mile on the frontage road, cut west for half a mile, and pulled into a long gravel driveway. Horses grazed in a fenced green pasture on his right. He'd killed a horse once. The experience had left him cold. They were dumb animals. Household pets offered only slightly more fascination.

Dr. Henry Humphries was a veterinarian. Englishman had never needed his veterinary services, but the good doctor had once sewn part of the Ukrainian's finger back on.

"I am not Englishman today," he said, parking by the large barn.

"Today I am simply . . ." He considered several choices. "*Un*man. I'm Unman."

He put the Buick in park, interlaced his fingers, and cracked his knuckles loudly. This was a cliché, of course. But he loved cliché because it had become so vogue to hate cliché. In truth, those who cringed at the use of cliché were their own cliché.

He stepped from the car and scanned the barn. His favorite movie was *Kill Bill*. Despite his general hatred of women, he liked Black Mamba because she fought like a man. And she wore yellow leather, which appealed to him for no reason that he could understand, no matter how much he thought about it.

Unman. Unman walked up to the door and wiped his black canvas shoes on a mat that read "All Animals Welcome, Whites Use Front Entrance."

For a moment Unman wished he was black. Maybe he was. He tried the door, turned the knob, and walked in without announcing himself.

Fireweed Mexican tile floor. White walls in need of a fresh coat. Clean at first glance but dirty under the skin, like most people. The place smelled of manure.

Manure and Johnny.

A man in a brown tweed jacket stood to the right of a workbench that held a large metal tub, something you might wash an animal in. Behind him, a dozen stalls housed a couple of horses, some pigs, and a lamb of all things. A fluffy white lamb.

The lamb bleated.

"May I help you?"

Unman took his eyes off the sheep and faced the man. White, fat, and old. Not fat-fat, but a good fifty pounds of blubber on his gut. Unman imagined the man without a shirt because he had both the time and the imagination to do so. Evidently sewing up animals didn't burn the calories as much as, say, kickboxing or jumping on a trampoline, either one of which would do the doctor good.

The man wore gray polyester pants and an untucked yellow shirt. He held a syringe in his right hand. If he was expecting any female company, he wasn't concerned with impressing them. Maybe Unman liked this doctor.

"What's your name?" Unman asked.

"I'm sorry, was I expecting you?" The man showed only slight fear. He filled the syringe from a vial and laid both on the table.

"I'm Unman. I'm looking for a man and a woman who stopped here last night. Good-looking fellow, about so tall, and a hot woman who tends to boss him around. The man had a small device buried in his skull that evidently didn't go off as it was designed to. We think someone here took it out, thereby sealing his own fate. So I guess I'm not really looking for the man who's all that, or the woman who bosses him around, but the doctor who helped them escape. Need to clean things up, if you know what I mean."

Surprisingly, the man still showed minimal fear. Interesting. Maybe Unman should drop the clever-meant-to-be-terrifying cliché and be more sinister. But that failed to interest him, so he continued.

"If you are that doctor, I'll need the implant. Then I'll have to kill you so that you don't tell anyone else about it. If you're not the doctor I'm looking for, then I'll have to kill you for knowing that I'm looking for a doctor to kill. So who are you, the doctor who needs killing, or the innocent bystander who needs killing?"

Now more fear showed on the man's face. Clichés and all.

"They were here," the doctor said.

"And the implant?"

The man produced a small box from under the bench in front of him and held it out.

Unman walked forward. He knew what would happen now. Any man who showed only a little fear when presented with the prospect of his own death had a plan. The doctor obviously thought he could survive this meeting.

The clichés weren't working as well as Unman had hoped. He wanted to get this over with and make the call.

He stopped twenty feet from the man. "Throw it here," he said.

The doctor made as if to throw the device with his left hand, but Unman didn't care about the implant. Syringe man was right-handed, and his right hand was under the bench top, holding something—probably a gun—that filled the doctor with confidence.

Unman could have waited for the man's hopeless attempt to distract him by throwing the implant.

He could have waited for the man's gun to clear the counter.

He could have even waited for the gun to go off. All of these would have been consistent with a tough villain defying death with elegance. Cliché.

But the time for cliché was gone, so Unman pulled a gun from his right hip and shot the doctor through his nose.

The man dropped like an elevator car, smacked the bottom of his jaw on the bench, bounced back with a few shattered teeth to go with his broken nose, and fell heavily to the ground.

In all likelihood, the doctor hadn't even seen Unman draw.

He walked to the window and pulled out his cell phone. Dialed the number. Two of the horses were looking at the barn, alerted by the gunshot. He wondered who would take care of the doctor's horses now.

"Yes?"

"The doctor is dead. I have the implant."

He could hear Kalman's breathing in the silence.

"Kill Saint first," Kalman said. "Then complete the contract."

"Thank you." Unman closed the phone.

Englishman hated Kalman, but he hated Johnny more. In fact, he'd been born to hate Johnny. Kalman didn't know this, Agotha didn't know, but Englishman knew. And now he was finally in a position to do something about that hate.

"Game on, Johnny," he said. Was that cliché?

26

Paradise was nestled in the Colorado mountains off the beaten path, several miles from the main road that passed through Delta.

The trees in Colorado were different from any Carl had ever seen. Tall evergreens that pointed to the sky mixed with deciduous trees similar to the ones that surrounded the compound in Hungary. The terrain was severe and sharp, with cliffs and huge outcroppings of rocks.

The Rocky Mountains. Carl watched from the car with fascination. It was familiar to him only because the boy had suggested it should be. Or did he remember?

They'd flown into Denver as Elmer and Jane Austring, knowing full well that Kalman could trace the false identities he himself had provided. But it would take even someone as powerful as Kalman at least a day to track them down. By then, they'd be gone. As soon as they'd visited Paradise, they would assume new identities and move on.

A taxi had taken them from Denver International Airport to a used car dealer off Interstate 70, where Kelly had paid $8,000 for the old blue Ford truck she now drove. They'd exchanged license plates with another vehicle in Vail, and then with yet another in Grand Junction. None of this would prevent Kalman from tracking them, but it would hold off the authorities in the event that Carl had been fingered as a suspect in the president's shooting.

News of the assassination attempt was everywhere. Shouting from all of the newspapers in the airport, all of the television monitors in the waiting areas, every station on the radio.

Carl was amazed by the reach of his one bullet. No one knew what to do with the information that the assassin's bullet had caused so little damage. The White House had released no specifics—a good thing, Kelly said. Any trained ballistics expert would know that the shot had been impossible. Better that the public didn't know.

"Why?" he'd asked.

She just shrugged her shoulders. "It's our secret."

He nodded. "Paradise, three miles," he said, reading a sign ahead on their right.

She took the turnoff and angled the truck up a narrow paved road. Within half a mile they were driving down a winding strip of black-top. The edge fell sharply on the right into a deep valley. A metal guardrail provided a measure of security.

This was the road to Paradise. It could have been the road to Mexico as far as Carl knew. None of it was more familiar than a suggestion.

"I like the mountains," Kelly said.

"They're nice," Carl said.

"Wait until you see the desert."

They both knew that if the boy had been right and Paradise was Carl's home, Kalman would know as well. Regardless of what happened here, they had to be gone by the end of the day.

They would go to the desert in Nevada.

Kelly glanced at him. "Do you recognize anything?"

"No."

"Maybe when you see the town."

"Maybe."

The road descended, took a sharp turn, and fed into a valley. One

moment they were watching trees rush by; the next they were looking down at a town.

Carl wasn't sure if it was Paradise at first. Then they passed a sign
that said it was. *Welcome to Paradise, Colorado, Population 450.*

He began to sweat.

"This is it," Kelly said. "Do you recognize anything?"

A large building with a five-foot sign that read "Paradise Community
Center" loomed ahead on the right. Beyond it, a grocery store with gas
pumps out front. Houses on the left, running up to a tall church with
a pointed steeple.

"Can you pull over?"

"Here?"

"Yes, pull over."

He didn't recognize anything, but his heart was hammering and he
thought that might be a good sign.

Kelly pulled the pickup truck onto a dusty shoulder a hundred feet
from the community center. "Do you recognize it?"

Carl stared ahead, searching his memory. This building had once
been something else. A burned-down pile of rubble. Or a theater. Or
maybe his mind was just making things up.

"Carl?"

"I . . . I don't know." He climbed out and faced the town.
Something had happened here, he could sense it if not remember it.
His body was reacting even if his mind wasn't. Kelly joined him,
exchanging looks between him and the town.

"Why can't I remember?" he asked.

"Agotha's no amateur. Only the strongest minds can endure her
methods. She told me she'd never seen a mind as strong as yours. She
was determined to either break you or kill you."

She looked up at the cliffs to their right. "She broke you," she
said softly. "She tore your identity down until it was nothing, and
then she rebuilt it, many times over. Your mind is still strong,

stronger than before, but now its walls are built around the wrong identity."

"Then it'll have to be broken again," Carl said.

She didn't answer.

"I don't know if I want to be broken again."

"I understand. But if you reclaim your true identity, you'll have fewer scars. You have a strong mind, Carl. A very, very strong mind."

Carl started forward along the road's dusty shoulder. Kelly followed. He spread his hands, palms facedown by his sides. A slight breeze passed through his fingers. He could smell the dust rising from his feet. The hot afternoon sun cut through the cool mountain air. He felt as if he was walking into a dream on legs of soggy cardboard and a body cut from paper.

The street was deserted. A bench . . .

Carl stopped and stared at the empty bench on a boardwalk in front of a rustic building called Smither's Barbecue.

"What is it?"

"Does that bench look familiar to you?"

She stopped beside him. "I've never been here—why would it?"

His breathing thickened. For a moment he thought he might start to shake and sweat like he had in the hotel room. A tingle lit through his fingertips.

He stepped out onto pavement and angled for the middle of the road. He wasn't sure why he wanted to walk down this road—maybe it gave him a better view—but he picked up his pace and crossed to the yellow dotted lines that split the blacktop in two.

The tingle spread from his fingertips into his bones. He pushed his feet over the dashes, striding with purpose. But in his mind it was all happening in slow motion. He was staring at the bench and marching into a mesmerizing dream without the slightest idea of where it would take him.

But he'd been here before.

"Carl?"

He veered to his right and angled for the bench. He fought an urge to run up to the bench and tear it from the ground.

His breathing came hard, pulling at air that refused to fill his lungs.

Something was wrong with the bench. He hated this bench. This bench was—

"Carl!"

He stopped.

"What's wrong?"

It was just a wooden bench. Sitting on the boardwalk, ten feet away now. He looked up at the restaurant behind the bench. Smither's Barbecue. Beside it the grocery store with the gas pumps. All Right Convenience. The large building behind and to his right. Paradise Community Center.

Carl slowly turned and studied the rest of the town. A dozen small businesses on the right side of the street. A hair salon, a flower shop, an automotive shop . . . others. Houses.

Houses were on the opposite side. A large lawn ran up to the church.

"I don't think I've ever been here," he said.

"Why were you running for the bench?"

"I don't know. Why was I shaking in the hotel room? Why did I believe that you were my wife? Why did I climb into a crate full of hornets? Why did I put myself in an electric chair to die?"

Kelly shifted her eyes. He'd hurt her feelings.

"I'm not complaining," he said. "I just don't know anything anymore. I used to know who I was. Now I don't. I wish we'd never gone to New York."

"Johnny?" A voice was calling his name.

Kelly's eyes darted over his shoulder. He turned and faced a medium-built man with dark hair who stood in the restaurant's open doorway. The man's eyes widened with a smile.

"Johnny Drake. Well I'll be . . ." He twisted his head and yelled through the door. "Paula, get yourself out here and see who's come back."

The man marched down the steps and across the boardwalk and was nearly upon him before it occurred to Carl that showing his ignorance would raise unwanted questions. He smiled.

"Give me a hug, boy!" The man took Carl's hand and wrapped his arm around his back, pulling him close. "Good to see you, Johnny." The man slapped his back.

Carl didn't know what to say.

"And who's your friend?"

"This is Kelly."

The man extended his hand. "Hello, Kelly. I'm Steve. Welcome to Paradise. Pun intended, always intended, although I can guarantee we don't always live up to the name."

A woman in a blue dress ran down the steps toward him. "Johnny? Johnny Drake, my goodness! We heard you were missing!"

Carl assumed she was the woman Steve called Paula. Their excitement in seeing him was infectious. He felt his face flush with an odd mixture of embarrassment and comfort.

They liked him.

Paula gave him a hug and kissed his cheek. "Are you okay?"

She smelled like a flower—a familiar and warming scent. He must find out what perfume she was wearing.

"Johnny?"

"Yes?"

"Are . . . Are you okay?"

"Yes. I'm fine. Just a little . . ."

"He's on pain medication," Kelly said, offering her hand. "Nothing serious. I'm Kelly."

"Hello, Kelly. You're . . ." Paula glanced between them. "You're not . . ."

"No, no." Kelly laughed. "Just good friends."

"Well, I must say, Johnny, you know how to pick beautiful friends."

"Thank you," Kelly said.

Steve patted him on the back again. "Well then, come in and have a drink. On the house, of course. It's not every day we get a hero coming home."

"Actually . . ." Kelly caught Carl's eyes.

"Actually, I would like to go home," Carl said.

"Of course you would," Paula said. "Does Sally know you're here?"

"Sally? No. Has she moved?"

"From town? Goodness, no. She really doesn't know? She's going to faint! You go on. Don't let us keep you. How long will you be in town?"

"Just a day," Kelly said.

"Only a day? Then promise me you'll stop by and fill us in. The others'll be thrilled to see you. Does anyone else know?"

"No."

"Most of them are at the fair in Delta, but they'll be back by night. We'll do something. Right, Steve? We could have a barbecue."

"Absolutely."

"Okay."

"Perfect. I haven't seen Sally today, but that doesn't mean much. We don't see her much these days. She's kept to herself lately. She might have gone to Delta, but she might be home. You go on, don't mind us."

"Okay."

Steve and Paula, presumably the proprietors of Smither's Barbecue, stared at Carl, clearly expecting him to go home.

"What perfume are you wearing?" Carl asked.

Paula seemed slightly taken aback, but she smiled. "You like it?"

"Yes."

"It's called Lavender Lace. Sally gave it to me for my birthday."

It was his mother's perfume!

"Can you tell me which house she lives in?"

Steve and Paula looked at each other, clearly baffled.

"You don't remember?" Steve asked. "You sure you're okay?"

"I'm sorry, it's just this . . . I get bad headaches . . . I'm trying out a new pain medication, and it's making me . . ." He searched for the word.

"Loopy," Kelly said.

"Loopy," Carl said.

"Well, loopy or not, it's good to have you home, Chaplain." Steve pointed down the street. "Third house on the right. The white one."

Carl turned and started to walk.

Kelly thanked Steve and Paula—*Something I should have done myself,* Carl thought—and caught up to him.

"Hold on, Carl. Please."

"What is it?"

She grabbed his arm and pulled him back. "Just stop for a second. I realize this is important to you, but we have to be careful. You can't be so obvious. We'll be followed here. Kalman will stop at nothing to squeeze these people for information if he suspects that you've told them anything that could implicate him. We were here—that's all. Nothing more."

"Obvious? Why am I obvious?"

"For starters, you *are* acting loopy. This is nothing like the calculating killer you were trained to be. *I* don't even know who you are anymore. I'm just asking you to be careful."

"I was a chaplain," Carl said. "Did I have faith?"

Kelly studied his eyes for a few moments. Her features softened, and she offered a consoling smile, touching his cheek with her thumb. "I'm sure you did. I'm sorry. Just try to be . . . normal."

"I'm not normal—Agotha saw to that. I want to be normal. You know that's all I want. But I don't even know if my true self *is* normal."

He glanced back down the street and saw that Steve and Paula were at the door of their restaurant, watching them. Kelly had a point—Kalman could cause them some trouble.

"I can be normal for them, as normal as I can bring myself to be. But with my mother . . ."

With his mother he didn't know what. He probably wouldn't even recognize her.

Kelly took his hand in hers and turned him back toward his mother's house.

"Come on," she said. "Your mother is waiting."

ENGLISHMAN WALKED the B concourse in Denver International Airport, wondering what it would be like to be the thin rail of a man who hurried just ahead of him. The man was late for a flight, judging by his periodic watch-check. Was he going home to his wife and children?

Was he flying to Boston for a meeting with powerful bankers the next morning?

Was he eager to catch a plane that would deliver him to his mistress in Dallas?

Was he going to die of leukemia in twenty years or get hit by a car in two days, or did he already have a terminal disease and not know it?

Why did this man even want to live? Didn't he know that it would all end soon enough anyway? Didn't he know that a billion people with two legs and two arms, full of vim and vigor just like him, had lived and died and were now just memories in a few people's minds? Assuming they were lucky—most didn't even survive as memories. They were simply gone.

The simple, terrible tragedy of life's story was that it all ended on the last page. It didn't matter what clichés or wonderful descriptions or clever words people used to tell their stories; the greatest certainty any person had was that it would be over in about four hundred pages or eighty years, depending on how you looked at it. *Hallelujah, amen, you are dismissed.*

Of course, there were those who believed in the afterlife. Englishman hated those people. Not because he thought that they were right, but because he knew that if by some small chance they were right, he would not be joining them in their new journey of bliss.

Englishman lost interest in the skinny man and entered the moving sidewalk, letting his eyes rove over the concourse.

Hundreds of people hurried to and fro or sat at the gates waiting for their planes. Tall ones, short ones, skinny ones, lots of fat ones, blond ones, brown ones, black ones, young ones, old ones. Meat, thousands and thousands of meat packages. And every one of them thought they were that one package that actually mattered.

Englishman could easily kill any one of them at this very moment and walk away to tell how their particular story ended.

This meant he actually had *control* over their stories. He could write the last chapter of their lives. The end. *Hallelujah, amen, you are dismissed.*

He could actually end a few dozen stories right now, at this moment, before the authorities managed to stop him.

Not catch him, mind you. Stop him.

Englishman wasn't proud of his ability to control others by writing their final chapter. He was simply fascinated by it. The killing itself had long ago become rather tedious, but the power he possessed to end them made his mind buzz.

He crossed his arms, spread his legs, cocked his head all the way back, and closed his eyes.

No doubt dozens of people were staring at him at this moment, wondering why in the world the famous actor named Jude Law was passing through the Denver airport without an armed guard, drawing so much attention to himself by striking such a presumptuous pose.

Small minds.

Paradise, Colorado, was a five-hour drive from the airport. Six counting the slight detour to collect the weapons stashed at the safe house they'd prepared in Grand Junction. If his intel had informed him that the lovebirds had caught on to his very good plan, he would have flown to Grand Junction and driven from there. But the pair was clueless, so he had plenty of time. And Englishman preferred to drive. It offered more flexibility and was safer.

Without looking, Englishman knew precisely where the moving sidewalk ended. He stepped onto the carpet and took five full steps before opening his eyes.

Johnny Drake's story was coming to an end.

27

Carl stood at the white house's front door, staring through the screen at the small, octagonal crystalline window that revealed a fragmented image of the inside.

Fragmented like him.

"Go ahead," Kelly said softly.

He lifted his hand, rapped on the screen door's metal frame, then stepped back.

Hello, Sally.

Hello, Johnny.

Are you my mother?

No one came to the door.

"Maybe she's not home," Kelly said.

Carl was about to knock again when the latch rattled. The knob turned. The door swung in.

A woman stood behind the screen door. "Sorry for the wait, I was—"

She froze, eyes round. Carl's heart pounded. He didn't recognize her, but it could be because the screen impaired his view. She was his mother, had to be his mother, would be his mother. Somehow everything was going to be okay now.

"Johnny?" She lifted a hand to her mouth. "Johnny!"

He was Johnny and this was Sally. His mother.

"Hello, Mother."

She flung the screen door open and rushed to him, throwing her arms around his neck. He staggered back a step and instinctively put his arms around her torso.

"Johnny, oh, Johnny! You're alive! I was so worried."

She kissed him on his cheek, then squeezed him tight and buried her face in his neck.

Carl, who knew he was Johnny, held her gently as she wept.

Are you my mother?

Surprisingly, he didn't remember her as he'd expected to. She was wearing a different perfume—roses. She was beautiful and her tears were real and her eyes were a light brown, like his, but he couldn't remember. He stood still, suddenly frightened.

Sally stepped back, took his face in both hands, and studied his features. "Look at you. You haven't changed a bit." Her eyes darted over his shoulders. "You've leaned out. Are you okay?"

"Yes."

He could see the questions flooding her mind. One of them was probably why he wasn't doing the things sons were supposed to do in reunions like this, whatever those were. Jumping up and down or whooping and hollering with joy? He could manage a handshake, no more than a cold handshake.

Carl stepped forward and hugged Sally rather awkwardly. "It's good to be home," he said.

She patted him on the back. "Come in, come in. Who's your friend?"

"This is Kelly. She's the woman that I'm in love with."

Kelly looked surprised, then quickly blushed.

"My, we are full of surprises," Sally said, smiling warmly. "Please, come in."

They walked into the house. Brown carpet. Tan leather couch and love seat. Kitchen with yellow daisies on the wallpaper. A counter divided the kitchen from the eating area. The hall ran past three doors on its way to the back entrance. This was the house he'd grown up in?

He stared hard, intent on remembering. If he'd spent eighteen years in this house, the memories would be here, in the darkness somewhere. They had to be. Just there, beyond the black veil.

It occurred to Carl that he was in darkness. He'd entered his tunnel. At the end of the tunnel he saw a light. That light was what, his identity? His childhood?

Sally was saying something about cookies, but Carl's mind was now running, running down the tunnel toward the light. He could hear his feet slapping on the wood floor. Hear his breathing, heavy in his pursuit.

The light seemed to moving away from him. The farther and faster he ran, the farther the light moved.

His mother was calling his name.

Johnny?

Sally was crying out for him to rescue her. Rescue him, trapped in this tunnel.

Johnny!

"Where are you?" he cried.

KELLY WAS standing by the sofa table with Sally when Carl bolted down the hall. He ran to the first door and threw it open.

Sally watched him go, dumbstruck. "Johnny?"

"Where are you?" he cried.

"Johnny?"

"Where are you?"

He spun from the room, took a sharp right, and slid to a stop by the next door. Opened it. Stared. Slammed it shut.

"Where are you?"

Confusion laced Sally's voice. "Johnny!"

Carl stumbled toward the last door, shrouded by shadows. He banged through and disappeared.

"What's wrong?" The blood had suddenly left Sally's face. "What's he doing?"

"I think he's looking for himself," Kelly said.

"That's his room. What's . . . ? Is he okay?"

How could she explain the horrors that had brought Carl to this place? "No. No, he's not okay, but I think he will be."

No sound came from the bedroom.

"What's he doing?" Sally asked again.

Carl suddenly appeared in the doorway to his bedroom and stared at them. He looked as though he might have seen an apparition intent on torturing his soul.

"Mom?"

"Johnny . . ." Sally's voice was twisted with anguish.

Carl walked down the hall, eyes fixed on Sally. Something had changed. His eyes were large and streaming tears. The sight brought a painful knot to Kelly's throat. How could she ever forgive herself for what she'd done to this man?

And yet, she was meant to walk this path with him. She'd known this would happen. Now that it really was happening, she wondered how she could have allowed herself to fall in love with him.

Johnny rushed toward them, blubbering like an open tap.

"Mom. I'm so scared." The rest of his words were garbled by a gushing sob. He ran into Sally's arms and hugged her with desperation.

Kelly began to cry.

Mother and son were both blurting things now, but their words were stepping on one another, so she couldn't make them out. Then she heard Carl say, "I'm sorry, I'm so sorry, I'm so sorry, please forgive me." He was blaming himself for what Kelly had done.

Kelly turned from them, walked into the living room, and eased herself down into the love seat. This was her doing.

Every switch thrown by Agotha as she stood silently by.

Every needle that had pierced his flesh.

Every drug that had weakened his resolve.

Every treachery, every betrayal, every moment of loneliness that he'd endured out of misplaced love for her.

"No, no, no," the mother kept crying. "It's not your fault. You didn't do anything. Please, Johnny. Please, I love you. I love you."

"I put you through so much pain," Carl cried. "I can't live with myself."

"No, no, no. Stop it, you can't talk like that. Whatever they did, it's okay now. You're home, Johnny. I'm here for you."

Kelly covered her face with her hands, put her head back on the cushion behind her, and joined them in their sorrow.

"JOHNNY," CARL said. "I want you to call me Johnny now."

"Okay." Kelly offered him a small smile. "Johnny."

Something in Carl had broken. He was now Johnny even though he still felt like Carl.

He'd caught up to the light in his tunnel, passed through it, and stepped into a new world in which Sally was his mother. The room he'd run into was the room he'd grown up in, he could remember that with perfect clarity. This was his house. They'd spent an hour in the house, and he'd viewed each room a dozen times, desperately mining his memory for more, more.

He still couldn't remember any details of what had happened during his childhood without being told, but when Sally told him, he did remember, however vaguely.

Did it matter? He'd found his mother. He was whatever she was.

Johnny stood up from the couch, walked over to where his mother was seated, and bent over and hugged her again. Then he returned to the couch, sat down, and swallowed a terrible knot in his windpipe.

"You've become very emotional," Kelly said.

He couldn't seem to stop the gushing.

"I'm still having a hard time believing all of this," Sally said. "A year ago you were a chaplain in the army, stationed in Kuwait. Now you're . . ."

Her voice trailed off. They hadn't told her about his mission or the extent of his training. Only generalities that suggested why he was so different from the way she remembered him. She deserved that much. The rest would come in time. Johnny was afraid she might take Kelly's head off if she knew the whole truth.

"I'm not an assassin," Johnny said. "I haven't killed anyone. I was only trained as an assassin."

"What about your faith? You were a man of great faith—surely that hasn't just disappeared."

"I don't know. I just learned who I was last night. I can't. My mind's still spinning."

"How can the United States government make someone forget their own mother? It's inhuman!"

"I remember you," Johnny said, fighting emotion again. "I do remember you." Although he wasn't really sure he did. Perhaps he was forming a fact in his mind now rather than actually recalling her face.

"The training was extensive," Kelly said. "And these people in Black Ops have developed ways of erasing a soldier's identity, not only his memories. Johnny's mind is much stronger than most, which makes his recovery even more difficult. Did Carl show any unusual . . . abilities when he was younger?"

"Johnny," Johnny said. "Please call me Johnny."

"Sorry. Johnny."

Sally looked at him inquisitively. "Not that I can remember. Do you remember Project Showdown?"

Samuel had mentioned the name. *Project Showdown still lives.* But Johnny drew a blank. "No."

"You can't remember anything about it?"

"No, why? What's Project Showdown?"

"Wow. Well, I don't know where to begin, really."

The phone rang shrilly. Sally ignored it.

"Do you remember the monastery up in the canyon?"

"No. I remember you and this house and what you've told me, that's all."

The answering machine kicked on after five rings. Sally's voice. "You've reached the Drakes. Please leave a message."

Drakes. Not Sally Drake, but the *Drakes,* as in more than one. She'd never given up on her son. It made Johnny want to hug her again.

"This is David Abraham. It's critical that I reach you, Ms. Drake. Please call me immediately on my . . ."

Johnny didn't wait for the rest. This was the old man from the hospital. Samuel's father. He went for the phone and snatched it from the cradle as David repeated his number.

"Hello, this is Johnny."

A pounding of machinery in the background filled a long pause.

"So you *have* gone home," the voice said.

Johnny looked at Sally and Kelly. "Yes."

"Thank goodness. How much do you remember?"

"I only remember who my mother is."

"They'll be coming for you. If *I* can find you, they'll find you."

"Yes, I know."

"How many people besides your mother have you talked to?"

"Just Steve and Paula. The Smithers."

"Good. Can you trust me?"

"Do I have a choice?" He *wanted* to trust the man. "I think so, yes."

213

"Then I want you to meet me in the canyon above Paradise. Do you remember it?"

"No."

"Sally can tell you how to reach it, but come alone. It's where all of this started. And it's critical that you leave no evidence of your visit. Sally has to leave town with Steve and Paula. Immediately. I obviously don't have to explain—"

"She's leaving in an hour," Johnny said. "We've already explained enough of the situation to persuade her to leave."

"Good. Meet me at the mouth to the canyon."

"Kelly will come with me. She's my . . . She's with me."

"Can she be trusted?"

"Without reservation."

"She's from the X Group."

Johnny turned to face the kitchen sink. "She loves me."

"I'm sure that you think she does. I don't know—"

"She's with me," Johnny said.

"Fine. Meet me in one hour. You'll have to leave soon."

"Where are you?"

"In a helicopter, headed your way. One hour, Johnny. You'll want to hear what I have to say, I can promise you."

THE AFTERNOON light was fading as Dale Crompton steered the rental car through the mountain pass on Interstate 70. The problem with labels like Englishman was that they tended to pigeonhole you, and he refused to be pigeonholed. Those strong of mind could be the Unman or Englishman or Dale Crompton or Robert De Niro, whichever suited them.

This afternoon he was Dale.

The car he drove was a Dodge Ram pickup, a powerful vehicle that would take him to Paradise quickly. He'd rented a sedan at the airport, driven to another rental location in Englewood, parked it in a nearby lot, and then rented the Dodge under an alias.

Renting the truck in Englewood had taken longer than expected because the clerk was belligerent in his feeble attempt to impress Dale.

The clerk's name was Lawrence. Twice Dale's size and as dull as a lump of charcoal. He expected Dale to pay him respect for those qualities. Dale drove away fighting a terrible urge to return and teach Lawrence a few lessons about life and death.

Dust to dust, ashes to ashes.

He was tempted to light this particular lump of coal on fire, thereby reducing him to ashes. Instead, he drove on, up the mountain, after more enticing prey. *Hallelujah, amen, you are dismissed.*

Dale removed his right hand from the steering wheel and formed a C above the cup holder between the seats. The Styrofoam cup in the holder began to vibrate below his hand.

Time after time he'd held back his power while they continued to strip Johnny of his identity.

The cup stopped shaking and rose an inch.

There had been days of reprieve, of course. Assignments to kill in which he'd shown his victims more than a bullet. But on balance, the whole experience had tried his patience to the snapping point.

He glanced at the cup. It flew vertically and stopped in his hand.

The question he had to settle in the next three or four hours was a simple one: Should he kill the mother now or use her as leverage if Johnny managed to surprise him?

For that matter, should he kill Sally first or Kelly first?

They both had five letters.

They both ended in *lly.*

They were both two syllables.

They were both dear, dear, dear to Johnny, Johnny, Johnny.

One had given birth to Johnny, which was an offense worthy of death in and of itself.

The other had humiliated Englishman a hundred times, which would earn her a place in the hall of wide eyes and open mouths on sticks.

He lifted the cup to his lips and drank the scalding coffee.

Which would it be? Maybe both. Yes. Why not both?

28

Do you see anything?" Kelly asked, adjusting the small duffel bag on her shoulder. They'd hidden the other bag with their papers, the money, and two pistols behind the seats and brought two handguns, the knives, and their personal effects with them.

Johnny studied the rocks ahead. "It's a canyon."

"I can see that. He's not here."

"He said at the mouth of the canyon. This has to be it."

"Maybe this is the wrong canyon."

"My mother was specific."

Johnny stared up at the towering cliffs on each side. Night was coming fast. Already the canyon was encased in deep shadows. The encroaching darkness was comforting.

"I think I've been here before," he said. "It's like a tunnel."

"You remember being here, or does it just remind you of where you've been?"

"No . . . No, I think I've actually been here." Johnny headed into the canyon.

"This is the mouth. We should wait—"

"I've been here!" He began to run. "It's coming back! I've been up here before."

She ran after him. "Johnny!"

Johnny spun around and skipped backward. He flung his arms wide and yelled at the tops of the cliffs. "I've been here! I've been here, Kelly. I can remember it now. I remember."

Kelly grinned despite herself. "That's good, Johnny." Her eyes scanned the sheer stone walls on each side. "Meanwhile, our truck's down in the town. Englishman's probably sifting through it right now. We should have left."

"We *are* gone. How will he know about this place?"

"I don't trust him."

"Then trust me! I've been here, and there's no way he knows about this place."

"Johnny!" The voice echoed softly through the canyon behind him.

Johnny spun. There, thirty yards up the canyon, stood the old man from the hospital. David Abraham.

"That's him," Johnny said under his breath. "Do you recognize him?"

"He was on the stage at the president's press conference."

They walked up to David. When they stopped twenty feet from him, he approached them, wearing a mischievous grin.

"The helicopter dropped me off twenty minutes ago. They'll spend the night on top of the cliff."

"And us?" Kelly asked.

David's eyes shifted to her. "Kelly, I presume."

"This is Kelly Larine," Johnny said.

David let his gaze linger on Kelly for several long seconds. "Welcome to ground zero, Kelly Larine. As for us, we will be spending the night around the corner. Come."

David turned on his heels and angled toward a massive boulder on their left. Johnny followed with Kelly hurrying to catch them. The wall behind the towering boulder split to reveal a second, smaller canyon.

"I've been here," Johnny said, picking up his pace.

The older man's chuckle bounced eerily off the cliffs.

Johnny grinned. He'd been here. He was so eager to embrace the memories triggering the distinct déjà vu that he began to sprint. Past David, around the boulder, up to the mouth of the smaller canyon, where he slid to a halt.

The smaller canyon ran thirty meters in and then stopped abruptly at a rock slide that rose sharply to the top of the cliffs. A small log cabin had been built on the sand at the base.

This was wrong. He didn't know why or what, but something was wrong with the scene. The déjà vu popped like a soap bubble meeting a needle.

"What happened?" Johnny asked.

"So then you do remember," David said. "The monastery that used to be here. Project Showdown."

"No. Samuel and my mother both mentioned Project Showdown. I . . . I know that I've been here, just like I know I lived in Paradise and that my mother is Sally. The rest . . ."

"The rest will come," David said. "Shall we?"

They walked to the log cabin in silence. Inside, an oil lamp burned on a crude wooden table flanked by two benches. There were no stairs leading to the loft over the kitchen, only a rather unstable ladder made of twine-bound branches. One bed upstairs. Two beds in a bedroom along the back wall. That was it.

"Outhouse is behind," David said. "It's not the Waldorf, but it allows me to get away and reflect on Project Showdown whenever I am tempted to doubt. If you ever find yourself in that same place, doubting, you may come here. In fact, I strongly recommend it. Please, have a seat."

Kelly and Johnny sat on one side of the table facing David, who still wore his mischievous grin.

"Your mother and the Smithers left Paradise?" David asked.

"She said she'd make the arrangements. They'll spend the next two days in Delta."

An image of the young boy who'd confronted them in New York filled Johnny's mind. Samuel was a younger version of his father. Staring at the older man now, Johnny was sure he did know them both as they claimed. Samuel had been his friend.

But that was impossible.

"How could I have known Samuel?" Johnny asked. "He's still a boy."

"Is he?" David looked at Kelly. "What I say tonight must stay with you. No one can know. Not a soul. I don't think anyone would believe you, but that's not the point. What I tell you tonight is sacred. I don't mind saying that I'm nervous about your hearing this, Kelly."

"Then maybe you shouldn't tell me. I've done my share of damage already."

"She has to hear," Johnny said. "Without her I'm lost. What sense does it make to love someone you can't trust? If I'm ever going to be normal again, it will be with Kelly's help."

"As you insist. But I don't think you'll ever be normal, Johnny."

Then I'd rather die. He kept the thought to himself and watched David's kind eyes. There was a mystery hidden there that Johnny had to uncover.

"You shot the president?" David asked.

Johnny hesitated. "Yes."

"He saved the president," Kelly said. "If not for Johnny, Englishman would have been given the assignment, and the president would be dead."

"I know. And so does the president. He's given us a window while he decides what to do. It won't be easy convincing the authorities that the president's shooter was actually his savior." David drummed his fingers on the table. "My, my, where to begin."

"Who am I?" Johnny asked. "Start with that."

"You're Sally's son. You grew up in Paradise—"

"Not my history. Who I am."

"You're someone who knows how to ask the right questions. That's a start."

David cleared his throat and continued when faced by silence. "To know who you are, you have to believe some things you may not want to believe. How do you think you managed to affect the bullet's flight path?"

Johnny thought about his training. Lowering the heat in his pit. The electric chair. He glanced at Kelly.

"By affecting the zero-point field," she said. "The quantum theory behind observable telekinetics. Are you familiar with quantum theory?"

"Quite. I was fascinated with the theory years ago. There's some merit to zero-point-field research, more than most realize, but I can guarantee you that Johnny's power doesn't originate in his mind."

"Then where?"

David took a deep breath. He drummed his fingers again. "Do you believe in the supernatural, Johnny?"

DALE CROMPTON parked the truck behind the large theater and strode down the yellow dashes of the lone paved street in Paradise, Colorado, imagining the showdown that once occurred here.

The town was empty, as far as he could see. He stopped in the middle of the road and studied the buildings in the waning light. It had all started here. Fitting that it would also end here. Even more fitting that it would end because of him.

A screen door slammed to his right. He turned slowly and saw her standing on the porch of a white house. Johnny's Sally. *Hello, Mommy.*

For a moment they just looked at each other. No surprise from either him or her. The stuff of a perfect plan. *May all ye who don't kiss my feet rot in hell. Amen.*

She stepped off the porch and made her way to the car parked on the street.

Dale broke his stare and strode for the bar.

"SUPERNATURAL?" JOHNNY said. "I don't know what I believe. I used to, I think. I was a chaplain, but I can't remember my faith. Do I still have a faith?"

"Your faith has clearly remembered you," David said. "Your power comes from your faith. At least partially."

"You're saying his power is supernatural," Kelly said.

"Regardless of what we believe or want to believe, there is evidence of a great power that supersedes anything explained by our current understanding of science. Yes, the supernatural. How is it possible for one man to see events that will happen hundreds or thousands of years after his death?"

Johnny had never heard of such a thing. Actually, he was sure he had, but he didn't remember.

"I don't know."

"It's a gift. Words that one day come to life. Do you think something like this is possible?"

"I don't see how, but obviously I should. So I'll say yes."

"Even agnostics can't deny the writings of Nostradamus and certain prophets whose words have come to life. Saint John. Trust me for now, the ability to know the future, however misunderstood by science, is not *unknown* by science."

"Fine. I'll take your word for it."

"Good. Because there's hardly a leap between knowing the future and changing the present. Do you remember a man named Samson? He was a prophet—a judge, actually, but like a prophet—in Israel thousands of years ago."

"Samson?"

"How was it possible for a man named Samson to kill thousands of Philistines with the jawbone of an ass? Or level a massive stone building with one hard push? You think it was a fable?"

Johnny blinked. There was something here that he could remember. Comic books with superheroes that he read when he was younger. Samson was a superhero.

"Supernatural," he said.

David grinned. "I won't give you all the specifics of Project Showdown yet—they would overwhelm you. All in good time. But let me tell you what you need to understand your power."

He sat back in his chair. "Twelve years ago a confrontation between good and evil of biblical proportions visited this valley. Many things happened that week. It was then that a student named Billy found, among other things, some books in the dungeons beneath the monastery. Ancient books that demonstrate the power of the word and free will. They were called the *Books of Histories*, first discovered by Thomas Hunter, whose life is documented in the three volumes simply referred to now as *Black*, *Red*, and *White*."

None of this rang a bell with Johnny. David saw his blank look and moved on without elaborating.

"Never mind. You don't need to know any of this to understand. But these books that Billy found held a power that few have been fortunate enough to witness firsthand. I mentioned Samson's strength. But there are accounts of hundreds of these sorts of things, manifestations of superhuman power that changed the course of history."

David drew a deep breath. "In the case of these books, certain things written in them would actually happen. Like the scrolls in John's revelation. Do you follow?"

Johnny put his elbows on the table. He didn't know what to think about any of this. None of it was harder to believe than a prophecy, he supposed, and he'd agreed to believe the possibility of at least that much.

"Books that create truth," Johnny said. "Things that happen because they're written."

"Correct. At any rate, an event occurred that week that was so inconsequential at the time that we hardly noticed it. Evidently you and two other children each made entries into the books and then promptly forgot about those entries. I don't blame you. There was no evidence at the time that your entries had any significance or would come true."

"What entries?"

"'Johnny was given great powers to destroy anyone who stood in the way of truth.' Those were your exact words."

"That's it?"

David smiled and cocked an eyebrow. "Pretty broad statement, isn't it?"

"What happened to the books?"

"Let's just say that as far as we know, they went missing forever. It wasn't until you earned your first Purple Heart in Iraq that I took any notice. You were a chaplain and braved impossible odds to save a colonel stranded at a post. The rest of your company had been killed. Yet you, a noncombatant, went back. You evidently faced a barrage of gunfire without being hit. I talked to the colonel myself. He described a scene that he himself had difficulty believing. But he was alive. You had to have done what he saw you do. Samuel began to watch you then."

"Samuel, who is just a boy."

"No, no, not just a boy. He was part of Project Showdown as well. He was the only survivor immediately affected. Since that week twelve years ago, my son hasn't aged a day."

Johnny wanted to say something to express his doubt, but he couldn't think of anything. He looked at Kelly, who was studying the old man skeptically.

"You saw him. I can prove a hundred ways over that he's lived for twenty-five years. If you need any proof that what I've said about Project Showdown is true, Samuel is your proof."

"And you're saying that I gained certain capabilities as a result of writing in these books," Johnny said.

"Yes, you were given certain supernatural gifts. Not unlike Samson. Samuel watched you closely and recorded a dozen instances where you used them. He approached you about your gifts when he noticed they were growing stronger. Evidently you weren't certain of your gifts even then. But you were a man of incredible faith, a profound believer who was willing to give his life for the defense of truth. Truth, Johnny. Ever since Project Showdown, you've been consumed with the truth."

And now I don't possess an ounce of truth. It's been stripped from me. I don't even know if what I'm being told is the truth.

"Then Samuel had his dream," David said. "He saw into the future."

He said it as though this new bit of information was the anchor that would awaken Johnny's understanding. It did nothing of the kind.

"He saw the assassination of a world leader, which we now know was the president, and he saw the resulting destruction of Israel. The killer came from the X Group. Samuel had never heard of the X Group, naturally. You can imagine his surprise to discover that there actually *was* such a group that did indeed undertake assassinations. It took him months to get to the bottom of it, or as near to the bottom as one can get with the X Group. He hatched the plan then."

"Hatched what plan?"

"The plan to get you into the X Group. They are connected to certain parts of the Central Intelligence Agency that sometimes gave assistance to the X Group. Samuel saw to it that the CIA suggested your recruitment. With your record, you were the perfect candidate."

Johnny stared at the kind eyes that watched him. He had been kidnapped and destroyed *because* of this man and his son, Samuel?

"Please, you have to know that neither of us had any understanding of how destructive their techniques were at the time," David said.

Johnny wanted to feel anger, but he felt nothing.

"We didn't know about the torture," David said. "Or the invasive identity manipulation."

"Why didn't you tell me?" Johnny demanded. "How could Samuel do this and call himself my friend?"

"No, never! When Samuel told you of his vision and the X Group, you insisted that you should do exactly as he suggested. You said it was the least you could do after what he did for you. You were a man of deep faith. In your mind, infiltrating the enemy's camp was the only right thing to do."

"I don't remember any of this! You make me sound like some kind of crazy superhero!"

"Superhero? Aren't we all? Isn't that what all men, women, and children of faith are? Isn't that what Project Showdown was all about? We, the ostracized few, given power to aid the very society that fears us? You just happen to have an extra portion, thanks to the books. You're this world's Samson, Johnny."

"I don't know what you're talking about."

"And I don't believe you," Kelly said. "What kind of person would actually think he could infiltrate the X Group without being killed?"

"A boy who once faced the vilest evil and walked away. A boy who survived Project Showdown: Johnny. And a person who would give his life for Johnny at a moment's notice: my son, Samuel." The tremble in David's voice vibrated along Johnny's nerves. "And I don't mind adding," the older man continued, calmer now, "they were right. The president's alive today because of what Samuel and Johnny did."

"You don't know that," Johnny said. "Assim Feroz ordered the hit on the president. Kalman won't back off just because I failed. For all we know the president will be dead in an hour."

"You're sure it was Feroz who ordered the hit?"

Johnny looked at Kelly, who nodded. "Yes. There's no way to prove it, but that was my understanding."

"If the world knew, Feroz might call off any second attempt. If he was implicated in any way, it would destroy his initiative to disarm Israel."

"No. He would deny it," Kelly said. "And he'd make the United States look foolish for suggesting it."

"It would be his word against ours, surely—"

"Your own CIA would probably also deny it," Kelly interrupted. "They're in bed with Kalman. You've put us in an impossible situation! Our lives, your life, Sally's life, the president's life, and who knows how many others'—they're all in Kalman's line of sight. Clearly you don't understand how ruthless he is."

"I've seen worse, believe me. Perhaps he should be dealt with directly."

"Kill Kalman?" Kelly said. "This isn't a simple matter. He's no longer in Hungary. Any sign of trouble and Kalman would move immediately. Even if I could find them, they would know I'd compromised them and take the necessary precautions."

"They've moved my pit?" Johnny asked, surprised.

"They've abandoned the camp, at least temporarily."

He wanted to ask when he and Kelly might go back, but he immediately felt foolish for even thinking such a thing. He was done with them. Wasn't he? Of course he was!

"How would Kalman suspect that he was in danger?" David asked.

Kelly shook her head. "He's tied in with all of them. Interpol, CIA, NSA, the Russians, the Chinese, the French—they all need him. They all want him. He has many, many guarantees. If he dies, every country that's ever used him will be exposed, and they know it."

"There has to be a way."

"If I supposedly once had power from these books," Johnny said, "isn't it possible that others also have a power from them?"

"Yes. Two others. But we've been watching them. The rest were confidentially integrated back into society for their own protection."

"How do you know it's only two? What if someone else used the books? Someone evil?"

"No." David motioned emphatically with his hand. "We'd have seen it by now."

For a few moments they each were lost in thought. Johnny tried to remember a conversation with a boy named Samuel about being recruited by the X Group, but he didn't have the slightest recollection of talking, much less agreeing. What kind of man would agree to such a thing?

A man of virtue. But he didn't feel like a man of virtue.

A man of great faith. But he didn't have any faith.

A man who was unique and powerful. But he didn't want to be either unique or powerful.

A man who was still expected to do great things. But Johnny was overwhelmed by a desire to be normal. Hadn't he paid enough of a price these last ten months? Hadn't he done what he and Samuel had agreed to do by saving the president?

He stood and crossed the room, suddenly angry. He couldn't remember the last time he'd been truly angry. It was the emotion he'd first learned to shut down in order to survive Agotha. But now, learning who he was or had been, he embraced the sentiment—enough of it to raise his pulse a few beats.

"Why are you telling me this?" He knew the answer, but he asked anyway and then answered himself. "What do you expect me to do, protect the president? I don't even know how to protect myself anymore. The skills I had were dependent on my singular focus." He shoved a finger against his head. "On my mind! Now I'm full of doubts. I probably couldn't hit a barrel at a hundred yards now."

"No one's suggesting that you need your skills to protect the president," David said.

"Then what?"

David interlaced his fingers and put both elbows on the table. "I don't know. I'm not the one with the power."

"I *have* no power! How can I convince you of that? Should we test it? Strap me to a bed, electrocute me, see if I can withstand the heat?"

They both stared at him.

"Do you want to place me in a box full of hornets, see if I can survive their stings? Shove a needle through my shoulder, see if I can withstand the pain?"

David's face was white.

"Has it ever occurred to you that I've only been able to do a few things beyond what's considered natural even after intense training and focus? Now that you've undermined my faith by introducing all of this nonsense that only a child could possibly accept, I'm a shadow of myself."

"Only by choice," David said.

"I don't want to be this person you're describing! I don't want to be Johnny if Johnny is anyone but Sally's son. I'm Carl! Everything else is foreign to me. I've tried, believe me—I've racked my mind trying to be someone else, but I'm not. I'm Carl, and Carl loves two things: Kelly and his pit."

Kelly stared at him. It occurred to Johnny that his anger could be justifiably directed at her. If he continued down this path, she would be faced with more pain than she could bear, and in front of David. He didn't want to do that to her.

Johnny let his anger dissipate. His outburst wasn't satisfying anyway. He wasn't sure he even understood it. Why *wouldn't* he want to be the person David described? Because he wanted to be normal. Just himself, as he knew himself to be.

Carl.

He could still control his emotions to some extent, which was good. Maybe he still had some of the other skills he'd come to this country with. Maybe he was still a good sniper. A good assassin. He hoped so. Their survival might depend on it.

He returned to his seat. "I hate to disappoint you, but I'm not the one with power either. I can't do anything more than nudge a bullet to follow a path ingrained in my head. And don't tell me I haven't tried hard enough. If there's one thing Agotha taught me well, it's how to try. I tried in ways most can't or won't, and I have the scars to prove it."

Kelly put her hand on his arm. Johnny closed his eyes and swallowed. He wanted to throw himself at her and beg her to hold him. To comfort him. But he could no more break down again than he could stand and run around the cabin naked.

They sat in silence, sifting through these agonies.

Kelly finally broke the silence. "Can you tell us more about Project Showdown?"

David stared at her. It took awhile for him to respond. "Why don't we eat something? I brought some steaks. Then I'll tell you about Project Showdown. I trust you're not given to nightmares."

29

It was midnight. The orange light that flickered in the cabin's windows had winked out an hour ago. Englishman—now clearly cognizant of how boring the name Dale really was after trying it on for a few hours—had seated himself cross-legged on a boulder fifty feet from the shack two hours earlier and watched in silence, listening to the soft murmur of voices inside.

All three had come out once to use the outhouse behind the cabin, but none of them had seen him staring at them from the shadows beyond the ring of light cast by their lamps inside.

The canyon rested in perfect peace under a half-moon's pale gaze. A pebble clicked on his right, dislodged by a lizard or a small rodent that scampered away. Then peace again.

He could hear the silence. Feel its stillness. Smell its crisp purity.

The town of Paradise was a disappointment. Nightlife was evidently something these mountain folk didn't regard with much interest. Obviously they'd given up their affinity for grace juice.

He'd considered making a bit of a ruckus in the town before going up the mountain but decided that now was not a good time to leave a trail. There was nothing the hapless mountain folk could offer him that he didn't already have anyway.

He had bigger plans. Johnny.

They were in a test of wills, a contest of choices, and thus far Englishman had made the superior choices. In all likelihood, Johnny was only now even learning that he had a choice.

The fast-approaching end to this game seemed rushed after nearly a year of patience. A shame that he wouldn't need to use his trump card after all. Part of Englishman didn't want to end it so quickly. Perhaps he should extend the game. The decision momentarily paralyzed him.

Being human wasn't always the easiest way to make a living. He let the angst fade.

Englishman stretched out his left hand, shoulder-high, and opened his palm, eyes still fixed on the dark cabin. Something whistled softly through the night. A stone slightly smaller than his fist smacked into his open palm.

He had half a mind to take this rock back to Hungary and bury it in Agotha's throat. *Are we impressed with lowering the temperature and nudging bullets, Agotha?*

He tossed the stone into the air. Instead of falling back with gravity, it reached its apex two feet above his hand and was summarily snatched away by the night behind him. He heard it strike the distant canyon wall to his rear, hardly more than a *tick*.

He stretched his arms and shoulders by crossing them in front of his chest, then reached for his feet. Two hours without moving had left him stiff. He put his hands on his hips and swung his body around at the waist, cracking his back with the motion.

The black leather coat over his shirt fell long, roughly a foot below his belt. He pulled both sides back and hooked them behind two holstered pistols like a gunslinger.

Black canvas shoes. Black nylon pants that stretched easily if his maneuvers required them to. The only part of him that wasn't camouflaged by the night was his sandy-blond Jude Law hair.

He hopped off the rock and landed on the sand with a soft *thump*. Careless, but with odds like this he hardly needed to creep up on them like a mouse. Still, he walked soundlessly toward the door, hands ready.

He withdrew one of the guns from his hip, a Colt Model 1911 .45 caliber. Jacketed hollow-point 230-grain bullets with enough kick to knock a man across the room. Single-action, recoil-driven semiautomatic with a magazine of 10 +1. Custom blue-steel barrel. Englishman's pistol of choice.

He stepped up to the door, took a deep breath, cocked the gun by his ear, and tried the door. Unlocked.

Here it was, then.

Dale twisted the knob and pushed the door open, leveling the gun as he did so. His eyes were fully accustomed to the dark, so before the door had completed its full swing, he'd taken in the table, the kitchen, the loft above the kitchen, and the bedroom door on the back wall.

Still not a sound.

Moving fast, he slid to the loft ladder, hopped up onto the fifth rung, and scanned the sleeping area. Bed with rumpled blankets. No body.

No body.

He spun and dropped, catlike. The wood floor creaked. All three must be behind the bedroom door, sleeping soundlessly.

Moving more on instinct than with calculation, Dale flew across the room, shoved the door open, and trained his weapon on an empty bed.

Empty bed.

Empty room.

Empty cabin.

"Don't move."

The voice, which he immediately recognized as Johnny's, came from behind.

"Drop the guns. All of them."

He could have leveled the man then and there, without even turning. But he did have a couple of challenges if he made a move now.

His first challenge was that any one of Johnny's bullets would kill him as quickly as any other man's. The less-skilled man would undoubtedly get off a shot before falling from Englishman's attack, and at this range, he wouldn't miss Englishman's head.

His second challenge was that he didn't know where the others were. They'd obviously been more alert than he guessed. Kelly might not be Johnny, but with a gun at close range, she could kill just as easily.

Englishman turned slowly, gun hand raised.

He'd turned three-quarters of the way around when Johnny shot him in his leg. "I said drop the gun. The next one goes through a bone."

Englishman felt the pain spread through his thigh. Flesh wound, right thigh, hardly more than a crease. Still, he dropped the Colt.

"The other guns as well. And the knives."

No sign of Kelly or the old man. Englishman searched the darkness for any clue of the woman. Nothing. If Kelly hid nearby, she was silent.

"Now," Johnny said.

Englishman complied. The other Colt from his hip. The two 9mm's at his back. Two knives from his calves. He'd misjudged Johnny, but if the chaplain knew the extent of Englishman's skills, he'd have shot him while he had the chance. Instead, Johnny thought he had the upper hand and intended to question him. Or use him.

Englishman let a shallow grin cross his mouth. Johnny still didn't know the truth.

He spread his empty hands. "Satisfied?"

The man who loved the dark stared at him in the pale moonlight. "Hello, Englishman. You walk too loudly. I'm surprised you found us as quickly as you did."

"It won't be your last surprise," Englishman said. "Why don't you kill me?"

"I'm going to. How did you know about this place?"

"Kalman knows many things."

"He's ordered you to kill the president?"

"We never fail, you know that."

"Yet you failed now. It seems that Kalman forgot to tell you about the trap door in the bedroom. Only a fool would build a cabin at the end of this particular box canyon without an escape route. David Abraham is no fool."

So Kelly and the old man had escaped through some sort of hatch in the bedroom floor. They were probably on top of the cliffs already. This meant that there was no gun trained on him, other than Johnny's.

"You should have gone with them," he said.

"After you tell me what I need to know. Where is Jenine?"

Englishman grew impatient. One of the knives on the floor began to float. It lifted three inches from the ground and slid horizontally above the wood floor.

Johnny glanced down, eyes registering surprise.

The knife sprang shoulder-high and sliced toward Johnny in silence. Englishman was prepared to dodge a shot from Johnny's gun, but it never came. Johnny was immobilized by indecision. Or he'd already concluded that shooting would guarantee his death, even if he did hit Englishman.

"I know other tricks as well. I suggest you drop the gun."

Johnny studied the blade at his neck, then lifted his eyes. They exchanged a long stare.

Englishman winked.

Johnny slowly lowered his gun. "You're affecting the zero-point field?"

"Drop the gun."

Johnny's pistol fell from his fingers and clattered on the floor.

"Actually, it's nothing so scientific as the zero-point field or any of Agotha's theories. I'm surprised that you, of all people, don't know that."

"Who are you?"

"I'm Dale Crompton. I'm Englishman. I am the personification of man's worst fears. I am Jude—"

A creak behind Englishman stopped him cold. He dropped to one knee and felt the sting on his cheek a thousandth of a second after he heard the crash of gunfire from the room behind him.

Kelly had returned for her lover. Her bullet smashed through the window as it exited the cabin.

He palmed a 9mm from the floor where he'd dropped it and was twisted halfway around when her second shot split the night. He rolled to one side of the door and brought his gun up for a clean shot.

From his peripheral vision he saw a blur.

Johnny was coming for him.

Englishman's momentary lapse in concentration had let the knife fall from Johnny's neck. Now he was forced to consider both Johnny and Kelly. But this wasn't a problem for Englishman. As long as he had direct sensory input from each of them, he could . . .

The window behind Johnny crashed.

In that split second, Englishman knew what had happened. Johnny wasn't coming for him. He had thrown himself backward through the window.

Englishman was already in the process of shooting a bullet into Kelly's head when this realization hit him. And with the realization came another: Johnny had just gained the upper hand. Evidently he knew enough about how these powers worked to know that Englishman needed a line of sight or sound to affect any object. He was removing himself from that line of sight.

So Englishman would simply kill the woman now and go after Johnny.

Unless going after Johnny proved more difficult than he'd estimated, in which case having the girl alive might prove useful.

All of this crossed his mind before Johnny crashed to the ground outside the window. Kelly was screaming something as her third bullet whipped through the bedroom doorway.

The Englishman reached around the door frame and shot the pistol from her hand.

She cried out and snatched her hand close to her chest.

"Stay!" he snapped.

"You want *me*, not him!"

Englishman jumped to his feet and bounded for the door. He could hear stones tumbling outside as Johnny climbed the rock slide behind the cabin, but the sounds were scattered. The thought of Johnny escaping him now mucked up his instincts.

Kelly was reaching for the gun behind him. Furious, he jabbed his finger back at her. "Stay!"

The gun by her hand flew through the air as if it were on a string. He accepted it with his open fist, stepped into the night air, and fired wildly at the mound of boulders behind the cabin.

He fired seven shots in rapid succession. But he knew as he pulled the trigger that he couldn't direct the bullets with so much confusion at hand. His bullets smacked into rocks, unguided.

Englishman cried out in rage. The man was escaping. He could kill the girl and go after him, but Johnny undoubtedly had another gun strapped somewhere to his body. Johnny didn't have Englishman's power, but his aim was astonishingly accurate. And he loved the dark even more than Englishman. Johnny could sit in silence at the top of the cliff and pick him off at his leisure.

Englishman threw one of his guns on the ground and walked back into the cabin, calming himself. Johnny knew Englishman wouldn't kill Kelly now. A hostage was too valuable given the circumstances. And Johnny made the judgment quickly. Much more quickly than Englishman expected.

He stared at Kelly, who was evidently still stunned by the flying-gun trick.

"Get up," he said.

"What are you going to do?"

"We're leaving for a place better suited to our objective. If Johnny doesn't follow, I'm going to kill you."

"He'll never do that."

"He'll die for you. Or do you think he was just pulling your leg?"

"He'll know you're just using me."

"It doesn't matter. He's foolish enough to love you; he'll be foolish enough to die for you."

The sound of a helicopter winding up on the cliff cut through the night. He cursed himself for not taking the time to scout it out and disable it earlier.

Englishman eyed Kelly, who had gathered herself and was scowling. He allowed himself a smile. The woman he'd allowed to toy with him for so many months was beautiful; he could never deny that much. And wearing her anger, she was downright fascinating. Little did she know how much she cared for him.

But Englishman knew. Deep down where the black and the white traded blows, Kelly was desperate for him.

He lifted his pistol toward her, thumbed the release, and let the spent clip clatter to the floor. "Round one, Johnny."

Englishman slammed a fresh clip into the gun, chambered a round, and let go of the handle. The pistol hung in the air unmoving, aimed at Kelly. He stepped away from the obedient weapon.

"Stay," he said. "If she tries to run, shoot her in the leg."

Englishman looked at Kelly, who had traded her scowl for a look of amazement. Some fear. Respect and admiration. She was smitten by him. It was a pity he hated her; they would have made a good pair.

So why was he making such a display about showing her his power? Was he trying to impress her? They both knew there was no need for him to release the gun. It would shoot just as well in his fist.

He was toying with her, rubbing her hopelessness in her face.

Or maybe he was trying to win her respect because he didn't hate her as much as he thought he did.

Englishman grunted, stepped forward, and snatched the weapon out of the air, his bad mood at having lost Johnny now fouler because of this minor indiscretion.

He pointed the gun at the door. "Go."

"Where?"

"After Johnny."

"Where is Johnny going?"

Englishman hesitated, deciding whether to demonstrate his flawless logic in determining Johnny's next steps, which he had indeed calculated in the last sixty seconds while unwisely indulging in this gun-floating trick. He owed her no explanation. But he gave her a short one anyway, perhaps to impress her once again. He chastised himself even as he spoke.

"He's going to prove his love for you."

JOHNNY RAN down the mountain, propelled by his need to save. To liberate. To kill.

With each plunging step through the underbrush, his decision to put so much distance between him and the woman he loved haunted him. He had to force his legs forward, down, over logs, through the branches grabbing at his legs.

But his instinct told him that his decision was a good one. Perhaps the only way to save Kelly. If Englishman guessed his course and prevented him from succeeding, on the other hand, this flight away from Kelly could prove disastrous.

The helicopter had wound up and left with David. He'd protested Johnny's insistence that he leave immediately, but a short discussion had persuaded him. If Kalman had sent Englishman after them, it would be for Johnny and Kelly, not David. The last thing they could risk was making the helicopter a target, which it would become if Johnny and Kelly were in it. Shooting a helicopter out of the air would be an easy task for Englishman.

More than this, Johnny wasn't interested in fleeing. He and Kelly knew they would have to deal with this threat directly.

He'd come instantly and fully awake at the sound of a distant rock hitting the cliff. Not rolling down with a series of clicks as others had done through the night, but striking a far rock wall with some force.

Unnatural. Then he'd heard the soft thump of two feet landing on sand and knew that Englishman was outside.

Now, Johnny broke from the brush onto a wide ledge that overlooked the sleeping, moonlit town below.

He'd been here. He'd seen something significant from this very ledge. The events that David had described hours earlier flooded his mind. He'd seen part of them from this vantage point. The only thing that was more difficult to believe than this story of David's was that Johnny had some power hidden in his bones today because of it.

But the details of his past weren't germane to his mission today. They would tell him who he'd once been, not who he was now. They wouldn't save Kelly or him. They would not kill Englishman.

Englishman, who evidently wasn't the same man Johnny had always known him to be.

Johnny turned onto the path on his right and continued his descent at a fast run. A shiver passed down his spine. He'd seen Englishman's knife lift from the floor as if manipulated by a magnetic field. Seen it floating toward him, picking up speed, flashing through the night.

His instinct told him to block the weapon before it reached his neck. His mind told him not to. It understood something that wasn't apparent to his instincts.

It understood that if Englishman could do this, he could easily kill Johnny at any time. Could kill Johnny at his leisure. If Johnny tried to stop the knife, he would only injure himself. Perhaps lose his fingers or a hand.

His mind buzzed with the implication of Englishman's power. Either Englishman had perfected control of the zero-point field, or he possessed a power far beyond any Agotha knew about. Or David Abraham, for that matter, because David had said that only two others possessed such power, and both were being watched.

Johnny had affected the flight of a bullet with supreme focus, but Englishman had done far more. Any direct conflict with the man would end disastrously.

He ran with a growing fear. What he was about to attempt was nothing short of impossible. Yet he saw no other way.

His fear gave way to anger as he approached Paradise. The town was in deep sleep when he ran past the Paradise Community Center, toward the blue truck. A dog barked at him from a front yard. He sprinted past, eager to get out of this hole from his past.

The keys were still in the wheel well where they'd left them. The money behind the seats. Blowing a breath of relief, he slid behind the wheel, fired the truck, peeled through a U-turn, and roared out of the valley.

Miles flew by in a confusing haze. The tunnel in his mind obediently formed, leading to the familiar light. Success depended on reaching the target before it was removed from his scope of operation. If he was too late, the mission would present him with significant new challenges that would set him back days.

He had money. He had a set of papers that identified him as Saul Matheson. And he had the skills of an assassin—the fact that he could so easily form his tunnel now under duress assured him of this much.

Johnny drove north, through Delta, toward Grand Junction, slipping deeper and deeper into his tunnel, energized by a growing anger that surprisingly didn't compromise his focus. In fact, this new fury boiling in him seemed to make the light brighter.

He reached the airport north of Grand Junction as the sun edged above the mesas. The guns he left in the truck; the rest he took.

The only seat available on the 6:49 flight to Denver was a first-class seat identical in every way to the rest of the seats on the nineteen-seat United Express turboprop. The first-class seat on the Boeing 757 to New York was more comfortable, but comfort wasn't a thing he could easily judge. In his mind, the pit was still his safest and by extension his most comfortable place.

He didn't belong in the pit. Not now.

Now he belonged behind a gun, preparing to send a bullet into a target's brain to save the one woman besides his mother whom he loved.

He would kill anyone to save her. Anyone or everyone.

The decision satisfied a deep yearning in his psyche to justify the hours of torment during which Johnny had become Carl. The training would be redeemed—it would now help him save the woman he loved.

He was really Carl, he decided. He would be Carl and he would do what Carl would do.

He would force Dale's hand by killing the man he'd crossed the oceans to kill.

30

Carl and Kelly had selected the Best Western in Chinatown as one of their two dummy rooms. The authorities may have traced him to the Peking Grand Hotel, where he met Samuel, but there was little chance that anyone had found the room they rented for a week at the Best Western.

If they had, Carl doubted they'd found the small stash of weapons in the toilet tank. He was right.

Carl pulled out the bag, ripped open the plastic, and spilled two 9mm handguns, two extra clips, two sheathed knives, and one cell phone onto the bed. He shoved both guns into his belt behind him, dropped the clips into the pocket of his jacket, and strapped one knife to each of his ankles.

Grabbing the cell phone, he strode from the room, hurried down the stairs, and caught a yellow cab at the curb.

"Bellevue Hospital," he said.

"Bellevue, First Street," the cabby repeated, punching his meter, which immediately began its count from $4.20.

"Please."

The car pulled into traffic. The late-afternoon sun was setting behind them as they angled northeast on Houston. Carl had never put much thought into whether a target deserved to be killed, at least not in his time of training with the X Group. But now he did, and he'd come to the conclusion en route to New York that this target deserved to die, no matter what the world thought of him.

This man deserved to die to save Kelly.

This man deserved to die because Johnny had sworn to kill him.

This man deserved to die because Carl had been trained to kill him.

KELLY WAS tempted to cry out to one of the security guards as they exited La Guardia Airport, but she knew the impulse was a bad one. Not only were they all on the wrong side of justice, but they were playing a game that no security guard or policeman would understand.

Englishman had driven her north to Grand Junction, where he'd found the blue truck parked at the airport. He grunted in satisfaction and then booked them on the 7:50 flight through Denver to New York.

Kelly had asked him questions on the drive from Paradise, but Englishman refused to respond. She wasn't sure if he was sulking or simply playing his cards close. Afterward, they didn't exchange a single word all the way to New York. He had her in a virtual prison. One wrong move and he would kill her with as little effort as it took him to cough.

Who was the man? Certainly not the same assassin she'd ordered around in Hungary. But he *was* the same man, which could only mean that he had been playing her the whole time. Did Agotha or Kalman know that he had these incredible powers?

No, she didn't think so. Agotha wouldn't have shown so much interest in Carl's small feats if she knew that next door there was a man who could float a gun around the room.

If she hadn't seen Englishman float the gun with her own eyes, she would still think the old man had spun a piece of pure fiction with his tale of magical books. She'd often thought of the Bible as precisely such a fictional book of fables.

But now she'd seen the impossible, and she was quite sure there was such a thing as supernatural power after all. On any other day, the revelation would have thrilled her to the bone.

Instead, it left her flat. Of course this power existed. She'd known it all along, somewhere beyond her immediate consciousness.

None of it mattered anymore. The man she'd fallen in love with was going to die. And if he was going to die, she was also going to die.

Englishman hailed a cab and held the door for her without meeting her eyes. She could swear he was sulking.

"UN Headquarters," he told the driver.

The cab pulled out, braked hard to avoid colliding with a sedan, then surged into the flow of cars.

"Why are we going to the United Nations?" she asked.

Englishman spoke to her for the first time since leaving Colorado. "To kill Johnny."

EVERYTHING IN Carl's mind was black except for that light at the end of his tunnel. The light of his plan, the light of Kelly's freedom.

"Could you pull over here?" Carl asked, motioning to a side street.

"Not Bellevue?" The man's eyes searched the rearview mirror.

"Pull over here."

The cab pulled over.

"Is this your cab?"

"Yes. I lease name and sign from company."

"I need to borrow it. Two hours, ten thousand dollars. Does that sound fair?"

The man looked back and waved a hand. "No, it is illegal. I cannot—"

"Fifteen thousand, then." This time Carl pushed three banded stacks of hundred-dollar bills through the hole in the Plexiglas shield that separated them. "You can buy a new car if I damage this one."

The driver gawked at him, either thrilled by such an extravagant offer or terrified by it.

"No questions. If you'd rather, I'll make the same offer to the next cab. I don't have much time."

"How will I get car—"

"Parked in front of Bellevue Hospital in two hours. Yes or no?"

The man hesitated only a second before taking the money and flipping through it. He cast a long, furtive glance back, then tapped his watch. "Seven o'clock, Bellevue Hospital?"

"Yes."

The man climbed out and looked around nervously as Johnny rounded the cab and slid behind the wheel.

He drove the car north, past Bellevue, past Thirty-fourth, past Forty-second, and parked near the UN Headquarters on the corner of First and Forty-sixth.

Most meetings on the original summit schedule had been disrupted by his attempt on the president's life, but according to the CNN report that Carl had seen in the Denver airport, the meeting now under way in the UN Building wasn't one of them.

Under any other circumstance, he would have set up with a rifle and taken a shot from a safe distance. But with Englishman undoubtedly in pursuit, he didn't have time for such luxury.

Carl waited in the cab patiently, staring with fixed eyes at the doors through which the target would exit, acutely aware of details that his training had taught him to absorb.

The man fifty yards up the street who ambled slowly with a bottle in one hand and a stick in the other, poking through each garbage receptacle he passed.

The child across the street who'd stopped with his mother to gaze at the UN entrance.

A bird on the street lamp twenty meters north, cocking its eyes at him.

The security guards stationed by the front door, who had cast frequent glances his way before crossing the street and accepting his explanation that he was waiting for an aide, whom he named from a memorized list.

Each limousine and cab that approached and passed, which he examined like a machine searching for defective eggs at a poultry factory.

Most of this occurred outside of Carl's direct focus. Only one objective mattered to him now, and that objective received most of his attention.

Carl sat with both hands on the steering wheel, drilling the doors with an unbroken stare, sweating with cold fury now. He didn't want to sweat, but he wanted to feel, so he let his body react normally to the anger that filled the black walls of his tunnel.

Only when a tremble overtook his fingers did Carl rein in his rage. Within seconds his fingers stilled, and within five minutes the sweat on his skin had dried.

Then the doors opened and a dozen dark-suited guards and dignitaries spilled from the UN Headquarters.

It was time.

31

Englishman had a choice.

He always had a choice. Choice, choice, choice, that was his middle name. But he knew what he would choose.

At the moment his choices were as follows: One, kill Kelly now, as she rode muted in the backseat of the cab, and then kill the cabby and take the car on his own. Two, kill Kelly and let the cabby live. Three, kill only the cabby and take the car with Kelly beside him. Four, kill neither Kelly nor the cabby and let the cabby do the driving under the persuasion of his gun.

This was only one set of choices. There were others, any of which would affect the desired end result. Which was what?

Which was to destroy Johnny. Not simply kill him, mind you. Destroy him.

Englishman had been sent to the X Group for the explicit purpose of bringing Johnny to his knees and then, when he was ruined beyond recognition, when he was a shell of the man he once was, destroying him. In the end, Johnny would die in humiliation, but only after he'd been brought to a place where he could appreciate the true horror of his own demise.

Only after he learned to hate.

Then and only then would Johnny's undoing satisfy their collective hate for Samuel and the others who managed to survive Project Showdown. Samuel may have once survived that creep Black's assault, thereby rendering himself untouchable, but his heart wouldn't survive Johnny's demise, not after what they'd been through twelve years earlier.

The turn of events at the cabin hadn't been planned, but even that played to Englishman's favor. Johnny was learning to hate in a way that he'd never hated, and that was the point. He would eventually hate himself. And then the end would come.

If Englishman could use his trump card now, Johnny's hand would be forced. But he couldn't, not yet.

"Pull over," Englishman said.

The cabby grunted something in another language and pulled to the curb. Englishman had made his choice and was happy with it. Reaching under his coat, he quickly affixed a silencer to the barrel of his pistol.

Kelly watched him. "What are you doing?"

The moment the cab came to a stop, he climbed out, hurried around to the driver's window, and shot the man through the temple. But he stopped the bullet in the man's brain so that it wouldn't make a mess.

The man slumped over so that his head lay across the bench seat. Englishman stuck his head through the window and winked at Kelly.

"Get up front, please."

She didn't obey at first, and he thought about changing his choice. If she became a problem, he'd find another way.

She evidently had figured as much and now came to her senses. "He's up there," she said.

"There's room for three."

Englishman climbed in, shoving the man out of the way. Kelly opened the front door, studied the dead body. A man dressed in a blue business suit approached the car, apparently dumbstruck. Englishman shot the man in the chest. This time he didn't bother stopping the bullet. A little distraction here, a block from the UN, might come in handy.

He jerked the driver upright to give Kelly more room. "Please, hurry."

Kelly obliged.

There was yelling on the curb when he pulled back into traffic, but nothing was so shocking in this city to generate immediate and forceful action. Another of Englishman's favorite movies was *The Terminator*. At the moment he felt a little like Arnold Schwarzenegger must have felt pretending to be a ruthless, emotionless killer from the future.

Unlike the Terminator, Englishman was real. And Englishman had emotions, and right now he was both happy and excited.

The UN Building loomed ahead on his right.

"You'll never get away with being so careless," Kelly said. Her tone reminded him of her cocky superiority back in Hungary. "They'll come down on us like the plague."

"I would think that would please you." A long line of black limousines waited patiently for their respective dignitaries. They'd arrived in time, then. Good.

"We are all implicated in this," she said, pushing the dead driver's head off her shoulder. The man slumped forward and struck the dash with his face. It was a good position.

Everything was working out. Good car, good timing, good hostage, good dead driver.

"Maybe we should work together," she said. "Last I remember, we were on the same team. If you insist on killing me later, fine, but don't get us all killed before our time."

"You don't have the slightest clue what you're talking about. Please be quiet."

Englishman scanned the street, much in the same way he remembered Arnold scanning the street in *The Terminator*. If she knew the full extent of his power, she wouldn't question his choices. She certainly wouldn't be trying this pathetic attempt to gain his confidence. Surely she realized that he knew how much she cared for Johnny. Love had been in her every glance in Hungary, and it lit her eyes even now.

Kelly was madly in love with Johnny. End of story. End of story soon enough anyway.

"I may not be—"

The dead driver's hand flew up and backhanded her across the face with a loud *smack*.

Then Englishman did it again, this time as she watched fully aware of what was happening. The dead man's arm lifted, stopped six inches from her cheek, and then patted her face gently.

"Please be quiet," Englishman said and let the arm drop.

She obeyed him.

The mission was going well. Very well.

And then suddenly the mission wasn't going so well, because suddenly the doors to the UN Building flew open and dignitaries began to pour out and Englishman hadn't yet spotted Johnny.

He searched the streets quickly. Dozens of cars of all colors, mostly black limousines and yellow cabs—Johnny could be in any one of them. Pedestrians of all stripes—Johnny could be masquerading as a businessman or a dignitary or a security guard for that matter. His time had been limited, but a killer as resourceful as Johnny could have adopted any one of dozens of personas.

Kelly was searching as well, and Englishman kept her in his peripheral vision, watching for her recognition. Love was a strange and horrible beast, binding in mysterious ways.

Englishman slowed the car, ignoring horns behind him. Another cab drove by on his right and cut in front of him, horn blaring. Englishman wreaked havoc on the other car's engine with a burst of frustration. He couldn't isolate the specific damage without being able to directly determine the engine's layout through line of sight or sound, but he could send disruption to the general vicinity.

The car's front grille began to boil white smoke. Radiator. Englishman pulled around the car, through the clouds of steam.

A dozen cookie-cutter agents had exited the building during his brief distraction. The target stepped into the sun. Still no sign of Johnny. Had he misjudged the man? Was it possible that Johnny was still in Paradise, plotting to recover Kelly through other means?

Unlikely.

A taxi pulled away from the curb and roared away from the scene without a fare. Odd, but not singularly odd in a place where a thousand cabs went a thousand places known only to the driver and the fare. Englishman dismissed the sight.

The target was getting in a large black limousine.

Still no sign of Johnny.

A train of black cars, two in advance of the target's vehicle and two behind, pulled into traffic just ahead.

Still no sign of Johnny.

Englishman searched frantically now. Pedestrians, security, black-and-whites, government officials, cameramen, news crews—the street in front of the UN Building was now a scene of mass confusion. Behind them sirens wailed—presumably headed for the man Englishman had shot a couple of blocks back.

He hesitated, expecting the assassin's approach at any moment.

Still no sign of Johnny.

Englishman cursed and floored the accelerator just as the target's limousine disappeared around Fiftieth Street, a quarter of a mile ahead.

CARL'S THOROUGH reconnaissance of these streets before his first attempt on the president's life gave him the knowledge he now needed.

He knew the target was headed for the airport. Which meant his entourage would probably turn on Fiftieth if they passed Forty-eigth, which they had. But to be sure, Carl waited at the alley two blocks west of the turn until they actually made it. If they continued past Fiftieth, he would have to circle north and catch them . . .

The first black car in the train pulled into the intersection and signaled. They were coming down Fiftieth Street.

Carl slammed the car into drive and sped down the alley, away from Fiftieth Street. He skidded to a stop fifty yards short of where the alley met Forty-ninth, exited the still-running cab, and ran to the trunk, stripping off his black shirt and ripping it in two as he did so.

He stuffed one half of the shirt into the cracks around the license plate, effectively covering it. The second half he looped around the sign on the roof that identified the cab as #651.

Then he doubled back toward Fiftieth at a full sprint. If someone stole the car in the few minutes it would take him to execute this leg of the mission, he would have to find another. It was a chance he was willing to take.

Both of his guns found their way into his hands as he ran. Closing on Fiftieth. Fifty yards. Twenty-five. He was going to make it. The first car drove by. Close, very close.

Carl ran into Fiftieth at a full sprint as the second of the two lead cars passed the alley. He came to an abrupt stop in the middle of the street, turned toward the fast-approaching armored car hosting the target, lifted the gun in his right hand, and fired a shot directly at the driver.

What Carl knew about bulletproof windshields proved true: most could indeed stop a bullet, but few could stop three if all three struck precisely the same spot on the glass. Virtually impossible unless Carl was the one pulling the trigger.

He sent the three bullets in rapid succession, confident.

The third bullet pierced the glass and struck the driver in the throat.

Carl shifted his aim and fired three more rounds into the passenger's side, where a guard was frantically groping for his gun. Once again the third bullet ended his attempt when it entered his throat.

Carl dropped the half-spent clip and slammed a fresh one home as he ran toward the car, which had swerved to a stop. There were no more guards in the car—Carl had watched them enter in his rearview mirror. But the passengers in the entourage were enough to concern him.

They'd pulled up short, thrown open the doors. Carl stood beside the target's car, panting. He raised a gun in each hand, one aimed at the lead cars, one pointed at the rear cars. A man rose from behind the passenger door of the first rear car, and Carl shot him through his right shoulder. A second gunman stood from the closest lead car and received a bullet alongside his cheek.

This would make them hesitate long enough.

Carl turned his attention to the target's car. Side windows were typically thicker than windshields and required five perfectly placed rounds, which Carl placed low and to the right, over the door lock. He reached in through the hole he'd created, unlocked the door, pulled the driver onto the asphalt, and slid into his seat as the first bullet from the guards snapped through the air where he'd stood.

But he was now in an armored car, safe from their bullets. A thick pane of reinforced glass separated him from the man in the rear seat. Carl paid him no mind.

He jerked the stick into reverse and surged back ten yards before reversing the direction of the car and roaring forward.

No shots. They wouldn't risk shooting into a car that held the man they were sworn to protect.

Carl sideswiped both lead cars as he passed, only to slow their pursuit. The light at Third Avenue was red when he cut across oncoming traffic to a chorus of horns.

He called 911 on the cell phone and gave the operator instructions that would lead an ambulance to the badly bleeding guard in the passenger seat within minutes. He'd hoped that neither would be mortally wounded—had he done that? The guard on his right was still breathing. Why had he shot the man through the muscle on the right side of his throat rather than taken him out with a head shot?

Because he'd come to kill the man behind him, not his guards.

Carl cut back onto Forty-ninth Street before the pursuit entered the road behind him. He braked hard, popped the lock on all four doors, jumped out, and threw the rear door open, gun extended.

"Out!"

Assim Feroz had a small pistol in his right hand, but he wasn't sure whether to use it. Carl slapped it out of his fist.

"Quickly!"

He grabbed the man by his collar and jerked him through the doorway into the street. Pedestrians scrambled for cover; a woman in a lime-green dress with pink and yellow stripes began to shriek.

Carl shoved the Iranian defense minister toward the alley.

"You have no right—"

"Run!"

Feroz ran.

"Into the alley."

His yellow cab waited, nose toward them.

"In the front seat."

The man Carl had come to America to kill scrambled into the car, followed by Carl.

"One word and I put a bullet in your leg."

Five seconds later they raced away from the parked limousine. He turned right two blocks up and pulled over long enough to remove his torn shirt from the cab's sign and license plate.

The Iranian was shaking with fury when Carl reentered the car. "I demand—"

Carl slammed his door and shot Feroz in his leg at the same moment, so that the two sounded as one.

"Ahhhh!" Feroz grabbed his leg.

"I said no talking."

JOHNNY WAS in the yellow cab that had just turned west one block ahead. A piece of black cloth flapped from the sign on its roof; this was how Englishman knew.

He'd followed the Iranian motorcade onto Fiftieth Street and came upon four of them, backing up traffic just as the fifth limousine screamed around the corner.

By the time Englishman blasted his way through the corner, Carl had already traded the black car for another. It was Englishman's quick eye that caught the flapping black cloth.

But then the yellow cab disappeared around another corner. He swore and floored the gas pedal. All he needed was one moment of clear sight, and he could reach out and touch Johnny.

He wiped the sweat leaking into his eyes with his palm. Beside him, Kelly was saying something about slowing down, but his mind was dangerously removed from her. He noted this and adjusted. She wasn't Johnny, but she knew how to kill.

"I'm going to end this now," he muttered.

"He's going to kill Feroz," Kelly said. "He's going to fulfill his original order from Kalman and his oath to serve his country."

"You're forgetting that I have you," Englishman said. "If Feroz dies, then you die—the fool must know that."

Kelly ignored him. "He's going to undermine Kalman by killing the party who ordered the hit."

Englishman had figured this much out in Paradise, but hearing her say it sent a shaft of fear through his mind. He hated Kalman, but he was under the strictest order to protect the integrity of the X Group at all costs.

Englishman could choose to follow or reject the order. Although he'd fantasized many times about killing Kalman, he knew that he never would. It would be like cutting off his own arm.

"No," she suddenly blurted. "He's going to . . . He's . . ." Kelly stopped.

But she didn't need to say it. They both knew what Johnny was planning to do.

Englishman took the car to seventy miles per hour.

CARL WAS just entering the next turn when the cab began to shake violently.

Assim Feroz cried out and gripped the dashboard.

It wasn't the kind of shake he would expect from mechanical difficulties but the kind that might come from an earthquake.

At first Carl thought it was just that, an earthquake. But a quick glance in the rearview mirror showed him a yellow cab racing around traffic, bouncing up over the sidewalk and back on the street.

Englishman.

Englishman was making his car shake.

Carl gunned the car through the turn, felt the back end buck at least a foot off the ground and then settle. They were out of Englishman's line of sight.

Carl now had only one objective: to reach Bellevue Hospital in one piece and hope the cabdriver who owned this car was waiting as agreed.

He saw an opening in traffic and cut left, across the oncoming lanes, into an alley that headed east toward the hospital. He didn't know how long Englishman needed to wreak havoc with his car— more than a passing moment judging by the fact that he hadn't already stopped them. Carl didn't intend to give him even a moment. Second Avenue fast approached at the end of the alley, dead ahead. He would cut right and then—

The car began to shake again, more violently this time, bouncing as much as shaking. Feroz shouted something unintelligible about Allah. Englishman's yellow cab filled the narrow alley a hundred and fifty yards to their rear.

Panic began a ferocious assault on Carl's mind, but he cut it short. Fifty yards to the turn.

He angled for a row of tin garbage cans on their right and blasted through them at high speed. *Chunk, chunk, chunk, chunk.* The large cans bounced high and tumbled over the car, spewing refuse as they flipped through the air.

Twenty yards.

Carl glanced into the mirror. What he saw nearly made him miss the turn onto Second. The garbage cans were now flying off at right angles, smashing into the alley walls. Not only the ones he'd hit but others farther back, filling the air with paper and plastic and large stuffed bags.

Then they were on Second, squealing through a right turn, side-swiping a green sedan, narrowly missing a large bus. He was in the oncoming lanes, diving into a sea of headlights blazing in the failing light.

But Carl had stored the layout of these streets in his mind with precision. Rather than swerve back into the right lanes, he shot toward another alley on the far side of the street. Bounced over the curb. Cut into the narrow passageway, scraping the right mirror off against the far wall.

Metal screeched. Sparks flew. Assim Feroz cowered, head between his knees.

First Avenue was now in sight. And half a block south, Bellevue Hospital. They had made it.

Carl slammed his foot on the brake pedal and brought the car to an abrupt halt.

THE GARBAGE cans were flying, and Johnny's car was bouncing, and Englishman was happy.

He grunted, amused by his own power. Nothing short of amazing. And Kelly was impressed, he could sense it, see her mouth gaping with wonder in his peripheral vision. He hadn't shown her the half of it.

He impulsively sent the rest of the cans in the alley flying, like rockets shot from canisters. They slammed into the walls and streaked up, free from gravity for a moment.

It was a mistake.

He'd removed his attention from Johnny for only a moment, but that moment had allowed him to exit the alley and disappear.

Something smashed ahead. Johnny had hit a car.

Run, Johnny, run. Like a bat out of hell, because hell is coming sooner than you think. Even if you escape me, hell is coming. You will be destroyed.

In the end you will be your own undoing.

You can't escape you.

Englishman exited the alley, braking so as not to pile into whatever Johnny had hit. Traffic had stopped, allowing him plain view of what had happened even in the fading light. He could see the rubber marks that chronicled the car's trajectory. Across the street. Into an alley.

Johnny was undoubtedly still in the alley. And the path to the alley was clear.

Englishman roared across the lanes and angled into the alley. It would be over now. He wouldn't be so careless this—

They collided with a large steel garbage bin that promptly tipped over and stopped the car cold. Englishman's head smashed into the steering wheel. Beside him, Kelly crashed into the dashboard with her elbows.

It took him a moment to collect himself. The car had stalled. But neither the car stalling nor the large steel bin that had stopped the car concerned him. In the confusion Johnny's car had exited the alley without his seeing which way it had turned. This annoyed him.

Sirens wailed from several directions, racing to the string of disruptions Johnny had left in his wake.

Englishman grunted and shoved the garbage bin out of his way with a thought. He started the car, sent the steel container flying vertically, and drove under it. The bin crashed back down on the cab's roof and tumbled off the trunk behind him.

You think you've made an escape, Johnny. You're wrong.

CARL BROUGHT the cab to a screeching stop in front of a stunned cabby. Assim Feroz had taken off his jacket as instructed while Carl rolled the garbage bin to block the alley behind them. He'd known the maneuver would only waylay Englishman momentarily, but he also knew there was no other way to block his line of sight before they exited the alley.

Carl snatched the jacket from Feroz. "Straight to the parking lot behind the building. One move I don't like and I'll shoot your hand off." He shrugged into the jacket.

The Iranian defense minister was white with fear. "My leg . . ."

"Your leg isn't broken. Swallow the pain and run." Carl shoved his door open.

The cabby rounded his cab, frantically eyeing the damage. "What have you done to my car?"

Carl pressed one gun to the cabby's gut while training the other on Feroz. Not lost on the Iranian. "If you want to live, you'll drive this car south one block and leave it parked on the side of the road. Get in."

"What? What is—"

"Now! Now, now, now! Before I change my mind and kill you."

The driver piled into the car.

"Get out in one block, before the bomb blows." Carl slammed the door shut and the car jerked forward.

"Run," Carl ordered the Iranian.

The man hobbled toward a sidewalk that led to the parking lot behind the hospital. Englishman would exit the alley at any moment, and when he did they had to be out of his line of sight.

If they could manage that much, Carl would save Kelly. If he could not reach the corner in time, both he and Kelly would die.

Under no circumstances would Carl allow Kelly to die.

32

They roared from the alley onto First Avenue. Englishman searched frantically for the yellow car among a dozen yellow cars strung up and down the street, a half mile in each direction. And then he saw it, a full block south, pulling to the side of the road.

Only the fact that the car was stopping convinced Englishman to hold back his full fury. What was Johnny doing? Surely he realized that he was in danger. Unless he knew that by stopping he would make Englishman hesitate.

"David Abraham knows that Feroz ordered the hit on the president," Kelly said, eyes on the car as it pulled over. "That means the president also knows by now."

"I'm quite sure I told you to keep your mouth sealed," Englishman said.

"Fine, but if you refuse to consider what I have to say, you'll have to answer to Kalman."

Englishman guided the car toward the yellow cab. "What makes you think I care about Kalman? You think I don't know what Johnny's up to? You think waiting until now to give me advice isn't an obvious ploy to distract—"

Englishman stopped. A man had tumbled out of the car. Even from this distance he could see that it was neither Johnny nor Assim Feroz. Who, then?

He quickly reaffirmed the cab's identification. Black cloth tied around the number. The side was badly torn and the mirror was missing. This was Johnny's cab. Unless . . .

Englishman slammed on the brakes. Tires squealed and the car behind them tapped their rear bumper. But Englishman didn't care. His eyes and mind were on the yellow cab a hundred yards up the street. The car that Johnny had managed to ditch. The car that another man had taken for a short drive before ditching it himself.

Why?

His secure phone chirped. Horns blared. Englishman searched for any sign of Johnny or Feroz. Nothing.

The volume on his phone rose one level as he'd programmed it to do if left unanswered after three rings. He smiled. But he didn't feel happy. Waves of heat spread over his skull and down his back. Still he smiled. He had to respect the simple victory that his enemy was about to take.

Englishman took a deep breath, pulled out his phone, and answered without removing his eyes from the cab. "Yes?"

"Carl has Feroz." Kalman's voice crackled in his ear. "He will kill the fool unless you let the woman go. I have no doubt he means what he says."

"Yes."

Englishman had decided in Paradise that Johnny would return to New York to take Assim Feroz hostage in exchange for Kelly. It's what Englishman would have done, because assuming it could be done, the plan was nearly fail-safe.

"If Feroz dies, our credibility will be crippled. We can't kill the people who hire us!"

"I know."

"Then let her go."

"He'll kill Feroz anyway."

"I'll take the risk. Let her go and drive south past Houston Street. Give her your phone. Carl will contact her when he's convinced she isn't being followed. When you've done this, I want you to complete the hit on the president."

"He'll kill Feroz anyway. It's what I would do."

Englishman was tempted to tell Kalman about his trump card. Instead, he closed the phone. There was no way to flush out Johnny now, and no way to estimate where he might have run off to. North, east, west, south? On foot? In another car?

"Look at the car, Kelly."

She followed his gaze and looked at the vacant yellow cab. Cars were now squealing around him, blasting him with their pathetic horns. Some drivers even had the gall to gesture, as if that would offend him.

"If you ever find Johnny, the real Johnny, tell him about me. The real me."

The yellow cab bucked as if a bomb had been detonated beneath it. The car rose ten, twenty feet into the air, turned lazily in a complete flip, then began its descent.

The ascent was silent, because the power that had lifted the car came from him, not a bang beneath. But the landing was thunderous. The cab landed on its roof with a mighty crash.

Cars and pedestrians spread from the vicinity like ripples on a pond. They no doubt thought that aliens had just commenced an attack on New York City.

"You may go," Englishman said, handing her his phone. "Tell Johnny that his end is in himself, his real self. But I still plan on facilitating."

CARL SNAPPED the phone shut and sagged against the wall. Kelly was coming to him. Englishman was gone, at least for the time being.

They waited at the base of a deserted concrete loading ramp behind the hospital. Half an hour had passed since his call to Kalman, and darkness had settled over the grounds.

Feroz sat on the ground staring up at him. His slicked hair flopped over his sweaty, hawkish face. This was the man who had gone to such lengths to kill the president. He'd paid an insane amount of money to hire the X Group, because he trusted only the very best to handle the murder.

But Carl had been sent to kill Feroz, not the president. Yes, it was a bluff, but he no longer would accept bluffs. They'd bluffed him for ten months, and this was their last.

Carl had also once been a member of the United States Army, sworn to serve the commander in chief. So then, his obligation was clear. He had used Feroz to save the woman he loved. He must now kill the man who had hired him to kill the president. He must kill Feroz.

"You have what you want. Release me." The man's face was scowling and dark, as if he thought he was in charge.

"You hired me to kill the president," Carl said.

No answer. Good. Any other answer would have been foolish considering the circumstances.

"But they told me I was to kill you."

The man spit to one side.

"I have also taken an oath to protect the president. Since your life is a threat to his, I have an obligation to kill you."

Carl could hear the sound of running feet, presumably Kelly's. She was coming to him. He lifted his gun and placed it against his prisoner's skull. He would wait until he was sure she was safe.

"You are nothing but a hired killer," the man said. "Do you know who I am?"

"You are a dead man."

"Johnny?"

Kelly stopped at the top of the ramp, panting.

"Are you safe?" he called.

She hurried down the ramp. "I doubled back. There's no way he could have followed. Thank heaven, Johnny. I thought—"

"My name is Carl" he said and pulled the trigger.

The 9mm bucked in his hand. The target's head snapped back, struck the concrete wall behind him, and then fell to one side. The gun's report echoed in the small concrete depression. Assim Feroz stared ahead through black, vacuous eyes. Dead.

Carl lowered his gun.

Who am I?

He began to tremble, suddenly terrified. Kelly was standing halfway down the ramp, staring at him, taken aback by his execution of Assim Feroz, perhaps. He didn't care. He would do anything to save her. But now that she was safe, he was terrified to be with her. To be seen by her.

But more than this, to endanger her life. Englishman would hunt Carl before he hunted Kelly. He had no choice but to leave Kelly for her own safety, at least until he made sense of the madness of these past three days.

"Johnny?"

Why was she calling him Johnny? He'd always been Carl to her. He didn't want to be Johnny any more than he wanted to be Carl.

He forced himself to look up at her. She was safe. Safe and deserving of more than he could ever offer her.

Feeling like a fool, he ran up the ramp past her.

"What are you doing?"

He stopped at the top long enough to throw out a useless, pitiful word. "Sorry." Then he added just as pitifully, "Stay away from me. Englishman will come for me. Save yourself."

And then Carl, who was Johnny, who wanted to be neither Carl nor Johnny, ran into the night.

33

W hat I'm telling you is that my son and I were right," David Abraham said. "And Johnny penetrated the X Group in full cooperation. He insisted we set him up."

"How can you be sure that it was Johnny Drake who tore up New York and killed Feroz?" Stenton demanded.

"His marks are all over it. You've heard the reports? They found no explosives on the car that blew up." David paced at the foot of the president's bed. "It's him! He's learning who he is!"

"Unless it was this other assassin, Englishman."

The name gave David pause. Englishman was a mystery. If it turned out that he rather than Johnny had flipped the cab, then they were all in a hopeless mess. He would leave it up to Samuel to sort it out.

"Perhaps. The point is, you owe your life and your presidency to Johnny. You must issue a statement that evidence implicating Feroz in your assassination attempt has surfaced, prompting a successful preemptive strike by our people."

"Johnny's not our people. He's a chaplain who—"

"A chaplain in our army!"

Stenton eyed David. "What evidence do we have that Feroz was behind this?"

"The sworn affidavits of Johnny Drake and a high-level operative from the X Group named Kelly Larine. They gave these statements to me verbally, but we can get them in writing if . . ."

"If?"

"They survive. I doubt this is over. The X Group has never failed to make good on a contract. Feroz has paid for your death—it doesn't matter that he's now dead. If you implicate the Iranian minister of defense with even a shred of evidence, two things will happen. The first is that his support for the initiative to disarm the Middle East will evaporate. A major victory. For this alone I would think you'd want the evidence needed to implicate him, particularly knowing it's true."

"And second?"

"The X Group will pull out all the stops to silence those who expose a paying client."

"Meaning they will come after me hard."

This much David had already accepted.

"And you're hoping Johnny can stop this so-called Englishman," the president said.

"He may be your best hope."

"Assuming that Johnny, not Englishman, has this supernatural power."

"Yes. Assuming that."

"I'm not sure which is harder, being caught in the wake of this Project Showdown, or believing it even exists."

"Clearly, being caught in its wake."

"Don't you ever doubt?"

This silenced him. They both knew he did on occasion. Anything unnatural was not naturally believed. Faith, in essence, was unnatural.

"On occasion," David said. "This isn't one of those occasions."

Stenton looked as though he'd aged ten years in the last two days. Perhaps he had.

"I want a sworn statement from you. I'll pass all of this by Ed Carter as soon as you leave. If the director is in agreement, we'll hold a press conference in the morning explaining how Feroz's own hired guns took him out to keep him from ever fingering them. There'll be plenty of international fallout, but I think you're right. When the dust settles, it'll go our way. If, and I do mean if, you're right about all of this, your Johnny may have just saved Israel."

"Which was undoubtedly why Samuel received the vision he did."

"Doesn't mean this Johnny is innocent. I've been given the green light to be discharged tomorrow. I think I'll move it up."

"Where will you be going?"

"To my ranch in Arizona. I think disappearing for a few days is in order considering all that's happened." He caught David's concerned surprise. "Don't worry, my ranch is armed to the teeth."

THE DIRECTOR of the Central Intelligence Agency, Ed Carter, now faced an impossible decision. He had thought betrayal would get easier with time.

It didn't.

What he and a small group of well-informed U.S. leaders were doing wasn't a true betrayal in that they weren't betraying their nation. Only their president, and only for altruistic reasons grounded in sound moral principles. The large sums of money flowing through their hands were enough to grease the wheels, but hardly motivation for assassination. So he'd told himself a thousand times.

There was good reason why virtually every nation in the world supported the Iranian initiative to disarm the Middle East. After more than a thousand years of bloody conflict, it was time to bring the region under control. The Iranian initiative had a better than average chance of doing just that.

The only person who stood in the way was Robert Stenton. One gunslinging president who had no right to subvert the will of the world or, for that matter, the will of the United States. They all knew that on balance the American people supported the Iranian initiative. If, as Stenton had repeatedly warned, Israel was ultimately destroyed by her neighbors, well then, the world would go on with one less brewing conflict.

As he saw it, disarming the region and putting a United Nations peace force in place was far less risky than allowing ideologically driven conflicts to fester.

His role was strictly to provide intelligence. Schedules, names, weaknesses in security. None of it traceable to him. With Assim Feroz now dead, Stenton would fan the shocked world into flame and kill the initiative. The agency couldn't contradict the evidence that Feroz was behind the attempt on the president's life without themselves appearing complicit.

The only way out of this mess was to continue as planned. Deal with the president. There would be a dozen Assim Ferozes willing to carry his torch in the absence of opposition.

Ed pushed his wire-rimmed glasses up on his nose and picked up the satellite phone. He called an attorney in Brussels. From there he was passed through no fewer than six filters before finally reaching Kalman within fifteen minutes. An amazing network the Russians had established, superior in every way to their own.

The phone clicked twice. "Yes?"

"The operative has fixed the customer. The other will be going home immediately. His withdrawal papers will be handled through normal New York channels."

Translation: *Johnny killed Feroz. The president will be going to his ranch in Arizona. Details of his location and the planned security measures will be left in the same subway tunnel used last time.*

"Yes, sir."

Ed Carter, trembling, set the phone down.

It was now out of his hands.

34

Carl decided to do the thing expected of him.

Children did what was expected of them, and he felt more like a child now than he had since last entering his pit. But that wasn't entirely true, because when he'd last entered the pit's familiar darkness, he felt warm and secure. Now he felt cold and afraid.

But he returned to Paradise anyway.

He caught a red-eye out of New York to Dallas and then an early-morning flight to Denver and on to Grand Junction. He was going back to Colorado because the blue pickup truck was there. He was going back to Paradise because the cabin was there, hidden up in the canyon where no one waited.

He struggled with the decision to find Sally again, but in the end realized that he couldn't go back to his mother because he wasn't sure that he was her son anymore. How many times had he been led down a path of "truth" only to discover that it was simply part of a grand scheme to convince him of a lie? More times than he could remember.

All he wanted was to be a son and a lover. Sally's boy and Kelly's lover. But by being Johnny he could be neither—not really, not if it meant that Sally and Kelly would be hounded by hell. If Johnny could be a normal person and an ordinary lover, then he would like to be Johnny. But Johnny wasn't ordinary and Carl hated him for it.

The problem was, Johnny hated Carl even more. For this reason alone, Carl decided that he would call himself Johnny, the lesser of two evils.

In the end he was just a lost boy who didn't belong.

In the end he was rejected by both worlds.

In the end he was numb, flying and driving and walking up the mountain in a haze, choking on the lump that had lodged itself so firmly in his throat that he was sure it would never leave.

He was regressing. He was becoming a boy. The only problem was that he didn't *know* that boy, and he didn't want to know the boy who had become Carl.

Johnny stopped on the ledge high above Paradise, trying to recall some of the fun boyhood memories that must reside somewhere in his mind. Running down Main Street chasing a girl with pigtails. Lazing behind the community center on a hot summer day, bragging about impossible feats.

Nothing came. There was only his blue truck parked behind the community center. No memories, no friends, no sign of Sally.

Johnny hated another thing about himself. He hated this sentimentality that riddled him with weakness. Carl would detest such a show of self-degradation. Carl did.

Johnny impulsively gripped his hands into fists and screamed at the valley. He closed his eyes, leaned into the cry, and shredded the still air with a blood-boiling cry until his lungs were exhausted.

Then he opened his eyes and listened.

There was no answer. No reaction at all. No one ran out into the streets of Paradise to attend to the call for help. Wind passed softly through the trees around him. Birds chirped nearby. A lizard scuttled through the underbrush on his right, undeterred by the boy's wail.

He was alone. No one cared.

He hated himself.

The tears broke through his protective shell when he stepped back on the path that led up to the canyon. If Kelly saw him now, eyes leaking, she might suggest a treatment from Agotha for his own benefit.

The suggestion sent a shiver through his arms. It was Agotha who'd hurt him, never Kelly. Kelly only protected him. She was as much a victim as he had been.

And neither of them was really a victim, because both had been made strong by the training. Carl was perhaps the best sniper who had ever walked the face of the earth! You couldn't get much better than that. As for Kelly, Agotha had saved her from a lonely and abusive childhood.

Kelly. She was another reason he was going back to the cabin, wasn't she? He knew that Kelly could find him here.

He walked into the canyon, bearing an ache in his heart that hurt worse than any needle he'd received through the shoulder. If Agotha could find a way to inflict this kind of pain on her subjects, she would strip them in less time than it took with electroshock or sensory depravation. Physical pain was a faint shadow of this pain in his mind.

Then Johnny was there, standing on the rocky sand, facing the cabin at the end of the short canyon that had once hidden Project Showdown.

He felt nothing but utter loneliness.

He wanted Kelly to come and hold him.

He wanted to die.

Johnny sat on the sand, failing to find the energy required to walk into the cabin. There was no reason to approach the cabin. No reason to leave the cabin.

He lay on his side, pulled his knees into his chest, and continued to cry.

SAMUEL HEARD the soft sobbing and ran to the cabin's window. He'd come?

His childhood friend lay on the ground twenty-five yards from the porch, rolled into a fetal position.

Samuel sat hard on the bench facing the window. Both he and Johnny had known that Johnny would pay a significant price for going under, but he'd never suspected the terrible lengths that the X Group would go to unmake his friend.

Johnny was only a shadow of the child he'd once been. And no one knew as well as Samuel that being a child was what it was all about.

Unless you become like a child . . . Unless you become like a child, you can't do much of anything good in this world.

But at what cost? What was the cost of following the path into this kingdom where power flowed beyond the comprehension of most?

Samuel stared at his friend, unable to hold back his own tears. Not only because he empathized with the pain Johnny felt as he lay in a heap, but because Samuel knew that the price had not yet been fully paid.

Johnny was desperate for the end, but he was only at the beginning.

Samuel's father had made the right call when he'd guessed that Johnny would return to the cabin. They both knew that if anyone could reach Johnny now, it would be Samuel, but even he wasn't sure Johnny could be reached by anyone.

Samuel's mind flashed back to that day in Paradise a dozen years ago when they'd first met. When heaven had collided with hell. Neither he nor Johnny had been normal since that day.

They were both outcasts. Unless Johnny embraced his alienation and stepped willingly into the role, he would fade into powerless obscurity—so it was with all of the faithful.

It took Samuel ten minutes to compose himself and wipe the evidence of tears from his face. Then he took a deep breath, stepped up to the door, and went out to meet Johnny.

THERE WERE only two places Kelly thought Johnny might go.

The pit in Hungary.

The cabin in Colorado.

The pit would be the more difficult destination. So she went to Colorado.

If there was a way to flog herself and thereby accept punishment for what she'd done to him, she would gladly accept each blow. If she could find a way to repay him, no matter how ludicrous or how great the cost, she would do so. Betrayal was a terrible, terrible thing.

She had betrayed Johnny by making him someone he wasn't. By stripping his identity and forcing another one upon him. By pretending to love him only to win his allegiance.

She'd never expected to fall for him. It cost her dearly, but not a fraction of what she was willing to pay to win his trust one more time, this time as the Kelly who truly loved him.

She wept openly on the plane, leaning against the window to hide her face from the other passengers but not caring if they stared, which they did. It was another lesson she was learning: when this much sorrow ravaged the heart, the mind shut down any respect for etiquette.

Assim Feroz was dead. That was good.

The president was alive. That was good.

Englishman was not only alive, but brimming with a power that Kelly had only dreamed about. This was bad.

But Kelly didn't care, because there was another power at work within them all, and this power was intent on destroying the only man she'd ever loved, with or without Englishman's help.

Back in the Egyptian desert, she'd been abandoned and abused before escaping. She remembered how it had felt to be rejected and alone, without a mother, a father, or a true sense of belonging. Humans went to great lengths to belong. To fit in. Agotha had taught her this, and together they'd leveraged the tendency against Carl, luring him to belong to them. To her.

They'd done the job well. Too well.

If they survived this ordeal, Kelly would take him to the desert, where they could heal together. To Nevada, where no one knew them. To the place she had always intended to take him.

If they survived. And if they died, she wanted to die in his arms no matter how melodramatic that sounded. They were all a page ripped from the story of life anyway. All humans were, whether they realized it or not.

Dear Johnny . . . Dear Johnny, what have I done to you?

THE FACT that Johnny had outwitted him turned all of Englishman's happiness into bitter anger. It didn't matter that he was the Terminator or that in the end the Terminator always won. This setback was humiliating.

There was still hope. More than hope, certainty. Even when Johnny won, he was really losing. But this didn't make Englishman feel any better. He would first kill the president, not because he had been ordered to do so, but because by killing Robert Stenton he would undo what Johnny had done in saving the man's life.

Then he would find Johnny, and he would reduce him to a desperate, blubbering fool.

And then, when Johnny was only a shell of himself, he would choose to kill him. That wasn't the original plan, but the original plan was now obsolete.

This new plan made Englishman happy. Not as happy as he'd once been, plotting and planning all these months, but still happy. He still had the trump card, and this, too, made him happy. But Johnny was turning out to be a more worthy adversary than he'd originally calculated.

He'd retrieved the information on Stenton's ranch and would soon board an airplane bound first for Denver and then Grand Junction, where he would collect all he needed from the safe house. He would then head for Arizona, where he would be free to level whatever paltry security they threw his way and take the man's life at his leisure. The Terminator would undoubtedly kill the whole family—father, mother, and son. So would Rambo if pressed.

So would Englishman.

He didn't need the information Kalman had provided, only the destination. But he had it nonetheless. Better not to be overconfident, considering a single stray bullet could end his life as easily as the president's.

Englishman began to whistle in the backseat of the cab that was taking him to the airport. But his whistle sounded hollow. In all honesty, none of these mental gymnastics were bringing him happiness. His identification with the Terminator and Rambo wasn't helping. He couldn't remember such a profound lack of happiness.

He stopped whistling.

When he met Johnny again, he would make sure that Johnny never whistled again. Ever.

35

Hello, Johnny."

Johnny opened his eyes.

"I remember the first time we met here," Samuel said.

Johnny pushed himself up on his elbow. The blond boy stood ten feet away, smiling at him. He was here? Johnny blinked. The image was still there. Samuel was here. He climbed to his feet, embarrassed to have been caught in such a vulnerable state.

"You remember?" Samuel repeated.

"No."

"You will. Give it time. My father tells me that you remember your mother."

"Some."

"Then the rest will come too."

Johnny felt dazed. Trapped in a hopeless depression. "I'm not sure I care anymore."

Samuel clasped his hands behind his back and paced. He stood under five feet, a short boy. His eyes were blue, like his father's, and his skin fair. He wore tan shorts that ended just above knobby knees. His beige socks were scrunched down around the lips of brown leather hiking boots. It was amazing to think that he was the same age as Johnny. But was that really true?

Even though Johnny no longer cared to remember his childhood, he couldn't deny the strong sense that he'd known Samuel before New York.

"My father told you about Project Showdown," Samuel said.

Was that a question? "Yes."

"And about our meeting to discuss the vision I had. Your insistence to enter the X Group."

"Yes. Do you know what I did in New York?"

"You saved the president and then killed his enemy."

So they'd found the body. Not that it mattered.

"Do you know if Kelly's safe?" he asked.

"I don't know."

Johnny nodded and turned to face the cliff. Samuel was undoubt-edly here to talk more nonsense about Project Showdown, but Johnny only wanted to be alone. Or with Kelly. For all he knew she was dead. The terrible sadness he'd felt earlier returned.

"You haven't finished the task, Johnny. You know that, don't you?"

He looked at the boy. At the man who looked like a boy. Samuel drilled him with soft, kind eyes. Did he like Samuel? Johnny did. Maybe even Carl did. But the person trapped between Johnny and Carl felt too lost to care about a man who looked like a boy and claimed to be his best friend.

"You haven't become what you're meant to become," Samuel said.

Johnny wasn't sure he'd heard right. "What I've done isn't enough for you?" He knew he was giving in to self-pity, but he felt justified. He couldn't imagine a man, woman, or child who'd been put through as much as he had been put through in these last few months.

"Enough? No. I know that sounds harsh, but you're not the only one to walk this path."

What on earth did the boy think he was saying?

"Unless you become who you were meant to be, untold harm will come to an untold number of people. You are chosen, Johnny. I would be more gentle if we weren't so short on time, but you may be the only one who can stop the X Group from killing the president."

"Me? You have the wrong person. I don't stand a chance against Englishman!"

Samuel blinked and stilled. "You've foiled him twice now. What do you mean?"

"Twice? You mean here and in New York. I was lucky that Kelly came back here, and I just managed to stay out of his line of sight as I fled him in New York. I wouldn't characterize either as foiling him. The next time he'll kill me."

Samuel stopped pacing and dropped his arms. "You . . . You're saying that Englishman has power?"

"You don't know?"

"My father assumed the reports were about you."

"Your father was wrong. I don't know who Englishman is, but he can maneuver physical objects with his mind. Knives and guns. Cars. I have no doubt he could walk up to this cabin and level it with a hard look. Me, on the other hand, I can change the temperature. Maybe the gift will come in handy when I find myself standing among the flames of hell."

Samuel's face had lightened a shade. Two shades. For a long moment he stood stock-still, staring at Johnny without so much as breathing, it seemed.

"You're sure . . ."

"Do you think I would have fled his initial assault if I thought there was any way to take him? The only way to keep Kelly alive was to force Englishman into using her as a hostage."

"That means . . ." Samuel had come upon a revelation of great weight. "Then he must be either a fictitious character or someone else who was given power by the books."

"Fictitious character? He's real, I can swear that much."

"Real, yes, yes, of course. But written from the books, not born of this earth."

"A demon?"

"Or a human given power by the books like you were."

"I don't have power! Why is it so difficult for you and your father to understand that? It isn't there!"

"I think it is. But I also think you're so lost that you no longer can truly imagine it. Belief begins with the imagination, you know. The day a faith loses imagination is the day it dies."

"I have no idea what you're talking about."

"Of course you do. You never read *Spider-Man*? Accepting your true identity means understanding that you are a stranger to this world. A freak, ostracized by the very people you want to help."

The words struck a chord. At least the bit about being a freak. But the idea of his being someone who had a unique power to dispatch evil seemed absurd. Even if it wasn't a fantasy, he honestly didn't know who he was or had been or wanted to be. He was trapped.

"I see it every day," Samuel said.

"Sure," he said. "There are thousands of superheroes running around this planet, struggling to find their magic."

"Not like you, no. Unless I'm mistaken, there are only two others, not counting Englishman. But the path you're on is essentially identical to the path all men, women, and children of faith finds themselves on. To be or not to be, that is the question, as they say."

Johnny honestly didn't know what the boy was saying. Samuel elaborated.

"Once born into childlike faith, brimming with belief, typical people begin to lose their faith. Society mocks them. Their friends smirk. They come to change the world, but over time the world changes them. Soon they forget who they were; they forget the faith they once had. Then one day someone tells them the truth, but they don't want to go back, because they're comfortable in their new skin. Being a stranger in this world is never easy. Look at me, I should know. Don't feel sorry for yourself, Johnny."

"Have you been in my pit? No? Have you been strapped to my hospital bed? No? Then you have no right to tell me anything, including how to feel."

"Actually, I do. I've been through worse. But I admit I'm being a bit direct. We are running out of time. And if you're right about Englishman, we may already be out of time."

"I don't want to be—"

"Stop it!" Samuel yelled at him. "Stop it!" His face was red, and a single vein throbbed on his temple. "This isn't about you anymore!"

Johnny was dumbstruck. His heart pounded and his face felt hot, but more than either of these, his heart felt sick.

Samuel just stared, his face slowly losing its bright red hue.

The sickness in Johnny's heart slowly rose to his throat. He was no longer sure whether the emotions that swallowed him were self-pity or profound anguish at his own pathetic excuses for not stepping into the role he was destined to take.

A tear leaked from his right eye.

"I'm sorry, Johnny. I'm truly sorry for what you've been through."

Johnny closed his eyes and fought the waves of remorse that crashed through his heart. He lifted a hand and rested it against his forehead, as if to hold back the pain in his head or to hide from it. He accomplished neither.

A cool hand touched his hand by his side. Samuel was standing next to him now, looking up at him with tears rimming his eyes. In that moment Samuel who was a man was only a boy. Johnny remembered this. He remembered Samuel this way.

"Will you trust me?" Samuel asked.

"Yes," Johnny said without thinking. Then he asked a very stupid question. "Will it save Kelly?"

Samuel smiled. "You see, you're still a child. Yes, I think it will. And it just might save you."

Johnny nodded.

"You should know that if you walk where I'm going to ask you to walk, there will be a price."

"I'll be strange. Ostracized by society. Rejected."

"Yes, that too. But more. I don't know specifics, but it'll affect you physically. Like me. I stopped growing."

Johnny considered the implications. "You're saying that I'll never be normal. That I'll be rejected by normal people. That I was chosen to be an outcast. And that if I manage to embrace this childlike faith of yours, I'll wear my abnormality in some debilitating way?"

"Yes. But you'll have the power to change the world."

"A freak with a magic stick."

"No magic. But a freak, probably. At least in the minds of most. In fact, the being-a-freak part will probably precede the power part."

"Will I be able to defeat Englishman?"

"Maybe. Maybe you've been chosen to die to rid the world of him. The rules are different in the supernatural reality."

Johnny nodded. "All of this assuming I can become like a child and believe like I once supposedly did."

"Yes. Will you?"

"I'll try."

Samuel let go of his hand and stepped back. "Okay. That's good. That's real good."

Johnny felt stupid, but he didn't know what he could do other than offer Samuel a stupid grin.

"Wow, that was easy," Samuel said, smiling.

"Not as easy as you think. Now what?"

"Now what?"

"What do I do?"

"You believe," Samuel said.

"Believe what?"

"Believe what you believed as a child. All of it."

"How do I do that? Just believe?"

"Well, yeah. Just believe. Accept who you are. Remember Spider-Man? My father talks of Samson. Believe."

Johnny wasn't sure what that meant. "Do I close my eyes?"

"Why? If you think it will help you focus, but believing isn't a matter of focusing. It's just . . . You just believe!"

"What if I don't?" Johnny asked.

"Well, do you?"

"What?"

"Believe. Do you believe?"

"It depends on what I'm believing."

They stared at each other, caught in their circular questions.

"I think I believe," Johnny said. "How will I know?"

Samuel stepped back. "Try it. Do what you do in your pit."

Johnny nodded and closed his eyes, focusing his mind to form a tunnel. The long, dark space formed easily enough, but he didn't know what to form as the objective.

He looked at Samuel. "What am I trying to do?"

"I think your gift involves affecting the physical world. Like the temperature. Or bullets. Stones. Anything physical. Probably not the free will of people, though. I'm guessing inanimate objects."

"Samson," Johnny said.

Samuel grinned. "Samson. But I like Saint better."

This time Johnny turned to his right and rested his eyes on a stone on the sand ten yards away.

He was able to enter the tunnel again.

He was able to step outside the tunnel and see the rock on the sand.

He was able to imagine the rock lifting off the ground and flying toward him, and he was quite sure that it was doing just that.

For a long time he watched the stone fly to him and around him. His pulse surged. Maybe everything Samuel had said was true after all. Maybe he really did have a supernatural gift as written in the book twelve years ago. Maybe he could do what Englishman did.

Johnny opened his eyes.

The stone lay on the ground, ten yards away, unmoved.

He stared at it, stunned. "It . . . It didn't move!"

No response from Samuel.

"I saw it move in my mind." He spun to the boy. "I gave it everything! You're wrong. I can't—"

"You're not believing," Samuel said. "You're focusing but not believing. This isn't some random force that you can tap into because Yoda says so." Samuel gripped his hand into a fist. "Believe, Johnny. Believe!"

"Believe in what? I believed that I was moving the stone, and it didn't even budge."

"Believe in the Maker of the stone to move it! Believe that he is alive and active and begging to move the stone if you allow it."

"God?"

"Of course, God!"

"What kind of belief do you have?" Johnny asked. "What is your power?"

Samuel hesitated, then answered steadily. "I don't have your kind of power, not since Project Showdown. For now I'm more than happy to exercise a gift called speaking the truth."

"And yet you expect me to—"

"You are chosen! We are all chosen, but you for a specific task, which depends on your belief. Your gift is to believe in a way that makes ordinary people seem stuffy by comparison. So believe!"

We're like two children arguing about which game to play, Johnny thought. He felt irritated, impatient. He knew how to focus on a level attained by few Zen masters, but he couldn't just believe in some unseen, unfathomable Creator who refused to show his hand unless properly summoned! It made no sense. The stuff of a child's fantasy.

Unless you become like a child . . .

The midday sun blazed high above them. A hawk screeched as it flew in a lazy circle above the cliffs. Here on the bare ground stood two boys trying to enter a kingdom in a different realm, beyond the rocks and cliffs and sand, beyond the hawk that called to them.

"Say it, Johnny."

"Say what?"

"Say you believe. Out loud. Shout it."

"I believe?"

"Don't mumble it like a question! Shout it out so that the whole world can hear it. You did it once; do it again."

Johnny imagined himself standing in a busy city square, Times Square, shouting out his belief for all the wayward to hear. It was a terrifying thought. Why? Because he didn't believe? Or because he was ashamed to believe?

Because he didn't want to be a freak. He wanted to be normal, accepted. His desire to be accepted was stronger than his belief.

Samuel walked toward him, drilling him with a stare. "Say it. There's no one here to hear you except me."

"I believe," Johnny said.

"Louder. Shout it."

He hesitated.

"What's the matter, Johnny? You're enslaved by the same pathetic weakness that holds the agnostic in chains? Hmm? It's not that you don't have the capacity to accept the truth. You don't *want* to accept it, and you hide behind your own logic and intelligence while the truth marches by. Step out and join it, for goodness' sake! Shout it out in full step! *I believe!*"

Samuel shouted the last two words, startling Johnny.

He impulsively matched the cry. "I believe!"

A mischievous smirk tugged at Samuel's mouth. "I believe!" he cried.

"I believe!" Johnny cried.

"I believe!" Samuel screamed, at the top of his lungs now.

"I believe!" Johnny screamed.

Samuel thrust his hand toward the stone. "Now move it."

Johnny faced the stone and brought the full weight of his belief to bear on the small fist-sized piece of rock, confident that it would rise and fly. He focused, he willed, he clenched his teeth. When nothing happened, he closed his eyes and entered the dark place, focusing until the rock was zipping around in his mind's eye.

When he looked again, the stone lay still.

For several long seconds Johnny stood in stunned silence. Then he closed his mouth, walked to a large boulder on his right, and sat down on top of it.

His utter foolishness swallowed him.

"We'll try again in ten minutes," Samuel said. "Time is running out."

"Then time *has* run out," Johnny said. "I'm not who you think I am."

"We'll try again in ten minutes," Samuel said.

36

Robert Stenton sat on the porch's bench swing, gazing out at the twin rows of tall pines that bordered the long paved driveway leading up to the ranch house. He'd built the place when he was the governor of Arizona. Here, the stress of the presidency was a distant reality. At least for a few hours.

Here, he was just Robert. Bob. Wealthy and savvy many would say, but just Bob, the rancher, a political outsider who'd upended Arizona's electoral traditions and taken the governorship by storm. The fact that he'd done the same in Washington never ceased to make him shake his head just to be sure it was all real.

It was. As real as the high-desert wind blowing hot through the trees that were scattered around the ranch.

A pile of huge boulders sat to the right of the house. At Jamie's suggestion, they'd hauled in the rocks to form a cave that reached nearly a hundred feet into the pile, then reinforced the boulders with a steel mesh to prevent them from slipping.

This was Jamie's Bat Cave. It said so on the wood sign at the entrance.

A tall electric fence that Robert had agreed to put up at the insistence of the Secret Service stood back three hundred yards and circled the house, the riding stables, and all of the outbuildings. Three hundred yards beyond this was another fence loaded with the most advanced surveillance technology available. Nothing within a thousand yards of the ranch house went unidentified.

Their lines of defense ended in a natural boundary three miles away. A long mound of massive boulders cut across the valley, offering both position and cover for more than a hundred men. Beyond the boulders, a ten-foot concrete wall nearly two thousand yards long connected the cliffs on either side.

The gentle hills behind the ranch house hid the fact that the property was technically in a box canyon. Six observation posts covered every square inch of the ranch from their positions on top of the hills. The Stenton ranch was as well protected as any piece of real estate in the United States.

David Abraham had come with them, but as was his normal practice when invited, he stayed out of the way, letting them "be a family," as he put it.

The screen door behind Robert slammed. Jamie walked out in bare feet, trailed by Wendy, who held two tall glasses of iced tea.

"Drink, Commander?"

"Commander?" Robert reached for the condensation-beaded glass.

"Jamie was just informing me of the difference between a good commander in chief and a bad one. We both agreed that you're a good one."

Jamie lowered himself gingerly to his seat on the swing beside Robert. He wasn't as strong as he'd been even last week, and his skin seemed paler, but it was hard to tell with his ghost-white complexion.

"With potential to become the best," Jamie said.

Robert smiled and smoothed his son's hair. Pulled him close. "I'll try not to disappoint."

Wendy sat down on his right. This was the Stenton family, three abreast, sitting on their front porch grappling with the latest of many challenges they'd faced over the years.

Although the struggles facing them now promised to be more intense than most. A sniper had just put a bullet through Robert's chest. Jamie was dying. Wendy was about to lose a son and feared for her husband's life.

"How's your chest?" Wendy asked.

Robert touched the bandage under his shirt. "Not bad considering a bullet passed through it three days ago. The painkillers help."

"You're sure this is the best place for us?" she asked. Her eyes always smiled, even when she was sad or afraid. An amazing thing, her eyes. At times Robert was sure he'd married Wendy for the mystery behind her eyes alone. They were certainly what prompted his interest in the beginning. No woman could have such a radiant face and not be as kind as she looked. So far she'd proven him right.

"No one knows we're here—that's a start," he said. "Sam's holding a press conference." He glanced at his watch. "Correction: just held a press conference, during which he made it clear without actually saying it that we are in the White House."

"Wouldn't take a rocket scientist to track us down."

"Blake told me that we have over a hundred National Guardsmen directed by a unit from the Special Forces," Jamie said. "And that's on top of the Secret Service. Do you know they have aerial reconnaissance on us at this very moment? Two unmanned Predator drones. Nobody gets within a hundred miles of here without us knowing."

Robert winked at his wife. "Yeah, Wendy. Quit your worrying. We're armed to the gills."

JOHNNY DID try again, half a dozen times, to no avail. One time the rock moved, possibly—Johnny couldn't be sure. Otherwise he experienced nothing except growing frustration and unbelief. If not for the image of Englishman, doing his tricks, gunning for them all, Johnny would have given up after the first attempt.

The afternoon wore on. Samuel didn't press too hard after the first failure, just enough to persuade Johnny to try again. And again, six times.

They talked about the past—about good times, about bad times. Slowly, like a cold honey pouring out, the memories began to come back. Unless they were simply new memories being informed by the details that Samuel fed him. *No, it was more,* Johnny thought. The more they talked, the more he recalled specific unrelated events.

"You do realize that when you find your power, more will be required from you," Samuel said after a particularly long pause. He was unrelenting. "I don't want you to walk into this blindly. You won't be able to come head-to-head with someone like Englishman and expect to defeat him with a bigger rock."

Johnny dismissed the notion with a quick word. "Sure."

Even though the superhero-making had been decidedly derailed, Johnny took some comfort in his friend, whom he evidently once loved like a brother. It was still amazing that such a wise, mature person could be embodied in such a young body.

Several times he took Samuel's hand and felt his young skin, awed by the appearance. If the power Samuel spoke of had done this, perhaps he could believe. Encouraged, he would agree to try his hand at stone-moving again.

Not even a budge.

With the setting of the sun, Johnny felt his own mood sink. Then fall. Then crash to pieces on the ground.

He was lost. He wasn't Carl, and he was proving that he wasn't Johnny either, not any longer. He couldn't be what he was meant to be because he'd become someone else over time. Recapturing his true childlike faith was impossible because a different life had beat it out of him.

Johnny excused himself from the cabin when it was night. He walked into the darkness, comforted by it. But then he remembered that he would never go back to the pit. The pit had been a lie.

Still, he liked the darkness.

Johnny lay down on the large boulder at the small canyon's entrance, stared at the stars, and let himself feel completely hopeless.

BY THE time Englishman reached Denver, his blood was very nearly boiling. And he still had another flight. The fact that a few thunderstorms had caused such delays could only be explained by the spineless nature of people who thought they were wiser than they were for shutting down the system to avoid a few bumps in the air.

He hated airports.

He hated the people who worked in airports.

He hated most of all gate agents who clicked away incessantly on hidden keyboards, rarely raising their eyes, summoning people, informing whomever they wished of whatever they wished, all of it bad. Gate agents were powerless power mongers.

Englishman sat in a hard plastic seat staring at the dark-haired, dark-skinned, dark-hearted, dark stain of a gate agent whose head jerked ever so slightly with her every keystroke. She'd told him twice already to have a seat and wait for his name to be called.

He had no intention of waiting in his seat for his name to be called. The plane was at the gate and they were boarding the first-class passengers and she was still ignoring him. This devil in the blue dress fastened by eight brass buttons that ran from her skinny brown neck to her knees was thinking of him even now, consumed by thoughts that immobilized her—all very flattering on any other day, but today he hated this devil.

He knew a thing or two about devils.

He also knew as an absolute matter of fact that unless the story

was about a man stuck in an airport terminal or an airplane—such as
The Terminal or *Airport*—movie stars never sat for two hours waiting for a devil in disguise to let them on the plane. In reality, most
movies skipped the airport scene altogether, because everyone knew
that it was no more interesting or eventful than pulling on your socks
or underwear after rising each morning. For the most part these
details were inconsequential.

And yet this woman trying so sincerely to hide her passion for
Englishman by avoiding his stare was making his boarding of the
plane consequential.

Englishman stood and approached the podium, further angered by
her refusal to confess her interest in him with even a casual glance.

He put both palms on the podium. "Pardon me, mademoiselle, but
I'm growing tired of this silly act of yours."

She looked up at him, feigning surprise. It took a serious amount
of self-control on Englishman's part not to strike her on the cheek. He
couldn't use his power to make her slap herself or gouge her eyes out
or begin screaming like a bloody lunatic, but he could do a few other
things that would ruin her day.

"I want to board the aircraft now. Please give me whatever docu-
mentation I need to do so at this time."

"Excuse me?" She was growing red. This pleased Englishman.

"Are my words too big for you? Let me restate. Please. Seat. Me.
Now."

For a moment she seemed too stunned to speak. Unfortunately for
her, she overcame her shyness.

"If you don't have a seat immediately, I'll have to call security.
Please sit and wait like everyone else. The flight is overbooked. Next
time I suggest you avoid flying standby."

She had no intention of putting him on, Englishman realized. He
wasn't going to his destination on this plane. And if he wasn't, no
one was.

"I must tell you something, mademoiselle. You are an ugly and pathetic woman. And you're upsetting me."

For an unbearable moment, Englishman forced himself into submission, ignoring the impulse to punch her in the face. Instead, he wreaked havoc with her keyboard, popping the keys out like popping corn so that they sprang loose and flew up to hit her on her chest and chin. He simultaneously fried the monitor so that smoke rose in a thin coil.

The agent jumped back and let out a startled cry.

Not trusting himself to stop there with her, he turned his back on the devil in the blue dress and walked to the window. The jet was parked just outside, taking on the last few bags from handlers who plopped them on a long conveyor belt that fed into the fuselage's belly.

Englishman made all the suitcases he could see fly from the belt with enough force to send them tumbling and skidding on the tarmac for a hundred feet.

He popped the tires on the plane as well. Then he sent one particularly heavy-looking bag flying into the engine with such force that he was sure it did some serious damage. The ground crew scrambled for cover like rats.

Satisfied, Englishman walked toward the sign that pointed to the rental cars. It was a good night for a drive anyway.

37

Johnny slept on the sand outside the cabin, uncaring, unwanting, unmade. He dreamed of nothing. Just the black tunnel without a light at the end. Somewhere in the fog of nothingness, he realized that he had finally and firmly been reduced to nothing more than a blind mole. His light had been extinguished.

He slept in blackness. It was his only reprieve.

A voice called to him from the dark. "Johnny?"

I'm not Johnny.

"Johnny." Something was shaking him. "Johnny."

Kelly was calling him. His pulse spiked. He wanted to be held by Kelly. He wanted to be comforted and loved and made alive by her love.

Do you love me, Kelly?

Yes, Johnny.

Do you mean that? Do you really, really love me?

Yes, I do mean that. I love you, Johnny.

Then will you hold my head in your lap and brush my hair from my forehead and smile down at me? Will you breathe your undying love into my mouth and swear to love no other man the way you love me?

Yes.

Kelly was crying.

Do you love me, Johnny?

Yes! I love you more than life!

Are you sure?

It's the only thing I'm sure of.

Will you kiss my cheek and my neck and hold me tenderly? Will you kiss my lips and breathe on my neck and tell me that I belong to you?

Yes.

Johnny opened his eyes. Someone was lying beside him on the canyon floor under the stars, crying softly.

Kelly was here?

He sat up, startled. "Kelly?"

She lay on her back, and her right hand covered her eyes. She was torn by sorrow or relief or another emotion so gripping that she felt unable to respond to him.

"How . . . How did you find me? Are you okay?"

No response.

"You shouldn't have come."

She still didn't answer. There was nothing else to say, so he laid his head beside her shoulder. He was glad she'd come, but his guilt at having endangered her life and reduced her to this wasted soul on the sand was too much.

Was this a dream?

No. He could feel her hand touch his head now. Stroke his hair.

She shifted to her side and whispered, "I love you, Johnny."

"Do you really, really love me?"

"I really, really love you."

"Then will you hold my head in your lap and brush my hair from my forehead and smile down at me? Will you kiss my lips and breathe on my neck and tell me that I belong to you?"

Johnny said it all before he realized that he was actually saying it out loud.

"As long as I live," she said.

They lay in silence a long time without speaking. What was there to say? Kelly was safe. As far as Johnny was concerned, she was all he had, and she was no small thing. He didn't know himself, but he knew Kelly and that was enough for now.

"How did you find me?" he finally asked.

Where else would he go? She knew him, she said. She told him about her cross-country flight. She'd rented a car in Denver after missing a flight because of thunderstorms.

"Englishman is out there," she said.

"He's going to kill the president," Johnny said. "No one can stop him."

"You don't have his power?"

Her bringing the subject up bothered him. He pushed himself to his seat and stared back at the cabin. To his surprise, Samuel was seated on a chair beside the front door, watching them.

"Englishman told me to tell you that your end is in yourself. That you'll hate yourself."

"And if you ever see him again, you can tell him that I already do."

"I think I know what he meant," Kelly said. "You don't feel loved. Your mind is too preoccupied with your own worthlessness to accept love."

"I know that you love me. How can you say that I can't accept love?"

"Why do you need to ask me, then?"

"To know, to really know."

"Exactly. Because you're unsure."

"I wanted to hear you say it."

"Why? To reassure yourself, which is the same as asking to know. You can't believe that I love you because you're absolutely certain that you're unlovable."

Johnny blinked in the moon's dim light. She did indeed know him better than he knew himself.

"Maybe you're right. But I don't see what that has to do with my not having Englishman's power."

"That's not what I care about," Kelly said. "Englishman can go rot in hell as far as I'm concerned. But I want the man I love to know how much I love him. I know now that unless you can believe you're loved, you'll ruin yourself, just as Englishman said."

"You don't want Englishman's power," Samuel said. He stood less than ten feet away. "Trust me, you want nothing that Englishman has. But I think Kelly's right, and I think love might be the key that unlocks your power, Johnny."

Kelly sat up and stared at the boy with Johnny. Samuel could take the slightest suggestion and turn it into a ray of hope; it was his nature to do so. *But this is a last desperate attempt,* Johnny thought. What did love have to do with power?

And then he thought about Samuel's own story.

"What do you mean?"

"I don't think you know how to love," Samuel said. "I don't mean to hurt you, but I've been racking my brain trying to think of the problem, trying to understand why you can't seem to believe the way you once did, and I think Kelly's right—it's love. Your inability to accept love, yes, but as a result, your inability to love."

Was that true?

"Not that I blame you, Johnny, but I don't think you really care about anyone other than yourself. You've had to focus almost exclusively on yourself in order to survive. As a result, you don't care about having the power to fight evil unless it threatens something you care deeply for, which no longer includes you because you don't even love yourself anymore. Make sense?"

"No. Yes."

Samuel rounded them, bright-eyed despite the darkness. "That has to be it. You can't believe because you are too preoccupied with yourself, which is the opposite of love. You have to learn to love so you can believe. You have to become selfless to fill the shoes you are meant to fill."

"Now I can add the inability to love to my list of failures?" Johnny said. "Splendid."

"You have to learn tonight," Samuel added.

"I think you're being just a bit unfair, don't you?" Kelly asked.

"Unfair? No. Direct, yes. We don't have time to be less direct."

"Your being direct will only push him away. Is this the way your father taught you how to love?"

No! She doesn't know what she is saying, Johnny thought. She couldn't understand how cutting and terrible her words were. Samuel watched her like a wise man looking on with patience.

Maybe Samuel was right. What did Johnny really know of love? What could a man learn about love while strapped to a hospital bed as those who claimed to love him shot electricity through his bones?

Love. He didn't remember everything about Project Showdown, but he was now remembering enough and had certainly been told enough to know that in the end it was all about love. About the discovery of love, no matter how terrifying the path might be.

"Love," Johnny said. He pushed himself to his feet, inspired by the notion that Samuel had hit upon something.

"Love," Samuel repeated. "Do you believe?"

"That would mean I don't really love Kelly at all. I need her comfort and I need someone to comfort so that I feel useful, but that's not true love. I don't love her at all."

Samuel's eyes flitted to Kelly.

"No, I do love her," Johnny said. "I do love you. And even if I don't, I want to more than anything, because you're the world to me. But what if Samuel's right and I'm really loving you for my own sake? That's not real love, right?"

"Do any of us really love?" she demanded. "This kind of talk can only conclude that there *is* no love in the world!"

"But there is love in this world," Samuel said. "I see it every day. Johnny's just had it beaten out of him."

"By me," Kelly said.

"No!" Johnny cried. "You were only doing what you thought was best for me. What else is a girl who's been sold into slavery as a child supposed to think?" He waved his hand angrily through the air. "Forget it. I love you. And if I don't, then I choose to love you now, from this moment forward."

"Love," Samuel said. "It's always about love."

"Love," Johnny repeated. There was something very familiar about this exchange. "Will you love me?" he asked Kelly, not wanting her to feel isolated.

"I do love you," she said.

"Samuel's right—this may be our only way of surviving Englishman. Englishman said I'd hate myself, so maybe I should learn to love myself."

"But then aren't you loving for your own sake again? So that you can survive Englishman?"

"No," Johnny said after a long pause. "I choose to love for your sake. To save you from Englishman."

"Tonight," Samuel said.

"Is love something you can just turn on with a switch?" Johnny asked.

"Yes, I think so. It can be. It has to be. Is knowledge a switch? Knowledge can turn the world on with a single throw of the switch." Samuel put his hands behind his back and circled to their right. "Do you have the power?"

Johnny stared off into the night, focusing on a pile of stones fifty feet away. Not one of them stirred. After a minute he gave up.

"Evidently not."

"Then forget about the power," Samuel said, turning back to the cabin. "Focus instead on love. True love. Selfless love in your heart."

"How?"

"Love Kelly, of course."

38

The night was failing in the high desert, giving way to a pale early-morning sky in the east. He'd driven from Denver to the safe house in Grand Junction, collected all he needed, and then broke every possible speed limit on his way to Arizona.

Twice the highway patrol had tried to pull him over. Twice he popped their tires and melted their radios. He was such a major stud.

It was cool outside, but the black asphalt still held some heat after baking in the sun for twelve hours the previous day. Englishman drove with the Honda Accord's windows down, left arm stuck out so that he could feel both the heat from below and the cool from above. Opposites.

Life was about opposites. Hot and cold, mostly hot. Hate and love, mostly hate. Fiction and flesh, mostly fiction.

That was him, anyway. Made by the monk, Marsuvees Black—quite literally made. Englishman had been given one objective in life: He was to watch Johnny Drake. If this person named Johnny ever began to manifest any unusual powers, Englishman was to destroy Johnny.

There were more like Englishman, created to wreak havoc at the appropriate time. Barsidious White, who'd played games with unsus-pecting travelers in abandoned houses, for example. A killer with interesting dimensions, to say the least. Black had failed in Paradise; White had failed in Alabama. Englishman would not fail. And nei-ther, for that matter, would the others. Learning, always learning and growing smarter.

Englishman had wandered aimlessly for years, prowling like a lion, until the day when Johnny had indeed manifested an unusual power. Just as predicted.

Englishman killed Dale Crompton and made himself exactly like the man. He liked Dale Crompton's body very much. Not only had it been conveniently located in the same camp with Johnny, but Crompton's body was quite a magnificent specimen of lean and finely sculpted flesh. He would keep it if everything worked out.

Whenever a car pulled up behind him, Englishman slowed, then cut into the left lane when they attempted to pass. After several attempts he let them pass, blasting their horns. He did this because it gave him power over them without so much as moving a finger or throwing a thought. He wrought misery by merely sharing the same space with these motorists.

He turned onto a gravel road and headed north, farther north. If they were worth half the salt paid for them, the security forces who had dug in to save the president had already spotted his car pulling off the highway. It was the only road that led to the ranch forty miles ahead.

Forty miles till showdown.

Englishman was happy.

39

Samuel awoke to the sound of screaming.

He jerked up and listened. Silence. The door to the bedroom flew open and Kelly stumbled out. "What was that?"

Then it came again, a fuller sound now. "Elieeeee!"

"Johnny!"

Samuel rolled from the mat and dropped out of the loft, bothering to touch only one rung as he did. Johnny must have awakened early and gone out by himself. Samuel yanked the door open and was through before thinking to let Kelly out first. Never mind, she was on his heels.

Dawn had broken. The small canyon was empty, no sign of Johnny.

His scream came again, echoing through the outer canyon, a furious howl that screeched with such intensity that Samuel felt momentarily frozen by fear for Johnny's life.

He ran barefoot over the sand, ignoring the rocks that dug into the soles of his feet.

Kelly kept up. "Samuel? What's—"

"I don't know."

Again the piercing scream. He still couldn't make it out.

He tore around the huge boulder on the west side of the canyon's mouth and pulled up sharply. Kelly clipped his shoulder and slid to a stop.

There, not thirty meters away, knelt Johnny, tearstained face raised to the sky, eyes clenched, arms spread wide, hands squeezed into fists, screaming.

"*I belieeeeeve!*"

Samuel gasped. The canyon was a hundred yards wide here, like a dry riverbed littered with hundreds of rocks that ran its length to the edge of the mountain.

But the boulders were not on the sand.

They were floating twenty meters above Johnny's head.

A thousand boulders, at least, all at the exact same height, moving very slowly toward the canyon mouth, as if defying gravity were a regular morning exercise.

Johnny screamed his belief.

Samuel's heart crashed.

Kelly grabbed Samuel's arm.

Johnny had found his power. Did he even know? And if not, would the canyon rain boulders if he became distracted?

The floating rocks above them looked like an asteroid belt that floated lazily, undirected except by a general force that came from Johnny.

Samuel wanted to shout out with glee. He wanted to jump up and down and pump his fist into the air, crying victory.

"Say nothing," he whispered.

He said it between Johnny's screams. But the sound of his whisper had been too loud. Johnny lowered his head and opened his eyes.

The boulders did not fall.

Samuel exchanged a long stare with his friend. He still didn't know?

"You've found your power?" Samuel asked.

Johnny slowly lowered his arms. "No. I don't care about the power. I just want to be Johnny again."

Samuel took a step toward him. "Then do you at least understand love now?"

"Yes, I think I do." Johnny's eyes darted to Kelly. When he spoke again, his voice was choked with emotion. "I really think I do. Forgive me for not truly loving you before. Forgive me, please."

Kelly was still speechless. Her eyes lifted to the sky above him, but Johnny did not notice.

"I feel . . . myself." Johnny staggered to his feet. "Real again." A grin tugged at his mouth.

"Johnny," Samuel said. Without raising his arm, he lifted one finger toward the sky. "What's that?"

Johnny looked up. Saw the floating boulders, a particularly large one directly above him. He shrieked and dove to safety, tumbling in the sand.

The rocks still did not fall.

"Whoa! What?" Johnny slowly stood and craned his neck to take in the belt of rocks above him. "What's happening?"

"I don't know," Samuel said. "You're making them float."

"Me? Are you sure?"

"It's not me."

"Englishman?" Kelly asked.

Samuel scanned the cliffs. He didn't think it was Englishman.

They watched the rocks, soaking in the abnormality of it all.

One of the rocks above Johnny jerked. He looked at Samuel, eyes wide.

"Try again."

Johnny looked up at the same rock. It hung still for a moment. Without warning it flew into the canyon with blinding speed, like a UFO accelerating from zero to sixty in a single, undefined moment. The rock streaked for the end wall, a projectile fired from Johnny's mind. It slammed into the cliff and shattered, bringing a shower of smaller boulders tumbling down.

Johnny and Samuel spoke at the same time. "Wow!"

"Wow," Kelly said.

Johnny raised both hands and moved them toward the canyon mouth. The flotilla moved with his suggestion.

"Wow."

He moved his arms back the other way, like a conductor instructing a symphony.

The boulders stopped on a dime and reversed their direction, flying toward the end of the canyon now.

Johnny whooped with enthusiasm and swept his arms toward the sky beyond the canyon, above Paradise, as if he were sending a fighter jet off an aircraft carrier. *Go get 'em, boys!*

The boulders streamed east, increased their speed, and then disappeared into the horizon.

Johnny stared after them, stunned. "When will they stop?"

It was Kelly who asked the question on all of their minds. "What if they fall? On Paradise?"

Johnny frantically flung his arms to the sky and motioned the rocks back, like the ground crew might wave a jetliner into the gate, only with twice the animation.

The tiny specks reappeared in the dawn sky. "They're coming back," Johnny cried, motioning with even more vigor.

The small spots became larger spots, and from Samuel's angle the boulders looked as if they were headed directly for Johnny at an unstoppable speed. He instinctively crouched.

Johnny stopped motioning and threw himself to the ground as the flood of rocks zoomed silently into the canyon. A thousand boulders blasted twenty yards over their heads. The flyby took less than a second, followed by a huge wake of air that nearly blew Samuel over.

The squadron of rocks slammed into the far wall with enough

force to shake the ground. Half the cliff caved with a thunderous roar. Dust boiled to the sky.

They stared at the destruction in awe. This time all three spoke at once.

"Wow!"

This is it, then, Samuel thought. *This is why I chose Johnny and why Johnny agreed to enter the X Group.* And yet he knew that it would take more than this to overpower Englishman.

"That's it," Samuel said. "Time to go."

"Did I really do that?" Johnny asked, staring at the rising dust. "Go where?"

"The president is at his ranch in Arizona, an hour by helicopter."

"You have a helicopter?"

"How do you think I got here? Top of the cliffs. The crew are running around like rats at the moment, trying to figure out what caused the ground to shake, but their orders are explicit."

"Don't . . . Don't you think I should practice or something?"

"Englishman has a full day on us," Kelly said. "The president's probably already dead."

"He's with my father, safe for the moment. But we have to leave now," Samuel said. "You can practice on the way. Find some barns to float or something. You have the skills and the training to use weapons—just think of this as a new weapon."

"You can't be serious!" Kelly said. "You can't just throw him to the wolves without proper planning!"

"We'll plan on the way."

Samuel turned and strode toward the cabin with resolution.

"Hold on."

He glanced back, saw that Johnny wasn't following him, and turned around. "We're not going to make it if we don't go now, Johnny."

"You said I couldn't defeat Englishman with a few boulders anyway. Do I have any other powers?"

The question caught Samuel off guard, but he didn't have time to explain his suspicions yet again. There was always a price. Even Samson's power had come with a condition.

"I don't know. You'll have to figure that out as you go."

Johnny measured him for a long moment, then turned his head to face a two-story boulder that rested at the base of the cliff.

"Do you believe, Samuel?"

Before Samuel could respond, the boulder rose soundlessly from the ground. It slowly floated toward Samuel and came to a rest two feet over his head.

Do you believe, Samuel? Truth be told, he was unnerved. Perhaps terrified. It wasn't every day his faith was tested by a boulder weighing several hundred thousand tons.

He reached up and felt the reddish sandstone surface with both hands. A vibration hummed through his palms, down his arms, and along his spine and shot to his heels. There was enough power here to level a city. Amazing.

"I do," he finally said.

Johnny smiled and winked. "Just checking to make sure I still have the power," he said. "I think Samson would be a bit jealous."

The boulder floated to the other side of the canyon and settled quietly on the ground.

"Let's rock," Johnny said, striding forward. "No pun intended."

It was then that Samuel first noticed his eyes. They seemed gray instead of brown. Or was it the light? If Samuel hadn't been expecting some kind of change, he probably wouldn't have noticed. Apparently Kelly hadn't. She would soon enough.

Samuel turned and led them toward the cabin. "The truth will set you free, Johnny," he said, staring forward. "Show them the truth."

40

The guards waited for him at the gate. He could see their tiny figures moving in the dawn light. Naturally, they'd been alerted to the sedan that had exited the freeway and made its way toward them. They would need to turn the lost tourist around.

Englishman could execute this bit of fun in an unlimited number of ways. He'd considered the possibilities on the long night-drive from Phoenix. But almost all of those ways failed to interest him.

The only way to execute this mission without boring himself to tears was to go right up their throat with a few fireworks to announce his arrival.

He would have to save Dale Crompton's body from all of the heavy metal they would hurl at him. He couldn't dodge bullets, but he had other skills.

"Dust to dust, ashes to ashes," he whispered. And then aloud but with a low voice, "Hallelujah, amen, you are dismissed. Every last hell-bound one of you."

Englishman stopped the car a hundred yards from the gate. With the high walls running both ways to the cliffs on each side, he would have to go straight through the entrance. Four armed men now stood before the gate, patiently waiting their turn to die. He would reward their patience by letting them go first.

He pried his eyes skyward, wondering if the drones were armed. A projectile in the back from a low-flying Predator would be most unwelcome. He'd have to keep moving and watch the skies. This could be slightly more challenging than he'd anticipated.

Now *that* was interesting.

One of the guards was waving at him. Stupid fool was motioning him forward. *Do you want me to come? Is that what you want, Jack Black?*

A Bradley fighting vehicle was parked on the right, and a tank was parked on the left. He saw now that their guns were manned and aimed at him. According to the docket that he'd breezed through on the flight from New York, the real threat would come from the second line of defense a mile up the road where the troops were dug in.

Englishman gunned the motor, but he kept it in neutral. Sweat tickled both temples. His heart was pounding like tumbling boulders. Now that he was here, staring down so many guns, he wondered if he'd been a little overzealous in choosing this particular approach.

A tremor ran through his fingers.

The sensation was so foreign to him that he found it impossible not to remove his eyes from the gate to look at his hand. Trembling with eager, joyous anticipation. And with fear.

Opposites. Love and hate. Good and evil. It was a good day for a showdown.

Englishman took a deep breath, blinked the sweat from his eyes, dropped the gearshift into drive, put both hands on the steering wheel, and slammed the accelerator to the floor.

The tires spun on the gravel road, caught some traction, and propelled the black Honda Accord forward.

JOHNNY PUT both feet on the helicopter's skid and readied himself to jump as soon as the pilot gave him the signal. They approached a guard post on a hill behind the main ranch buildings, the largest of six similarly equipped hills.

Something was wrong with his eyes, but he wasn't sure what. Even now, looking down at the passing ground, he thought his vision was somewhat impaired. The stones and bending weeds were slightly out of focus.

Kelly had been a wreck since their departure, breaking into tears for no reason, it seemed. Yes, he might be headed into danger, but his training was superior.

It was his eyes, she finally told him. She wouldn't elaborate, but his eyes seemed to scare her.

Riding the side of the helicopter twenty feet in the air, Johnny was struck by the change in himself. He wasn't the same person he'd been even three days ago. The thought of jumping from this height wouldn't have bothered him in the least, but now even looking down put butterflies in his gut.

He was being whisked into a battle that he was suddenly terrified of. The good news, supposedly, was that no attempt had yet been made on the ranch. All Johnny could think about was the bad news, namely, that this frail man named Johnny was their hope.

If Englishman had the same power as he did, how could Johnny be their hope?

The helicopter swept in low and flared to a hover a few feet above the rocky earth.

"Go!"

Kelly placed a hand on his shoulder. He turned around and saw that she was crying again. She gazed at his face, then quickly averted her eyes.

Something was wrong with his eyes. He should find out what,

but the prospect of throwing himself into battle with Englishman dominated his concern.

Kelly wrapped both arms around him and spoke into his ear. "I'm afraid, Johnny."

He smoothed her hair, at a loss for words. He didn't even know what he was supposed to do up here on the hill. They'd developed no real plan other than for Johnny to do something if Englishman showed up.

Samuel held a pair of sunglasses out to him, the mirrored kind that pilots wore. "Wear these."

He didn't know why Samuel thought he should wear them, but maybe they would help his eyesight. Maybe it was the sunlight that distorted his vision. He took the glasses and put them on.

Was he going blind?

"The truth, Johnny. Show them truth." Samuel nodded, as if this should mean something to him. "The truth will set us all free."

Johnny returned the nod.

Kelly released him and he jumped from the skid, landed on a patch of hard sand, and ran toward the four soldiers who waited in the outpost. The helicopter blades lifted the bird up, then toward the ranch house with a blast of hot air.

The ten-by-ten post was built of half walls and sandbags that gave the soldiers inside a 360-degree view of the valley. Four large machine guns were mounted to cover all four sides. Johnny ducked his head under the eaves and faced a Special Forces lieutenant and three guardsmen. He knew this by the insignias they wore.

It occurred to him that he could remember these details. And now that he thought about it, he could remember more.

The lieutenant eyed him. "Pardon my ignorance, but remind me what it is you're supposed to do here?"

Good question.

"We don't have a place for you to sit."

Johnny stuck out his hand. "I'm Johnny. They want me to watch over . . . things."

The commander took his hand without enthusiasm. "Watch what, the weeds grow?"

The radio under one of the grinning guardsmen squawked. "We have a situation at the front gate. Black sedan's headed our way at high speed. Unresponsive. Do we shoot?"

A crackle of static.

"Blow his tires out."

"Copy. Disabling veh—"

The radio went abruptly silent.

The guard manning the radio keyed the transmitter to no avail. "What was that?"

"I don't know."

But Johnny knew, and the knowledge immobilized him. Englishman had come. So soon?

He looked past the gun on his right to the ranch below, where the helicopter was just now landing safely. The horizon offered only a gray morning sky above distant cliffs. Or were his eyes making the sky gray? He removed the sunglasses, but the sky was no less gray, so he replaced them.

He was going blind, wasn't he?

"What happened?" one of the guardsmen asked.

The lieutenant hesitated, scanning the forward perimeter. "We may have some trouble." He jabbed a finger at Johnny. "Sit."

Instead, Johnny walked out of the post.

One of them yelled something at him—his heart was pounding so loud that he couldn't hear the words. He walked twenty paces and faced the south. No sign of Englishman. That was something to be thankful for. But he knew his gratitude would be short-lived.

A chorus of frantic calls barked over the radio in the post. The lieutenant leaned out of the post and shouted angrily at him,

Barking orders about getting his butt back inside, punctuated with obscenities.

Johnny faced the man and floated a dozen sandbags from the ground. He held them suspended in front of the man.

"Holy—"

All four soldiers stepped back, silenced and slack-jawed.

Johnny let the bags fall. "Please," he said, pausing to catch his breath over the panic that was gripping him. "Let me do my job."

ENGLISHMAN WAITED until he was absolutely sure they were about to fire before making his first move.

It was a thought more than a move, but it did move some things. Three things to be precise. The guardhouse, the Bradley fighting vehicle, and the tank. He moved them up and out of the way. Fifty very quick feet straight up. The underground electrical wires that fed the guardhouse separated in a spray of sparks as the shack flew up before coming to a sudden stop next to the tank and the Bradley high above the gate.

The guards lucky enough to be left on the ground seemed disturbed by the sudden skyward display. Englishman made their guns hot, instantly hot enough to fry their hands.

He couldn't hear their cries because the car was roaring and the windows were down, but he could see their faces. They dropped the guns.

Johnny wouldn't have. Even in Hungary he would have controlled his reaction to the heat long enough to get off at least one shot, and one shot from Johnny was enough to kill even Englishman's flesh-and-blood body.

"Ha!" He couldn't resist the cry of delight. In the space of five seconds he'd neutralized the front gate.

Englishman slammed his foot on the brake pedal, and the sedan skidded sideways before coming to a dusty stop. The sharpshooters would be climbing out of their holes at any moment. Guns from the sky would begin blazing. Missiles even. They would unleash all hell without the foggiest idea of what hell really was.

He stared up at the floating guardhouse and saw that someone had thrown open a window and was bringing out a rifle. On each side, the hatches to the tank and the Bradley were flopping open, and crew members were poking their heads out.

Englishman let the guardhouse, the tank, and the Bradley fighting vehicle fall to the ground together.

The earth shook. Amazingly, the tank bounced a good five feet before slamming to rest on broken tracks. Its suspension had survived the fall, which was certainly more than could be said for those inside. The Bradley's undercarriage shattered upon landing. And the guardhouse became a pile of kindling. *Dust to dust, ashes to ashes. You are dismissed.*

Englishman floored the Accord. He sent the metal gate flying into the sky, not just fifty feet or even a hundred feet this time. He launched it far into the valley as a warning to the forces hunkered down to meet him.

The Englishman cometh.

41

What Johnny first mistook for a bird flying through the sky grew as it hurtled toward them and became a pair of metal gates. They flew in an arc like debris lobbed from a catapult and crashed into the ground several hundred yards from the ranch house.

One of the guards voiced his shock. "What the . . . ? Did you . . . ?"

Johnny did the only thing he knew to do in that moment. He pictured the gates flying back.

They flew. Like gangly missiles propelled from a silent canon, in precisely the same trajectory in which they'd come.

A huge line of boulders ran across the desert floor two miles away, effectively blocking Johnny's line of sight to the front lines, but with any luck Englishman would see his shot returned.

Or had that been a mistake? He'd just announced himself to Englishman!

A strong voice cut through the radio chatter. "The gates are down! I repeat, the gates are down and we have an intruder. Black sedan coming in like a bat out of hell. Blasted through the front guard, tank and all. Get the drones over here and take him out!"

The earth began to rumble. A long line of dust rose from the valley floor in front of the boulders nearly three miles out.

"What . . . ?"

The line of boulders was moving. Hundreds of ten-, twenty-, and thirty-foot rocks rolled across the ground toward them. Englishman had turned the barrier into an army of rock!

Johnny watched in horror as a flight of smaller rocks broke off from the boulders and streaked forward. Toward the ranch house.

Johnny quickly envisioned the rocks flying back, but they came on, faster now. He couldn't affect the flight of objects in Englishman's control?

The rocks were going to crash into the ranch house. Johnny's blood turned cold. Could he move the house? No, that would as easily kill them!

His vision fogged over.

The rocks gathered into six groupings, turned sharply in differing directions, and blasted toward the hills. The rocks were going for the outposts, including the one twenty feet from where Johnny now stood.

Before he fully knew what was happening, one of the groupings streaked out of the sky like a comet and slammed into the hill on his left, driving the outpost and everything inside it below the ground. The earth shook.

Dust rose.

Johnny's legs were rooted to the ground. Englishman had seen the gates flying back over his head, concluded they had come from Johnny, and fired the first salvo. Men lay crushed and broken under tons of rock where only a moment ago the four-sided post had topped the hill. Not only here, but at the other five outposts as well.

He jerked his head back to the valley. The line of boulders was picking up speed as it rumbled across the flat ground, barreling down on the ranch house where Kelly had taken shelter with the president.

Kelly . . . He was here to save the president, but his mind was now on Kelly, whom he loved for her own sake. He didn't know how to stop the boulders! He tried in vain to stop them by focusing on them, but they were impervious to his power.

Fear and uncertainty overcame him. Johnny ripped his legs free and sprinted down the hill toward the house. He didn't know why he was running; he was only running.

"WE HAVE to get you out now, sir!" Bruce Wyatt was the president's most trusted Secret Service agent. He grabbed Robert's arm. "The chopper's ready."

"What's that noise?" Robert demanded.

David Abraham ran from the window, motioning to the first family, Samuel, and Kelly. "No, you can't leave. He'll destroy the helicopter as soon as it takes off. You have a shelter?"

"The basement."

"In the basement! Now!" David spun to the other three Secret Servicemen who stood with sidearms drawn. "Everyone! The house is going to be hit. Let's go!"

"Hit? By what?" Robert asked.

He still couldn't wrap his mind around what David's son, Samuel, had suggested to him moments earlier. The notion that two men with supernatural powers were duking it out in his front yard wasn't making it through his reality grid.

Elijah had fought the prophets of Baal—an event recorded by an ancient writer. Samson had pushed over some pillars, another story written down by another ancient writer. Johnny had saved his life by affecting the flight of a bullet, an event that was recorded by an X-ray. But here in the backyard of the president's ranch, stories of soaring gates and flying tanks were in an entirely different category.

They were real. Happening now.

This stuff wasn't supposed to be real. Not unless you were David Abraham and had broken into the supernatural plane with Project Showdown.

Robert repeated his question. "Hit by what?"

"Boulders," Samuel said.

ENGLISHMAN DIDN'T know how many soldiers had been hidden in the broad line of boulders, but they were all dead now, crushed under the great stones before the sharpshooters got off a single shot. Englishman owed this fortuitous turn of events to Johnny. It could even be said that Johnny had saved him, although he knew that this was an overstatement. Still, it could be said, would be said, had been said, and it excited Englishman.

He'd sent the gates flying into the valley, roared past the crumpled tank, and piloted the dust-spewing Honda Accord a third of the way down the straight road toward the huge line of boulders when the gates had suddenly come flying back, over the rocks, across the dull blue sky, over his head like a giant twisted metal bird.

Johnny! Johnny was here! Englishman nearly drove off the road in his exuberance.

He had intended to use his power to accelerate the Honda Accord to a speed far beyond its limits. He would have blasted through the narrow gap in the defenses like an unstoppable roadrunner from hell. *Beep-beep.*

Then the gates had come flying back and Englishman changed his mind. He sent the boulders rolling. He couldn't see the ranch house yet, but he could just make out the outposts on the distant hills, exactly where the documents had put them. He decided to take them out now, ahead of schedule.

Englishman did not laugh. Laughing at a time like this would be far too cliché. If it was just the president up there waiting to die, he might have allowed himself a cliché or two. But now that Johnny had inserted himself into the mix and demonstrated that he knew a thing or two about gate-flinging, Englishman would avoid cliché.

He parted the boulders like a Red Sea in motion and increased the Honda's speed. The car shook with hammering vibrations, the sky boiled with dust, the air thundered with the sound of a million tons of rock rolling, rolling, crushing, crushing, pounding, pounding.

The small Honda Accord followed directly behind, splitting the dust with an unseen shield. He pushed the car even faster, drew abreast the boulders that were less than twenty yards away on each side. Tumbling, tumbling, crashing, crashing, roaring, roaring. He couldn't see any body parts in there. Englishman might have allowed himself a laugh then. He couldn't be sure, because the sound was so deafening he couldn't hear himself.

He leaned back, looked directly ahead, and blasted through, easily pulling ahead of his massive rear guard. They would be able to see the lone, small Honda Accord leading the charge now, assuming they had the presence of mind to take their eyes off the big show to realize that *he* was the big show.

The air was crystal clear this morning. With the dust behind him, he could see all the way to the large grouping of trees and scattered boulders that presumably surrounded the ranch house.

If Johnny had a rifle, he might be able to take out Englishman now. The thought sent a chill down his back.

Am I ready to die?

No.

Was Johnny ready to die?

Yes.

Do I want to kill Johnny?

Yes.

Have I destroyed Johnny?

Yes.

Then why was Johnny throwing gates back at him?

Because Johnny didn't know about Englishman's trump card.

He blinked. Still, it was a good question that hadn't presented itself until now. Johnny had some power, more power than yesterday, enough power to throw gates around.

Wasn't it understood from the beginning that Johnny might find the power before he was utterly destroyed?

"Yes."

And he has found the power. So now you have to kill him. Crush him, defeat him, pulverize him, decimate him, ruin him, shred him, chew him up and spit him out. Minus the cliché.

"Dust to dust, ashes to ashes, hallelujah, amen, you are permanently dismissed."

Englishman hated Johnny. He despised him in the worst way, so much that in that moment, he realized not having Johnny to hate might be *his* end.

If Johnny dies, I might die.

The thought made him sweat again. Heavily.

JOHNNY GOT halfway down the hill toward the ranch house and pulled up panting. He wasn't going to make it! On top of that, he didn't have a plan.

What could he do down there that he couldn't do from up here?

The boulders were bouncing high as they tumbled forward, traveling at a speed of at least fifty or sixty miles an hour. They would reach the ranch house in less than thirty seconds.

Could he block the line? He glanced up the valley and quickly determined that there wasn't enough material to block the massive amounts of energy in these thundering behemoths.

Then he saw the car blazing a dusty trail just in front of the boulders, which had parted to let it through.

Englishman.

His mind flipped through options as if they were playing cards fanned by a thumb.

Stop the boulders. No.

Stop the car. He tried. It was being controlled by Englishman. No.

Divert the boulders. Again, under Englishman's control. No.

Stand in the way of the boulders. No, that couldn't possibly be a good idea.

Lift the boulders off the ground so they would fly over . . .

No, no, no. Nothing could be done to the boulders.

But to the car . . .

Johnny scanned the valley floor for a large rock, found one, lifted it a hundred feet into the air, and then sent it flying toward the car.

Fast. Faster than he could see. A streak of granite packing enough striking power to bury the car a hundred feet under the ground.

Englishman was still too far away for Johnny to make out any detail, but he did see a few things.

He saw the car skidding to a stop. He saw a boulder rise from the line behind the car, streak toward the rock he'd sent, and slam into it in midair. He saw a hundred fragments rain down around the car.

He saw that the line of boulders was still thundering for the ranch house, in front of the car now.

Johnny began to panic. The valley filled with the sound of other-worldly bowling balls crashing down the lane for the target.

His heart skipped a beat. *Down?*

He swung his eyes to the ground two hundred yards in front of the granite army and told it to move. Dust immediately swirled in a long straight line across the high-desert floor. The sand lifted into the air, like a long row of fountains blasting skyward.

He dug the trench deep, the entire width of the valley floor, sending excavated sand and stone up to the clouds, where they hung in suspension.

Englishman's line of boulders reached the wide trench, bounded into the air, and dropped out of sight.

As long as the boulders were beyond Englishman's senses, he couldn't control them.

Johnny dropped the excavated sand and stone back into the trench.

The boulders were now gone under an uneven line of dirt that formed a mound across the valley. No sign of Englishman.

Silence seemed to echo.

He'd done it? Johnny's heart pounded, a heavy, thick bass drum in a hollow chest. He'd really done it?

"Johnnyyyyyyyyy!"

His named drifted over the valley floor, barely reaching him. Englishman was where? On the mound of dirt? He couldn't see too clearly.

With alarm Johnny realized that the sky was darker now, definitely darker than it had been just minutes earlier.

He really was going blind.

Show them the truth, Samuel had said. *The truth will set us all free.*

The truth had turned Samson blind.

Englishman cried his name again. "Johnnyyyyyyyyy!"

The cliffs at the entrance began to crumble. He saw the car then, emerging from behind several tall boulders, like a bat out of hell.

Johnny ran. Down the hill. Like Elijah racing the rains, down, down, stretching each leg in front of the other, afraid to look up. Knowing that Samuel had been right. He couldn't win this battle with a few boulders or a ton of boulders. A single large chunk of granite from the sky would destroy the ranch house—there was no way Johnny could protect them forever.

He had to get to Englishman before Englishman got to them.

The ground over the now-filled trench flattened before the car. Johnny cut to his right, hoping that he could intercept the car, but even as he ran, he knew Englishman would beat him to the ranch house.

He passed a small wooden outbuilding at the base of the hill—perhaps a tool shack. He could hardly see the distant tumbling cliffs, but he could tell that they were floating in large broken chunks. Englishman was gathering an armada. This time it would float. Their end was clearly in sight.

Or not so clearly.

Johnny ran faster, on level ground now, terrified as much by his failing sight as by the coming catastrophe. He could make out forms, but they seemed shrouded in dusk. A faint glimmer followed the edges of most things. The rocks, the trees on his right, the speeding car angling in from his left.

The faint glimmer of light that surrounded the objects seemed to have intensified. But the world that held the objects was most definitely darker.

Maybe every time he used his power, he lost some of his eyesight.

Was it the sunglasses? He lifted them with his mind and was rewarded with a blast of air that stung his eyes. The light on the edges of this dark world was bright enough to hurt his eyes.

He let the glasses drop back onto his nose.

Englishman raced on, his jagged armada flying above him. Johnny was halfway to the ranch house when he acted more out of panic than with any real plan.

He emptied the trench again, straight up into the air, but not as high as the last time. The sand, the dirt, the huge boulders rose, and Johnny flung it all back in the direction it had first come.

Light glimmered and crackled on the surface of the flying debris. His wall of rock collided with the massive chunks of stone that Englishman had gathered for his assault.

The valley filled with the sound of a thousand detonations. It was nothing more than a distraction; he was only providing Englishman with more rocks to fling.

His enemy had already filled the trench again, making the path smooth for his car. They were locked in an impossible duel. He had to slow the car!

"Englishmannnnnnn!"

As if on cue, the car slowed to a crawl, a hundred yards from the house.

Johnny headed for Englishman. Why didn't he just take out the house? *Because, Johnny, you, not the president, are his target. He knows you are all that stands between him and the rest.*

The sky to his right blossomed with an exploding ball of light. He ducked. Samuel had mentioned drones. Englishman had just taken one out. As if in answer, a second explosion rocked the dusty sky.

Englishman was out of the car, around the car, standing with hands on hips, waiting for him in brimming light, like a gunslinger with one last cowpoke to kill before he called it good.

Johnny slowed to a walk, then stopped, thirty yards from the man.

Englishman grinned. "Hello, Johnny."

42

Englishman strode to within ten paces of Johnny, ready to pre-empt his slightest move. But Johnny neither moved nor made anything around them move.

The kid was wearing dark reflective glasses. Odd. No, not odd. Cliché. Still, the sight of those black, shiny glasses unnerved Englishman.

He put both hands on his hips, planted his feet in the sand, and faced the boy he'd waited so patiently to crush.

A rock came screaming out of the north toward him. Did Johnny think he could accomplish anything with a stray stone? He lifted a large boulder near the hills and flung it at the incoming projectile. The two collided with a loud pop a hundred yards out. Dust hung in the air as a hundred shattered fragments fell harmlessly to the ground.

"It will take more than a few boulders," Englishman said.

He saw his reflection in Johnny's silver glasses, and the sight amused him. *Two of me, one of you.* A fitting symbol. Did the boy actually think he had a chance against Englishman? Surely Johnny didn't think he could get the upper hand with some stone-throwing.

Another boulder came hurtling in, from the south this time.

Englishman destroyed it with another while it was still small in the sky. He grunted with disappointment.

The pain came out of nowhere. A sharp jab that sliced through his right shoulder. He knew immediately that Johnny had tricked him by drawing his attention to the boulder in the sky while bringing a much smaller stone in from behind.

Englishman did the same to Johnny even as he dropped his body flat.

Johnny gasped and staggered forward.

But one was not enough. Englishman lifted a hundred small stones into the air behind Johnny and poised them to strike.

"Behind you, Johnny."

Johnny glanced behind. Saw the stones. Swung back around.

"Behind you, Englishman."

He didn't have to look to know that Johnny had already placed as many stones in the air behind him, but he did anyway. He was right. More than a thousand, maybe ten thousand. Englishman rose to his feet.

"There is no way to deflect a thousand stones," Johnny said. "You can kill me, but know that before I die, I'll do the same and you'll die as well."

"And you should know that I've taken similar precautions. You will deeply regret any real attempt to kill me."

"How so?" Johnny asked.

"Because although you think you returned to Paradise and hugged your mother and learned the truth about who you are in the canyon above, nothing could be further from the truth." Englishman was happy to finally offer up these nuggets of information. He could hardly stand the pleasure of it all. "Aren't we clever? Two hounds of hell trading tricks."

"I'm no hound of hell," Johnny said. "I did hug my mother. I do know who I am. The truth *is* with me."

"Is that why you're trembling?"

"I'm trembling because I finally figured out who you are."

"Is that so? And who am I?"

"Who am I?" Johnny asked.

"You're the boy who caused so much trouble in Paradise," Englishman said without missing a beat. "An innocent fool."

"And you are the monk who came to destroy Paradise. Guilty as sin."

"Ah, but there you are mistaken. So much for the truth being with you."

"You're wrong. You may not have his face or his hands, but you are him in all the right places, born of hell and determined to drag the rest down with you."

Englishman wanted to destroy Johnny now by stripping the boy's faith from his underbelly, he really did, but the talk felt satisfying after so much secrecy.

Johnny circled slowly to the left, and Englishman kept the stones at his back. He walked to his left and knew that Johnny returned the favor. They were two circling vultures, each guarded by a flotilla of stones to keep things even.

"Do you believe, Johnny? I mean really, really believe?"

"How could I not with all of these flying rocks?"

"I'm not talking about the power that moves the rocks. Do you really believe that this power comes from some benevolent God in the sky? Because if you do, you're sadly mistaken."

"What do you mean?"

A soft, comfortable warmth filled Englishman's veins. The time had come to tell Johnny the truth.

DAVID ABRAHAM studied the images on the large flat-screen, frozen by what his eyes had witnessed. The pictures were being relayed from a C140 reconnaissance platform that was circling the ranch at twenty thousand feet, but they were amazingly clear.

A squadron of F-15s was on its way from Nellis Air Force Base in southern Nevada, because the compound's defenses were quite literally crushed. Even the two drones. Only what remained of the interior guard remained, and none of them were volunteering to go stand in the way of the massive bowling balls that had crisscrossed the valley.

Robert Stenton stood by his side, watching the picture, face white. "They've isolated the target on their radar," he said quietly. "This— I don't have any words for this."

"You won't need any words for this. As far as the rest of the world is concerned, this isn't happening."

"How's it even possible?"

"Do you know how small those huge boulders look from the vantage of a Boeing 747 flying overhead? Like specks of sand. Imagine how small they look from the moon. Now Mars. Now the other side of the solar system."

"Meaning what?"

"Meaning what you're seeing today is nothing more than ants' play from a thirty-thousand-foot vantage point."

One of the Secret Servicemen flung the door wide. "Sir, the fighters have a lock on the target. Waiting your order."

"No," David said.

He faced the screen again. Both Johnny and Englishman were in clear view, circling each other and surrounded by a cloud of levitating stones.

"Even if you could isolate one of them, what makes you think Englishman will just stand by while a missile streaks in to obliterate him? He'll more likely send it back on its own heat trail. I'd tell the planes to stay out of visual and keep their fingers away from any triggers for the time being."

"Then what?" Stenton demanded. "For that matter, what are *they* doing?"

"I think they're getting down to the truth of the matter," David said. He headed for the door. "I'm going out there."

"David—"

"I'm going. The rest of you stay here."

43

"If the power came from a benevolent God, wouldn't he hand out more of it so that mortals could rid the world of nasty men like me?" Englishman asked.

Johnny was remembering now. Dogma embraced during his tenure as a chaplain flooded his mind. "Because I'm an exception, just like Samson was an exception. But you're right, I am going to rid the world of you."

Englishman didn't speak for a long time. The world was a charcoal gray, highlighted by bright edges. It was clear to Johnny that his coming out to meet Englishman without a plan would end badly. He was facing off like the local sheriff while thinking about how to make it back into the hills in one piece. At least he was stalling the attack on the ranch house. In this way he was fulfilling his mission.

In every other way he was lost. And going blind.

Englishman's shoulders suddenly relaxed. He crossed his arms. Johnny heard a smile in his voice. "Well, well, well. You've gone and done it. Congratulations, Carl. Your training is complete. You've done well—far better than we had hoped." Englishman walked toward him.

"Stop."

He lowered his arms, totally relaxed now. "I realize you may be confused about this. I was too. But it's over. You've just completed your final test. We've reintegrated you into your own history, most of which is true."

"What do you mean, *integrated*? That's a lie. I'm Johnny."

"You are. And you were a chaplain as well. And you did volunteer for X Group. And now you are Saint. All of it's true. The continuing story of Project Showdown, on the other hand, is a fabrication. It's Agotha's version of a crutch. Like religion. It gave you a reason to believe that you could move mountains and rocks. You were hitting a wall in Hungary, so we set this up for you."

Englishman spread both hands, indicating the valley. "This, my friend, is *you*, not God. It's all you and me. I'm the only other person who's succeeded in manipulating the zero-point field."

"I don't believe you." Johnny was feeling nauseated. The world was black, like his pit, and maybe that was good. Maybe he did belong in the blackness of a pit, only surviving to kill.

"I denied it too," Englishman said. "I stood right here and screamed my bloody head off. It took me a week before I could move another rock, and only then when I finally realized that I had done it with my own power, not with some power from the sky."

Englishman tapped his head. "It's up here, Carl. A simple matter of quantum physics. The zero-point field. And believe me, you've done well. Statistically, fewer than one in ten million humans have the mental strength to pull off what you have, and only then with considerable training. Gurus and such."

Johnny stared at Englishman, stunned by the possibility, however thin, that he was hearing the truth. But even then, he knew it had to be a trick. It had to be! He'd lost himself in their lies once, a hundred times. He couldn't accept them this time.

"You're wrong. I've finally discovered who I am, and it begins with

Project Showdown. Now you have the gall to think I'd just throw it all out for the same lies Agotha fed me for a year? What do you take me for?"

"Please, Johnny. If you insist, we can resort to drug therapy."

"Kelly knows the truth. This is crazy!"

"Kelly is the same person today that she was a month ago! A woman willing to betray you for your own sake. She does love you, but she's under no delusion that this exercise is anything more than a very carefully executed hoax to help you believe in yourself. Believe, for crying out loud! Believe, but believe in yourself, not some faceless god!"

"I *can't* believe in myself."

"You can. As of this moment, you can. You're finally understanding who you really are. You are Johnny. You love Kelly and Kelly loves you. You did not kill the president because we didn't want you to. You did kill Feroz because you were meant to. You were put into the most inhumane pressure cooker of a test to draw out your strength, and it has succeeded. Everything else is a sham! Everything! Even your mother. It wasn't Sally you met. She was one of ours."

The claim blindsided Johnny. "That's impossible. I . . . I felt her love."

"You felt what we wanted you to feel," Englishman said. "The woman you wept over in Paradise was not your mother. We stashed Mommy away in a safe house the day after you bolted from New York. It was all a lie to bring you to the point you've finally come to." Englishman nodded at the floating stones. "And it was well worth it, don't you think?"

Johnny's head swam in confusion. He simply couldn't accept that Sally wasn't his mother. Reuniting with her was the beginning of his awakening. If she was a lie, then the rest was a sham.

Or was it? He refused to let down his guard. The woman he'd embraced in Paradise *was* his mother!

"Samuel," he said. "David Abraham . . ."

"Unwitting accomplices we used because of their connection to you. It was all a setup, beginning with Samuel's vision, which was nothing more than a simple case of strong suggestion in a drug-induced state, followed up by numerous uncanny confirmations. It was *our* vision, and we made sure it came to pass. Does Samuel have any powers? I don't think so. He's a thirteen-year-old boy who knows only what we've wanted him to know."

This was incredible. "What about his age?"

"So he has a growth issue connected to Project Showdown. So what? That doesn't change the fact that we pulled his strings all along."

"David Abraham?"

"Fed off of Samuel's vision."

"The president. You're saying that even—"

"No. You shot him, remember? But it wasn't your bullet that struck the president. It was mine, and I was much closer. I have the power to affect a bullet's path. I did. Your bullet went where our scope told it to go, far over his head. Not that you couldn't have pulled off the hit, but we didn't want a dead president on our hands. At some point we will retrace every last detail and explain it for you. Trust me, it all fits like a glove."

Johnny's worlds were colliding. Did Englishman know about his eyesight? Was that also part of the deception?

There was a sound of hard rain behind Englishman. Johnny's stones, falling to the sand. He didn't mean for them to fall; they just did.

He had supposedly passed the greatest test of all time and felt only desperation. Neither the anger nor the righteousness he would expect to feel at this moment.

"You," Johnny said. "You don't fit."

Englishman smiled. "I fit perfectly. I'm the only person on the globe who has the power you have. I know your pain. Unless a seed falls to the ground and dies, it can't bear fruit, isn't that the truth? We've been destroyed so that we can live, and frankly I hate that. But there it is."

"Why?" Johnny asked. "Why did you do this to me?"

"Look around. You just moved a mountain! You tested off the charts on your military entrance exams and were noticed. Then followed for three years before it was determined that you'd make a good candidate. Now you've proven them right. And to prove it to me, there's one last thing I need you to do."

"What?"

"Kill the president."

Outrage flooded Johnny, then ebbed. He swallowed. "I thought you didn't want him dead."

"Not until after you'd killed Feroz. With Feroz and the president out of the way, the Iranian initiative can move forward without the threat of two idealists duking it out."

"No." He clenched his fists. The stones behind Englishman sprang back into the air. Courage filled his chest. Englishman was lying.

"I don't believe you. You're here to kill me. Samuel and David have told me the truth. Sally is my mother. You're taking me for a fool!"

Englishman took a long time in answering. "Then you are a fool, Carl. And in this business, all fools die. You decide today: either you believe me when I say you were deceived in Paradise, or you believe them that I'm lying. One way you kill the president and live, the other you die."

"I found the truth in Paradise. I embraced my mother."

For a moment Englishman just stared at him. A loud wrench of tearing metal split the air. Thirty yards behind Englishman, the trunk hatch on the Honda Accord flew to the sky.

A large object tumbled from the trunk and rolled toward them. As if manipulated by unseen hands, it was jerked upright not fifteen yards off. Johnny saw then that it was a body.

A woman. With long hair and wide eyes, bound with rope and silenced with gray duct tape. His heart hammered.

"One wrong move and she dies," Englishman said. "Is this the woman you embraced in Paradise? No, I don't think so. Say hello to Mommy."

The tape ripped from her face. She screamed, terrified. "Johnny?"

This was not the woman he'd embraced in Paradise. Johnny began to tremble from the bottom of his feet to the base of his head.

"Johnny," the woman whimpered.

The sound of her voice haunted him. *Are you my mother?*

"Mother?"

"Johnny, what have they done to you?"

He knew then that this woman was his mother. And he felt powerless to move.

"The woman you found in Paradise was an operative. A rather brilliant operative, as you can attest. We orchestrated it all, Johnny."

"Let her go," he said. Emotion choked him. "Just let her go!"

"You are like me, Johnny. You're a pretender who doesn't believe in what he's pretending anymore. You're a child of illusion who's been fed dogma and doctrine as a form of manipulation."

Johnny had been here before, on the barely surviving end of a hundred less-distorting games. What was one more?

"Will you?" Englishman asked.

The question echoed through Johnny's skull. *Will you?* He tried to focus on Englishman and was struck again by the darkness. Maybe his blindness was psychosomatic and would soon end.

"How?" he heard himself asking.

"Just walk in and kill him. You're their hero. They won't question your return, particularly if I've given a show of surrender."

From the beginning this had been their intention. To break him as he'd never been broken before and to kill both Feroz and the president at the same time. This was the mission he'd been so carefully trained for.

He exhaled slowly to calm himself. The familiar resolve that had been his friend in so many tests lapped at his mind. There was comfort there, in the dark tunnel where he was safe by himself.

"Johnny!" David Abraham stepped out from behind a large boulder and marched straight toward them. "Don't listen to his lies, Johnny."

"The old fool has come out to die." Englishman rolled his eyes.

"Is she my mother?" Johnny asked.

David stopped twenty yards from them and glanced at Sally. "I thought you met her in Paradise."

David knew Sally from before. And this was her. "Not her," Johnny said.

David's eyes widened slightly.

"Game over, old man," Englishman said. "We have all firmly in hand. Your presence is no longer required."

"Samuel told me about your eyes, Johnny," David said. "They show the truth. The truth will set you—"

Before David could finish, a hole blew through his shirt. He gasped and stared at a growing stain of red blood over his left breast pocket. Englishman had sent a pebble through the old man.

Johnny spun back to Englishman as David Abraham fell to the ground.

"One wrong move and she dies too," Englishman said.

"Stop it!" Johnny screamed. It sounded silly, but he felt so overwhelmed that nothing else came to mind. So he yelled it again. "Just stop it!"

"Only you can stop it. Kill the president, Johnny."

David's last words still rang in his ears. His eyes. There was something about his eyes . . .

His mother stood shaking, hands tied tightly behind her. She was crying now, begging him to do something. He saw her more in shades of light and shadows than in full color, but oddly enough, this way of seeing didn't compromise his ability to understand exactly what he was looking at.

"Trust David, Johnny," she said. "Use your eyes."

THIS MATTER *of the eyes again,* Englishman thought. He didn't care for the black stare. He preferred looking a man in the eyes before killing him.

Oh yes, he was indeed going to kill Johnny. As soon as Johnny killed the president. That was the deal, the new deal, the deal he should have made long ago.

Johnny looked at him dumbly—those shiny, silver-coated glasses made him look like an alien. They bothered Englishman immensely.

"My eyes?"

"Enough with the eyes crap, Johnny," Englishman said. "Either you kill the president, or I do the lot of you. This is growing old."

"I think something might be wrong with my eyes," Johnny said. "I thought I was going blind. But it's stopped now."

Blind? He wasn't sure why the idea of blindness sent a shaft of fear through his chest, but he knew about opposites. He knew that when darkness encroached, the light was often just over the horizon.

"I see glimmers of light on the edge of everything. Otherwise it's dark," Johnny said.

"Enough!"

"David told me to show you the truth." Johnny reached up and lifted the sunglasses from his face. "Do you know what he meant?"

Englishman's nerves stretched to the snapping point when he saw Johnny's eyes. Behind him, the mother gasped. Johnny didn't have eyes in the common understanding of the word. No blue or brown or green irises with black dots dead-center.

Instead, where his eyes should have been were two white orbs. If they didn't actually seem to glow, Englishman would have thought they were Johnny's eyes turned back into his head.

But these were solid white, like fluorescent cue balls.

"What's wrong?" Johnny asked.

He didn't know. Johnny really didn't know.

Englishman spoke the simple truth. "Your eyes are white."

And then they weren't white. They were black and monstrous and flowing with blood. Not just any blackness or any monstrosity or any blood, but Englishman's.

He was staring directly into himself.

Into hell.

Behind him, the mother screamed.

JOHNNY KNEW that something had changed the moment he removed his sunglasses. One look at Englishman, gawking at him, and Johnny knew that whatever had preceded this point, Englishman was now seeing the truth, and whatever that was, it stunned him.

"What's wrong?" he asked.

"Your eyes are white," Englishman said.

This, too, was the truth, spoken plainly. Englishman was only being truthful, and he, Johnny, was responsible for the man's truthfulness. And the truth was that his eyes had become white.

But what if there was more truth to be shown?

Realization dawned on Johnny so suddenly that he blinked. Then blinked again. Blindness was his price. He could give up his eyesight—for what?

He drilled the man with a hard stare, willing the layers of truth to be laid bare.

Englishman's mouth flew wide, and his eyes filled with terror. He began to suck in air and shove it out like a pump that had lost its prime.

The stones suspended all around them hailed to the ground. He was dumbstruck. The confidence and strength he'd felt in the canyon above Paradise flooded his mind, quickened his breathing, and hammered through his chest. Sally had dropped to her knees and shielded her eyes with both hands.

Johnny bore down on Englishman again, baring layers of truth that he himself could not see.

"Take it," he said.

Englishman began to shake violently from head to foot. His torso vibrated as if it had been crammed into a blender, and his head jerked from side to side, slowly at first, then gaining speed until it shook back and forth like a spring-loaded punching bag, fast enough to obscure his features, all except his black mouth, gaping obscenely wide.

Johnny took a step forward, gripped his fists tight, and leaned into whatever power flew from his eyes. His muscles were stretched tight, and he was still breathing hard.

"I believe," he said. "I believe, Englishman. I am not the lie. You are the lie!"

A piercing wail came from the man's throat. Not animal. Not human. More insect. Englishman was seeing the truth about himself, and he didn't like what he saw.

Johnny began to scream. An openmouthed, wordless scream of rage and remorse and terror and love and belief all wrapped around a single chord that he leveled at the lie with enough force to hurt his throat.

Englishman's entire body became a screeching blur of agony. The thing's terrible insectlike shrieks rose in pitch until they overpowered Johnny's cry. The desert air was cut to ribbons with this earsplitting shriek of anguish.

The blur that was Englishman suddenly became an empty shirt and trousers that hung in the air.

Johnny's scream caught in his throat.

Silence.

Then the *whoosh* of falling clothes, which plopped lightly on the ground between two shoes. A thin tendril of smoke rose from the shirt's collar. Englishman occupied space with his unfathomable contortions one second, and became empty air with a twist of smoke the next.

Johnny took a step back, legs like spaghetti, heart hammering. He turned to face David Abraham's fallen form, the dark stain of blood discoloring the desert sand, and if his world weren't so twisted, so fractured, he might have thrown up. Instead, he swallowed hard and faced his mother, who wept through her fingers.

Somehow he managed to replace his glasses, but his legs were giving out. He sank to his knees, dumbstruck and spent. The world spun around him.

With a failing conscious effort, he released the cords that held his mother. Sensed more than saw her rushing toward him. Felt her arms crash around him. Heard her sobs of relief.

Someone was wailing, high-pitched. Samuel, tearing at them from the ranch house.

Then Johnny's world went black.

44

Johnny and Kelly stood hand in hand, staring at the town of Paradise from the overlook high above. Sally stood beside them, arms crossed, sober.

Johnny had spent a week hidden away here with Kelly and Sally, discovering himself—his new self, his old self. His mother, his old friends, his place of birth, and his place of new birth.

He'd spent half that time in tears. Tears of sadness, tears of gladness, tears of relief and shame and love.

Samuel's world had imploded with the death of his father. He'd fallen on his body and wept for an hour before allowing them to pull him away. They buried David Abraham four days ago, and the funeral had been a terrible mix of good and bad for Samuel.

Good because the president had given his father a burial of highest honor, which his father deserved.

Bad because in his speech, the president vowed to bring all involved in the assassination attempts and the death of his beloved friend to justice. This, Samuel learned in short order, included Johnny.

He'd attempted to kill the president of the United States of America. Still faint from sorrow, Samuel had rushed back to Paradise and convinced Johnny to disappear. In good time, he would turn himself in. In good time.

Not now.

The threat from Kalman still loomed. The X Group had reportedly gone deep, but they would rear their heads again—these kind always did. Samuel wondered if Johnny wouldn't quietly put an end to them in the next week or so. He certainly had the means to do it.

The press still had no idea about what had happened this last year. They probably never would know. What they did know for certain was straightforward:

The president was alive.

His would-be assassins were a man named Dale Crompton, better known as Englishman, now dead, and Johnny Drake, now missing.

Assim Feroz, who had masterminded the president's assassination attempt, was now also dead, killed by his own hired guns.

Robert Stenton vetoed the Iranian initiative, and no other world leader had yet come forward to resurrect it.

Samuel approached them and studied the peaceful town. "Have you decided?"

"We are going to the desert," Johnny said. "To Nevada."

"Nevada. Plenty of desert."

"Plenty of desert," Johnny said. "Have you heard any news about the president's son?"

"His condition continues to deteriorate."

Johnny frowned but offered no comment. He maintained that it was Jamie who'd first broken through his shell and got him thinking about a father figure, which David ended up being.

"Any change in your eyes?" Sally asked, placing her hand on his shoulder.

Johnny turned his head south so that he faced neither of them, then lifted his glasses for a moment before lowering them back into place.

"No."

"I don't think it will ever change," Samuel said.

Johnny remained silent. The burden he bore with this new gift was hardly imaginable.

He wore the mirrored glasses for their sakes as much as his own. He could see well enough, but not the way the rest of them did. No color. Only black and white. With definition and acute depth perception formed by a thin crackle of white light that outlined everything, he said.

Samuel had looked into the whites of his eyes only once and then very briefly. The horror that had blazed a trail through his mind in that moment was a thing he'd never forget. He wasn't sure how it would affect Johnny and Kelly's relationship. She'd seen enough on the helicopter, when his eyes were just starting to go milky, to swear off ever looking into his eyes again.

"And the other abilities?" Samuel asked.

"Nothing."

He nodded. Johnny's blindness had remained. His other powers had left him. In some ways he was like Samson, who had lost his powers and gone blind. But Johnny's greatest gift was his revealing sight. Imagine what he could do in a session of Congress with those eyes.

"I think it could return," Samuel said, speaking of his other power.

"I'm not sure I want it to."

"Then it won't."

Kelly reached up and kissed Johnny lightly on his cheek. "I love you the way you are."

He placed his arm around her and kissed her forehead. "And I love you the way you are."

They returned their gazes to the valley. "Are you ready?" Johnny asked.

"I am," Kelly replied.

Johnny had become a man of faith, but he was still unsure about his role. For now he was a brooding hero trying to stay alive long enough to come to terms with who he was.

"So this is it," Sally mused. "There really is no alternative?"

"The authorities will be in Paradise by nightfall. This is it. I either turn myself in or buy some time. Would you rather I stay?"

"No," Sally said. "Run. But promise me you'll come back."

"I promise."

Samuel wasn't sure what to think about the other two who'd written in the same book that had given Johnny such power. Or if there were still other characters like Englishman lurking, created by the monk Marsuvees Black before his demise.

Samuel extended a hand to Johnny. "Take care, my friend. Try not to get lost in that desert."

"I think I've been lost enough for one lifetime." He clasped Samuel's fingers and smiled.

Samuel stepped forward and hugged Johnny, who returned the hug with strong arms. "Be careful."

"I'll see you again, Samuel. I just need some time."

"You know I'll have to tell them that you went into the desert."

"I know. Keep your nose clean. I have a feeling I'll be needing your help again."

Samuel pulled back, kissed Kelly's hand, and let them go. Johnny kissed Sally. Tears brimmed in her eyes.

"I love you, Mother."

"I love you, Johnny."

Kelly and Johnny walked away, hand in hand.

"Saint."

Johnny turned back. "Saint?"

"Remember what I said about your power," Samuel said. "The giver of the gift doesn't take it back so easily."

Johnny stared at him as if unsure of what he meant. Then he smiled, turned back down the mountain, and stepped onto the path.

"Remember that, Saint."

"I will," Johnny said without turning. "I will."

SKIN

CHAPTER ONE _____

When the rain isn't so much falling—be it in bucket loads or like cats and dogs—but rather slamming into the car like an avalanche of stone, you know it's time to pull over.

When you can't see much more than the slaphappy wipers splashing through rivers on the windshield, when you're suddenly not sure if you're on the road any longer, and your radio emits nothing but static, and you haven't seen another car since the sky turned black, and your fingers are white on the wheel in an attempt to steady the old Accord in the face of terrifying wind gusts, you know that it's so totally time to pull over.

Wendy leaned over the steering wheel, searching for the yellow lines that separated the two-lane highway. No real shoulder that she could see. What was to keep another car from rear-ending her if she pulled over here?

She'd seen the black clouds pillaring on the horizon as she headed across the Nevada desert. Heard the tornado warnings on the radio before it had inexplicably fried. The fact that this wasn't tornado territory had the announcers in a bit of a frenzy.

Wendy had ignored the warnings and pressed on into evening. She'd given herself two days for the long haul between San Diego and western Utah. The call from her mother asking her to come had frozen Wendy for a good ten seconds, phone in hand. Had to be Thursday, this week, her mother had insisted. It was now Tuesday night. Wendy wondered if she'd see the rest of the Brotherhood cult, or just her mother. The thought of either was enough to keep her awake at night.

The tribe, as the leader Bronson called it, was a somewhat nomadic group of twenty or so members, going where God led them. God had evidently led them to remote Utah-Nevada now.

Wendy had been born into the cult and had managed to escape seven years earlier, on her seventeenth birthday, the day she was to wed Torrey Bronson as his third wife. Twice she'd hired private investigators to locate the tribe and report on her mother's condition. Twice the report had come back favorable. But the investigators had never actually talked to her mother—speaking to anyone from the outside world was strictly forbidden. Even making eye contact was good for a day in isolation. Physical contact, heaven forbid, was grounds for severe punishment.

Inside the cult there was plenty of touching and hugging and kissing, but no physical contact with strangers ever, period. That was the Brotherhood way.

Wendy had fallen in an Oklahoma ditch when she was seven years old and broken her leg. A farmer had heard her cries and taken her to the others who were searching. Before setting her leg, Father Bronson had beaten her severely for allowing unclean hands to touch her. The lashing hurt more than the broken leg. It was the last time Wendy had touched or been touched by anyone outside the tribe before escaping.

And when Father Bronson had taken it upon himself to break her two thumbs and her two forefingers as punishment for kissing Tony, another thirteen-year-old in the tribe at the time, he'd made it excruciatingly clear that he'd claimed her for himself alone.

She'd fled the cult, but not the wounding of such a perverse childhood. Few knew the extent of the damage; she hid it well behind soft eyes and a light smile. But to this day even the thought of physical contact with men unnerved her.

No issue in Wendy's tumultuous life consumed her as much as this failing. Touch was her personal demon. A beast that prevented her from expressing the deep caring she'd felt in any relationship with men, isolating her from love, romantic or otherwise.

Now, driving through nature's fury, she felt oddly isolated again. It was suddenly clear that her decision to continue into the dark clouds had been a mistake.

As if hearing and understanding that it had played unfairly with her, the storm suddenly eased. She could see the road again.

See, now that wasn't so bad . . . Time to retreat to the nearest overcrowded motel to wait out the storm with the rest of the traveling public.

She could even see the signs now, and the green one she passed said that the turnoff to Summerville was in five miles. Exit 354. A hundred yards farther, a blue sign indicated that there were no services at this exit.

Scrub oak lined the highway. Freak storm. Flash floods. Truth be told, it was all a bit exciting. As long as the storm didn't delay her, she kind of liked the idea of—

Her headlights hit a vehicle in the road ahead. Like a wraith, the cock-eyed beast glared at her through the rainy night, unmoving, dead on the road. A pickup truck.

She slammed her foot on the brake.

The Accord's rear wheels lost traction on the wet pavement and slid around to her left. She gripped the steering wheel, knuckles white. Her headlights flashed past scrub oak that lined the road.

For an instant Wendy thought the car might roll. But the wet asphalt kept the Accord's wheels from catching and throwing her over.

Unfortunately, the slick surface also prevented the tires from stopping her car before it crashed into the pickup.

Wendy jerked forward, allowing her forearms to absorb most of the impact.

Steam hissed from under her hood. Rain splattered. But Wendy was unhurt, apart from maybe a bruise or two. She sat still, collecting herself.

Oddly enough, the airbags hadn't deployed. Maybe it was the angle. She'd hit the other vehicle's front bumper in a full slide, so that her left front fender had taken the brunt of the impact before becoming wedged under the grill.

She picked up her cell phone and snapped it open. *No Service.*

No service for more than half an hour now.

She tried the door. It squealed some, then opened easily before striking the smallish pickup, which she now saw was green. She climbed out, hardly noticing the rain. The pickup was missing its right front wheel and sat on the inner guts of the brake contraption—which explained the tire she now saw in the road. Her eyes returned to the pickup's door. The side window was shattered. The front windshield seemed intact, except for two round holes punched through on the driver's side.

Bullet holes.

Of course she couldn't be sure they were bullet holes, but it was the first thought to cross her mind, and having done so, she could hardly consider that mere debris had punched those two perfect circles through the glass.

Someone had shot at the driver.

Wendy jerked her head around for sign of another car or a shooter. Nothing she could see, but that didn't mean they weren't out there. For a moment she stood glued to the pavement, mind divided between the drenching she was receiving from the rain, and those two bullet holes.

She remembered the pistol in the console compartment between her Accord's front seats. Louise had talked her into buying it long ago, when they'd first met at the shelter. Wendy had never received the training she'd intended to, nor fired the gun. But there it lay, and if there was ever a time for it . . .

She flung the Accord's door wide and ducked inside. Finding and dislodging the black pistol case from between the seats proved a slippery, knuckle-burning task with wet fingers. Yet she managed to wrench it out. She disengaged the sliding mechanism that opened the case, snatched out the cold steel weapon, and fumbled it, trying to remember what the safety looked like.

Meanwhile her butt, which was still sticking out in the rain, was taking a bath. The gun slipped from her hands, thudded on the floor mat. She swore and reached for it, found the trigger, and would have blown a hole in the car if the safety had been off.

Thank God for safeties.

Now she found the safety and disengaged it. However unfamiliar she was with guns, Wendy was no idiot. Neither was she anything similar to gutless.

Whoever was in the truck might still be alive, God forbid even injured, and out here in this storm. And Wendy was the only one who could help. Sniper lurking or not, she would never abandon anyone in need.

Wendy turned the key in the Accord's ignition. The car purred to life. It was still steaming through the hood, but at least it ran.

She turned it off, took a calming breath, then slipped back out of the car and hurried around to the truck's passenger door, staying low.

With a last look around the deserted highway, keeping the gun in both hands down low the way she'd often seen such weapons wielded on the big screen, she poked her head up and looked through the passenger window.

Empty.

She stood up for a better look. The driver's window was smeared with something. Blood. But no body. Someone had been shot. The truck had apparently sideswiped another car and lost its front wheel before coming to a rest.

Wendy scanned the shoulder and ditches for any sign of a fallen body. Nothing.

Still no sign of a shooter, no sign of any danger.

"Hello?"

No response to her call.

Louder this time. "Hello? Anybody out there?"

No, nothing but the rain drumming on the vehicles.

She started to shove the gun into the back of her Lucky jeans, which were now drenched right through to her skin, but a quick image of the gun blowing a hole in her butt stopped her short.

It was then, hand still on the pistol at the small of her back, that she heard the cry.

She jerked the gun to her left and listened. There it was again, farther down the road, hidden in the growing dark. An indistinguishable cry for help or of pain.

Or the killer, howling at the moon in victory.

The cry did not come again. Wendy crouched low and ran down the roadside toward the sound, gun extended. She wanted to yell but was torn, knowing that in the very unlikely case the sound *had* been made by whoever had shot at the truck, she would be exposing herself to danger.

That she was now running away from the safety of her car through the dark rain, toward an unidentified stranger, struck her as absurd. On the other hand, she would gladly spend the rest of her life pulling little girls with broken legs out of the ditches into which they had fallen, regardless of the consequences.

She'd run less than fifty yards when a van loomed through the rain. She pulled up, panting.

The van had swerved off the road and down the shallow embankment on the left, where it now rested in complete darkness. It wasn't the kind of minivan in which moms hauled their children to soccer matches. This was the larger, square kind—the kind killers threw their kidnapped victims into before roaring off to the deep woods.

A streak of fear passed through her. Refusing to be gutless was one thing. Acting foolishly out of some misguided sense of justice was another. This was now feeling like the latter.

MOVIE EDITION
AVAILABLE
OCTOBER 2007

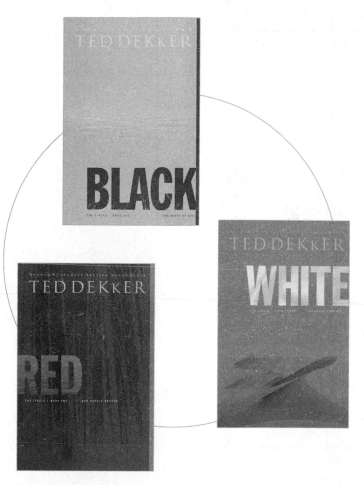